Praise

CAPTAIN K

"A well-written, realistic sea yarn—loaded to the gunwales with violence, blood and guts, powder and shot, broadsides, pikes, sabers, tall ships jargon, wine, whiskey, and considerable sex, including adultery."
—*The Star Democrat*

"It's unusual for novels set during the age of 'wooden ships and iron men' to be written by authors with actual naval experience. But with his new book, *Captain Kilburnie*, retired U.S. Navy Vice Adm. William P. Mack has joined the ranks of Capt. Frederick Marryat of *Peter Simple* fame as a writer who has seen naval life firsthand . . . *Captain Kilburnie* swashbuckles quite nicely."
—*Sailing* magazine

"Compelling. The book has plot, the character have motivation, the action is exciting, and the background is authentic."
—*The Annapolis Capital*

CAPTAIN KILBURNIE

A NOVEL

William P. Mack

BERKLEY BOOKS, NEW YORK

A Berkley Book
Published by The Berkley Publishing Group
A division of Penguin Putnam Inc.
375 Hudson Street
New York, New York 10014

PRINTING HISTORY
Naval Institute Press hardcover edition / January 2000
Berkley trade paperback edition / May 2001

The Penguin Putnam Inc. World Wide Web site address is
http://www.penguinputnam.com

Library of Congress Cataloging-in-Publication Data

Mack, William P., 1915–
  Captain Kilburnie / William P. Mack—Berkley trade paperback ed.
    p.   cm.
  ISBN 0-425-17826-9
    1. Great Britain—History, Naval—18th century—Fiction. 2. Nile, Battle of the,
  1798—Fiction. I. Title.

  PS3563.A3132 C3   2001
  813'.54—dc21   2001020216

PRINTED IN THE UNITED STATES OF AMERICA

10 9 8 7 6 5 4 3 2 1

Contents

Captain Kilburnie

I

IRELAND

Young Fergus Kilburnie ran the currying brush over the glistening flanks of Lord Inver's favorite mare. He had finished the horse's grooming several minutes ago, but it gave him a convenient vantage point from which to watch the efforts of Lord Inver's beautiful daughter Shannon to saddle and bridle her own horse. His six feet of growing young body topped by a shock of light brown hair and a ruggedly handsome face made it easy for him to see over the horse's high brown back.

As Shannon reached up to put on her mare's bridle, Fergus's blue eyes could see her white cotton blouse pulling at her well-formed breasts. Her long riding skirt did little to conceal her shapely hips as she leaned over to adjust her stirrups.

Fergus sighed, and he could feel his desire rising. When he had first arrived at Lord Inver's estate Shannon had been a spindle-shanked redhead running about her father's estate. Now she was a young beauty, her long, gleaming red hair caught in a ribbon at the back of her graceful neck, her green eyes flashing in her tanned face as she concentrated on her task.

When the horse was rigged to her satisfaction, she stood back and looked at it, pulling at her skirt to settle it over her hips. She brushed the dust off

I

her gleaming black boots and pushed the errant ends of her blouse back into her skirt top.

As the mare lifted its hooves in anticipation Shannon turned and looked at Fergus. Her smile was at once innocent and devilish, as if she knew Fergus had been admiring her.

Fergus sighed, knowing what was coming.

"Fergus," she called, "I'm going to ride over to the old churchyard for a picnic. Won't you join me?"

Fergus sighed even more deeply, torn between the desire to be with her and the certain knowledge that if he gave in to such temptation trouble would probably result. He took a deep breath. "I don't think I can. I have two more horses to finish."

He put down his curry comb and brush, went over to her, and held her knee in his hands as she mounted. He was sure she purposely brushed her breast against his cheek as she lifted herself into the saddle. She looked down at him, her green eyes dancing. "I'll be in the churchyard at least an hour. Do try to make it."

He opened his mouth to protest, but before he could get the words out, she hit the mare lightly with her crop. Eager to run, the mare headed for the open gate at a fast trot. As soon as they cleared the gate she ran toward the open fields as fast as she could go, her hooves sending up small clods of green turf. Shannon had been riding for years, and she gave the eager mare her head.

Fergus watched her, the curry comb motionless. He said in a low voice, "Deliver me from temptation," and turned to his chores, hoping the exercise would calm him down.

As he curried the other horses, he thought back to the first time he had seen Shannon. As a seventeen-year-old boy he had arrived at the Inver estate seated next to his father and mother on a large wagon filled with household goods they had brought from their farm at Fairlie, on the coast of Scotland near Kilmarnock. Fergus's father had been hired to supervise the estate of Lord Inver, an Irish peer and a member of the Irish parliament. Lord Inver raised horses as a business but, like all wealthy Irishmen, he was an avid horseman and maintained a string of race horses.

In the 1790s many Scots formerly of a relatively high social class came to Ireland to manage the land of the Irish gentry according to the latest techniques of farming. The Kilburnie estate was large, almost as large as Lord Inver's, and had been in the hands of the Kilburnies for a century. Like many

Scots the Kilburnies had become cash poor but remained land rich. They came to Ireland to avoid having to sell part of their land.

As the wagon pulled up young Shannon stared up at Fergus. He raised his hand in a salute of acknowledgment and her stare turned into a smile. To Fergus her slim body appeared to be formed of sticks, but he also noticed it had a certain grace of movement, like that of a thoroughbred foal.

After his arrival, Fergus helped his father with Lord Inver's large stable of horses. Both a quick study and a lover of horses, he was now in complete charge of the stables and was paid handsomely.

Shannon had learned to ride before Fergus arrived, but Lord Inver gave him the task of teaching her to care for, saddle, and train horses. Fergus spent many hours with her, teaching her in the large barn and paddock, and riding with her over the fields and trails of the surrounding countryside.

Without realizing what was happening, he let her growing beauty captivate him. At first he resisted, knowing that Lord Inver would never permit him to court his daughter, even though in Scotland the Kilburnies held high positions in their clan and so were the social equals of the Invers. To Lord Inver, however, Scottish distinctions meant little. He considered the Kilburnies little better than his Irish tenants.

Fergus knew something was happening between them, and the sight of her lithe form disappearing over the turf made his blood surge.

He finished his work quickly, saddled his own horse, his movements so fast he pinched the belly of his stallion in the girth. The pained horse reared, but Fergus spoke soothingly to him, fixed the offending pinch, swung into the saddle, and in a few minutes the large mansion began to disappear behind him as he let the horse have its way.

He was so preoccupied he almost missed seeing Lord Inver riding up on his best horse from an outlying field. For a moment it appeared that Lord Inver was calling to him, but he was too far away to hear, and Fergus deliberately looked away so he would not see him if he waved his hand.

As he rode, he thought of Shannon and tried to sort out a future for them. He knew he could not do anything rash. Lord Inver's temper was well known. Fergus was big enough and strong enough to stand up to him, but always there was the family's position to think of. Lord Inver might send the Kilburnie family back to Scotland. Despite the beauty of Ireland, Fergus cared little for it, but he was also sure he didn't want to leave Shannon. He gritted his teeth as he rode, thinking he should have taken more notice of Lord Inver as he rode off. Now Lord Inver would know where he was going.

He shrugged his shoulders; the attraction of Shannon was too strong. He spurred his horse, and it picked up its pace. As to direction it did not need any urging. It had been to the churchyard before.

Twenty minutes later Fergus stopped his hard-breathing stallion on the crown of the slope leading down to the old churchyard. The church was no longer used, but occasionally someone was buried there to be near their relatives. It was poorly maintained, but lush grass, weeds, and wildflowers grew among the stones, and stands of trees lined each side of the church-yard. No houses were visible, but curls of smoke rose lazily from houses deep behind the trees. Off in the distance directly over the church Fergus could see Donegal Bay, and to the left he could see spires of the churches of the city of Donegal deeper within the bay.

He lowered his gaze to the casual jumble of old headstones in the church-yard, and he spotted at once against the carpet of long green grass the white and brown of Shannon's riding costume. She was leaning against a low gravestone, saddlebags beside her. Her horse was tethered to a small tree nearby, slowly cropping the lush Irish grass.

Fergus rode slowly down the slope, his horse picking its way between the gravestones, and dismounted near Shannon's horse. He tied the reins to a low-hanging branch. After removing the saddle, he pulled off the saddle blanket and carried it over to the grassy area where Shannon was sitting.

She looked up at his approach and giggled. "I knew you'd come," she said in the lovely lilting voice tinged with a brogue she saved for intimate moments with him.

He grinned. "Sounds like you've forgotten your expensive school English."

"Oh, Fergus, you Scottish dolt. It's no worse than your Scottish burr."

He spread his blanket and sat down. She picked up the saddlebags and moved over beside him. "I waited for you. It's all here, and there's plenty. I know how hungry you get."

He sighed heavily and blurted, "Oh, God, Shannon, I'm not just starved for food. We can't go on meeting each other like this."

She looked up at him, her green eyes cool under her long black lashes. "Whyever not?"

"Your father wouldn't approve of me. Besides, you're too young."

She reached out and caressed his shoulder. "I don't care what he wants or doesn't want, and I'm not too young. I'm almost seventeen, and Father constantly talks about finding a husband for me."

Shannon then began to tease him, alternately making some amorous approach, rubbing his arm, smiling playfully, and then, when he leaned over for a kiss, offering him a sandwich or piece of cheese. Soon, Fergus was smiling, too.

Once he brushed aside a sandwich and tried to kiss her, but she put a finger on his lips. "I want you to be well fed and strong," she said with mock seriousness.

"You sound like your father talking about a horse before a race," Fergus retorted. When the last bit of picnic lunch was gone, Shannon smiled mischievously and held out her arms to Fergus. "Now, my hero."

Fergus hesitated. He knew he shouldn't, but just the same he drew her to him. She didn't resist and responded so quickly he almost lost his nerve. Instead of the awkward, almost innocent meeting of their lips that they had allowed themselves before, he found himself kissing her passionately. He knew he couldn't stop, and he kissed her so hard he was afraid he would bruise her full red lips. Shannon responded with equal fervor.

Fergus pulled away, shaking his head. "No. It's not right."

She wrapped her arms around him and pulled him down beside her on the blanket. "Oh, Fergus, I've wanted you so much. Don't stop now."

For an instant, Fergus tried to control himself, but then he kissed her again with as much passion as before. It was too late. He began to unbutton her blouse, and she helped him to pull it back. He groaned with pleasure as he caressed the full young breasts he had admired so often. At other times they had been covered by a variety of clinging clothes, but now they were naked under his touch. He began to pull up her full skirt, and when she told him she was not wearing anything under it, he began to press against her. He knew he could not stop. He reached back and pulled one side of the blanket over them, even though he knew there was no one around for miles.

He kissed her again. Then, seemingly in the distance, he heard the neighing of horses, but he was so intent on Shannon that he paid no attention.

The soft swish of a horse's hooves in the grass, followed by a pounding on the ground, and the creak of leather, was unmistakable. Fergus looked up. Atop his black hunter was Lord Inver, his face flushed purple with rage. Staring down at them, for an instant he was silent as he looked at the two young lovers. Then in a booming voice he shouted, "Dammit, girl, get up from there. Adjust your clothing and go home. I'll tend to you later!"

Shannon gasped. Although she had acted surprised at first, Fergus thought he caught an impish look on her reddened face. She rose slowly, pulling her skirt down with one hand and adjusting her blouse with the other.

It suddenly occurred to Fergus she was not afraid of her father, and as if to prove it as she ran beyond him she turned toward him and stuck out her tongue.

Watching his daughter leave, Lord Inver saw her gesture of defiance and his face became even redder. Fergus was sure he was going to have apoplexy. His horse seemed to sense his anger and began to rear, but Lord Inver got the trembling beast under control. Turning toward Fergus, he leveled his riding crop at him and said in a voice cold with contempt, "Make yourself presentable and get back to my farm. You have twenty-four hours to get off my land and if I see you again near my daughter anywhere, I'll run my sword clear through your damned belly and then I'll cut off your manhood!"

Before Fergus could move, Lord Inver gave him one final contemptuous glare, wheeled his horse, and pounded off after his daughter.

Fergus disconsolately realized his churning blood had turned from passion to lead, and he laid back on his saddle blanket. If only he had not obeyed his impulse when he had passed Lord Inver and had gone to meet him. If only he had stayed in the stable . . . if only he had listened to his conscience . . . if only. . . .

Now it was too late, and he had ruined whatever chance he might have had of courting Shannon some day. He thought he had disgraced his family and endangered their position, and maybe even their land. He sighed deeply and looked up at the tops of the trees surrounding the churchyard. Now what was he to do? His despair was a weight in his stomach.

Fergus got up, finished straightening his clothing, picked up the blanket and saddlebags, and walked slowly to his horse. He threw on the blanket that had so recently covered their near-coupling, put on the saddle, and threw the saddlebags behind the saddle. He rode slowly out of the churchyard, but shortly looked back at it. Only a few short moments before it had seemed a place of paradise. Now he saw it for what it was, a place of death for his passion, and the end of his relationship with the girl he loved. The ride back was only three miles, but it seemed to take three hours.

When Fergus returned to the estate he avoided the barn and paddock and instead rode to the front gate of the fence around the modest overseer's cottage in which his family lived. He had no wish to look into the knowing eyes of the stable boys and hear their giggles.

Fergus's father, Angus Kilburnie, was waiting for him, hands on hips and a querulous expression on his angular face, framed by graying sideburns and equally gray hair.

Fergus looked at him and his mother, Elizabeth, a slightly plump and pleasant-faced Scotswoman, standing near the front door. He slowly dismounted, tied his horse to the gate post, and turned to face his father.

Before Fergus could say anything, Angus held up his hand and said in a surprisingly calm voice, "Well, lad, tell us about it. Whatever you did, Lord Inver rode up here, his face red and swollen, and said he wanted you off of his property in twenty-four hours. I thought he was going to have an apoplexy."

Fergus sighed deeply. "Let's go inside first. We'll all need a nip of that terrible Irish whiskey."

When Fergus's younger sister had been firmly banished to the garden, the three adults sat down around the kitchen table. Angus poured whiskey into three tumblers and Fergus handed one to his mother. "Here, Mother, you're going to need this more than either of us."

Elizabeth Kilburnie smiled. "I'll take it, son, but your news just might be good for me to hear."

Angus said, "No more shillyshallying, son, tell us what happened."

Fergus shook his head slowly. "I did a terrible thing today. I should have controlled myself and thought more about what might happen to my family."

His mother sipped her whiskey. "It was Shannon, wasn't it? I have seen how you two have been looking at each other."

Fergus nodded. For a moment he couldn't speak, and his father said impatiently, "From Lord Inver's shouting, I take it he caught you in the act."

Fergus finally found his voice. "Not exactly. We really hadn't done anything wrong when he rode up. I just hope he won't do anything harsh to Shannon."

His mother shook her head. "He won't. He worships her."

Fergus nodded. "I'll admit we were getting close. Lord Inver may want the rest of the family to leave."

Angus snorted. "Fine. We want to leave anyway. Your mother and I have wanted to leave for the last year."

Elizabeth Kilburnie laughed. "I can hardly wait to get back to my own kitchen and to get away from the Irish."

Angus reached over and patted her arm. "We'll leave next week. I have to give him that much notice."

Fergus asked, "But will there be room for all of us on the family farm?"

Angus pointed to a packet of letters on the mantel. "I haven't told you this, but your grandfather wrote to me that his health is failing, and there is no one on the farm but your older brother and a hired boy to take care of it. So many people have left the country that help is hard to find. He wants us to come back and take over. He will stay with us in the big house. Your brother will move into the little house as soon as he marries, which will be soon."

"But he'll want to take the farm over from you some day," Fergus replied.

"And so he will. I can see that you don't like farming anyway."

Fergus grinned. "I like horses, but the rest you can have."

Elizabeth broke in. "I think you could plan to do something else as soon as we are settled. We have enough saved to send you to the University of Edinburgh."

Fergus sighed. The university meant a profession. Law, medicine, the clergy. "I'll think about it, but right now I have to get ready to leave."

Elizabeth rose. "I'll pack some food for you and give you a big breakfast early tomorrow."

Fergus and his father sat before the fire talking until the bottle of Irish whiskey was finished.

Just before dawn Elizabeth called the men, and they sat down to the big breakfast they had been promised. Angus pushed a leather packet over to Fergus. "Here's twenty pounds. It's a lot of money, but after you pay your fare to Glasgow give the rest to your grandfather. You shouldn't have to sell your horse."

Fergus placed the packet securely inside his shirt. "Thank you, Father, I think I can stay by the roadside some nights and save a little money. I'll go via Omagh, Craigavon, Dungannon, and Lisburn."

Angus nodded. "You should make the docks at Belfast by noon of the fourth day."

Elizabeth said, "Please be careful. There are highwaymen along the way."

Angus got up, took a foot-long, thin dagger from the mantel. "This is my skene dhu. It's been in the family for years. Tie this scabbard to your calf upside down under your trews. Tie the dagger in the scabbard with a light piece of yarn so you can reach down and release it in a hurry."

Taking the weapon Fergus said, "Thank you, Father. I'll give it back to you when you reach home. But what will you have to defend yourself with on the road?"

Angus pointed to a long sheathed broadsword, a claymore, leaning against the corner of the kitchen. "That's what I'll use." He smiled. "Never liked those skinny little daggers."

After breakfast, Fergus saddled his horse and tied a bundle of clothes wrapped in a blanket to the back of his saddle. His mother brought out a pair of bulging saddlebags and tied them to the front of his saddle.

After hugging his mother and sister and shaking hands with his father, Fergus mounted his impatient stallion. He waved as he went out the gate.

As he started down the road to Omagh, he looked back toward the big house on the hill. He thought he could see the curtains on a window in Shannon's room move, but he couldn't be sure.

2
TRAVELING TO SCOTLAND

he ride down the road to Omagh was the longest day of Fergus's life. Not even the beautiful spring day, the green grass in the adjacent fields, or the wildflowers lining the road cheered him.

Only his horse, happy to be out of the paddock, was in good spirits. All Fergus could think of was Lord Inver's red face towering over him and Shannon's quick cry. He realized that it was a sound of anger at being disturbed, not an admission of shame or fear. She was a strong person, even at sixteen, and Fergus couldn't help but grin as he remembered the sign of defiance she had made to her father and the quick smile she threw him over her shoulder as she moved to mount her horse. Fergus knew he probably would never see Shannon again, but he realized he was deeply in love with her, and it would be a long time before he was interested in another woman.

Now he would have to concentrate on doing something with his life besides breeding horses. He thought about his grandfather, who had left the family farm fifty years ago and joined the Royal Navy. After rising to the rank of lieutenant, however, he had resigned and returned to the family farm. He had realized that as a common Scot in the eyes of the English he would never rise higher in a service dominated by the aristocratic hierarchy.

Fergus always had been interested in his grandfather's stories about the navy. In the snowy winter months, he taught him how to use a quadrant for taking sights of the sun and Polaris and how to use charts for navigation. In the summers Fergus learned to sail in the small sailboats kept at a pier on the family farm that bordered on the Firth of Clyde. Three summers he had gone to sea as a deck hand on a large fishing boat sailing out of Glasgow. He felt he was well qualified to join the Royal Navy or to go back to the fishing fleet. If there was a choice, it would be the Royal Navy. There wasn't much adventure in fishing but, on the other hand, he had heard that life in the navy was tough. Still, his grandfather had become a lieutenant, and that was probably better than smelling fish all day.

As darkness approached, Fergus was sure he could not reach Omagh that evening without riding on a strange road at night. He rode into a copse of trees in an area that did not seem to be inhabited. About a hundred yards into the trees he found a sheltered clearing. He unsaddled his horse and tied it to a tree with a long length of rope to allow it to graze. A few yards away he spread the horse blanket and took out the food his mother had packed in his saddlebags.

He made a small fire and heated some water to make herbal tea. After a cold supper, he leaned against his saddle and pulled the second blanket from his blanket roll over him. He remembered that the horse blanket he was lying on was the same blanket that he had shared with Shannon the day before. He could still smell her cologne on the rough fibers. He sighed deeply, vowing never to part with the blanket.

Fergus tried to sleep to ease the stiffness in his muscles from the long hours in the saddle, but his mind kept coming back to his troubles. About midnight he drifted into a troubled light sleep, so light that at what he judged was a few hours before dawn he became aware that his horse was stamping its feet. He opened his eyes, suddenly aware that something was not right. In the dim light of the dying fire he could see a figure working to untie the long rope that held his horse.

He reached down his leg to where the skene dhu was attached, undid the yarn that held it in its scabbard, and slowly withdrew the weapon. Quietly he pushed back the blanket, eased to his feet, and stealthily approached the figure. When he was only a step away, his foot broke a small stick, and the figure in front of him started and froze. Seeing his chance, Fergus reached out with his left arm and encircled the figure's neck. He brought the skene dhu up to the figure's ribs.

Fergus said in a steady voice, "Don't move or you'll have six inches of steel in your chest."

The figure moaned, but did not move in Fergus's strong-armed grip.

Fergus said, "Turn around slowly toward the fire so I can see your face."

The thief turned slowly and began to sob. In the dim light Fergus could see enough to realize he was a young boy of about twelve. Stunned, he released the arm around the boy's neck but did not lower the dagger. Fergus had heard of thieves fourteen years old being hanged and did not want to take any chances. "Come over to the fire and sit down."

The boy sat down slowly, shaking and still sobbing. Fergus put some sticks of wood on the dying fire and sat down across from the hunched-over young boy. "Now tell me why you were trying to steal my horse."

The boy struggled to regain his composure. Finally able to speak, he said, "I'm sorry, but my family is starving."

"You were going to eat my horse?"

"Oh, no, sir. I was going to sell it and buy food."

"Do you no ken I could have killed you?"

The boy raised his head. "Yer a Scot?"

"Aye, and on my way back to Scotland. If you'd copped my horse I'd have had a long walk."

The boy rubbed the tears from his face and looked up at Fergus. "Please let me go. My mother will be worried if I don't come back by dawn."

"Where do you live?"

"About a mile down the road toward Omagh."

Fergus put his skene dhu back in its scabbard and took some food out of his saddlebags. "All right. Go home, and take some of this food with you."

As the boy rose he said, "You might like to stop by our cottage. My mother would like to meet you and give you some breakfast."

Fergus laughed. "I thought you were starving."

"We are. All we have to eat is boiled greens and an egg or two when our hen lays. Sometimes my sister finds wild oats for porridge."

"Good luck. If I stop by I won't tell your mother about what happened tonight."

The boy walked off toward the road, but then stopped and said over his shoulder, "Sir, if you stop by the road tomorrow night, either build a bigger fire or go farther away from the road. You'll be safer."

At dawn Fergus stamped out his fire, saddled his horse, and rode east toward Omagh. As the young Irish boy had said, he came to a small cottage a mile down the road. There was no one in sight except a small girl playing with a makeshift ball.

Fergus dismounted and called the small girl over to the gate. He took about a pound's worth of coins out of the small leather bag in his coat pocket. It was money he had kept out of his pay, separate from the money his father had given him. He counted his money and realized he still had a little over twenty pounds.

The little girl ran over to the gate and looked up at him. He held out the coins and said in English, "Give this to your mother."

The child took the money and looked at it carefully. She said a word in Gaelic, but Fergus couldn't understand it. He pointed at the cottage and said, "Mama." The word was almost the same in any language, and the little girl closed her fist on the coins and ran off toward the cottage door. Fergus mounted and rode off. Perhaps, he thought, that might help to save one small boy from the gallows.

Fergus's horse, eager to run, carried him through Omagh before noon. By dusk he had reached the outskirts of Dungannon, and he stopped at the stable next to a small inn.

As he unpacked his horse he thought about the years of his faithful service to him. He had trained him in Scotland three years ago and had brought him to Ireland with him. Now he didn't want to have to sell him for passage, and he resolved to find a way to take him home with him.

The hostler at the stable tipped his hat. "Let me have your horse, young sir, but you'd better take your saddle in with you."

"That bad?" Fergus asked.

The hostler shrugged. "I sleep in the stable every night, but I'm getting old, and I don't hear so well. You shouldn't take a chance."

Fergus unsaddled his horse, shouldered his saddle and equipment, and entered the inn through the stable door. A fresh-faced Irish girl met him. She laughed and reached out to take his saddlebags and bedroll. "Ye've got enough tack for two horses," she said in a thick brogue.

Fergus smiled. The arch of her neck, the round lines of her breasts thrusting against her blouse, and the roll of her ample hips as she lifted his equipment reminded him of Shannon. "Do you have a small room for me?"

She nodded toward a man behind the bar. "Best see him, he's the master. I'm sure he'll take you in. I know there's a small room left on the upper floor." Her white teeth flashed. "It's close to mine," she added with a grin as she walked away. Obviously she had not missed Fergus's appreciative glances.

Fergus dropped his saddle in front of the bar. The landlord put down the glass he was polishing. "Ye'll be needing a room?" he asked Fergus.

"For one night," Fergus said. "And some supper and a very early breakfast."

"Aye, we can take care of you very well. There'll be a joint and some potatoes ready in half an hour." He nodded toward the barmaid. "Enya will give you breakfast." A smile passed over his rugged Irish face. "Seeing as you're such a well set-up young man, she'll probably give you anything else you might want."

Fergus grimaced. "I'm afraid I won't have time for that."

The landlord laughed. "Suit yerself, but when I was yer age I didn't have time fer anything else. I'd have made time for that one."

Fergus grinned. "Aye, maybe I'll change my mind."

The landlord called out, "Enya, take this lad up to the top floor, and come right back. Supper is almost ready, and I'll need you to serve."

Enya picked up Fergus's saddlebag and bedroll again and started up the stairs. She looked back to see if Fergus was following her. Fergus was watching her ankles as they flashed in and out of the bottom of her skirt as she went up the steps. "Like what you see?" she asked playfully.

Fergus blushed. "Aye, and I'm sure the rest of you is even better, but don't expect much from me. I've just had to leave the girl I wanted to marry."

They reached the top floor, where they stored Fergus's equipment in the small room. Enya laughed. "Got caught, did ye?"

Fergus blushed again. "Aye, and I've been told never to return."

Enya looked into his eyes and said, "Then what do you care if you're never coming back?"

"I shouldn't, but I do."

She deliberately brushed against him as she went out the door, but even the feel of her full firm breasts failed to entice Fergus. Resigned, Enya turned and said, "Come right down to supper, or there won't be any left."

Fergus followed her down to the main room and took a seat at the long crude table. Thinking about Shannon had set his stomach churning. When the serving dishes were passed around, he took small portions.

The landlord's wife noticed and said, "Lad, yer eating like a child. This is good food."

Fergus nodded. "Yes, Mistress, it is, but I've not been eating much lately."

Enya, busy at the bar nearby, heard him and said mischievously, "He's lovesick, ma'am. Maybe we can help him."

The landlady shook her head. "If you can't, I can't either."

The landlord's face clouded. "And don't yer try."

After supper, the inn's guests sat around the fire, drinking and talking. Fergus, exhausted by his day's ride, went back to his room, did his best to clean up with the primitive facilities, and, after placing his skene dhu under his pillow, stretched out on the small bed fully clothed. He thought about Enya for a few minutes, but Shannon's memories gradually overcame his thoughts. He shook his head, took several deep breaths, and was asleep in moments.

About midnight he was aware that the door, creaking slightly, was being opened. He slowly reached under his pillow, drawing the slim dagger. As the door opened wider, he could see it was Enya holding a candle. She quietly entered the room and moved toward his saddlebags that were piled near the washstand. He waited with the dagger to see if she was going to rifle the saddlebags, but she placed the candle on the washstand and made her way to the bed, sitting down on the edge of it. Her hand reached out and began to undo the buttons on his shirt. He put his hand over hers. She started and gave a little gasp.

"I'm sorry," he said. "You're a very pretty colleen, and I know what I'm missing, but I really meant what I said."

She smiled a little sadly and pulled back her hand. "Could I just lie down beside you in case you change your mind? I don't have a chance to meet many young men. Most who stay here are old and fat." She giggled. "Or they would rather talk about politics over punch."

Fergus laughed and moved over on the narrow bed. "I guess we can talk. I haven't had a chance to meet many young girls either. They are not interested in a Scotsman, especially a Presbyterian."

Just before dawn they awoke. Fergus dashed cold water over his face and neck while Enya went downstairs. When he came down with his equipment, Enya had fried eggs, porridge, and strong tea ready. She sat down and joined him, and by dawn he was ready to leave on the next leg of his journey.

By now the landlord and his wife were up, and Fergus paid his bill. Although he knew passage to Scotland for him and his horse would cost most of his money, he gave Enya a shilling. She blushed and smiled. "Thank you," she said. "You're quite kind."

Fergus spent the next night rolled in his blankets in a wooded area near Craigavon. This time he remembered the advice of the young Irish lad and kept a large fire going. He slept lightly, wondering if he would be lucky enough this time to hear any thief approaching and hoping that if he didn't the thief would be no more fearsome than the twelve-year-old boy. When he woke up slowly the next morning, he saw that the horse and his meager belongings were safe.

By noon Fergus was winding his way through the busy streets of Belfast to the waterfront, his horse picking its way among busy pedestrians of all classes, carts of produce, barking dogs, and mounds of trash scattered over the cobblestones. Sailors strolled along the streets, arguing with peddlers, and stopping to hail Fergus as he passed.

Fergus didn't have time to take in the details of Belfast and kept his eye on the tall masts that marked the wharves. In an hour the main street opened to an area of open water lined with piers and moles. A dozen sailing ships were moored to the long wharfside. Most were fishing vessels, but some, slightly larger, were packets that took passengers as well as cargo up and down to the ports on the Irish Sea. Crudely lettered signs on the piers adjacent to the individual ships listed their destinations.

Fergus stopped at a sign that read PRESTWICK-ROTHSAY-GLASGOW. An elderly man wearing a brimmed hat and an eyepatch lounged against a round bollard on the wharf near the brow, a wide plank that led up to the gangway in the side of the ship. He wore a yellow slicker top and white duck trousers that were covered with tar and paint spots and tucked into black gum boots. His tarred straw hat had been through many a storm. His face was cast downward, as if inspecting his boots, and from a short pipe in his mouth came clouds of tobacco smoke.

The ship, bigger than most and very sturdy in appearance, appealed to Fergus. He tied his horse to a nearby bitt and walked over to the old man.

When Fergus stopped in front of him, the old man looked up at Fergus appraisingly, slowly removed the pipe from his mouth and, after breathing out a mouthful of smoke, said, "Can I help you, lad?"

Fergus touched his forehead with the knuckle of his right hand and grinned. "Yes, sir, I'd like to see the captain about passage."

The old man said, "Yer talking to the captain of this here vessel, the *Marianne*. Where do you want to go, and what do you want to take with you?"

"I'm bound for Kilburnie, but I'll have to disembark at Glasgow."

"That's right, laddie, and it'll cost you ten pounds for you and ten pounds more for your horse, unless you're thinking about selling him."

Fergus sighed. "I don't want to. He's a very good horse, but I don't think I have enough money to pay full passage for both of us. Could I possibly work to pay for part of our passage?"

Puffing at his pipe, the captain looked Fergus over from head to foot with his one good eye. "Lad, just how big are you?"

Fergus said, "One fathom high. Fourteen stone."

The captain whistled. "Yer bigger than you look, and you seem to have a lot of muscle under those clothes. Do you know anything about sailoring?"

"Aye. I can navigate, including using a quadrant for sun and Polaris sights. I can take bearings and keep dead reckoning and read a chart, steer a course, and heave a lead. I've been to sea for three summers on a fishing schooner about this size."

The captain took off his hat and scratched his head. "Well, lad, that sounds good, but can you work aloft?"

Fergus took a deep breath. "Try me."

The captain looked up at the small crosstree of the main mast of the two-masted schooner where the ratlines were secured to the mast about two-thirds of the way to the top. "Climb up to the crosstree, look to see how the tide is doing, and come back down."

Fergus grinned and bounded over to the port shrouds. He climbed up rapidly, making sure the captain could see that he had his hands on the vertical shrouds and not on the horizontal spreaders. At the top he stood up on the small crosstree, put his arms around the mast, and looked out over the harbor to where he could see the flotsam floating by to indicate the tide was ebbing. Then he grabbed a single stay leading to port, hooked a leg over it, and slid down to the main deck.

As he reached the deck, he unhooked his leg, landed lightly, and walked over to the captain. "Sir, the ebb tide is beginning. You have about three hours until maximum ebb. The wind out there is about the same as it is in here. You should be able to go out all the way on the port tack."

The captain laughed and extended a calloused hand. "I'm Captain Leary, and you have a job. I'll take your horse to Glasgow for ten pounds. You'll earn your own passage as a seaman and by helping me navigate. Now report to Mister Hamilton, the boatswain, over there, to help hoist your horse aboard. We leave in two hours to catch the tide."

Fergus grinned. "Thank you, sir, and I promise you won't regret it."

He walked over to the stout man who had been pointed out by the captain as the boatswain. Hamilton's gut barely stayed inside his broad belt, but under the layer of fat were strong muscles. His face had not seen a razor for several days, and his hair was overly long. Fergus guessed he would do well with the local ladies if he was cleaned up.

The boatswain stopped work and looked at Fergus. "Mr. Hamilton," Fergus said, "the captain said I was to report to you as a seaman for the next voyage and as his assistant navigator."

Hamilton looked at him curiously. "You can't be both. Which is it?"

Fergus cleared his throat. "Well, at least I know I am to be a seaman in port, and I'm supposed to help load and take care of my horse over there on the pier."

Hamilton laughed. "Sounds like the old man thinks this is a man-of-war with a navigator and all."

Fergus shrugged. "I'll just do what I'm told."

Hamilton cocked an eye at Fergus's horse, standing quietly near the bitt. "Nice animal. You'll have to work on him if you want to keep him that way. There's hay, oats, and water enough aboard. Also curry combs and brushes. Just see that he gets the forage and the care."

"Do you have any other animals aboard?"

"Aye. Two cows, two hogs, and a horse. Not as fine as yours, though. You'll have to take care of all of them. As you can see, the main boom above is still rigged for hoisting from the pier over to the main hold. Take that sling and cloth over to him. Once he's blindfolded, you'll be able to rig the sling around his belly. Keep talking to him as we lift him up and swing him over. Then run aboard and go down to the hold. Just keep on talking to him as we lower him into the hold. As long as he can hear you he'll be all right."

Fergus went over to the pier, took off his saddle, and carried out the boatswain's instructions. His horse was apprehensive and whinnied loudly as its feet left the surface of the pier, but Fergus soothed him, and in a few minutes he was standing in a pile of straw on the orlop deck between a cow and another horse. Fergus unrigged the sling, took off the blindfold, and held some oats up to his horse's mouth. In a few minutes the horse was relaxed and eating.

Fergus laughed. "Take it easy, Prince, and soon you'll be a sailor, too. This is the same thing you did when we came over here." He checked the spars rigged between the animals to make sure they would withstand the ship's movement and went back on deck.

The boatswain had only two other deck hands, both slim young boys, and he seemed to welcome Fergus's strength and willingness to work.

About two o'clock, the captain bellowed, "Make ready to sail in five minutes. Kilburnie, take the helm."

Fergus went aft to the wheel, hoping he could remember the commands he had learned on his summer cruises.

The captain climbed creakily up to the port bulwark, looked over the side, and yelled, "Take in the brow and all lines. Heave round on the anchor cable."

Fergus noted that the anchor cable led out the starboard hawse hole to a location he judged to be about fifty yards off the starboard bow. After the brow and lines had been brought aboard by the young seamen, the boatswain and the two seamen manned the capstan bars and heaved around, straining to bring in the cable and its anchor. The anchor cable tautened and then took a strain. Drops of harbor water began to drip back into the dirty surface water, and the bow slowly began to move out to starboard into the river.

The captain climbed down from the bulwark, adjusted his yellow slicker, and came aft. "I'll take the helm. Kilburnie, help the boatswain make sail."

Fergus knew what had to be done next, and without waiting for the boatswain's orders he cast loose the mainsail halyard and began to hoist the large mainsail. The boatswain left one man securing the anchor, and he and the other man joined Fergus. The mainsail went up rapidly, and Fergus secured the halyard to its cleat and stored the excess line. The sail flapped slowly, began to fill, and the ship moved slowly toward the harbor entrance a few miles away. Soon the ebbing tide caught the slow-moving schooner and speeded its progress.

The sailors quickly began to hoist the jib. The captain called Fergus back to the helm and picked up an ancient brass telescope that had been leaning against the compass binnacle. He put it to his good eye and began looking ahead for the channel markers. Out of the corner of his mouth he shouted, "Hamilton, get that damned jib up smartly. We ain't got all day. Kilburnie, steer for that white church spire."

Fergus found the spire and held the bowsprit steadily on it. The captain lowered the telescope and scanned the waters ahead with his good eye.

"Well, Kilburnie," he said, "you can steer a straight course all right. How'd you like to sail with me permanently?"

Fergus laughed. "I think I'd like it and maybe I'll come back, but first I have to help my family get settled."

After the ship passed out of the harbor entrance, the captain set a course for Scotland, using a dog-eared chart marked with coffee stains. After a cold supper, one of the seamen relieved Fergus for the first watch. Fergus went below to feed and water his horse and then came back on deck. He walked aft and looked toward the disappearing Irish coast. The setting sun outlined the higher buildings of Belfast and the hills behind them. Soon the dusk blotted out even this view. Fergus sighed, realizing that he might never see Ireland again and also would never see Shannon again unless she left Ireland.

He took one last look toward Ireland and then turned to look forward. One of the young boys had the wheel watch, steering by a small compass in a box on the deck, and the captain stood next to him, bending over a battered chart. The windward side of the chart was held down to the deck against a fresh breeze by the captain's telescope. The remaining two corners were anchored by two chipped coffee mugs. Fergus chuckled. Now he understood where the coffee and tea stains on the chart came from.

Beyond the group at the wheel, Fergus could see the staysails, two triangular sails designed to be hoisted fore and aft between the two masts and used instead of a foresail on this schooner. They were carelessly secured with their sheets and halyards against the bulwark. Fergus looked up at the mainsail, a sail rigged aft from the mainmast. The jib bellied forward from the foremast, its forefoot secured to the jib boom.

Fergus walked over to the captain. "Sir, I estimate we could make another knot if the staysails were rigged. Shall I hoist them?"

The captain straightened up, rubbed his ancient back, and adjusted his eye patch. "Well, lad, thank ye, but we don't need the knot, and I sure don't want you lads tending those two extra sails if we have to tack in the dark."

Fergus scratched his head. "Sir, aren't you in a hurry to get across the channel?"

The captain laughed. "You young'uns are always in a hurry. Take a look at this chart."

Fergus bent over the flapping chart and measured the distance across the channel.

"Well?" the captain asked.

Fergus said, "I make it about thirty miles to the nearest point of land."

"Exactly, and I don't want to get there in the dark. At four knots, which we're making now, we'll see the lights of Ballantrae just before dawn. We're steering nor'east, and the current will be light. Even if I'm a little off my reckoning, and if we miss Ballantrae, we'll be able to see the loom of the land long before we run aground."

"I see, sir. The weather should stay clear, and there'll be a half moon, well up before dawn."

"Ye've got it, son, soon as we see the loom of the coast or the lights, we'll turn a point to port. Ought to get us into Prestwick about late afternoon."

The next morning Fergus had the wheel watch. Shortly after dawn the captain came to the wheel, carrying two mugs of hot tea. He gave one to Fergus.

Fergus said, "How did you heat the water?"

"Oh, I have a sand box in a corner of my cabin. As long as the weather is good, I can make a small charcoal fire on it. The rest is easy."

Fergus drank deeply from the rich, hot brew. "This makes the long night shorter."

"Kilburnie, I ask you again. Will you ship with me?"

"I'd like to, Captain, but my uncle, who served in the Royal Navy, says a small vessel like this or a fishing vessel can smell worse than the bilges of a man-of-war."

"I can't argue that, but the bilges of a man-of-war really stink. I fell into the hands of a press gang once and spent a cruise in a seventy-six-gunner. Food stunk. Bad stuff."

"The food stunk?"

"Oh, yeah. When you passed the galley just before midday meal, you had to hold your nose."

"Why?"

"There were barrels of opened sauerkraut, salt beef, and wormy biscuit standing around having the stink let out before they was cooked. The salt horse had to be soaked in water for twenty-four hours to get the salt out. Then it was boiled for hours in a big pot, and the fat all came to the top."

"So it could be thrown out?"

"Hell, no. The cooks sold it to the crew on the sly."

"I'm starting to dread my breakfast."

The captain laughed. "The food on a coaster is always better because you're in port so often and there aren't as many mouths to feed so it won't be bad. I always stock up before I get under way. We'll eat and drink well for a week. Maybe you'll like it enough to stay with us."

Fergus pressed on with his curiosity about navy life. "Tell me, were you flogged?"

The captain was silent for a moment. When he spoke it was slow and steady. "I've still got a few lash scars on my back."

"What did you do to get them?"

"I was a little slow taking my hat off when the captain spoke to me," he replied with a tinge of bitterness in his voice.

"My uncle said some captains were like that, but some were good. He says you just have to take a chance that you'll get a good one."

"Your uncle is right," Leary said.

"How long did you stay in?"

"Just one cruise. There was no war to fight, so the ship was put into ordinary, the crew was paid off, and the officers were sent ashore to wait for another ship. As soon as the ship paid off, I came back to Belfast. Took me twenty years and a little luck with cards to save enough to buy this ship."

"You seemed to have learned enough in the navy to command her."

"I knew plenty before I was pressed, and I was a quartermaster's mate and kept my eyes and ears open on the quarterdeck. Learned a lot about handling men." He paused. "And how not to."

"Well, Captain, maybe I can learn something, too."

There was no reply. Fergus turned to see the captain going below. Fergus had the feeling he had dredged up memories the captain would rather have forgotten.

It was still dark when the glass was turned at 5 A.M., marking the end of the first hour of Fergus's watch. One of the young boys on watch in the bow as lookout called out, "Lights one point on the starboard bow."

Fergus picked up the telescope and looked at the lights. Must be Ballantrae, he said to himself. He called to the boy, "Tell the captain land is in sight."

The lookout went aft to the captain's small cabin and notified him. In what seemed like only an instant the captain was on deck, looking at the lights. He clapped a hand on Fergus's shoulder as if to say, See, I knew what I was doing.

Fergus grinned.

"Come one point to port," he said to Fergus.

As the sun rose from behind the hills, the green of the shores of Scotland slowly became visible. Fergus welcomed the sight of his native land, all thoughts of Ireland except those about Shannon driven out of his mind. After the end of his watch he stayed on deck, watching the waves break against the occasional groups of rocks.

Just after noon the lookout sighted the entrance to Prestwick's port of Ayr. After the *Marianne* anchored, a barge came out to the ship, and the cow and some other cargo were unloaded onto it. By dark they had completed their unloading and at dawn were under way for Rothsey, across the Firth of Clyde.

By that evening they had entered the small port, unloaded the other horse, the hog, and some cargo, and had left the port. Prince now occupied the hold in solitary splendor, now enough at ease in his strange surroundings to be left alone, although Fergus spent his off-watch time feeding him, currying his smooth coat, and giving him an extra ration for the trip he would have to make the next day from Glasgow south to Kilburnie village.

The small schooner began the trip up the channel to Glasgow at dawn and by mid-morning was moored at a pier. Fergus helped unload his horse and the rest of the cargo and by noon had said goodbye to the captain and the crew, mounted Prince, and headed south. Fergus was familiar with Glasgow and the road to Kilburnie, and his well-rested horse cantered most of the way.

By mid-afternoon Fergus was on the crest of the hill north of Kilburnie village. He stopped and looked at the Kilburnie farm spread out below him from the road to the Firth. Copses of trees dotted the area and other trees surrounded the main house and the nearby small cottage.

Fergus rested his horse for a few minutes while he surveyed the familiar landscape ahead. The buildings and trees seemed unchanged in the three years he had been away, but the herds of cows and the flocks of sheep seemed bigger. He could see a man riding along a path leading from the main farmhouse to the fields where the cows were grazing, and a young lad and two silent and obedient collies herding the sheep.

On both sides of the Kilburnie farm were dense stands of trees, obviously marking streams coming from the hills to the Firth. The land also belonged to the Kilburnies. Fergus remembered the salmon in the streams and the times he had fished for them with his grandfather.

Small sailboats bobbed at their pier. Smoke rose from the chimney of the main house and seemed to be beckoning to him. Before he rode down the hill, he stopped, dismounted, and walked to the high point of the hill. The sky was clear, and from that point Fergus could see fifty miles across the Firth toward Ireland. He knew the coast of Ireland was another hundred miles farther away, and then there was another hundred and fifty miles across land to Donegal.

Three hundred miles away, he thought, and it might as well be three million. He shook his head sadly and tried to hold back the tears. He knew he would never be able to go back to Ireland. Somehow Shannon would have to come to him. He passed his sleeve across his eyes, walked back to the waiting horse, mounted, and rode slowly down the road. He dug his heels gently into his horse's flanks, and Prince started down the hill at a slow canter. Fergus Kilburnie was home.

3
AT HOME

Fergus pulled his horse up to a walk to avoid injuring him on the potholed road. Halfway down the gently rolling hills he paused again. The young boy carefully shepherding the flock of sheep with two collies was strange to him. Remembering how he had wished passing travelers would acknowledge him when he was a boy, he waved at him casually.

Fergus rode into the stable area and the huge barn near the big house, dismounted, unsaddled his horse, and stabled it in a vacant stall. After feeding and watering Prince, he walked to the back door, pushed it open, and walked into the large kitchen. His grandfather was sitting at the long kitchen table nursing a mug of tea. Since retiring from the Royal Navy he had insisted on using a mug instead of a cup and saucer. Fergus laughed. "Hello, Grandfather, I see you're still the old sea dog."

Strath Kilburnie, still vigorous and erect in his eightieth year, squinted at Fergus, recognized him, and shouted in his quarterdeck voice, "Boy, what the hell are you doing here?"

Fergus came round the table and wrapped his arms around the beaming old man. "Grandfather, I've come home, and the rest of the family should be here in about a week."

Old Strath sighed and sat down again at the table heavily. "God knows ye couldn't have come at a better time. We need ye and none too soon."

Fergus poured tea from the pot on the table and sat down across from his grandfather. "Tell me what's wrong."

"Nothing's really wrong, lad, it's just that I'm getting old. Hired help is hard to find, and your brother wants to get married."

Fergus nodded, drew deeply from his tea cup, and said, "Help is here. Father, Mother, and Sister are anxious to get back, and Father will be glad to take over. What does my brother want to do?"

"He wants to marry a fine young girl he knows and then to move into the small cottage. I'm sure he'll stay and help your father because I know he wants to take over the farm some day. Can you help for a spell?"

Fergus shook his head slowly. "I'll help for a while until the rest of the family is settled, but then I want to join the Royal Navy."

Old Strath snorted. "Good God, lad! Do you know what ye'd be getting into? You could just as well go to the university."

"Yes, Grandfather, you've told me enough. But I like the sea itself, and I think I can succeed. I've done well when I've been aboard ship so far, and you've taught me a lot about the navy and going to sea."

"But Fergus, don't ye realize that no matter how good you are, as a Scot you can only rise so far in a British Navy commanded largely by the English aristocracy? As a Scottish commoner you might be before the mast all your life. If you are lucky, like I was, you might become a lieutenant."

"But isn't promotion possible for performance in battle in this year 1793? I understand we're building and manning hundreds of ships in preparation for the war with France."

"Sure, lad, if you survive and are very lucky, you might be promoted. But being a Scot won't help ye. Some Englishmen find us comical, others openly despise us as rebels."

"What should I do to find good luck?" Fergus asked, deliberately choosing to avoid a discussion of Scotland's image in the eyes of Englishmen.

"Well, for one thing you can study hard to become an expert seaman, navigator, and gunner. Keep your eyes open and ask questions. Ask to be made a member of a gun crew near the quarterdeck. There you'll be under the eyes of the high-ranking officers of the ship."

Fergus interrupted. "But if I do that won't they think I'm trying to curry favor?"

Strath laughed. "Hell, no, more men get killed near the quarterdeck than any other place on the ship. The Marines on other ships are trained to shoot at the quarterdeck personnel first. They'll welcome ye because you might stop a bullet meant for an officer."

Fergus scratched his cheek. "I'm willing to take that kind of chance."

Strath nodded. "Some high-ranking officers realize early on that to win in battle it takes good gunners first, good gun captains, and good junior officers. If an ambitious officer finds out you're good, he'll want to take you to other ships and promotion will follow. That is, if you last through the battles in one piece." Strath took a sip of tea and started to go on. "And that . . ."

Fergus stopped him. "I know what you're going to say. Even then I can advance only so far, maybe to lieutenant. Then my patron will retire or get killed and some fop or martinet will be sent aboard to replace him and I'll still be stuck as a lieutenant."

Old Strath glowered into his tea mug. "Ye've got it. That's why I finally came ashore."

Fergus brightened. "But you said my mother's brother, my Uncle Jeris Fairlie, stayed in the navy in a civilian capacity and is now a clerk to one of the sea lords and has some influence."

"Ha! He's just a clansman like all the rest of us Scots, and then not even a member of the Kilburnie clan, but the Fairlie clan. He doesn't have a title or a number of seats in Parliament in his pocket."

"Don't both sub-clans belong to the MacTaggart clan?" Fergus retorted.

"Well, yes," Strath said, his tone softening somewhat, "and he's always liked our family. Says he feels like he's part of it, and of course he's related to you by blood. Jeris never got any further than I did at sea. Just a lieutenant like me. I left the navy and came back here. He lost an arm and an eye, and after he recovered he was given a clerk's job in the office of one of the sea lords, thanks to his old captain. He's just a pen pusher, but I think he knows how to pull strings by now. In the Admiralty, the clerks aren't just scriveners. They have a lot of influence, sometimes more than the members."

"But you once said he just about ran the ship assignment section of the Admiralty."

Strath laughed. "Well, maybe I was telling a little sea story. But then again Jeris is pretty smart. I suspect he'll know a lot by now and may be able to help. He does know everything that goes on in assignments and writes and sends out all the officers' orders. Still, a flunky appointed by the king is actually in charge and nobody not on the king's list of friends or acquainted with someone on it gets a command. Not even of the smallest letter-carrying packet."

"Are there no exceptions?"

Strath pursed his lips thoughtfully. "Well, maybe sometimes. A fellow named Nelson made it. But even he needed some coattails to ride. Sometimes others get to command transports, but there isn't much money to be made in them since they don't usually take prizes. I'm sure there is a war with France coming on, and if it happens promotions will loosen up, and maybe even commands."

"I'd think the navy would need good officers in the war and particularly if many ships are to be built. Do you think they will be?"

"Aye, many will be needed. The French have us outnumbered even now."

"How about the Spanish?"

"When and if they come in against us, we'll really be in trouble. The combined enemy fleets would outnumber us two to one, or even more."

Fergus got up to fill the tea mugs. "I'll take a chance. At least I'll be able to forget the last weeks."

Old Strath's eyebrows shot up and a sly smile crept across his face. "Ah, lad, now we get to the real reason for your return. Tell me before I paddle your bottom like I used to."

Over another cup of tea, Fergus told his grandfather about his growing love for Shannon and ended with the final scene with Lord Inver in the churchyard. The words came at first slowly, and then with a rush. As he came to the final scene, tears began to form in his eyes, and he got up abruptly and went out to check on Prince.

In a few hours Fergus's older brother, Ennis, rode in from the fields where the cattle were grazed. Ennis was a larger and older version of Fergus. Both showed the fair skin, light brown hair, and blue eyes of the invaders from the north who had raided and settled in Scotland centuries ago. Ennis greeted Fergus warmly. "Little brother, this is a wonderful surprise. But why are you here and not in Ireland?"

Fergus sighed. "A long story, Ennis, I'll tell you all about it at supper."

Ennis laughed. "You may be too weak by then. I'm the cook since Grandfather began to show his age."

"Do you run the whole farm now by yourself and still do the cooking?"

"Just about. I have a village boy who tends the sheep with our two collies and a second lad on weekends. As you can see, the place is getting run down. I need your help. I want to get married. The girl I'm engaged to sometimes helps with the cooking now, but she would rather work outdoors than cook, and so would I."

Fergus grinned. "Help is coming. The rest of the family will be here in about a week."

"Why did they decide to come back? I thought they were being paid well."

"They were."

"Then why did they leave?"

"It was my fault. I got involved with the daughter of the lord of the estate."

Ennis laughed. "That isn't like you." He stopped talking and looked appraisingly at Fergus, noting how well muscled his big frame was and how handsome his face had become. "Well, that wouldn't be like you were when you left Scotland, but I see you've changed."

Fergus nodded. "I thought I'd grown up over there, but I've matured a lot more since I left Ireland."

Fergus spent the next several days doing what he could to restore the buildings, drainage system, and roads. The first thing he did was to use one of the work horses to drag a heavy sledge over the approach road. He harnessed Prince beside the work horse. At first Prince reared in protest but soon settled down under Fergus's gentling voice. Over the next week repairs to roof leaks, broken furniture, and even the sailboat followed.

Fergus was just coming in from a trip on Prince to observe the tending of the sheep flock when he saw a wagon appear at the top of the hill. He kicked Prince's flanks gently and started off at a canter.

Fergus dismounted on the fly and ran over to embrace his smiling mother and sister. Angus was more reserved and extended a rough hand to his son. "How is everyone?" he asked Fergus.

Fergus shook his head. "I think we're just in time. Grandfather is getting feeble physically, although his mind is still as sharp as it ever was. Brother Ennis is overworked and can find little help. Grandfather is ready to turn the farm over to you."

Angus looked down toward the house and nodded. "Three years ago I left because it looked like he wanted to run the place forever."

"Well, he's changed now. Let's ride on down to the big house and see him."

Fergus's father and grandfather talked for hours, while Fergus's mother and sister took control of the kitchen. A huge meal soon was on the large kitchen table.

Ennis came into the house on the run and took his mother in his arms. "I saw you drive in, but I couldn't leave the cattle until I had them in their pens."

Suppertime was full of general talk, but when the men gathered before a peat fire in the living room after supper, talk turned to the future of the farm.

Grandfather Kilburnie said in his booming voice, "Angus, I want you to take over the farm. Ennis will help until he gets married."

Ennis put down his tea mug. "Yes, Father, I'd like to go to work for you after my wedding. Eileen has already started cleaning the small house. We'll be very happy there."

Grandfather Kilburnie sighed. "I always expected to finish my years in that small cottage where your grandmother and I started, but I know I can't live alone. Angus, if you and Elizabeth will have me, I'd like to stay with you here in the big house. I can still do small tasks."

"Of course, there's plenty of room."

Fergus cleared his throat. "There'll even be more room when I leave."

Angus whirled toward Fergus. "What? Where do you think you are going? The university?" he asked, his voice full of hope.

Fergus shook his head firmly. "No. I've talked this over with Grandfather. I'm going to go to London and join the Royal Navy."

Grandfather Kilburnie carefully studied a corner of the ceiling. Angus turned toward him inquiringly. "Father, how could you tell him so? You remember what it was like for you, and I think you'll agree it's a tough life for a lad."

Old Strath sighed, and his normally booming voice was subdued. "I know, but Fergus has more natural ability and intelligence than I had, and more maturity at his age. Also, there'll be more opportunity ahead now with the war expanding. War with France will mean that the king will need every man he can lay his hands on. Even Scottish commoners may be needed as officers. Furthermore, he will have influence. Remember, your brother-in-law is an Admiralty clerk."

Angus was silent, looking into the fire.

After a few minutes Grandfather Kilburnie rose slowly, yawned prodigiously, and said, "I'll leave you two to make the decision. I've got to go sling my hammock, even if it is just a regular bed now."

Fergus and his father talked until after midnight, and as the fire died out Fergus finally won the argument. Angus shook his head in defeat. "All right, lad, you may go in a week. That should give us time to put things right here."

Fergus brightened, but then he remembered how the change in the family's fortunes had come about, and he said, "Father, I'm sorry. All this is my fault. If I'd controlled myself, you might still be in Ireland."

Angus snorted. "Except for your loss of that beautiful lass, everything turned out just fine. Your mother and I had had enough of Ireland, and you can see we're all needed here. Your brother says he was about to send word to us that we should return as soon as possible. As for Shannon, Lord Inver made it clear to me that as a son-in-law he had an eye on the heir of the estate next door, the son of Lord Malin. He would never have considered you as a son-in-law, although he liked you as a groom."

Angus rose and stretched, reminding Fergus, as he watched, how much he resembled his grandfather when he had been younger. Angus said, "In a week then, you can leave for London by stage. I can spare enough money to get you there. Your Uncle Jeris will take you in, I'm sure. Remember, you can always come back home if you decide not to go to sea."

"Thank you, Father. I don't think you'll need me permanently, and I'm sure Ennis will want to take over the farm some day. I want to give the sea a good try."

Angus shook his head. "Ye're as stubborn a Scot as the rest of the clan."

4

In London

A week later Ennis drove Fergus to Glasgow in the wagon. Following Grandfather Kilburnie's advice, Fergus traveled lightly, with only a change of clothing and a warm knit hat and gloves his mother had made for him. Fergus had protested that they couldn't be worn on deck of a man-of-war as articles of uniform, but his grandfather insisted that he could use them on cold night watches, and that enlisted men did not necessarily all wear the same uniform.

Fergus had money that his father had given him hidden under his undershirt for his stage fare to London and for his meals, and a little extra his grandfather had given him privately. "Have a little go in London before you turn yourself in," he had said. "Maybe you can find someone to help you forget your Irish colleen."

Fergus shook his head. "I don't think so. I'll remember her all of my life."

His grandfather nodded. "Aye, that's what you say now."

In Glasgow, at the tavern where the stage would leave, Fergus and Ennis had a last beer together. All too soon Fergus boarded the stage, electing to sit outside in the cheaper top seats. When they reached open country south of Glasgow, the driver whipped up the eager horses, and the stage began to roll and buck as it negotiated the ruts and bumps in the country roads. An elderly man sitting next to Fergus held on to the rail with one hand and kept his top hat on with the other. "Worse than on a packet in the channel," he said. "I'm not used to this violent motion."

Fergus grinned, taking the motion without trouble. "More like the open sea," he replied.

Within an hour the old man was hopelessly sick, and Fergus realized that his brief training at sea was doing him some good. Without realizing what he had done, he had automatically taken the seat on the windward side of the heavy stage, and the old man's breakfast shot harmlessly over the side of the stage down wind.

"Can I help?" Fergus asked.

The old man grinned painfully. "Not unless you can slow this contraption down."

After a few miles the horses tired, and the motion became more tolerable, but not enough to suit the old man, who continued to spatter the passing landscape with whatever was left in his stomach.

The next few days were a blur of three hundred and fifty miles of roadside fields of grain, waving children, scared cattle, and the plunging horses in the groaning leather harness. The stage made stops at roadside inns for lunch and tea. At the nightly stops Fergus tried to conserve his meager funds by eating lightly at the inns where the stage stopped. The old man who had shared the stage top with Fergus invited Fergus to share his dinner, which proved to be enormous.

"Can you really eat all that?" Fergus asked.

The old man laughed. "I have to eat enough now to last all day tomorrow. Once I get up on top of that coach I can't eat any more that day."

On the sixth day the stage rolled into London and stopped at a tavern acting as a terminal. Fergus quickly found an inexpensive roominghouse where he could rest for the night and have his clothes washed and ironed. While the landlady was gone with his clothes, he took out the letter his grandfather had written for him to take to his Uncle Jeris. If the glowing description of Fergus and the equally eloquent plea for help did not impress Uncle Jeris, nothing would.

Fergus remembered his uncle well, from when he had taken salmon fishing vacations at the Kilburnie farm, but he was not sure his uncle would remember the gangling ten-year-old lad who had carried his fishing equipment and dogged his footsteps walking up the salmon streams. He might recall, Fergus mused, his constant pestering for more tales of his service in the Royal Navy.

The next morning, carefully dressed in his clean clothes, with his letter and remaining money securely fastened inside his shirt as his grandfather had advised him, Fergus got directions from the innkeeper to the Admiralty and set off on foot to find the famous building.

London was a vast change from the country lanes of Kilburnie and even from the fairly orderly roads of Glasgow. In London the streets were filled with noise and confusion. Beggars and peddlers pawed at Fergus, speaking in strange local accents. Most were dirty and unkempt and several had legs, eyes, or arms missing. Large drays pulled by four or more clattering horses made crossing a thoroughfare hazardous. Horse manure and garbage filled the streets, and the stench was overpowering.

The walk took almost an hour, but after asking for directions several times from the mayor's guards and private watchmen on streetcorners Fergus found himself in front of the main Admiralty buildings, near the buildings of Parliament. He stopped and looked at them carefully. The two large yellow edifices were set back from the main street, as if trying to maintain their privacy and dignity in the midst of confusion and noise. The main buildings were protected from the heavy dray traffic of the street by a screening wall along the street with a gate large enough to admit carriage traffic to the courtyard.

Fergus slipped inside the gateway, narrowly avoiding a rumbling carriage carrying a visiting admiral. Ahead he could see the four large columns supporting the roof of the portico in front of the main structure. He walked up to the colonnade, looking with awe at the impressive architecture. It was far fancier than anything he had seen in Glasgow. As he approached the big double doors to the inner part of the buildings, he was aware of a man standing next to them.

As he watched, the visiting admiral slipped something into the hand of the man at the door, who grinned and touched his hat. The doorkeeper was middle-aged, past his physical prime, but obviously still well muscled and physically strong. As Fergus approached, the man cleared his throat loudly and held out his hand, raising his bushy eyebrows expectantly.

Fergus stopped. "I'm Fergus Kilburnie, nephew of Jeris Fairlie. I've come to visit him. He's a confidential clerk to the Third Professional Lord. I have a letter for him. Can you direct me to his office?"

The man cackled. "Sure I can, lad, just put a pound or at least several coins in me palm first so I can remember correctly. Otherwise you might not get in the door."

Fergus bridled. "I don't think I'll do that. I'll find it myself. Just who are you to try to cozen a poor Scot from the country?"

"I'm the main door usher. Every visitor from midshipman to admiral tips me. You ain't no exception, you damned Jacobite!"

Fergus turned red. "I am an exception. I'm not in the Navy yet, and if you don't stand aside I'll have my uncle take care of you."

"Haw! He ain't here, you impudent rascal. I'll give the letter to him when I have time."

Fergus strode toward the doorway, pushing the usher aside with his muscular shoulder. He pushed so hard the usher landed on a lieutenant. Fergus quickly walked inside the massive door, leaving the usher to pick up the gasping lieutenant, who began upbraiding the usher.

Inside Fergus turned right and began to scan the big brass door plates for his uncle's name. A hundred feet down the corridor he found the one he wanted: JERIS FAIRLIE, Confidential Secretary to the Third Professional Sea Lord. Fergus knocked firmly.

"Come in," a voice responded. Fergus turned the big brass knob, opened the tall mahogany door, and went in. Behind a modest desk was a man, obviously a Fairlie. He had a black patch over his left eye and his left arm of his black coat was pinned up to the elbow. Even with the eyepatch, his face looked so much like his mother's that Fergus had no trouble recognizing him and, strangely enough, his uncle seemed to have no trouble recognizing Fergus. "Fergus, isn't it?"

Fergus grinned. "Yes, Uncle Jeris, it is, all the way from Kilburnie. I didn't think you'd recognize me."

Jeris laughed. "Lad, you've grown a lot, but you're still the image of your grandfather, with a bit of my sister thrown in." He rose, shook Fergus's hand warmly, and said, "Sit down and tell me what brings you to London and why you left God's country up in Scotland."

Fergus took out his grandfather's letter. "This, sir. I'd like your help in joining the Royal Navy."

Jeris frowned and took the letter. After he had read it, he looked over at Fergus and grinned. "Aye, old Strath still spreads it a bit thick, but I've no doubt you're as good as he says you are. But why do you want to join the navy? Isn't the family farm doing well?"

"Yes, Uncle, it is, but with my father still young and my brother coming along, there is very little future for me there. I'd like to go to sea."

Jeris nodded. "I can see that. It's just what you said when you were a lad. From your appearance, your knowledge of the sea, and your general character, which I know well, you should do fine, but I must warn you, I have little influence in appointing midshipmen. I know who is to be appointed, and I write and deliver all the orders for the officers and captains of our ships of the line down to midshipmen, but the king and his ministers keep a firm hand on the list of those to be appointed, and the Third Professional Sea Lord, a naval officer, signs all of the orders. Frankly, there aren't many Scots among them."

Fergus nodded. "Grandfather told me as much, but he thinks the Royal Navy will need all the officers it can get, regardless of their origins, if the war with France expands. I assume the best I can hope for is to enlist as an ordinary seaman and hope to work my way up through the ranks over the years. I am willing to take that chance."

Jeris nodded, obviously relieved that Fergus did not expect too much from him. "I presume your grandfather gave you good advice as to what to do once you got aboard ship."

"Yes, sir, he did. Now all I need to know is where to go to find a ship."

Jeris laughed. "Not so fast, young man. I want you to come home with me for a day or two before the Navy gets ahold of you for good. My wife will want to feed you well, and we'd both like to get to know you better. I remember you well from my trips to Kilburnie. We've never had children but I wish we had a dozen like you. I'm about through for the day. Let's go off to my quarters."

Jeris rose, locked his desk with a large brass key, and walked out his office door, locking it with a second, even larger key. As they walked toward the outer door, Fergus said, "Uncle, I must confess. I had to knock the usher about a bit to get in to see you. He asked me for a pound and I didn't have any to spare for him. Certainly not that much."

Jeris guffawed loudly, the sound echoing off the marble walls. "What? The old bastard wanted a whole pound? Anything you did to him will be common gossip in the Sea Lord's daily meeting tomorrow. If you did enough to him, they may want to make you a boatswain right off."

Fergus and his uncle walked down the Mall to Haymarket Street and across Shaftesbury Avenue to Soho. The large, heavy drays thundered as their wheels clattered across the heavy cobblestones. Fergus was apprehensive as they crossed streets between drays drawn by four and sometimes six horses. Carriage drivers shouted as they tried to urge their horses to slip between breaks in the steady stream of traffic. On the narrow sidewalks peddlers and beggars accosted Jeris and Fergus, but Jeris raised his cane when they came too close, and they melted away. Fergus at first tried to protect his uncle, but soon realized that his uncle was really shielding him.

Fergus sighed. "This isn't like Glasgow. Even Belfast was cleaner and safer than this."

Jeris laughed. "You'd get used to it if you made the walk every day like I do."

"I thought you owned a carriage."

"I do, but I need the exercise."

"Don't you get tired of all these beggars pestering you with their cries?"

Jeris wielded his stick, and a gap opened in the mass of humanity ahead. "No, they're bothering us because they see you. When I'm alone, they see my empty sleeve and my eyepatch and think I'm one of them. When you are with me, they think you are an easy mark and that I've gotten to you first."

In fifteen minutes Jeris stopped in front of a medium-sized flat in Soho. The front was brick, carefully whitewashed. "This is my final billet," he said. "Let's go in. Martha will be glad to see you."

Fergus grinned. "I'll be glad to see her, too. I remember how nice she was to me when you used to visit us. She was almost another mother to me."

Jeris unlocked the red front door and ushered Fergus into a long, softly carpeted hall. The wonderful smells of good cooking wafted from the kitchen, obviously somewhere at the rear of the hall.

Jeris raised his voice. "Martha! Put down your spoon and come here. Our nephew Fergus Kilburnie is here from Scotland. He has news for you."

A robust female figure burst out of the kitchen door, large spoon in hand, and a radiant smile on her face. She ran to Fergus and enfolded him in her arms against her ample bosom. "Laddy! Laddy! I haven't seen you for years!"

From deep in Martha's bosom, between the clean smells of soap and the aroma of a roast, Fergus laughed. "Aunt Martha, you haven't changed a bit. You used to hold me close just like this when I was ten."

"Aye, and I loved you like a son even then." She released him and stood back. "Jeris, why are we so fortunate?"

Jeris smiled at her happiness. "It's just for the weekend. He's going to sea Monday."

"Well, at least we can feed him up a little. Go into the parlor and have a hot toddy. Supper will be ready in a half-hour. Save all the gossip for me, particularly about my sister-in-law. My cook and maid are off for the day, and I do love to get back in my kitchen."

Jeris led Fergus into a large room off the hall. Paintings of sea battles and of ships of the Royal Navy hung in the middle of one wall. A sword, obviously Jeris's, hung on another wall. Comfortable chairs and chaises surrounded a fireplace in which a small coal fire glowed. Soft carpets covered the wood floor that shone between the edges of the carpets.

Jeris gestured toward an overstuffed chair. "Sit down, lad, and I'll bring you a spot of grog. Knowing your mother, I don't think you drink yet, but this is a good time to initiate you into the qualities of drink. You'll find times at sea when you'll want to draw your grog ration and enjoy it instead of saving the equivalent in money. It will do a lot to cheer you up at the end of what will be some long and tough days at sea."

Fergus eased into a chair and looked around the room. Jeris filled the glasses and gave him one. He sat down and raised his glass. "To your naval career. May it be long and successful and may your ships take many prizes."

Fergus raised his glass. "Thank you, sir. I can do without the prize money if I can survive."

The light brown liquid burned his throat and watered his eyes.

Jeris laughed. "You'll get used to it." He took a sip of his own drink and smiled appreciatively. "Now, Fergus, don't be too easy about rejecting prize money. If you wish to live well and get your family ahead, you need money. I know men who went to sea as poor as church mice and are now addressed as 'Sir John' and are rich men."

Supper was delightful. The grog warmed Fergus's stomach and loosened his tongue. He quickly brought his uncle and aunt up to date on the Kilburnie family history and even, after being prodded by his aunt, told them about Shannon and the reason his family had left Ireland. With the passage of time, and a little alcohol, he could talk about it more freely.

"Sounds like a wonderful girl, even if she's the daughter of an Irish squire," Jeris said. "I don't blame you. I'd have done the same."

Martha laughed. "You old stick-in-the-mud. You wouldn't even have ridden after her in the first place."

Jeris laughed. "Maybe not. I never did like picnics."

On Sunday Jeris took Fergus out walking in the streets of London. "Keep close by. I don't want you to get in the hands of a press gang."

Fergus laughed. "I'll be careful. I'm just glad I didn't get picked up the other night."

"Probably because you weren't in any tavern."

Fergus nodded. "I stayed in my room and did my laundry."

Jeris led Fergus along the bank of the Thames, pointing out the naval facilities and ships lining the banks on both sides of the narrow, winding river. On the way home, they swung by Westminster Abbey, the Houses of Parliament, Haymarket, and the Admiralty. Jeris pointed to the entrance to the Admiralty buildings. "I hope some day you'll be summoned to see one of the Lords of the Admiralty," he said.

Fergus shuddered. "One trip was enough. I'm not sure I want to go in there again."

Jeris interrupted. "You can be summoned for good reasons as well as bad. Now let's get back home. Martha will have a joint ready for us, and we need a little grog in us to get us ready for it."

After supper, Jeris excused himself and left for the back of the house. In a few minutes he was back with two canvas sea bags. He dropped them on the parlor floor. "Here, Fergus, you can manage these better than I can. Open them and spread out the contents."

"What are they, Uncle?"

"My old sea gear. Most of it will fit you. You can't use the lieutenant's uniform yet, but I'll save it for you. The rest of the clothing, particularly the foul-weather gear, is usable by any seaman."

Fergus pulled the bag's contents out and spread them on the floor under Jeris's direction. All the usable clothing was put back into one of the bags. Jeris said, "You'll be entitled to two months' pay when you go aboard and are enlisted by the captain. The purser will complete your outfit out of his stores, and that will take most of your advance pay and all of your bonus. Because of the articles I'm giving you, you should have some pay left on the books."

"Uncle, it sounds like I'm well taken care of."

Jeris smiled with satisfaction. "Oh, yes, lad, but more important I have in my pocket a set of orders for one of the finest lieutenants I know, name of Kittrelle."

"And this just happened accidentally?"

"Good Scot's luck, I guess. He's just getting out of the hospital. He was badly wounded on his last voyage, and I had arranged for my carriage to pick him up at the hospital Monday morning and then come here to pick up his orders before he goes to his ship."

Fergus asked, "What ship?"

"He was the first, or senior lieutenant, of the *Athena,* a thirty-six-gun frigate. She's down the Thames at a shipyard finishing repairs after a battle."

"How'd she do?"

"She's very fast, but like most frigates she carries light guns, twelve-pounders and some eights. The twelve-pounders fire a shot about two and one-half inches in diameter. Weighs about half a stone. When fired with six-pound powder charge, the ball will carry about a thousand yards, more or less. Close in, say at one hundred yards, the ball will penetrate twenty-four inches of oak. It is a powerful gun, but of course it can't match twenty-four and thirty-two-pounders."

Fergus whistled. "She could do a lot of damage even with that light armament."

"Not against big ships of the line carrying more and bigger guns. Frigates are designed to be scouts for the fleet and to use their speed. If they are alone, they have to be careful not to attack large ships and to make sure they maneuver so as to be able to get away from larger and slower adversaries. In her last battle, the captain got too close to a French third-rater, a far superior ship. Lost a lot of good men and almost lost Kittrelle."

"He'll be all right?"

"Oh yes, a very tough man," Jeris chuckled. "I understand he gave the hospital staff hell, though."

"What was wrong?"

"Nothing really. He just wanted to get out of the hospital and get back to his ship and go to sea. He was afraid the captain would ask us for a replacement."

"Then I am to go to the *Athena*?"

"Yes, lad, that would be a good ship for you. Tomorrow morning, when Lieutenant Kittrelle arrives, I'll ask you to leave the room to pack your gear. Then I'll make arrangements with him to take you with him and have you enlisted on board."

"Won't I need some training?"

Jeris laughed. "Not you. You already know more about going to sea than half the seamen and all of the midshipmen. Many of the men are pressed and have no training or experience at all."

Fergus had heard about the "press." Whenever the Royal Navy needed men, as it did now, any man who looked able to go to sea and even those who didn't were liable to be picked up by groups of men known as "press gangs" and taken aboard a ship whether they wanted to go or not.

"If you'd gone into any of the taverns here or been out on the streets at night you might have landed in the navy the hard way, by way of a press gang. Now, by enlisting voluntarily, you will be eligible for an enlistment bonus and a lot better treatment."

Fergus smiled, but Jeris cut him short. "Don't get too happy. You won't see much of your bonus, or your pay either, until the ship's cruise is over."

Fergus sobered. "I don't really care about the pay, I just want to go to sea. But what happens to my bonus and wages?"

Jeris laughed. "As I told you, the purser will get most of your bonus for your initial outfitting. The rest is usually held by the captain."

"But won't I get it later?"

"It seems to disappear. A little here, a little there. The captain doesn't actually steal it, but he subtracts money for your sick-bay expenses and extra food. There is always something for you to pay. It depends on the honesty of the individual captain and his purser. You should have something left. Your captain is very honest."

"What if I become an officer?"

Jeris laughed so hard his eyepatch almost came off. "You're a Scot, remember?"

Fergus colored. "And proud of it. Won't I get promoted if I do well?"

"Only if the ship is far away from England and several officers are killed. Even then you have to be liked, or at least known by the officers and particularly by the captain."

Fergus was silent for several minutes, staring into the fire. Then he sighed heavily. "I'll take a chance. If I stay alive and do well, fine. If I get killed, it won't matter anyway. Tell me more about the ship."

Jeris leaned over the fire, took out a hot poker, and thrust it into his mug of wine. "Lieutenant Kittrelle, I've told you somewhat about. He owes me a favor, and I'll ask him to look after you."

Fergus shook his head. "But, Uncle, I want to make it on my own."

Jeris nodded. "You will, lad, but Kittrelle will see that you have a fair chance."

"Will there be problems?"

"Oh, yes, all the senior officers in the navy have friends at Court or at the Admiralty. Even the lieutenants and midshipmen are assigned to ships by favoritism. Some pay a lot of money for their commissions and assignments."

"Isn't there any other way?"

"There is. Make yourself so expert they'll have to promote you in their own interest. Somebody has to run the ship, and the politically promoted officers usually aren't very good. First, you will be made a member of a gun crew. If you become the best man in the crew and learn what the gun captain does, they'll turn to you when a new gun captain is needed. Do each job better than anyone else, and each time you are promoted begin to learn the job of the next higher rank. As I said, captains need people to navigate the ship and fight the enemy."

Jeris leaned closer. "There's something else I want you to hold in confidence."

"Yes, Uncle."

"When I came up to Scotland your grandfather and I, late one night, made an arrangement for your future. We both agreed you might want to join the navy, and we wanted you to have every chance to succeed."

"I agree, sir, and I'll do my best."

"But that alone won't do it. If you are to make lieutenant at an early age, you would need six years of service. I had a friend much beholden to me for helping him to get command of a first-rater. He agreed to put your name on his rolls as a midshipman."

"But I was never there."

Jeris laughed. "Never mind, lad. This is done every day on every ship. For five years you accrued service as a midshipman on the books of that ship and also on the records of the Admiralty. Now, after one more year of service, you will be eligible for lieutenant."

"It can't be that simple."

Jeris laughed. "Of course it isn't. You have to be at least nineteen—you're already twenty—and you have to be appointed by a captain and nominated to take the examination. I have no doubt you can pass it."

"Thanks, Uncle, for the help and advice. Now all I have to do is carry out my part."

"I'm sure you'll do well. Now off to your bed with you and get some sleep. The next time you turn in will be in a hammock. Your Aunt Martha will want you up bright and early so she can start feeding you."

The next morning Fergus was up early, checking again the contents of his sea bag and then restowing it carefully. He went out in the morning freshness, knowing it might be months before he saw trees, grass, and flowers again, except in the distance. Back in his room he began to smell bacon frying and other delightful kitchen smells, and he went below to see his aunt.

She saw him coming. "Come on in, dear laddy, you need a little something before breakfast. Maybe some coffee and toast, or a little bacon?"

"Just coffee, please, I want to save my appetite." Fergus sat at the kitchen table chatting with his aunt until he heard a loud knock on the front door. Jeris, just coming down the stairs, said, "I'll answer it. The maid isn't back yet."

Fergus heard the door open. A deep, strong voice said, "Ah, Jeris, we meet again. I've missed you."

Jeris said, "And I you, Jonathan. Come in. Breakfast will be ready in a few minutes. While we wait, I want you to meet my nephew."

Fergus could hear Jeris call to him, and he pushed his empty coffee cup back and went into the parlor.

Lieutenant Jonathan Kittrelle was standing with his back to the fireplace. Today the fire was going at a faster rate. His hands were behind him. Fergus noted his thick black hair, cut short. Then he noticed his equally black eyes, large and keenly focused. They dominated his face, even though his nose, mouth, and chin were strong. His lieutenant's uniform was spotless, from his white stock, topping a frilled white shirt, to his white-lapeled blue coat, white knee-breeches, and white stockings. Below the stockings black pumps were anchored with small gold buckles that caught the fire's reflection.

Jeris noticed that Fergus had come into the parlor behind him and said, "Lieutenant Kittrelle, this is my nephew, Fergus Kilburnie."

Kittrelle smiled warmly, walked forward, and extended his hand. "I am honored to meet you. Any friend of your uncle's is a friend of mine."

Fergus was so flustered his jaw dropped, but he soon recovered, stepped forward, and took Kittrelle's outstretched hand. "I, sir, am the one who should feel honored. My uncle has told me much about you."

Martha came in, greeted Kittrelle, and announced that breakfast was ready.

When they were seated, Jeris led the conversation, inquiring about Kittrelle's health and catching him up on what had been happening at the Admiralty while he was in the hospital. Finally he said, "I guess you are wondering about the *Athena*."

Kittrelle's face darkened. "Wondering! I've been worried that she'll sail without me. Those damned bounders at the hospital, er, pardon me, ma'am, wouldn't listen to me. They wanted to keep me another week."

Martha laughed. "Oh, Jonathan, I hear lots worse from this old sea dog every day."

Jeris said, "Your ship will be ready to sail in a few days. She's provisioning now. I have your orders in my pocket for you to rejoin her, and my carriage will take you to her after breakfast."

"Good. Now all I have to worry about is rounding up the rest of the crew."

Jeris coughed discreetly. "Fergus, you seem to have finished your breakfast. Please go and check over the equipment I gave you yesterday."

Fergus, remembering his uncle's instructions from the day before, said, "Certainly, Uncle."

Jeris turned to Martha. "Dear, if you'll excuse us, we'll take our coffee into the parlor."

When the two were settled in front of the fire, Jeris said, "With regard to your ship's crew, your captain told me a few days ago he has a lot of men but not very much quality. I have a proposal that will add to that quality. My young nephew wants to go to sea."

Kittrelle's eyebrows shot up. "Egad! I'll take him if you say so."

Jeris laughed. "Not so fast. I'm not just pushing him on you. He's a real jewel. He's big and strong, as you can see. His grandfather retired as a lieutenant and has taught him everything he could about seamanship, navigation, and gunnery. The only thing the young man hasn't done is fire a large gun, although I'm told he's very good with a fowling piece."

"Has he been to sea at all?"

"Oh, yes. Three summers on a fishing schooner, but that was some time ago."

"Even with that he's better qualified to go to sea than most of our seaman, all of our midshipmen, and even some of our lieutenants."

"My only request is that you look out for him."

"Of course."

Jeris relaxed. "I don't mean for you to show him any favoritism. Just give him assignments where he can show what he can do. He'll take care of the rest."

"You say he knows navigation?"

"Yes. He can take sun and Polaris sights, work them out, and plot them. He can run a line of dead-reckoning, read charts, take soundings, and read a compass and steer a course. Also he speaks and writes well."

Kittrelle's black eyes sparkled as he rubbed his hands together. "Wait until the captain meets him. The only question is whether the captain or the master will take him on as an apprentice quartermaster. I'll wager the captain will let the master have him."

After a final cup of coffee, Fergus's sea bag was stowed along with Kittrelle's duffel in the back of the carriage, and the horses clomped down the cobbled street toward the Thames River and the *Athena*.

Kittrelle looked at Fergus out of the corner of his eye while still keeping a close watch on the traffic ahead. "Lad, your uncle says you are well qualified to go to sea. I'm going to see that the master takes you on as an apprentice quartermaster."

Fergus hesitated. "Sir, would I still be a member of a gun crew?"

Kittrelle grinned. "Damned right. You'll be a member of the crew of the after gun, less the stern chasers, on the starboard battery. You'll be right under my nose since I command the battery, and the captain on the quarterdeck just aft of the gun will see everything you do, good or bad."

Fergus grinned. "Thank you, sir. If I have a chance I won't let you down."

A large carriage cut in front of them. Kittrelle grabbed the edge of the top and thrust his head out the side. His bellow at the other driver hurt Fergus's ears. "Avast, you bloody lubber! We had the right of way! Shape up or I'll twist the tails off your damned horses!"

The other driver leaned out and unleashed a stream of cockney oaths, most of which Fergus had never heard before and could not understand.

Kittrelle sat back and grinned. "That didn't do any good, but I feel better. When you get to sea, you'll hear a lot of these exchanges. They shouldn't always mean anything to the man who receives them, except that the man who delivers the hot air feels better. Don't pay it any mind."

After an hour of dodging heavy traffic, the carriage pulled up alongside a man-of-war moored with heavy hempen lines to the wharf. Fergus looked up with awe. It was the biggest ship he had ever seen, yet he knew it was less than half the size of the navy's largest ships.

Kittrelle noted his wide eyes. "Lad, she's not that big as war ships are rated. She's a fifth-rater carrying thirty-six twelve-pounders and eight-pounders. But she's a very fast sailer. Her lines were taken from a French frigate of note. Used properly by admirals, she's a very valuable ship. Used improperly by her captain, she can run into a lot of trouble."

Fergus started to make a remark, but thought better of it and climbed down from the carriage. Kittrelle climbed down from the other side and headed for the brow. Fergus pulled all the baggage out of the back of the carriage, waved in thanks to the carriage driver, and walked toward the brow. He put down the baggage and looked up at the masts and their rigging. They seemed to soar upwards forever. "My God!" he muttered. "Can I ever climb that high?"

Kittrelle said, "Son, this is the last time you will see the outside of this ship for about a year when our cruise ends. I have to take a look at her side to see what the crew has done to her while I've been gone. Come with me and we'll both take a good look."

"Thank you, sir, I'd like that."

Kittrelle started toward the stern at a brisk walk, Fergus following close behind him. When they got there, Kittrelle pointed to the carved and gilded decorations. "Those are very modest for a man-of-war. I don't hold with them, but the captain likes them."

Kittrelle turned around abruptly, almost knocking Fergus over, and walked slowly along the *Athena*'s side, looking at it carefully. He stopped, looking at a gun port. "Look at that! I'll have the carpenter's ass!"

"The carpenter is in charge of the gun ports?"

"Damned right, and he has neglected all of them, this one in particular. Look at that sheave on the lifting rig. It's foul. In this condition he and his mates would take too long to raise the port when we beat to quarters. We'd lose time to the enemy. Yes, I'll be all over him."

Kittrelle started up the wharf again. Fergus noted that the *Athena*'s side, from the barely noticeable copper strip below the waterline to the bottom of the gun ports, was painted black. The gun ports were also black, but the spaces between them were lemon yellow. Up above the gun port line, to the bulwark, the intervals were also painted black.

Kittrelle walked up the remaining part of the side and paused at the bow. Fergus could see the figurehead just below the bowsprit and in front of the head structure. The whole arrangement was under a protruding jib boom.

"Look at that figurehead!" Kittrelle said. "Damned beautiful, isn't she?"

Fergus could see the figure of a woman, head held royally back, arms missing, but breasts thrust firmly forward. The entire figure had been freshly gilded. He was reminded of Shannon, who had been as beautiful as the reproduction of *Athena* and certainly a lot more lively.

Kittrelle said, "Athena herself! Truly a goddess! I love it!"

Fergus nodded, not quite understanding Kittrelle's enthusiasm. "Very beautiful, sir."

Kittrelle looked up at the space on the ship below and aft of the figurehead. "Kilburnie, up there is the head. You'll see it several times a day, but you'll never be able to foul that beautiful woman."

Fergus was puzzled. "Sir?"

Kittrelle said, "A square-rigged ship can only sail about thirty degrees into the wind. That's why our elders, years ago, decreed that the head would be in the bow. No matter how hard you try, the wind will always be from astern, and your best efforts will always be blown forward."

Fergus pursed his lips. "If you say so, sir."

Kittrelle turned abruptly. "Let's go aboard. Obviously I've got a lot to do."

Fergus followed Kittrelle astern to the brow, picked up all the baggage, and followed him aboard.

Kittrelle saluted the midshipman on watch at the top of the brow, and then the colors flying at a staff aft. Fergus, still a civilian, walked aboard behind him and put down the baggage on the quarterdeck.

Kittrelle said, "Leave the baggage there. I'll need a little time to talk to Captain Burbage. You can walk about the topside and get acquainted with the ship. I'll call you to the quarterdeck at the proper time."

When Burbage saw Kittrelle approaching, a huge smile broke out on his regularly featured, well-shaved face. His body, in his carefully tailored uniform, was well formed, but not as husky as Kittrelle's. Fergus thought his face was not handsome, but it was pleasant. His eyes were gray and steady, and he had an air of quiet confidence. Perhaps, Fergus thought, part of it came from maturity. He was definitely older than Kittrelle.

Fergus liked the looks of him, and after all he had heard about others he knew he was lucky to have drawn a good captain. He silently thanked Uncle Jeris.

Burbage said, "Ah, Kittrelle, I heard you'd be back soon. I'll bet the hospital crew was getting pretty tired of you. I'm very glad to see you made it back aboard. As you can see, I'm not doing very well with all this myself. Young Lieutenant Brashear is doing his best to fill in for you, but I need you badly."

"I'm ready to go to work, sir, and I hope Woolwich dock yard has done well by you."

"No complaints. Now let's get to work."

5
THE ATHENA

ergus had watched Kittrelle as he walked aft, and now he raised his eyes to the forest of masts, yardarms, and rigging above. There were three masts, the largest the mainmast, stepped about in the middle of the ship. The forward mast, or foremast, was about halfway between the bow and the mainmast. The third, or mizzenmast, was about halfway between the mainmast and the stern. A long horizontal boom, called the jib boom, protruded out about fifty feet from the bow. A smaller boom stuck out thirty feet astern from the mizzenmast. Three sets of horizontal spars, or yardarms, were hung from each of the three masts.

On the mainmast, a sailmaker and his mates were rigging a new sail. It was pristine white, in contrast to the gray of the two sails already rigged and furled to their yardarms. Fergus could guess as to the difference in color. The thousands of coal-burning stoves in London threw up a blanket of black soot each night which in the daytime descended on the sails, the bare wooden decks, and indeed on all of London. The sails on the other masts had not been rigged yet, and were safe below from the blackening fog.

From his time on the fishing schooner, Fergus knew that the three or four triangular flying jibs would be, in contrast to the square sails on the masts, rigged with their forefeet fixed to the long jib boom, and the thin top of the sails hoisted aloft by halyards.

Astern was another triangular sail, called a spanker, rigged to the after boom.

Between the masts, Fergus knew that additional triangular sails, called staysails, might be rigged if needed for additional speed. His grandfather had taught him well.

Fergus looked down at the bases of the three masts. Around each was a table-like structure, about waist high, into which were fitted thin wooden pins known as marlinspikes. The ends of the long rigging lines leading aloft could be secured to them and the excess line wrapped around their tops. The resulting gaggle of tarred black lines looked like a nest of orderly snakes to Fergus.

Fergus looked up, trying to follow the paths of the black lines to the blocks, called sheaves, secured at various points on the upper parts of the masts and then running back down to the sails. Fergus shook his head, knowing he would have to master the names and functions of the halyards used to hoist the sails and the sheets used to control the sail directions.

Fergus looked around the upper deck of the ship. All around the side was a heavy wooden structure about four feet high, known as a bulwark. Like the entire ship, it was made of heavy oak. Apertures were cut in it at intervals for guns. Inside was an arrangement of light line put together to resemble a net. Stowed in this netting, which was secured to the bulwark, were the crew's hammocks, lashed in a sausage-like shape, and then doubled and lashed again. The result was good protection from incoming iron shot and also from musket balls.

Fergus looked aft to where Captain Burbage and Kittrelle were still in intense conversation. From the mizzenmast aft to the stern was known as the quarterdeck. Just aft of the mizzenmast was a square mahogany box about three feet high known as the binnacle, containing a magnetic compass calibrated in compass points for steering, a second compass with a ring calibrated in tens of degrees for taking bearings, and a lantern arrangement for reading the compass cards at night. Aft of the binnacle was a huge double wheel. From a drum between the wheels a leather rope led down through two holes to the deck below and back to the massive wooden rudder. Large wooden spokes on the wheel gave the helmsmen leverage with which to turn the wheels.

Around the quarterdeck were eight twelve-pounder guns, their bronze carcasses resting on heavy wooden carriages painted a deep red. Aft on the quarterdeck were two eight-pounder chasers mounted on swivels.

Fergus turned and started up the port side. The area from the mizzen-mast forward to the foremast area was known as the waist. On each side of it was a narrow walkway next to the hammock nettings. Over the rest of the waist area three pulling boats, which could also be rigged for sailing, were secured firmly. Two small utility boats were nestled in between them and a half dozen spars for replacements for the yardarms and even a piece of spare mast were lashed down.

As Fergus walked forward he looked down at the hammocks. Each was plainly marked in black paint with a name and billet number. He knew he would soon have his own hammock stowed there.

The forward part of the ship, known as the forecastle, was rimmed with two more eight-pounders. Fergus went to the forward part of the bulwark and started to look over the side. He was surprised by the head and shoulders of a seaman climbing inboard over the bulwark. "Hello," Fergus said.

The seaman smiled. "Just back from a trip to the head. I thought I'd be able to water the lady down there, but I couldn't quite make it."

"You mean you thought you could because the wind is from ahead instead of from the beam like it is when you are at sea?"

The seaman looked at Fergus curiously. "You're dressed as a landsman, but no landsman would know that."

"Perhaps I'm not a landsman," Fergus retorted with more than a little amusement at the sailor's perplexed tone. "Or at least I won't be one for long."

They were interrupted by a boatswain's whistle. Fergus turned around. A struggling sheep in a belly sling was being hoisted aboard. Fergus watched as it disappeared down an opening just aft of the forecastle.

The seaman said, "He's bound for the manger below to join five other sheep and two hogs."

"You'll eat them at sea?"

"For a few days. The captain and the officers will get the choice cuts. We'll get ours mostly in soup."

Fergus considered the rationing. "With three hundred men to feed, they won't go very far." He thanked the seaman and went aft to the area near the gangway. Near the baggage he stopped and looked toward Kittrelle and the captain. They were standing near the rail, out of the way, anxiously watching the parade of crewmen, yard workmen, and stevedores crisscrossing in front of them, bearing equipment, barrels, and boxes, while continuing to converse.

Fergus noted that Kittrelle was rapidly taking charge. His piercing black eyes closely followed the work parties, while at the same time he kept up a conversation with the captain. Now and then he raised his voice and spoke to a petty officer. Kittrelle seemed to remember all the names of the petty officers although he had been absent at the hospital for several weeks.

Realizing that Kittrelle was rapidly taking a burden off his shoulders, Fergus saw the captain begin to relax. He noted that the captain's uniform was much like Kittrelle's but of finer materials, and he wore one golden epaulette on the shoulders of his coat, signifying that he was a captain of a fifth-rater.

Kittrelle apparently finished his conversation with Captain Burbage. As Fergus drew closer to the two officers, he could hear Kittrelle say, "I can see that you miss me, and I'll stow my gear and get right to work. But first, I have a small surprise for you. A recruit who is worth ten pressed men. He is young, strong, smart, has been to sea, and wants to serve on a fast ship. May I call him over and present him?"

The captain looked past Kittrelle's broad shoulders and saw Fergus standing by the baggage. His eyebrows shot up, though whether in delight or dismay Fergus could not tell. Burbage said noncommittedly, "By all means bring him over."

Kittrelle turned and motioned to Fergus, who trotted over and came to attention in front of the captain. The captain looked Fergus up and down, exchanged a glance with Kittrelle, grinned, and extended his hand. Fergus, not quite sure of protocol, took the captain's hand and shook it firmly but tentatively.

The captain noticed Fergus's uncertainty. "Lad, you won't be shaking hands with me again after I've enlisted you unless it's on the occasion of a promotion." He then turned to Kittrelle. "Sir, I accept him. Put his name on our list and assign him to your battle bill. Now we all have to get to work."

Kittrelle saluted and turned smartly on his heel. Fergus did the same before picking up the baggage and falling in behind Kittrelle.

At the forward edge of the quarterdeck, Kittrelle stopped. "Well, lad, as soon as I put your name on the captain's list you will be considered legally 'enlisted.' From then on you will belong to the king and to the Royal Navy but, most important, to Captain Burbage, and to me."

Kittrelle looked about as if searching for someone. "In a few minutes you'll also belong to the master. First, though, leave my duffel here. My servant will pick it up. Bring your sea bag with you, and I'll take you below to meet the purser."

Two decks below Kittrelle found the purser holding forth in his storeroom, piled with clothing and equipment. "Smollet, this is our newest enlistee. See that he gets a good outfit, and don't cheat him or you'll answer to me."

The purser was a short, rotund man with a two-day beard, a slight lisp, and a foul breath, both evident as he started to talk. "Sir," he said, "I'll treat him like I treat everybody else. Fairly."

Kittrelle snorted. "That's what I mean. Treat him better than that or you'll answer to me."

Kittrelle turned to Fergus, "When you're through here have Smollet show you to the master-at-arms. He's just across the ship. He'll issue you two hammocks and their equipment and show you how to make them up navy style. He'll also assign you a place to keep them during the day. Tell him you are going to be assigned to the after starboard gun crew and their mess.

"Smollet, tell the master-at-arms the same thing I told you. New hammocks—not something he's been wiping his feet on."

Smollet watched Kittrelle until he was out of sight. Then he turned to Fergus. "All right, lad, let's get at it. I've got my sailing orders, and I don't want to get across the bows of that one."

An hour later, outfitted and billeted, Fergus went back to the quarterdeck. Kittrelle was in a deep conversation with an older man Fergus would have taken as a merchant had he not been warned by his grandfather. He knew the man standing there in the plain black jacket, white breeches, and a tricorn hat was probably the master.

Fergus stopped in front of Kittrelle and saluted. Kittrelle watched him with an amused look. "Ah," he said, looking up and down Fergus's new clothing articles. "I see the purser heeded me. For a man who's never been to sea in a man-of-war, you look, well, acceptable."

Fergus wanted to laugh, but realized his relationship with Lieutenant Kittrelle was now on a more formal military basis, and he managed a straight face. "Thank you, sir."

Kittrelle turned to the master. "Mister Montgomery, this is the young recruit I've been telling you about. He's yours as an apprentice quartermaster. But his duties under you are not to interfere with his presence at gun drill."

Montgomery, rubbing his short grey beard, looked Fergus over, obviously assessing him. He smiled, showing two missing teeth in his lower set. "Well, Kilburnie, if what Lieutenant Kittrelle tells me about your knowledge of navigation is true, I'll welcome you. Now I can get a little sleep when we are out to sea."

Kittrelle asked, "What's the matter with your apprentice and the midshipmen?"

"The apprentice can't add, and the midshipmen can't see very well."

The first night aboard Fergus slung his hammock in his assigned billet. On each side of him, fourteen inches away, were other hammocks, occupied by other members of his gun crew. He was slumbering well when he became aware of a shrill call on the boatswain's pipe, and a deep voice shouting, "Rise and shine! Show a leg! Turn out or I'll cut you down!" Fergus swung down out of his hammock and put on his new clothes. The purser had issued him a pair of white duck trousers that reached down to his low-cut black shoes. He stepped into the trousers and then pulled over his head a horizontally striped blue and white jersey. A short brimmed black hat completed his uniform. Others dressing nearby wore completely different uniforms.

Dressed, he turned to unrigging his hammock, squeezed it together like a huge sausage, and lashed it with a piece of line designed to allow him to put exactly seven hitches, no more, no less, around the rolled-over canvas.

When he had lashed it as tightly as he could, he cast loose two other lashings holding it to two large iron hooks in the overhead beams.

Fergus tossed the lashed hammock over his shoulder and started topside, following his mess mates. The hammock hit the overhead several times before Fergus learned to bend his knees and keep low. The beams overhead were only five and a half feet above the deck. Once topside, he put his hammock in a netting.

His gun captain, already there, looked at his hammock and frowned. "Not very good, Kilburnie. Tonight I'll show you how to do it right. I'll put it in the bottom of the netting under mine today. If the master-at-arms sees it like this, he'll make trouble for you."

Fergus nodded gratefully, looking over the gun captain he had met only late yesterday. Quantril was not quite as big as Fergus, but then only a few members of the crew were as big as Fergus. His hair was red and unruly, his complexion very light and, as Fergus would find out, seemingly always sunburned. Powder burns marked both cheeks and his forehead. Quantril saw Fergus looking at the scars and said, "Got too close to the touch hole a couple of times back in the days when we used slow-burning matches."

Fergus followed Quantril below to the area of the gun deck set aside for their mess. A light canvas curtain hung on either side of the area to give some privacy. Fergus wrinkled his nose at the odor of stale grease.

The mess cook had lowered the mess table from the overhead and was busy wiping it with a dirty white rag. Fergus asked, "What's that?"

The mess cook held up the rag, casting an amused look at the gun master. "A pair of Quantril's wife's pantalettes."

"What?! I didn't think sailors got married."

The mess cook laughed. "He isn't. That is, not permanently. Like all the officers and petty officers, he keeps a woman aboard when the ship is in port. Most British captains allow women to stay aboard in port. For legal purposes most of those having women aboard say that she is their wife."

"I haven't seen any women aboard."

"You won't. The old man told the master-at-arms to kick them off the ship two days ago. A hell of a ruckus, too. Those that didn't want to leave that early were thrown off, either over the brow or into the water." He laughed at the memory.

Fergus couldn't believe women were given such rough treatment. "Did any of them take a swim?"

"Two. Both drunk and couldn't swim." At the look on the young man's face he added, "Didn't drown, though. We fished 'em out with a grapnel."

"Wouldn't that hurt them?"

"Nah. They wear a lot of clothes, and this was a small one, just for rescuing men overboard."

"The master-at-arms must be plenty tough."

"Fiftal? Yeah, he's a bastard. Keep well clear of him."

Fergus was not surprised. He knew he couldn't expect the entire crew to be as decent as Kittrelle, so he changed the subject. "By the way, isn't the captain married?"

"No. Not many British captains are married."

"Can't he keep a wife ashore?"

"Sure, but captains can't go ashore."

"You mean the captain can't go ashore?"

"Not in England, anyway. Only if the Admiralty sends for him. I'm going to the galley to draw our ration. Sit down at the table and wait."

There was a burst of noise nearby. When Fergus got up and poked his head around the end of the screen, a young midshipman greeted him with a string of profanity. He ended with "Get your damned face out of here or I'll stripe it for you!"

Fergus hurriedly pulled his head back and retreated to the mess table. While he was waiting for the mess cook to return, he noted that the cloth table covering was stained and greasy with the remains of several meals visible. The smell was almost unbearable. He pulled the bowl, spoon, and fork he had drawn from the purser off the table and moved it in his lap.

In a few minutes the mess cook was back with a steaming tureen of oatmeal gruel and a pot of what appeared to be hot coffee, but was really hot water mixed with parched grain. As soon as the tureen was on the table, the other members of the gun crew appeared as if on signal, laughing and joking. They plunged their forks into the fabric of the table covering to clean them of the last meal and wiped their spoons on the edges. Fergus, sitting at the far end of the table, resolved to find a different way to clean his utensils, and he got to serve himself from the tureen last. He was lucky to find half a bowl of gruel when the tureen reached him.

Quantril noted his raised eyebrows. "Not much of a breakfast," he said. "You'll learn to look out for yourself soon."

Fergus shrugged and started eating. "Not bad. Typical Scottish breakfast." As he finished the last of his meager meal, the boatswain's pipe shrilled again. "All hands except idlers topside and turn to."

When Fergus reached the upper deck, the bright sunlight hurt his eyes, which had been conditioned to the gloom of the lower decks. He looked around the upper decks. The crew and the men from ashore were as busy as they had been the day before, but now Fergus could recognize some purpose in the seeming confusion.

Kittrelle stood next to the captain, shouting orders. When he saw the crew gathering on the upper deck, he said to a nearby lieutenant, "Brashear, take four gun crews and finish loading the water casks."

Quantril's crew drew the assignment of bringing aboard the twelve-pound iron balls for the guns from a large dray on the pier. Fergus found carrying two of the black balls up the brow and down below to the storage racks not too exhausting, even though the gunner in charge seemed to be a hard taskmaster.

When all the shot had been loaded, Fergus joined a group loading barrels of salt beef and salt pork. Quantril made a face. "Eating this stuff is bad enough without having to bring it aboard."

Next they loaded barrels of sauerkraut, biscuits, and even a few barrels of lime juice. After that came hundreds of butts of water, beer, and rum. By nightfall loading was completed, and the word was passed that the ship would get under way the next day.

Early the next morning, Fergus made a better job of lashing his hammock and managed to pass Quantril's inspection. Breakfast was also better. Fergus got to the mess early and took a seat in the middle of the table. The gruel was the same, but he managed a full bowl.

As Fergus finished the last of his so-called coffee, a messenger stumbled through the gloom. "Kilburnie?" he said, looking around.

"Here," Fergus answered.

"Lay up to the quarterdeck. The master wants to see you."

Fergus ran up the nearest ladder and then aft. The master, Montgomery, was standing next to the binnacle. Fergus stopped in front of him and saluted. "Yes, sir?"

Up close the master appeared to be an older man, with a short, gray beard. Fergus guessed that he would look younger if he shaved. The master wore a broad floppy black hat and a black jacket without ornamentation or insignia. Like the other officers, he wore white breeches, white stockings, and low black shoes.

The sailing master gave no reply except for a grunt and turned to complete his inspection of the table-like wooden binnacle, the compass inside of it, and the long glasses and barometer stowed inside the bottom. Finally, apparently satisfied that he had seen everything, the master turned to Fergus. "Kilburnie, this binnacle looks like birds have been nesting in it. Get it cleaned up."

Fergus saluted again. "Aye, aye, sir."

An hour of brushing, dusting, and scrubbing brought the binnacle and the compasses inside of it back to the state of cleanliness approved by the master. While cleaning Fergus noticed that the compass card on the steering compass was a little fancier than the one he had steered by on the fishing schooner, but easily readable. The bearing compass was even easier to read. The ten-degree marks were very legible. As he finished he heard the boatswain pipe, "Hands stations for getting under way."

Bare feet thudded on the deck as the crew raced to their stations, but apart from the shout of the boatswain not a word was spoken. Fergus remembered that his station was on the big wheel next to the binnacle. Soon he was joined by the other apprentice quartermaster senior to him, who held out his hand and whispered, "Hello. My name is Poston. You're supposed to be on the port side of the wheel."

Fergus held out his hand and started to say something. Then he remembered he had to stay silent and whispered, "Thanks. I'm Kilburnie." He shook Poston's hand quickly and moved to the other side of the wheel.

Fergus watched as Kittrelle prepared the ship for leaving the pier. First, one of the long boats was lowered, manned, and brought under the bow where a towline was lowered to it. Kittrelle directed the boatswain to order the oarsmen to pull together and at the same time directed that all mooring lines be brought aboard except the stern line. As the oarsmen heaved on the oars, the ship's bow slowly began to move into the black, oily waters of the Thames. Then the slow current caught the bow and the ship began to swing faster, still held by the stern line. When the sailing master nodded approval, Kittrelle ordered the stern line brought in, and the boat returned to the ship and was hoisted aboard.

Fergus turned to Poston and whispered, "I wondered how the ship was going to head downstream when the bow was pointed upstream and the wind was holding us on the pier."

Poston nodded and whispered, "Now you know. The sailing master will hoist sail and we'll move out from the pier on the port tack and then down the channel. The captain likes to have him handle the ship."

The master opened his bearded mouth and let loose a series of orders to the seamen aloft on the yardarms and at the base of the mast where they were manning the halyards and sheets. Fergus was bewildered. Some of the orders he understood from his fishing schooner days, but the sails carried by the *Athena* were far more numerous and their rigging much more complicated than that of a small schooner.

Then the master turned to the wheel. "Steer south by west."

Poston shouted, "South by west, sir."

Poston spun the huge double wheel, using the heavy spokes. Fergus was caught off guard because he was looking at the compass card, noting the point on the card that the master had just called for. After listening to a few more orders Fergus was able to sort out the orders to the wheel from the stream of orders to the men working the sails. Soon he was able to look at the compass card and help Poston turn the wheel. He realized he was sweating heavily from the tension, whereas Poston seemed to be cool and dry.

Poston grinned. "You're learning faster than any apprentice I've been with. By tomorrow you'll be able to stand wheel watches and take charge of one of the seamen."

By now the *Athena* was well down the straight, wide channel, and Kittrelle ordered the chief boatswain, "Set the sea watch, port watch."

Poston said, "You're on the starboard watch. I'll go below and see you in a few minutes. Then I'll hang around while you get settled in."

"You mean I'll be in charge of the wheel watch?"

"Sure. The officer of the watch won't be giving many orders. We'll be on a straight course down the channel until we clear it and then we'll turn south tomorrow morning some time. You won't have any trouble in weather like this."

"And if the weather makes up?"

Poston shrugged. "You're stronger than I am. The wheel won't throw you. Just listen carefully for the orders to the wheel and sing out loudly after each order, repeating it exactly as you hear it."

At the end of his watch Fergus started below but the loud voice of the master-at-arms stopped him. Fergus had seen Fiftal inspecting the hammock nettings. Fergus had managed to escape Fiftal's attention so far, and after the mess cook's description of him he wanted to avoid him if possible.

Fiftal's beefy pockmarked face was screwed into a snarl as he looked directly at Fergus. "Kilburnie, you Scottish oaf, get over here to the netting and relash your hammock. It looks like a rat's nest, which is probably what yer dungheap of a Scottish house looks like." Fergus flushed red at Fiftal's insults. Fiftal saw Fergus's face go crimson and prodded him further. "Don't like that, do you, Kilburnie, me talking about yer home in Scotland? You ignorant Scottish bastard."

Fergus clenched his fists until they hurt, but he didn't say anything.

Fiftal noticed and moved closer to him. "Go ahead, Kilburnie, I'd like nothing better if you'd strike me. Then even Lieutenant Kittrelle couldn't stop the captain from flogging yer back raw."

Fergus loosened his hands slowly. Fiftal smiled, again with no mirth. "All Scotsmen, I said all Scotsmen, are dirty, thieving rascals. Fit only for a gibbet," he snarled. "Yer fooling yerself if you think yer any different." He spat at Fergus's feet and walked away.

The rest of the day Fergus thought about his confrontation with Fiftal. He wondered if he should talk with Quantril but considered that perhaps that might show him to be weak. He decided to keep his mouth shut. He knew that Fiftal would be at him again and again, trying to goad Fergus into hitting him. And Fiftal was right, the captain could flog his back raw for striking a petty officer. He would have to take it, but he would get even some day.

That night Fergus stood a watch on the wheel. At 4 A.M., when he was relieved and started to go below to turn in in his hammock, Montgomery appeared on deck, stroking his beard and yawning.

"Just a minute, Kilburnie, we need to take a Polaris sight at 5 A.M. Get my quadrant and chronometer. Be careful with them, and tell Poston to come up with you and help carry them. You'll be helping me take the sights and Poston will record the times. Then we'll plot them, and just after we make our plot, we should be in position to head south around the North Foreland, the most eastern part of England up here."

Fergus sighed, fighting back his fatigue and his desire for sleep. "Aye, aye, sir."

Fergus roused Poston, and with Poston grumbling about being awakened the two carefully carried the quadrant and the heavy Harrison chronometer in its shiny mahogany box to the quarterdeck. The master said, "That's not all we need. We won't do well until we have a good cup of coffee. Go forward to the galley and tell the cook I said to send three mugs up here." The master laughed. "Tell him if it isn't hot I'll put him on watch."

With a cup of hot coffee, Fergus thought, he might just be able to make it until breakfast.

Around the quarterdeck the men of the port watch joined the members of the starboard watch, who had been called at 4 A.M., and were holystoning the wooden decks. Fergus stepped around the large stones and the men who were pulling them back and forth with short lengths of cotton line fixed in holes in their ends and made his way down to the galley forward.

The cook, busy with his pots, saw him coming and laughed. "Yes, I know, the old gray bastard wants some coffee. Well, I'm ready for him. Carry the mugs carefully and bring them all back, or you won't get any more tomorrow."

Fergus took a huge gulp of the steaming black liquid from one of the white porcelain mugs and made his way back to the quarterdeck where he delivered the other two mugs to the master and Poston.

In the growing daylight, he noticed that the captain had come to the quarterdeck with three of the older midshipmen. Fergus looked at Poston and raised his eyebrows questioningly. Poston said, "The captain teaches navigation to the midshipmen since we don't have a schoolmaster aboard. They'll take their sights, plot them on their charts, and the captain will compare them with the sailing master's results."

Dawn was breaking, and the North star, Polaris, was quite bright on the port side. It was the only star navigators of the day knew how to use, and it was always in the north and approximately at the altitude of the place from which it was observed. An accurate measurement of its altitude with a quadrant gave the navigator his latitude at the time of observation after entering corrections to the reading from some tables provided by the naval observatory at Greenwich.

The master looked around the clear sky at the thousands of visible stars twinkling in the clear sky. He shook his head. "Too bad," he said. "Some day someone at the observatory at Greenwich will figure out a method of navigating at sea using all of those beautiful stars."

Poston piped up, "Sir, the horizon is becoming visible to the north. Are you ready?"

Montgomery, the master, put his coffee mug down on the binnacle that housed the magnetic compass and looked at the horizon, now faintly visible in the predawn light. "Kilburnie," he ordered, "take a sight on Polaris."

Fergus was taken by surprise, but he hoisted the heavy metal quadrant toward the bright star, looked at the star through the eyepiece, brought it down to the horizon by manipulating a large screw, and walked the tiny image back and forth across the horizon using a fine adjustment as his grandfather had taught him to do. When he was satisfied, he made a small final adjustment, called out "mark" to Poston, noted the reading on the metal scale, and handed the instrument to Montgomery.

The sailing master noted the reading and then took his own sight, also calling out "mark" to Poston. He looked at the scale and then at Fergus. In the brightening dawn Fergus could see his eyebrows rise. "Not bad," he said. "Within about two miles of my sight. Take my reading and the slate here that has the night's course changes and log readings on it down below and plot them all on the chart."

Below, Fergus, with Poston hanging over his shoulder, plotted the ship's course and speed from the slate kept on the night watches by the officer of the watch and his quartermaster, and brought the dead reckoning up to date by plotting the distances run and the direction made. Then he plotted the latitude line from the Polaris sight. Where it crossed the course line, he made a small neat circle at their intersection and labeled it with the time of the Polaris sight.

Poston looked at it and sighed. "Seems pretty good. I've got a lot to learn."

Fergus nodded, "I'll be glad to teach you what I know about navigation. You can help me with a lot of other stuff that goes on about the ship."

In a few minutes, Montgomery came below and looked at the reckoning on the chart that Fergus had just finished. He nodded approvingly and then went above to consult the captain. Soon Fergus could hear him bawling orders to the men aloft on the yardarms, and the ship heeled slightly to port as it changed course to the south.

When the ship had steadied and the noise topside had subsided, Poston said, "Let's go to breakfast before the rest of the mess eats it all."

After breakfast, Fergus and Poston polished the wood of the binnacle and the brass of the compasses and cleaned the area around the wheel. As they finished the task, the boatswain's pipe shrilled, and the boatswain and his mates ran the length of the ship, leaned down the hatches, shrilled their pipes, and passed the word, "All hands to battle station for gun drill."

Most gun crews messed near their guns and kept the equipment either in the overhead on hooks or secured against the outer bulkhead. The crews of the upper-deck guns messed below in special areas set aside for them and kept the equipment for their guns near their messes.

Fergus knew he would have trouble getting below against the traffic of emerging men on the narrow ladders, so he went directly to his gun.

Soon Quantril and the rest of the crew came up the ladder with the "worm," a corkscrew-shaped instrument used for cleaning burning debris and unburned powder out of the gun. Another man carried the rammer, an eight-foot-long piece of heavy hempen rope, stiff enough to be pushed down the barrel to ram a cartridge home but also flexible enough to be bent around the muzzle from the inside of the gun port so that the man using it would not be exposed to enemy fire. One end of the rammer was fitted with a piece of unwoven hemp secured in such a manner that it also served as a swab, or sponge, to extinguish any burning bits of powder or wadding left after the firing.

Quantril also carried the quills and a flintlock, and if firing was scheduled a young boy known as a powder monkey or powder boy would carry up small, cylindrical "cartridges" of black powder contained in red flannel bags and kept under his coat or carried in leather bags for protection until they were needed.

Quantril's goose quills, carried in his belt, were filled with choice black powder and were sharpened at one end. After the powder bag was rammed down the bore of the muzzle by the rammer, a wad, an iron shot, and then another wad were inserted and rammed home down the long barrel. When the round was ready to be fired, Quantril would thrust a quill down the touch hole. The sharp end would puncture the powder cartridge, and a continuous train of black powder would then be ready. The flintlock, when fired, would initiate the rush of flame through the train and the cartridge would go off, propelling the heavy iron ball out of the muzzle. This much about the mechanics of the gun Fergus knew from his grandfather, but he had never seen or heard a big gun fired.

A collection of empty boxes and barrels had been tied together and topped by a piece of scrapped sail flying from a broken oar. It now floated forlornly as the ship pulled away, and the master maneuvered to bring it abeam at about five hundred yards.

While the ship moved into position, Fergus looked over the rigging for handling the gun to see that it was in safe and proper shape. Two large pieces of line known as "breeches" led from a round fitting on the rear of the gun known as a "pomelion" to strong ring bolts in the side of the ship. Two sets of tackles led from fittings on the sides of the wooden gun carriage to fittings in the inner side of the ship. When the gun was fired, the breechings let it recoil inboard until it reached their lengths and then the gun stopped with the muzzle just inside the gun port, a square hole in the side.

Fergus realized that anyone caught behind a recoiling gun could be crushed. It was like being kicked by a horse, and he resolved never to be caught behind a gun.

From this position next to it the gun could be cleaned. Burned and unburned powder could be removed using the worm, if necessary, and the swab on the rammer. After reloading, it could be run out the gun port again by the two tackles manned by several men on each side of the gun. The gun was elevated by the gun captain inserting small wedges, or "quoins," between the gun barrel and the wooden carriage. Small adjustments in horizontal direction were made by inserting a pry bar under the gun carriage wheels and traversing it from side to side. Like everything associated with gunnery, this process of aiming was slow and difficult, and the whole process was crude, tiring, and laborious. Yet without constant practice, a ship's fighting efficiency deteriorated rapidly and an inefficient ship was useless.

Fergus grew apprehensive as Quantril and the rammer man loaded the gun and it was run out. Quantril stepped back and picked up a flintlock. Then he squinted down the length of the gun, adjusted the quoins, and passed back orders to the gun crew to stand clear of the area where the gun would be recoiling.

Kittrelle had given orders for the guns to fire individually on his orders from forward aft. The wind, coming from aft, would blow the gun smoke forward and give the captain and Kittrelle an opportunity to watch the fall of shot of each individual gun and judge how well the gun captains had done in aiming and laying their guns.

The first gun to be fired was a bow chaser. Even though it was the length of the ship away, the booming noise hurt Fergus's ears and caused him to jump a little. Snickers came from somewhere close, and Fergus flushed with embarrassment. As the other guns began to fire in succession, however, he became more used to the noise and remained still.

Finally Kittrelle called out the number of their gun, thirty-four. Gun thirty-four was the after twelve-pounder on the starboard side, and guns thirty-five and thirty-six were the two eight-pounder chasers aft. Quantril bent over the gun for one last sight on the bobbing target. When he was sure the ship was on an up roll, he stepped back, grasping the lanyard to fire the flintlock in his hand into the touch hole. There was a whoosh and a puff of black smoke as the quill full of powder fired, conducted a ribbon of flame down the touch hole, and ignited the cartridge. Then came a thunderous boom as the monstrous gun belched gray-white smoke. Its carriage leaped back and came to a crashing stop against its breechings.

Fergus, as a new man, had been assigned to the starboard tackle, and he watched as the gun was swabbed and reloaded. Then Quantril, using hand signals, pointed forward, and the men on the tackles heaved on the lines and the gun inched forward, pointing its brass snout out of the gun port, ready for the next firing.

Again the signal to fire was given. Again the gun thundered and jerked back, and again the routine started. After three rounds had been fired by each gun, the firing was ordered to be ceased, and the men stood easy by their guns.

"How'd we do?" Fergus asked Quantril anxiously.

Quantril shrugged. "Don't know. The target has been destroyed, but only the captain and Lieutenant Kittrelle know which guns hit it."

As the crew turned to clean the gun, Fergus realized that his shirt was stuck to his back with sweat and that his arms ached from the effort of pulling the gun back. Sweat stung his eyes and his ears still rang from the combined concussions of the frigate's guns. Quantril saw him shaking his head. "Just be thankful you're not on a sloop or cutter."

Fergus looked at him quizzically, still rubbing his ears.

Quantril explained, "They carry six- or four-pounders and when they shoot, they give a nasty crack that will have your whole head hurting for days."

The smell of burned powder lingered on as the guns and equipment were cleaned. There was much to gunnery that he needed to learn, Fergus thought, but for some odd reason it seemed more interesting than navigation.

After gun drill, Fergus and Poston went below to Montgomery's cabin, picked up his quadrant and chronometer, and took them to the quarterdeck where the master was talking to Kittrelle. Fergus knew the master already had calculated the approximate time of local apparent noon, the time when the sun would reach its highest point in the sky for that meridian of altitude. Finding the exact time of that event, and comparing it with the time on the chronometer, keeping Greenwich time, would give them their longitude. Crossing the longitude line with the latitude determined by the sun at an earlier time or Polaris sight gave an approximate navigational position known as a fix.

When the chronometer showed about five minutes to go Fergus nodded to the sailing master, who was lounging near the bulwark, still speaking with Kittrelle. Montgomery came over, took the heavy quadrant from Fergus, pointed the quadrant at the sun, and brought the sun's lower limb, the bottom of the round disc, down to the horizon by moving the arm. By manipulating the arm, he could adjust the reading on the scale. He watched the image for a few minutes, satisfied the sun had begun to dip again and that he had caught the maximum altitude for that day. Then he called "mark" to Poston. Montgomery called off the angle and handed the quadrant back to Fergus. Fergus, followed by Poston, carefully carrying the large chronometer, started below.

As they went down the ladder, Fergus said, "I noticed the ends of several scars under the sailing master's beard."

Poston nodded, "Yeah. I understand he used to be a bare-knuckled boxer."

"I thought all fighters were bare-knuckled."

"They are when they fight in the ring, but professionals pickle their knuckles in saltwater to make them tough. When they practice they wrap their knuckles in rags so they won't hurt them or their sparring partners. When they fight they become bare-knuckled and can cut a man's face badly."

"He grew his beard to cover up the scars?"

"Right. The captain gave him permission. His knuckles are battered, too. You can see from the swelling that he has rheumatism in them. That's why he wants you to take the sights and do the plotting."

"Was he a pretty good fighter?"

"I don't know. I never saw him fight ashore in the ring, but I do know he has one hellish punch."

"Yeah?"

"One day a foretopman, a big muscular guy, gave him a smart answer when he was coming down the ratlines. When the foretopman stepped off on deck, Montgomery floored him with a right-hand punch. I never saw one harder or faster. The foretopman was out five minutes."

"Didn't the captain do anything?"

"Sure. He turned and looked over the other side."

6

İn Battle

or three months the *Athena* beat to the south against the wind. They had been ordered to patrol the area off Ushant looking for merchantmen transitting from the Indies to Brest, but few enemy ships appeared that far north.

Captain Burbage grumbled about the stupidity of his shorebound superiors in the Admiralty who had sent his ship to this station. "They ought to be out here. They'd quickly find out we're wasting our time."

Watches were called every four hours to change course across the wind, which required resetting and trimming the huge square sails each time. But by making course changes at the changing of the watch, the master could add the off-going watch personnel to that of the on-coming watch and make the changes quickly and with minimum tiring of the crew, whom, everyone knew, the captain wanted as fresh as possible for battle.

Fergus, standing wheel watches, was spared the demanding chore of going aloft, and whenever he could he honed his knowledge of navigation under the master. He also began to memorize the commands he heard Montgomery use for the sail handlers, and he sorted out the multitude of lines leading to the corners and tops of the sails used to hoist and trim them. Gradually the maze of lines began to make more sense.

At the daily gun drills, Fergus asked Quantril for permission to take the place of each member of the gun crew, including the rammerman, who swabbed out the bore to clean out any powder that might remain, and rammed the powder, wads, and shot down the bore. When he was sure he knew each man's job thoroughly, he began questioning Quantril, asking questions about the aiming of the gun and finally asking if he could take his place occasionally. Quantril laughed. "My God, Kilburnie, you must want my job."

Fergus shook his head. "No, I just want to be able to take your place or those of the other men should any of you be killed."

Quantril explained the use of the quill and flintlock system and let him aim the gun by giving orders to the men placing the quoins between the gun and the carriage. After a month Quantril gave in. "All right, Kilburnie, you're qualified to be a gun captain. Now leave it alone."

At the end of the third month, the *Athena* had completed her first patrol and was supposed to change station to south of the latitude of Gibraltar and a thousand miles to the west. Fergus, standing watch at the wheel, overheard Kittrelle talking with the captain. "Sir, I don't think we should be discouraged because we haven't sighted anything. After all, we are right where the Admiralty sent us."

Captain Burbage nodded. "I agree with you. Their intelligence could be right, but just as often it's wrong. Nevertheless, this is the usual time for the French merchant fleet that comes from the Indies to the Mediterranean to arrive."

This was the first indication Fergus had of the ship's mission. As he had plotted the *Athena*'s positions on the chart, he wondered why they were going so far east. When he shared his knowledge with Quantril, the gun captain said, "Don't worry. We'll sight something soon." The older sailor smiled and rubbed his hands with glee. "I'd like to be in on the taking of a fat prize or two."

Fergus said, "All I want to do is beat the French."

Quantril raised his bushy eyebrows. "That's all well and good, lad, but I've been at sea long enough to think beyond that, and by that I mean I want the prize money. So does the captain, Lieutenant Kittrelle, and even that bastard Fiftal. Gold in your pocket beats patriotism by a hell of a lot."

Suddenly a commotion began topside. Excited shouts and the sound of rushing feet came from the deck. Fergus followed Quantril up the ladder. On deck Quantril stopped a passing seaman. "What's going on?"

"The lookouts sighted a sail to the west. That's all I know."

The crew gathered where they could along the leeward rail eagerly searching for the sail along the horizon. "Damn me!" one grizzled sailor said. "I hope it's a Frog."

"Aye," said another, "maybe a nice, fat merchantman stuffed with gold from the Spanish main."

Fergus tore his eyes from the horizon and looked at the quarterdeck. Most of the officers were there, clustered around the captain. An officer with a telescope hung over his shoulder by a lanyard broke away from the group and bounded up the mizzenmast's rigging. It was Kittrelle and, by his rapid ascent, it appeared to Fergus that his leg was now completely healed. His bulging calf muscles moved freely under his clean white stockings. Fergus wondered if the heat of the moment had just dulled the pain. Kittrelle climbed to the level of the yardarm, steadied his glass on a shroud, and studied the distant ship.

On deck a sailor whispered hoarsely, as if he feared a shout would scare away the Frenchman. Fergus turned to the rail and the horizon. He could see the sails of the approaching ship. But what was she? American, French, or British? As if to answer this question, a foretopman who was an experienced lookout said, "It's a Frenchman, all right. The cut of those top sails gives her away, as well as the color of the canvas." Fergus glanced at the *Athena*'s topsails. He could tell the difference.

The captain's voice, booming through a speaking trumpet, cut through the buzz of the crew's voices. "Mr. Kittrelle! What do you see?"

"French frigate, sir. It looks like a forty-four!" Kittrelle raised the glass to his eye again. "Sir, he has turned toward us!"

The captain looked at the advancing Frenchman, pausing as if to digest the information. Then he raised the speaking trumpet to his lips. "Very good, Mr. Kittrelle! Very good!" Kittrelle snapped his long glass closed and with it swinging from a lanyard descended the rigging expertly, landing lightly on deck.

Immediately upon hearing Kittrelle's report, the sailors on deck began to talk. Their voices swirled around Fergus. "We'll run; the Frog's bigger than we are." "Captain Burbage is full of fight; he'll not run." "Aye, Burbage will close; he's game for a fight." "If the Frenchman doesn't like the look of things, he can outrun us."

Fergus had his own opinions. The boatswain's pipe shrilled above the low-toned murmurs of the crew. "All hands, assemble aft!" The men scurried from the rail toward the quarterdeck, pressing close about the area.

Captain Burbage stepped forward. "Men, yonder is a French frigate," he said in his best quarterdeck voice. "By heading toward us"—at this many heads turned involuntarily to look at the approaching sail—"it appears that the French captain means to gobble us up." He paused and leaned forward. "But, by God, the *Athena* will stick in her throat." At this the crew cheered heartily, almost wildly. Fergus joined in the cheer, his heart thumping madly in his chest. Around him faces were red and eyes blazed with an almost animal light. Thoroughbreds, thought Fergus, the men were like thoroughbreds before a race, stomping like horses and shaking their heads, eyes wild, nostrils flared, impatient to run.

The captain raised his hand and the men fell silent, tense with anticipation. "Mr. Kittrelle," he shouted, "clear the ship for action!"

A wild cheer went up, drowning out the first few words of Kittrelle's orders " . . . for action! Drummer, beat to quarters!"

The marine drummer began the long roll, but the men were already racing to their stations to prepare the ship. Fergus stood transfixed until Quantril laid a hand on his shoulder. "Go to the gun, lad. Start to get her ready."

Fergus ran to the gun and began to loosen the tackle. As he worked, he caught glances of the preparations for battle. Powder monkeys streamed out of the hold, carrying the leather bags containing cartridges for the cannons. Some men walked down the decks, slowly spreading sand to prevent men from slipping on blood and bits of human flesh. A net was rigged over the waist to protect the men from falling spars and tackle. Red-coated marines clambered up to the fighting tops, clutching muskets and buckets of grenades. Other marines went below to stand by ladders to prevent men from running below; still others stood in loose file in the waist of the ship, ready to repel boarders and pepper the enemy with musket fire.

Fergus could hear the partitions in the captain's cabin and the officers' staterooms falling as they were unrigged and taken below. A quick movement caught his eye, and he turned to see the *Athena*'s battle ensign hoisted. It hung limply for a second, but then caught the wind and streamed out boldly. He strained his eyes to look at the Frenchman, now closer; a splash of color appeared on her as a large tricolor soared into the wind, her vibrant colors a bold and defiant acceptance of the *Athena*'s challenge.

Soon Quantril and the rest of the quarterdeck gun crews came up on deck. As he had learned, Fergus tied a kerchief around his forehead to prevent sweat from streaming into his eyes, and he stripped to the waist. Like most of the crew, he rarely wore shoes on his feet to give better traction.

As he tightened the cloth about his head, Fergus looked about the quarterdeck. Poston was on the wheel, as was Davis, a Devon man who liked to claim that an ancestor had been helmsman for Sir Francis Drake. Montgomery stood slightly behind the captain, his gaze shifting slowly from sails to helmsmen to compass and back to sails, with no obvious thought for the approaching enemy. The captain stood almost directly behind the binnacle, buckling on his sword as he conversed with Kittrelle and Mr. Kerry, the warrant gunner. Kittrelle and the gunner stepped back, saluted, and went to their posts. The warrant gunner caught Fergus's eye and, putting on an unpleasant scowl, made straight for Fergus.

A huge, heavyset man, he had a bulging paunch, but his arms and chest were massive. He despised Kilburnie, for he considered Fergus's eagerness to learn an indication of Fergus's desire to replace him as warrant gunner. The fact that Kittrelle had brought Kilburnie aboard only increased his dislike for the young Scotsman. "Stop yer gawkin', Kilburnie, and attend to yer gun," he said sharply in the brogue of the Dublin streets. "Don't think of runnin' and hidin' below. If you do, you better hope a bootneck catches you first, for if I do I'll. . . ."

"Move on, Kerry," snapped Quantril.

Kerry gave a snort of contempt. "He's a lickspittle with his eye on a warrant and no stomach for fighting." The Irishman jabbed a thick finger at Fergus. "Watch yerself. One bad move and ye'll be triced up to grating." He paused to bring his face close to Fergus's. "Or worse." Scowling at Quantril, Kerry turned on his heel and clambered down the ladder into the waist of the ship.

"Irish bastard," muttered Quantril savagely. "Damn him to hell. He's worse than Fiftal." He looked at Fergus. "Few men on this ship would mourn if a French ball took off his head." The rest of the gun crew murmured in agreement.

Fergus forced a laugh. "Well, one woman would certainly rejoice."

Quantril looked at him, puzzled.

"Mrs. Kerry," Fergus said.

The gun crew laughed, and Quantril slapped Fergus on the back. "Always seeing the good side," he said.

The *Athena* was cleared for action in less than ten minutes, a fact that greatly pleased Captain Burbage. He looked for a long time at the oncoming French frigate and examined the sails. "Mr. Nash," he called for a midshipman.

"Yes, sir," the midshipman said, doffing his hat in salute.

"Order the purser to fetch grog for the crew. Serve them at the guns. Have the loblolly boys help if needed."

"Aye, aye, sir," the midshipman replied in a cracking voice and turned to deliver the message.

"And Mr. Nash," said Burbage. The midshipman stopped in his tracks and turned about. "Have my steward bring me a bottle of wine, claret." The midshipman acknowledged his orders and dashed off. Burbage turned to Kittrelle. "You are wondering why I gave such an order?" Kittrelle colored slightly; the captain had interpreted his expression perfectly. "The wind is dropping a bit, Mr. Kittrelle. We won't engage for some time now."

Soon a man came by Fergus's gun with a bucket filled with grog, measuring out a tot for each man. When Fergus's time came, he hesitated. With his stomach churning with excitement, he did not want to risk vomiting the rum back up.

"Go ahead," said Quantril, beaming. "It'll put fire in your belly."

Fergus drained the measure, feeling the warmth of the diluted rum run down his throat and into his stomach. As it always did, the taste of rum made him think of his grandfather and Uncle Jeris. Today, though, he couldn't help but concentrate on Uncle Jeris's empty sleeve and eyepatch. Was that how he would end this day? With the hawk-nosed surgeon hovering over him, plucking heated instruments from a pot in order to cut his flesh and saw his bones? He shuddered.

Quantril punched him lightly on the shoulder. "I told you it would put fire in your belly!" Fergus smiled weakly, thankful that Quantril could not sense his thoughts.

The captain's steward bustled by, holding a tray on which was a bottle of wine and two glasses. "Will you join me, Mr. Kittrelle?" Burbage asked quietly. Kittrelle stepped forward. A captain's invitation was tantamount to an order. The steward carefully poured the wine and offered the tray to the captain. The captain took a glass, followed by Kittrelle. Burbage raised his glass slightly. "Success to the *Athena*."

Kittrelle raised his glass. "Damnation to our enemies." They drank, replacing the glasses on the tray. They were immediately refilled and again offered to the officers.

"God, but that Burbage is a cool one," muttered Franklin, the gun's rammerman, observing the officers' ritual. "Kittrelle as well."

Watching as Burbage and Kittrelle stood there, drinking wine and talking as if at a gentlemen's house in London, Fergus nodded in agreement. He remembered his grandfather's stories of captains who "stood five and a half feet on ordinary days—six and a half feet during battle." With a large French frigate bearing down on them, Burbage seemed detached, almost unconcerned, as he chatted with Kittrelle. Fergus considered his own excitement and wondered what allowed Burbage to be so cool. Was it confidence in himself? Well, he was an experienced officer and had been in many fights before.

"Kilburnie!" Quantril's voice snapped him from his thoughts. "Take the boy's powder." Fergus turned to see a young powder monkey holding out a red flannel bag of powder. The boy was skinny, with gaunt features and somewhat sad brown eyes that flickered nervously.

"I have a sister of your age," Fergus said with a smile as he took the powder.

The boy stepped back, eyes wide. "Suffering Christ!" he said in mock horror with a voice straight from London's docks. "Some Scotsman wants me to feck his sister." With that, he turned and scampered down a ladder. Fergus's mates and the men at the nearby guns laughed uproariously as Fergus stood crimson-faced and dumbfounded at the boy's coarse remark.

As the laughter calmed, Fergus murmured angrily to Quantril, "I'll box that little beast's ears when he comes by next."

"Ah, don't be too hard on the lad," Quantril said. "Besides, a French bullet might kill him first." He caught Kilburnie's puzzled look. "Yes, Kilburnie, ask the bootnecks, the marines. Besides the officers and mates they aim for the powder monkeys. With no powder, no guns can be fired." He shrugged at the equation. "The French do the same."

Fergus looked across the quarterdeck to where another powder monkey was delivering a cartridge. "There's more to war than drinking wine on the quarterdeck, Kilburnie," Quantril said, his voice suddenly hard. Fergus turned back to his gun captain, whose blue eyes had suddenly gone a flinty gray. Those eyes moved to meet Fergus's. "Remember," Quantril added, a sardonic smile creeping across his face, "no flowers grow on a sailor's grave."

Before Fergus could reply, Kittrelle announced to the captain, "The Frenchman is closing." Fergus looked up, craning to see over the bulwark. The two ships were closing eagerly like fighting cocks. Captain Burbage raised his long glass to his eye. After a moment he lowered the glass and said, "Master, change course one point to port. I want to open with our starboard guns."

Fergus turned to Quantril. "Did you hear that? We get to start."

Quantril nodded. "Don't be so eager. There will be enough of that Frenchman for everybody."

The range decreased rapidly as the two ships stood toward each other. The men stood to their guns, made final checks of their equipment, and crouched at the ready. Apart from the creaking of the hull, yards, and spars, and the low whistle of the wind in the rigging, silence cloaked the *Athena*. Suddenly, from amidships, a tin whistle's warbling notes floated back to the quarterdeck. Fergus cocked his head at the music. The tune was familiar, but the words didn't come immediately to his mind. He looked questioningly at his mates who were smiling broadly. Suddenly, as if of one mind, the crew began to sing—just as suddenly Fergus realized what the tune was.

Rule, Britannia! Britannia, rule the waves!
Britons will never, never, ever be slaves!

A flash of light and a blossom of gray smoke came from the French frigate, followed by a hollow boom. She had opened fire with her bow chasers. Three more shots came in rapid succession, the smoke ballooning out around her stem and passing back along her sides. The balls splashed harmlessly in the water about two hundred yards short of the *Athena*'s plunging bow. The men seemed to take this as a signal to sing louder, bawling forth their defiance.

Fergus looked back at Captain Burbage, who stood with legs spread apart, as if braced for a heavy roll, his eyes fixed on the enemy. Fergus's heart raced wildly. He swallowed hard and tried to lick his lips, but his mouth was too dry.

The Frenchman fired again. Three shots fell close ahead, and one penetrated the forward bulwark, scattering several hammocks and caroming over the side. The singing continued, louder still. "One point to port, Mr. Montgomery, if you please," Burbage said, his voice calm.

Montgomery gave the order to the helmsmen, whose soft repetition was lost in the rough chorus of the voices.

"The French bastard will have us in pieces before we open fire," Fergus muttered as the two ships came even closer.

"Quiet, lad," snapped Franklin. "Captain knows what he's doing."

The captain looked at Kittrelle and Kittrelle nodded. "Time for silence," the captain said.

Kittrelle turned forward and bellowed, "Silence forward!"

The command spread forward from gun to gun and in seconds the singing stopped and there was complete silence. Again the soft soughing of the wind in the rigging and the slapping of wavelets against the weather waterline could be heard plainly.

Kittrelle looked at Burbage. The captain said, "Now we're ready."

"Two more points to port, Mr. Montgomery," ordered the captain, his voice suddenly loud in the silence. As the ship steadied on its new heading, the captain turned to the fidgeting Kittrelle. "Mr. Kittrelle, sir!" he said, his voice seeming to rise from the deck. "Let's see what the starboard guns can do."

His face showing apparent relief, Kittrelle moved rapidly forward to the quarterdeck limits. "Starboard battery!" he bellowed, disdaining a speaking trumpet. Faces turned toward Kittrelle. "Lay your guns and commence firing from forward! Fire as you bear!" A savage cheer went up from the crew.

Burbage's maneuvers had put the *Athena* in a position slightly off the Frenchman's bow, crossing at a shallow angle. The French captain could not turn to give the *Athena* a full broadside, for to do so would put him directly into the wind and almost dead in the water, a perfect target. He would have to take the first broadside and then attempt to maneuver for a better position.

The first gun fired from forward, the loud reports carrying aft. With the wind aft, however, the smoke blew away from the *Athena*, giving her gunners a clear view of their target. Fergus grinned. Another advantage from Burbage's cleverness at keeping the weather gauge. The reports came closer to Fergus's gun and then it was their turn. Crouched low, well behind the gun, Quantril took one final glance down the barrel and, satisfied, moved to one side of the gun and pulled the lanyard. For an instant, there was only a spark but then the priming powder ignited with a swoosh, followed almost immediately by the throaty roar of the main charge going off. The gun belched smoke and heaved back against its breechings. The men sprang to the tasks they had practiced so often before. The gun was sponged out. The charge was rammed home, followed by a wad, a twelve-pound ball, and another wad. Quantril fitted a quill down the touch hole, poured in the priming powder from his horn, and reset the flintlock. So busy was Fergus with the set tasks that he could not look over the bulwark to see what damage they had done to the Frenchman. By the third shot, he had all he could do to respond to Quantril's command, "Run her out!" Heaving on the heavy hemp lines made them slippery with perspiration.

Fergus was aware of cries of pain and shouts of command mingled with the booms of the cannon, and the rattle of the muskets from the fighting tops and about the deck. He felt the deck tremble under his feet but whether it was from the firing of the ship's guns or from shot slamming into the hull he could not tell. As he waited for his gun to fire again, he stole a glance toward the bow. A gun lay on its side with bodies sprawled around it, some moving, others still. Men moved toward the scene and began to carry those who were wounded below deck to the cockpit where the surgeon awaited them. Fergus's eyes grew wide as some men tried to right the gun while others picked up limp, lifeless corpses and threw them overboard. Fergus felt bile rising in his throat and a strangled cry choked him. He forced it back down. No flowers on a sailor's grave, he remembered. A flash of red caught his eye and he looked up at the mainmast rigging. A marine, dead or alive, he could not tell, was tangled in the lines, hanging by one foot.

Above the marine, Fergus noted that sails hung in tatters and that yards and lines drooped down. The mainmast bore a scar of exposed wood where a French ball had hit it. Further up, he noticed that the main top was leaning at a crazy angle. The French were concentrating on the *Athena*'s rigging, trying to slow her down and make her an easier target.

"Ready!" shouted Quantril, raising his hand. Fergus grabbed the hemp lines, ready to heave. "Run her out!" Fergus heaved. And then came a noise like a great low moan and a loud crash, the loudest sound Fergus had ever heard. He was hurled to the deck onto his back, stunned, his ears ringing. For a few moments the sounds of battle seemed far off, as if heard through cotton. As Fergus shook his head, the sounds grew clearer. He tried to move his legs but could not. Something was pinning them down. He raised his head and opened his eyes. A man lay stretched across Fergus's knees, his back toward him. "Get up, you clumsy bastard!" Fergus shouted, kicking at the man. The body was immobile. "Damn you! I said get up!" Fergus kicked again, this time more savagely, and finally freed his legs. The man rolled limply over on his back. His face and chest were pulverized by splinters and blood gushed from his throat onto the deck.

Horrified, Fergus came up on his hands and knees and moved back a few feet. "Quantril!" he called. There was no answer. His right hand went into something wet and sticky on the deck. Looking down, Fergus saw that he had backed into a pool of blood. He leaped to his feet and looked down. Whatever had hit the *Athena* had also taken Quantril's head off. Still twitching, his body lay on the deck, blood oozing in a pool. Fergus's breath came fast, and his stomach convulsed. He looked at his blood-covered hand and then around the deck. Of his gun crew, two were dead and another writhed on deck, splinters in his right arm and legs. Only Franklin was unscathed and was standing by the gunwale looking dumbly down at the carnage. The gun next to him was on its side; three men were scrambling about, trying to right it with handspikes. The rest of its crew were dead, slumped over the gun or pinned under it.

Fergus felt blood under his feet and looked down at Quantril's lifeless body. It gave a sudden twitch. A wave of nausea hit him and he dropped to his knees, retching on deck. Franklin was suddenly by him. "Kilburnie! Kilburnie!" he shouted. "Are you hurt?"

Fergus shook his head and looked into Franklin's eyes, which were wide and wild but not filled with fear or horror. Instead, he saw ferocity; Franklin was angry. Suddenly Fergus felt the same anger rising in him. He came to his feet, feeling a strange and sudden calm. He took a deep breath and looked at Franklin. "Thanks, Franklin," he said.

Fergus examined his gun. There were gouges in the black paint covering the brass, but it seemed serviceable. Fergus went over to the other gun. "Where's the gun captain?" he shouted.

One man pointed mutely toward a bearded man sprawled on his back, his chest ripped open and his eyes staring dully at the sky. Fergus shook his head to clear it. "Let's get one gun in action." The men paused, looking at the blood-stained Kilburnie and then at each other, but they moved over to Fergus's gun.

Fergus shouted to be heard over the din. "Get those bodies over the side." The men stooped down and began to drag the bodies of Fergus's crew toward the bulwark. Franklin and Kilburnie picked up Quantril's body and heaved it over the side. Before they tossed it over, Franklin said, "He was a good sort, eh?" Fergus nodded, but had trouble saying anything.

Fergus turned back to the task of organizing his new gun crew. "You be the rammerman," he said to a wiry fellow with a scraggly beard and few teeth. "Franklin, you load." Franklin nodded. Then Kilburnie remembered that the gun was already loaded and had not been fired. On the deck the lanyard lay in a pool of blood. Fergus wordlessly picked it up and looked down the gun barrel. There was no need to aim. The French frigate filled the opening in the bulwark. "Ready!" he shouted, raising his hand. Then he stepped back from the gun, moving as he remembered Quantril doing. Fergus yanked the lanyard, and the gun roared and recoiled, the tackle groaning under the strain.

As the new crew sprang to their tasks, a powder monkey ran up and handed Fergus a cartridge. It was the same rascal who had annoyed him earlier. The boy looked at Fergus for a moment and then asked, "Yer the Scotsman who wanted me to feck yer sister, ain't ya? Now ye've got a new job." Despite himself, Fergus found himself smiling at the boy's brazen manner. He raised his hand as if to backhand the boy, but the boy realized he was not serious. He turned and trotted for the ladder below.

Fergus turned to his work, putting the quill down the touchhole and filling it with priming powder from Quantril's powder horn, making sure to leave enough for the flintlock to ignite. "Run her out!" he yelled. Straining at the ropes, the men heaved and the gun rolled forward until its snout protruded from the opening in the bulwark. And so it went, for what seemed like an eternity. The men went through their tasks like machines, their sweaty torsos gleaming in the sunshine as it filtered through the smoke. Lungs full of smoke, ears ringing, and eyes stinging from sweat and smoke, they loaded, fired, and reloaded. Just when Fergus was sure he could drive his crew no longer, the order came, "Cease fire! Cease fire!" The gun crew was so exhausted they sank down to the deck. Fergus staggered over to the side and looked over the bulwark.

The French frigate's stern was toward the *Athena,* and the range was opening slowly. Fergus could see that the French ship had been punished severely. The stern gallery bore many shot holes and the ornamental rails were badly gouged and many pieces were missing. The French sails had many holes in them, although not as many as the *Athena.* The Frenchman had enough sail area left to sail away.

Fergus looked back toward the quarterdeck. Captain Burbage was sitting in his chair, his coat and hat off, his waistcoat and trousers spattered with blood. His right sleeve was rolled up and another wound was visible through a rent in his trousers. The surgeon was hovering over him, pulling out splinters with some bright instrument. Standing nearby were Kittrelle and Montgomery.

Grimacing with pain at the surgeon's probing, Burbage spoke to Kittrelle. "We didn't sink her, Kittrelle, and we didn't take her." He clenched his teeth and looked menacingly at the surgeon. "But we beat hell out of her in spite of all her bloody guns." He shot another angry glance at the surgeon. "Damn! Pull out what you can and bandage the rest of it." He looked at Montgomery. "How long before we can make way?"

Montgomery looked up at the sails and rigging, much of it cut to pieces by the French fire. "It will take us at least six hours, sir." He paused to rub his chin reflectively. "Maybe more."

The captain shifted his glance. "Kittrelle?"

Kittrelle apparently was not wounded, but sweat and smoke had stained his uniform. "I agree with Mr. Montgomery. At least six hours for repair of the sails. Besides, there is other damage." He gestured forward at the shambles along the upper deck; not all of the French shot had gone high.

Burbage scowled and drummed his fist on his chair. "Damn!" he snapped. "That means we have lost her." He looked at the surgeon, who was tying a bandage around his arm. "Aren't you finished yet?"

Without a word, the surgeon stood. "Yes, sir, and I may say I have taken men's legs with less fuss."

Burbage's eyes widened slightly. A sly smile crept across his face. "You may have, sir, but this is still my arm." He waved his hand. "Now go below to those men who really need you." The surgeon packed his case and moved down the ladder.

The captain heaved himself out of his chair. He picked up his coat as if to put it on, but seeing the blood and the holes in it he dropped it on the chair in distaste. "Montgomery, see to the repairs."

The sailing master doffed his hat in salute and went about his duties, his eyes already running over the masts and rigging as he moved away.

"Kittrelle," the captain began, but he stopped as he sensed that something was amiss. Then he looked over Kittrelle's shoulders and directly into Kilburnie's eyes. Fergus turned quickly back to his gun, where Franklin was directing the cleaning of the bore. In a few minutes Fergus heard footsteps behind him.

He turned. It was Kittrelle. Fergus stood at attention. "Kilburnie," Kittrelle said, "the captain said the gunners did splendid work today." Fergus nodded. Kittrelle went on. "He also mentioned that you rallied the gun crews after . . . ," he paused, "after the men were killed. The captain ordered me to make you a gun captain permanently."

"Thank you, sir," Fergus responded.

Kittrelle smiled. "I realize that Mr. Kerry won't like this." Fergus grinned. Kittrelle tried to suppress a smile. "But he'll just have to get accustomed to it." He gestured lightly. "Now get back to your gun."

"Yes, sir," Kilburnie said, turning back to the gun.

"Oh, Kilburnie," Kittrelle called.

Fergus whirled around, "Yes, sir?"

"The captain said one more thing." A broad smile crossed Kittrelle's face. "He said, 'I doubt this will be Kilburnie's last promotion.'"

"Yes, sir. Thank you for telling me."

Kittrelle nodded and walked back over to the captain. The captain's voice boomed out. "Mr. Nash!" The midshipman presented himself to the captain. "Mr. Nash, present my compliments to the purser, and tell him to double the measure of the grog for the crew." Nash saluted and moved off on his task. The captain called after him, "And a double measure, Mr. Kittrelle! A double measure, because they fought like lions! Lions!"

Kittrelle calmly surveyed the deck. "They did indeed, sir."

Neither Kittrelle nor Montgomery was right. Repairing the rigging and replacing the battered sails took all of the night and part of the next morning. First they had to cast loose the spare mast part in the waist lashed to the exposed portions of the frames and hoist it into position to replace a section of the foremast that had been cracked with a speeding ball. Replacing several yards was easier, because they were lighter to handle and hoist, but still time-consuming. With this done the rigging could be spliced and the sails, already patched, could be hoisted.

Just after the usual meager breakfast of porridge and scorched grain coffee had been fed to the surviving members of the tired crew, the surgeon, Doctor Pollitt, a lean, gray Welshman, walked unsteadily up the two ladders from the sickbay below, paused to get his breath, and walked aft to the quarterdeck. As he walked aft, Burbage could see that his normally white shirt, trousers, and stockings were completely soaked with blood and his arms were red to his elbows. Burbage was leaning on the binnacle. "Surgeon, how goes it?" he said wearily.

Pollitt sighed. "I've cut out the last splinter, taken the last stitches, and cut off the last limb. Now time will have to do the healing. I've finished my work for now and I'm almost finished, too, but Captain, I told you when I sewed you up to stay in your cabin for at least two days and to get off of your leg. If you don't, it may swell badly and even get infected, although I've cleaned it out as well as I can."

Burbage smiled patiently. "I know, but I couldn't stay below. There's too much going on up here. I'll send for a chair. How are the dead?"

"Twenty-two bodies, sir, all sewed in their hammocks with a shot at their feet. All fine men who have gone back to their maker. I suppose you know that young Lieutenant Brashear was killed early in the fight."

Burbage nodded. "Thank you, I did. I understand he did very well."

Kittrelle, who now stood behind Burbage, said, "Very well indeed."

Burbage nodded again and turned to Kittrelle. "Let's bury the dead right away. If you'll assemble the crew, I'll read the service."

Kittrelle said, "Right away, sir. This is one of the few times I wish the Admiralty could have spared us a chaplain."

The captain shrugged. "They're short a lot of things these days—chaplains, schoolmasters, and even ships. We'll have to do the best we can. Pollitt is too exhausted to sing a hymn. My reading of the service will have to do."

After the brief but moving ceremony, Burbage said to Kittrelle, "We've all done the best we could. Now let's get under way."

The master began shouting commands, and the tired crew ran up the rigging, out along the spars, and spread the mended sails. Slowly the *Athena* gathered speed, her wake became visible trailing back from her stern, and soon she was making all the sailing master could coax out of the repaired rig and patched sails. He shook his head and turned to the captain. "Sir, we'll make better speed as soon as the sailmaker and carpenter have had time to make more permanent repairs."

Burbage nodded. "Let them rest for a while first. This will do for now."

After another month of cruising to the east, the *Athena* fell in with another British brig, HMS *Arcturus,* on a similar patrol.

There was a flurry of excitement when her sails were first sighted, but with a trip to the foremast Kittrelle had quickly identified the sails as British in color and cut. Burbage, obviously disappointed that she was not an enemy ship, said to the nearby master, "Let's close her and see what she knows."

Captain Burbage was senior to the other captain and therefore he ordered the *Arcturus* to join him. The two ships backed their sails and lay, wallowing without way on, in the green Atlantic water.

Fergus watched the gig of the other ship row over with her captain to call on Burbage. As the gig approached, the boatswain glowered at the seamen loitering about the upper decks and shouted, "Clear the upper decks and quarterdeck! Side boys man the side!"

Fergus, on watch by the binnacle, watched the six side boys, seamen in their best uniforms, form two ranks on either side of the gangway, a space cut out of the bulwark just over a set of steps leading up from the waterline. The boatswain looked over the side, watching the approaching gig, and piped it as it pulled alongside.

When the visiting captain climbed up the side, and his head appeared, the boatswain started the second pipe and held it until the captain passed through the gangway and the saluting side boys. The visitor stepped on the gleaming holystoned oak of the quarterdeck and saluted the officer of the watch and the colors aft. He turned to Lieutenant Essex, who had the watch. "Permission to come aboard, sir?"

Lieutenant Essex returned the salute. "Permission granted, sir."

Captain Burbage stepped forward to greet the visitor. "Burbage here," he said. "Welcome aboard. Please follow me below for a little refreshment."

Fergus, watching Essex carry out the ceremony on the quarterdeck, asked Poston, who was standing at the wheel with him, "What do you think of Lieutenant Essex and the way he's conducting himself?"

Poston shrugged. "Looks like a bit of a fop to me. I think he's a lieutenant because his name is Essex and because he's an English aristocrat. I hear he gambled away all of his inheritance at cards and horseracing, and his father, heavily in debt because of him, sent him to sea to get rid of him. He'd been carried on a ship's rolls for six years so he would be able to enter the Navy as a lieutenant. I don't think he knows much about the navy except ceremonies."

"He's in charge of the port gun battery."

"Yeah, and you'll see that the captain will always use the starboard battery when he can."

Fergus scratched his chin thoughtfully. "Somehow I don't think he's that bad. I used to listen to him when we were both on watch. Usually the master tried to tack when the watch changed. Essex and his relief, Brashear, would stand there and watch the members of the watch going aloft. Essex would always poke Brashear in the ribs and try to get him to make a bet on which man would come down first off the yards after they had reefed."

"Did Brashear take him up?"

"Very seldom. Only on a sure thing."

Poston laughed. "Essex bets on anything, and he always loses. I don't think he ever has any pay left."

Fergus thought for a moment. "Well, I still like him, and I liked Brashear. We'll miss him."

Half an hour later the *Arcturus*'s captain came on deck, took his departure, saluted the resplendent Lieutenant Essex, and climbed over the side and down to his waiting gig. After the *Arcturus* had hoisted her gig, Burbage turned to the master. "Mr. Montgomery, make sail. Course west."

Burbage turned to Kittrelle. "Double the lookouts. I think we'll sight a convoy soon. Captain Perry of the *Arcturus* said he had hailed a neutral merchantman yesterday who said a French convoy is headed this way only a day or so off. We don't want to miss it."

Two days later, at dawn, the lookouts aloft sang out, "Many sail ahead."

Kittrelle went aloft with his long glass and soon was back on deck, smiling hugely. "Captain Perry was right. It's a convoy on an easterly course. We can't miss them, and we have the weather gauge."

Burbage grinned. "It's been a long time since we've had a chance. Now we've got to get into this as soon as possible." He turned to the officer of the watch. "Lieutenant Essex, make signal to the *Arcturus* to prepare to engage. Take the ship to starboard as your target." He turned to Kittrelle. "Clear the ship for action."

Kittrelle did not wait for the captain's orders. He shouted to the boatswain, "All hands to quarters! Drummer, beat to quarters!"

Fergus heard the order and was the first to reach his gun. In minutes it was cast loose, loaded, and ready to fire, with the crew nervously looking toward the closing convoy. The breeze coming from astern ruffled Kilburnie's short hair, and he took off his shirt and ordered the rest of his gun crew to do the same. He looked aft toward Poston, who was now in charge of the wheel at quarters. Poston grinned and waved his hand. Fergus waved back.

Fergus looked forward again. Over the bulwark forward he could see the sails of at least twenty ships. By now he could tell the slight differences in color between British and French sails, and he knew the ships were enemy. He heard Kittrelle, who was examining the convoy through a telescope, say to the captain, "I see two frigates out in front of the main body of merchantmen. They've turned toward us. I'd say they were at least thirty-fours. They won't be easy to take."

Burbage's face was grim. "No, they never are. We'll change course to port and head for the left-hand frigate. I've ordered the *Arcturus* to take the starboard ship as her target. Ours is to port. Open fire when she's in range."

Essex quickly moved to the rail and supervised the sending of the signals.

Then Burbage turned to Montgomery, who was waiting expectantly. "Master, change course one point to port. We'll try to open with our starboard battery again."

Fergus could see the two French ships, all sails set, standing steadily toward them like two border collies protecting their sheep. Behind them he could see the convoy begin changing course to the north. When the range was down to two thousand yards, just out of the twelve-pounder's range of about eighteen hundred yards, the French ships opened fire with their bow chasers.

Burbage grumbled, "Waste of powder."

Not unexpectedly, the shots fell short. Today even Kittrelle seemed satisfied as he watched the salvo raise geysers of water ahead.

This time, maybe a little earlier than he had done during the last engagement, or so it seemed to Fergus, Burbage ordered another slight change of course to port, and when the ship steadied Fergus was able to lay his gun on the mass of canvas over the hull of the left-hand ship. The gun was at its maximum elevation of about twelve degrees. Fergus could feel his heart pounding and his mouth was dry, but this time he knew what to expect. His hand tensed on the lanyard, and he was eager for the fight to start.

The next French broadside straddled the bow, and he could hear a low whistle and ragged smack as the shots plunged into the water.

Fergus turned and looked at Burbage. The captain stood with his hands behind his back, unhurried and calm, teetering slightly on his toes.

"Mr. Kittrelle," he said, gesturing toward the French. "If you please, sir."

Kittrelle relayed the order to the starboard battery and Lieutenant Essex shouted to his port battery to stand by when they were needed.

The rolling crash of the forward guns calmed and settled Fergus, and he leaned over and looked out over the gun to check the laying. It was still on target, and when gun thirty-seven's turn came, he fired the flintlock. In his eagerness, he got a little too close to the touch hole, and he could feel the scorch of burning powder on his cheeks as the fire spread down the touch hole and to the powder cartridge waiting below. The gun leapt back beneath him like a live thing. He remembered Quantril's burned cheeks and resolved to stand back a little farther from the gun from now on.

After six or seven salvos the action of the gun crew became almost automatic. With each salvo they got better and faster at the action of loading and handling the brute weight of the gun, but at the same time fatigue slowed them down.

On the next salvo, a shot hit two guns forward, and parts of bodies flew all over Fergus and his gun and gun crew. Almost without thinking his crew brushed the parts of flesh away, and if they didn't foul the parts of the gun near the touch hole, Fergus ordered them to leave them alone. "Later," he said. "Now we keep firing."

Only one wounded man was left from the two adjacent gun crews, and Fergus ordered two men from his crew to take him below. Their job was to haul the gun into position after it fired, and Fergus had to take their positions himself. After firing the gun, he had to run back and grab the line, slippery with perspiration and blood, and haul with the strength of two men to bring the gun back. Even his large muscles quivered as he strained to pull on the line. After two salvos the men returned to take their places again. "How is the man?" Fergus asked.

One of the men shook his head. "Not good," he said.

When the ship tacked, Fergus took the opportunity to look at the opposing frigate, but his men slumped on the deck, not caring what was happening to their enemy. Fergus thought the French frigate was on its last legs. Her yards were askew, but her masts were still standing. Cut rigging hung like black spaghetti from her yards. A few guns were firing, but sporadically and not accurately.

Then their ship steadied on course, and Fergus got his crew up to resume shooting. They got up slowly, obviously exhausted, but they loaded the gun and Fergus took careful aim at the frigate and fired.

The next half hour was a blur of noise, flames, blood, and flying splinters of oak, and he drove the sweating gun crew beyond exhaustion. Rigging, sails, and pieces of spars fell around them, but Fergus ordered his crew to push the debris aside, and the gun kept firing.

Just as Fergus thought his gun crew had reached its limit of endurance, the whole world thundered, and an intense bright light filled Fergus's eyes and numbed his brain. Every man in the gun crew was thrown aft, sliding along the quarterdeck and into the bulwark aft.

When Fergus was able to get up from the deck, he felt his body to see if any bones were broken. They seemed to be all right and there was no bleeding. Around him the members of his gun crew were slowly getting up and did not seem to have any broken bones or arterial bleeding. He looked forward over the bow. Where the French ship had been, there was only a seething patch of debris-filled water. A few larger pieces of spars and equipment whirled about in the dirty water. There were no large pieces of the frigate remaining. Only a cloud of grayish-yellow smoke rose slowly.

"My God!" Fergus shouted. "The damned ship blew up!"

On the quarterdeck Burbage and Kittrelle also picked themselves up. Burbage looked incredulously at the wreckage of the French ship. "Bloody hell! We didn't mean to do all that. The bastard's magazines blew up. Now we won't be able to take her in as a prize."

Kittrelle looked off into the distance beyond the remains of the frigate. "Right, sir, now we'll have to track down one of those merchantmen. If we can find a big one, it may be worth more than a frigate anyway."

Burbage took a deep breath and leaned on the binnacle to ease the pain remaining in his wounded leg. "Master, bend on all the sail we have left and catch us a merchantman."

He turned to a midshipman who had assumed the watch. "Officer of the watch, make a signal to the *Arcturus* to proceed independently with his prize."

Kittrelle smiled. "I'll get the sailmaker cracking on repairing the sails."

"Please do. We can't come out of this fight with nothing. The crew has done too much."

By mid-afternoon, the *Athena* was again under full sail, and the nearest and biggest merchantman was hull down to the east. In his eagerness the captain tried to pace the quarterdeck, but after a few paces Kittrelle's disapproving glance forced him to retire to his chair.

Kittrelle said, "Sir, you must take care of yourself. We all depend on you."

Burbage rolled his eyes. "All right, I'll get in my damned chair, but if anything ever happens to me you'll do better than I ever did."

Kittrelle shook his head. "No, sir, we need you."

Slowly the *Athena* overtook the fleeing Frenchman and by late afternoon she was in gun range of the *Athena*'s bow chasers.

Kittrelle examined the Frenchman carefully through his spy glass, lowered it abruptly, and looked at the captain expectantly. Burbage said, "Put a round across her bow and see if she'll stop."

Kittrelle gave the order, and a single shot boomed out from one of the bow chasers.

Burbage watched the ship ahead anxiously. The twelve-pound shot raised a geyser ahead of the Frenchman, but the large ship stood on.

Kittrelle studied the ship as the *Athena* closed. "I see a lot of soldiers on deck as well as sailors. Like all French merchantmen, she doesn't carry any guns."

Burbage pulled at his chin and shifted his weight off his bad leg. "Guns or not, all the soldiers aboard make boarding her a tough job. She must be returning some French soldiers from the Indies."

Kittrelle said, "I agree. Shall I give her a salvo from our bow chasers and try to disable her?"

Burbage shrugged. "Aim a four-gun salvo at her sails. We want to encourage her to stop and surrender to us, but we don't want to damage her too much. We'll need to be able to sail her home. I don't mind if a few shots go low and take off a few of those damned soldiers."

Kittrelle grinned. "I understand, sir. We can always repair or replace sails."

"Yes, just don't shorten her masts."

Kittrelle gave the order, and the bow chasers under Essex boomed. Holes appeared in the Frenchman's lower sails, but she stood on.

Burbage shook his head. "Stubborn bastard. We'll have to board her in spite of all the soldiers on her topside. Master, lay us along side her starboard side. Lieutenant Kittrelle, have Lieutenant Essex get ready to lead the boarding party over the port side. Also tell the captain of marines to have his men fire at the French soldiers and to spare the sailors. They can shoot all the soldiers they want, but if I see a sailor fall, I'll have their hides. We'll have to use them to sail her home."

Kittrelle went forward to instruct the captain of marines and Lieutenant Essex.

At his gun, Fergus heard the conversation on the quarterdeck. He realized that his gun wouldn't be firing during the initial meeting, but would serve as backup for the port battery when it boarded. They would have to be ready to board if the port battery needed them on deck on the French ship or to defend their own ship if the Frenchmen overcame the boarders.

Quietly he armed himself with a long pistol and a cutlass from the weapons stowage on the starboard bulwark. Other members of his crew picked up cutlasses and some added seven-foot-long pikes.

One of the men with a pike said, "What the hell do I do with this silly pitchfork?"

Fergus laughed. "You look like a farm boy. Just pretend it's a pitchfork, even it doesn't look like one."

The man examined the end of the pike. "It has only one tine, like a broken pitchfork."

"You're lucky. Whatever fighting you have to do will be seven feet from your face."

Fergus watched the distance between the ships decrease rapidly as the master began giving exact orders to the wheel and the sail trimmers. As the ships overlapped, he eased his crew back to protect the personnel on the quarterdeck.

The marines, stationed in the top and behind the bulwarks, began to fire at the soldiers. They were hiding behind their own bulwarks. Although not many of them were hit, they could not fire at the crew of the *Athena*.

The master, standing by the binnacle, gave additional quiet orders to Poston on the wheel and the *Athena* rapidly overhauled the Frenchman at just the right angle to bring the *Athena* alongside. When the *Athena* was almost abreast of the Frenchman, Montgomery motioned to Poston, and the quartermaster spun the big wheel to port. The gunfire of the marines was so loud now that the master had to use hand signals to Poston.

The *Athena*'s hull crashed into the French ship, and Kittrelle ordered grapnel hooks thrown over to keep the ships together. As the grapnels fell, the lines were drawn taut by the men on the *Athena*'s deck. On the Frenchman's deck, sailors began to cut the *Athena*'s lines with axes. The marines, heeding their orders, didn't fire on the sailors. Two grapnel lines were cut, but Lieutenant Essex leaped up on the *Athena*'s bulwark, ran forward on its wide slope, and began to slash at the French sailors' arms with his cutlass.

Fergus noted that Essex's weapon, originally a standard navy cutlass, had been ground down to little more than the thickness of a foil and was apparently razor sharp, both at its point and on its edge. Essex nimbly ran the entire length of the bulwark, seriously wounding at least six French sailors trying to get at the grapnel lines to cut them. The others rapidly stepped back to avoid the deadly blade of the flashing cutlass, and the grapnels held. Still the French soldiers remained under cover from fire from the marines and did not fire at Essex.

Essex turned and ran back amidships. He waved at his gun battery, signaling them to board. He yelled some oath that Fergus thought might be a school yell, but which the crew did not understand. They cheered anyway and followed him as he jumped to the deck of the French ship. The marines tried to pick off soldiers who moved toward them.

Fergus watched Essex use his lightened weapon to cut and thrust at three French soldiers who had come out from cover. A broad swing of the cutlass decapitated one, a second soldier took a thrust to the chest, and a third lost an arm to another swing. Essex moved up the deck, followed closely by members of the boarding party. Fergus could hear cries of rage and moans of pain as the crews hacked at each other with cutlasses, handaxes, and pikes, and Fergus lost track of Essex in the surge of battle and the milling men on the bloody deck.

A small group of Frenchmen who had concealed themselves behind the nettings aft rose and clambered aboard the *Athena*. Fergus saw them coming and realized they were intent on taking over the quarterdeck and the captain, master, and other persons on it. He shifted his gun crew aft and spread them in front of the wheel and the captain. The French group was led by a huge, bearded African swinging a heavy sword. The boarders headed for the captain, and Fergus stepped in front of Burbage, who was quite evidently the captain and, Fergus knew, would be the target. The gun crew closed about him.

The African shouted some obscure oath and raised his heavy weapon. Fergus stepped forward as his grandfather had taught him and thrust his cutlass at the charging African. In the confusion he forgot that he was carrying a long pistol in his left hand. His cutlass was lighter than the heavy Claymore he was used to, but he had no trouble spearing the African deep in his chest. Still, the African's blade was descending, and Fergus caught it on his pistol. The pistol shattered and took most of the blow. The deflected blade caught the point of Fergus's shoulder, and Fergus could feel its blade slice a thin edge off of his shoulder.

The members of Fergus's gun crew managed to blunt the charge of the rest of the boarding party, and soon only two Frenchmen were alive. Fergus started after the survivors but Burbage, behind him, shouted, "Kilburnie, move over and give me some room to swing my sword! This one is mine!"

Fergus moved aside, and Burbage, game leg and all, managed to finish off one of the remaining Frenchmen. A pike thrust killed the last one.

Fergus reached down and pulled a thick gold band off the African's upper arm and took a fine gold chain bearing a symbol made of a crescent and star off of his neck. He held them out to the captain. "For you, sir."

Burbage grinned. "I'd like the chain and symbol as a memento, but you keep the armband. It's solid gold and worth a lot. You've earned it."

Fergus looked forward again. Kittrelle was standing on the bulwark looking down at the French ship. "Dammit, Essex, I told you to spare the sailors!"

Essex yelled back, "Sir, the soldiers are all dead or very badly wounded. Also the captain and the officers are dead. I'm trying to gather up all the remaining sailors and make them surrender to us."

Kittrelle seemed to be satisfied, and he yelled at Essex, "Gather the sailors on the quarterdeck, put them under guard, and come back aboard."

Kittrelle dropped nimbly to the deck and came aft to the quarterdeck. "Sir," he said, "I report the capture of the French ship *Mystique*."

Burbage returned his salute and smiled broadly. "Well done. She seems to be in reasonably good shape. Now we've got to figure out what to do with her."

Kittrelle raised his bushy eyebrows and turned to the captain. "Surely you jest, sir. We know what to do now. She's our prize, and we have to get her back to England and the nearest prize court."

Burbage sighed. "Just trying to lighten the tension. Of course we know what to do, but who will do it? Our junior lieutenant was killed. That just leaves you or Lieutenant Essex to be the prizemaster. You can't leave, and I don't trust any of my midshipmen, although two of them are reasonably competent navigators."

"How about Lieutenant Essex? He can't navigate, but he's a competent sailor."

"And a hell of a fighter. I estimate he killed at least a dozen Frenchmen, and he didn't even get a scratch. He was running up and down that bulwark like it was a race course."

Kittrelle looked a little confused. "Sir, I think you are jesting again."

Burbage sighed. "Yes, yes. I am. I think he did a wonderful job."

Kittrelle said, "Any way you look at it, he's a good man with a cutlass."

"Why the cutlass?"

Kittrelle said, "Ah, sir, I think something has passed you by. I notice you still carry a sword in battle."

Burbage was puzzled, "Yes, I do."

"You'll note that the rest of us put on a cutlass when battle is imminent. The sword is for ceremonial purposes, but it won't cut it, if you'll pardon a jest. We need a heavy, strong-edged weapon. Also the cutlass has a better guard on the handle to protect the hand."

"I notice that young Essex had sharpened his weapon."

"Yes. Maybe a little too much, but he's had fencing lessons, and is more confident with a foil weight. The blade is still very sharp on the edge as well as on the point and strong enough to take a side blow."

Burbage stroked his growing stubble. "Please ask the gunner to prepare a weapon like Essex's for me." He beamed. "Oh, yes, and that's the first requirement of a naval officer, to be a fighter. Call him back here and let's get started."

Kittrelle turned forward and beckoned to Essex. Essex trotted back, his special cutlass banging against his leg, and saluted. "Yes, sir?"

Kittrelle said, "The captain has appointed you prizemaster of the French ship. Take Midshipman Arlen, a quartermaster's mate, a sailmaker's mate, twenty seamen, and six marines, and go aboard and take her over."

Burbage, listening carefully, said, "You did well, Essex. My compliments, and I hope you use your prize money for something else beside gambling."

Essex frowned and colored slightly. "I don't think I'll ever gamble for money again, sir."

Burbage looked doubtful. "Why and when have you made that decision?"

"I've decided that risking a few pounds isn't much of a thrill. I've just risked my life several times and won every time. This is the ultimate in gambling, and I like it and want to make it my career. I plan to send my father all my prize money to help pay off the debts I left him with. The navy will be my home from now on."

Burbage extended his hand and Essex eagerly grasped it. Burbage said, "Good luck, lad. We'll be anxious to get you back, and whatever you do, don't let us get out of your sight. You'll need us to defend you if a French force turns up. We'll see you in Gravesend in a month."

Essex saluted and turned to leave. Burbage stopped him. "Oh, Essex. By the way, I'm sending my best midshipman navigator with you. I expect you to learn navigation from him by the time you get to England."

In an hour the *Mystique*'s sails were repaired, and she was on the way. Burbage and Kittrelle watched her head north.

Burbage said, "We'll have to keep an eye on her. She doesn't have any defense."

Kittrelle smiled. "I'd hate to be any Frenchman who tried to board her and had to face Essex's sword."

Suddenly Kittrelle said, "My God! We don't have any lieutenants left except me."

Burbage laughed. "You'll have to stand watch twenty-four hours a day."

Kittrelle scratched his heavy beard, unshaven since before dawn, "We've got to promote someone. Do you consider any of the midshipmen qualified?"

Burbage moaned. "Hell, no. Maybe I haven't been a very good teacher, but the material I was teaching wasn't much. These young men we get as midshipmen are only here because their fathers paid a lot of money to get them to sea."

"Then we're agreed, sir?"

Burbage looked puzzled. "About what?"

"Kilburnie."

Burbage laughed. "Of course. Who else? I'll make him an acting lieutenant. It's all I'm empowered to do. If he does well, I'll do the best I can to get permission for him to take the examinations to make it permanent when we get back and he can get to the Admiralty. We may have trouble. He's only been in the navy for over a year."

Kittrelle said, "But, sir—"

Burbage nodded thoughtfully and interrupted. "And look at Essex and many others these days. Essex doesn't have any more sea time than Kilburnie has, and I take it Kilburnie is nearly twenty-two and has one year service."

"That's partly right, but his uncle told me in confidence that some captain has carried Kilburnie on his rolls as a midshipman for five years."

"My God!" Burbage exclaimed. "That's the answer. If he can pass his examination he'll have made it. The Admiralty will certainly accept my nomination based on his recent heroic conduct."

Kittrelle nodded. "They will. Now the navy needs all the good men and officers it can find."

Burbage was thoughtful. "That's what I'm counting on. He may not be an English aristocrat, like Essex, but he has a good friend where it counts."

"Yes, he does."

Burbage grinned. "I hear you have one, too."

"Maybe so, but in the last war, as I remember it, Commodore Nelson was a lieutenant at nineteen and a post captain at only twenty."

Burbage raised his eyebrows. "Are you sure?"

Kittrelle pursed his lips. "Very sure, but I don't expect it to help me."

"Well, we'll give Kilburnie a chance. If Nelson, with his puny physique and poor health can do it, Kilburnie can do better. I never saw a stronger or healthier man. You used to be one when you were younger and before you were wounded. I wouldn't be pessimistic, if I were you. I expect you'll make it."

"He certainly will have his chance. The rest will be up to him."

"And a few more lucky opportunities."

"Oh, yea, that's the navy for you. You can be potentially great, but you have to be lucky, too."

"And you have to come through when you get the chance."

"Well, Kilburnie did."

Burbage was pensive. "So did Essex, but I can't see him as a post captain some day."

Kittrelle shrugged. "We have a lot worse today."

7

Lieutenant Kilburnie

ergus was directing his gun crew in cleaning the exterior of the gun, swabbing out its interior, and mopping the blood from the deck. One of his gun crew, vigorously pushing his mop back and forth, said, "Kilburnie, this ain't going to work. It's still dark red."

Fergus looked down at the bloodstains and shook his head. "You're right. We'll have to wait until morning when we can holystone it." Suddenly he was aware of Kittrelle's voice calling him. He looked aft. Kittrelle, standing on the quarterdeck with the captain, motioned to him.

Kilburnie put a man in charge of his gun crew, ran aft, stopped, and saluted Kittrelle. "Sir, I'm sorry to be out of uniform, but we're still cleaning up."

Kittrelle looked down at Fergus's powder-blackened and bloody trousers and then at the dirty bandage on his shoulder showing through his shirt. "Well, you won't need that uniform anymore. Get out of it, clean up, and go see the purser for some new uniforms."

Fergus looked bewildered. "Sir?"

Kittrelle laughed in a friendly manner. "You've been appointed an acting lieutenant by the captain. If you do well, and we all live through the rest

94

of the cruise, he may recommend you to take the examination for permanent rank."

"But I'm not eligible. I only have a year in service."

"Kilburnie, you are too honest to live. Hasn't your uncle told you that he's had you on a ship's rolls for five years as a midshipman?"

"He mentioned something like that."

"Well, he has, and that gives you six years service and you are eligible for promotion."

Kilburnie frowned. "But, sir, that wouldn't be honest."

Kittrelle shrugged. "Maybe not, but it's done everywhere." Then he lifted his black eyebrows. "Kilburnie, the Admiralty has a record of you as a midshipman. You wouldn't want to make liars out of those fine gentlemen, would you?"

Kilburnie was completely confused. "Would I get in trouble?"

"You and a hundred others. Just relax. Let your uncle take care of it, and study for your examinations."

Fergus grinned happily, now convinced. "I won't disappoint you, sir. Thank you for the opportunity."

Burbage, quiet until now, spoke up. "I don't think you will either, lad. Now go scrub yourself down, throw those rags over the side, and get into uniform."

Fergus saluted and started forward, but Kittrelle stopped him. "How's the shoulder?"

Before Fergus could answer, Burbage moved next to Kittrelle and said, "He's lucky he didn't lose the whole thing to that giant with the sharp sword, and I'm lucky he was there with his crew. He saved my life."

Fergus cleared his throat with embarrassment. "It's not too bad, sir. Just a dozen stitches."

Kittrelle looked surprised, but he said, "Kilburnie, I didn't know about that. Go ahead forward." When he was out of earshot, Kittrelle said, "Sir, what was that all about?"

Burbage became serious. "Just what I said. He was smart enough to anticipate what the enemy might do. He formed his gun crew around the quarterdeck to protect it, and, of course, he took care of me."

Kittrelle interrupted. "I should have thought of that. I guess I was too busy with the boarding."

Burbage nodded. "You were, and you were doing your duty. The rest was up to me. I would have given the necessary orders, but young Kilburnie seemed to know what he was doing, so I gave him his head."

"You were attacked?"

"Oh, yes, by a huge African with an enormous sword escorted by a dozen Frenchmen who came streaming over the after bulwark and rushing aft like Napoleon was chasing them. Kilburnie's gun crew took care of most of them, but Kilburnie took on the African himself."

"Did he get wounded then?" Kittrelle asked.

"Well, the African was big and strong and he managed to get in a good whack at Kilburnie, who tried to catch the blow on his pistol. Then he skewered the man with his cutlass. Altogether a brave and neat job."

"I see."

"After we had disposed of the other Frenchmen he leaned down and took off the African's arm a huge gold band and a necklace and gave them to me." Burbage opened his shirt and showed Kittrelle the gold chain with its pendant crescent and star that he was wearing underneath.

Kittrelle looked at it in amazement and crossed himself. "Sir, that's a heathen ornament, a Muslim religious symbol. You shouldn't be wearing it."

Burbage laughed wickedly. "I'll be all right as long as a chaplain doesn't see it, if we ever have one. Since we probably never will, I'm safe."

Fergus stopped by his gun crew and pointed to the husky young sailor he had left in charge. "Wheeler, you're the gun captain from now on. Get the gun in shape. The deck is all right. It's white again."

Wheeler looked up. "Who says?"

Fergus tried to keep from grinning. "Lieutenant Kilburnie says."

"What?"

"Yes, me. I've just been promoted."

Fergus left the gun crew cheering and went forward to draw a bucket of water to use to wash his dirty body. On the way he stopped by the purser's quarters. The purser saw him carrying the bucket of water and held his nose. "Jesus, Kilburnie, you look awful, and you probably smell worse. You'll need some new clothes for sure."

Fergus grinned. "Yes, Purser, two white shirts, two pairs of knee breeches, two pairs of white stockings, and a lieutenant's jacket and waist coat."

The purser's jaw dropped. "What?"

Fergus laughed. "That's what I said. I've been made a lieutenant."

The purser closed his mouth and then opened it again. "Well, I'll be damned!" Then he recovered and reclosed his mouth. "Kilburnie, go clean yourself up. I'll put your clothes in your stateroom."

Now it was Fergus's turn to be surprised. "What do you mean, stateroom?"

"Sure. You rate one. There's one vacant now that we've lost a lieutenant. By the way, you'll need a cocked hat, too, unless you want the captain to blast your hide when you appear on deck without one."

Fergus nodded and picked up his bucket. "Thanks for the advice. I'll take a cocked hat and anything else you can think of that I'll need. How do you happen to have these uniform items in your slop chest?"

"Simple. Everything is basically the same for all officers and warrant officers. The extra stuff I sew on or, rather, I get the sailmaker to do it. We split the difference. You won't look as good as Lieutenant Kittrelle looks, but who can? You can pay a tailor in port some day to make a better jacket. They'll come out to the ship even if you can't go ashore."

An hour later, in the privacy of his new stateroom, Fergus tried to put his new uniform on properly, remembering how Lieutenant Essex had looked in his uniform. "Damn!" he said, as he tried clumsily to secure the bottoms of his knee breeches over the tops of his stockings.

His spare uniforms hung over a peg in the overhead, and a second pair of black, low-cut shoes and some underwear occupied a corner of the six-foot by six-foot room, the walls of which were made of thin maple and designed to be taken down and stored below when battle was imminent.

Fergus vowed to find a way to swing a hammock in the space of his stateroom in lieu of the small cot on which he was now sitting, which was also designed to swing. Maybe he would have to swing it out in the wardroom. He guessed the cot would be uncomfortable in a beam sea if he didn't swing it, but then he had gotten used to a hammock.

After fifteen minutes of pulling and adjusting, he felt he had done the best he could with his stockings and breeches, and he went up to the quarterdeck. When Kittrelle returned his greeting without smiling, he felt his uniform must be acceptable. Just the same, he surreptitiously adjusted his jacket and pulled down his cuffs. The jacket was too tight across his chest, and the sleeves were too short. He hoped the sailmaker could make them a little longer. All the other items were of universal size, and they fitted reasonably.

Kittrelle said, "You, I, and the senior midshipman, Paltrey, will be standing a watch in three. You can expect that the captain will come up to the quarterdeck frequently, particularly at night when you and Paltrey have the watch, until he is confident that you are well qualified to stand watch by yourself. I don't think it will take long for you to qualify, but I don't know about Paltrey."

Fergus nodded, remembering the hours he had spent learning the rigging and sails and the commands required to change and adjust them. He was confident of his navigation skills and his ability to read the weather and its expected changes, and he knew he could stand better watches than he had seen Lieutenant Essex stand. He took a deep breath and said, "Sir, I am confident I can qualify quickly."

Kittrelle smiled, looking casually at Kilburnie's short sleeves. "So am I. Otherwise I wouldn't have recommended to the captain that you be promoted to lieutenant. Now go forward and about the ship and get acquainted with your new responsibilities, particularly the port gun battery. By the way, the sailmaker can help you with those sleeves."

Newly promoted Lieutenant Kilburnie walked forward behind the guns of the port battery and stood proudly, fondly patting the rounded pomelions of each gun and admiring the shiny red carriages. He looked over each gun to make sure all of the equipment was there. Crews were cleaning their guns, and some of the men looked up at Kilburnie as he passed behind them. By now all of them knew he was their new lieutenant. Some smiled at him in a friendly manner. Others stared blankly, and a few even looked away. He shrugged and pulled down his sleeves. He knew he would have to earn their respect before they all reacted the way he wanted them to.

When Kilburnie finished his inspection, he headed below to his stateroom for a well-earned rest. As he was about to enter the door, the gunner Kerry came out of his own stateroom nearby and glared at Fergus.

"Kilburnie, a word with you," he said.

Kilburnie stopped and watched the gunner's burly figure approach. The gunner came so close that Kilburnie could see the small lines around his eyes and smell his foul breath. "What do you want?" Kilburnie asked.

The gunner scowled, and his meaty face screwed itself into a sneer. "I hear you've managed to hornswoggle Captain Burbage and Lieutenant Kittrelle again. I suppose you think you're senior to me now."

Kilburnie nodded. "That's the way it is, and I hope we can get along together."

"Ha!" the gunner said. "Never, and I don't suppose you've got the guts to take me on with your fists and settle this right now."

Kilburnie took a deep breath. "If that's what it takes, I'll do it. But first let me take off this jacket, waist coat, and shirt. It's the only clean one I have."

The gunner laughed wickedly. "You'd better get rid of it before I bloody you *and* it."

The boatswain, the only other officer living in the area, poked his head out of his stateroom. "What's all this noise?" he asked.

Kilburnie said, "The gunner wants to fight me, and I can't talk him out of it. Would you please act as referee for us? Also, I think it would be wise to keep everyone else out of the area. It isn't very big."

The gunner laughed derisively. "I suppose you don't want anyone to see your beating."

"No, that's not it. This isn't entirely legal, and I don't want it to get to the captain."

"It won't from me," the gunner said. "Now get ready for your beating." The gunner raised his fists threateningly and moved toward Fergus.

By now Kilburnie had his shirt off and moved away from the gunner to give himself room to maneuver in the restricted area. The gunner came at him, swinging wildly with both hands. Kilburnie stepped to one side and jabbed the gunner with a string of left-hand punches. The gunner blinked and scowled but kept moving forward. "Come on and fight, you prancing fop," he said between gritted teeth.

Kilburnie kept moving as best he could in the cramped space, watching the gunner intently and refusing to be baited by his challenge. The next rush drew a left from Fergus to the gunner's swelling eye, followed by a right to his soft belly, but the right-hand punch pulled at his recently wounded shoulder, and he resolved to use only his left hand if he could.

The gunner gasped, and right then Kilburnie knew he had him. Now it was a question of wearing the larger man down to his size.

The gunner's accuracy was flagging, and his punches were missing wildly. A right uppercut bounced harmlessly off Fergus's forearm and swept upward where it hit a low overhead beam. The gunner bawled with pain, drawing back and examining his bruised knuckles.

Fergus stepped back. "Had enough?" he asked.

The gunner put his fists back in front of him. "Hell, no, you sniveling bastard. Stop prancing around like a chicken and fight like a man."

Fergus sighed. "All right. You asked for it."

The boatswain tried to step in. "Gunner, you're getting beat, why don't you quit?"

The gunner glared at the boatswain. "Keep out of this or I'll take you on next."

Fergus said to the boatswain, "Thanks, but I'll have to finish this off." He turned back to the swaying gunner and let loose a string of lefts.

Most of Kilburnie's punches either produced welts on the gunner's fatty tissue or tore small gashes in his face. Kilburnie suffered little, occasionally being backed into a corner. When he was trapped, he ducked and moved to one side. The gunner bellowed again, "Come on and fight, coward," but he was becoming so winded his voice was mushy.

After fifteen more minutes, the gunner was gasping deeply and swinging even more wildly.

Almost in pity, Kilburnie moved to his left, feinted twice, and finished him off with a strong right hand deep in his fat gut. It hurt his shoulder badly, but he didn't think he would have to use his right hand again. The bloodied gunner staggered and then fell face down on the equally bloody deck.

The boatswain leaned over the prostrate form. "Well, that settles that. Kilburnie, if he bothers you again, let me know. I don't like the bastard either."

There was no fresh water available, but the boatswain found a cold cup of coffee in a corner and poured it on the back of the gunner's head. The gunner groaned and struggled to get up, but fell back again, breathing deeply and groaning.

The boatswain turned to Kilburnie. "You'd better go get cleaned up. I'll take care of this hunk of fat, and I'll guarantee he'll never bother you again. He knows if he did I'd spread the word around about what happened, and I don't think he could take that. The crew would laugh him across the deck and right over the side."

The next morning Kilburnie had the morning watch. The master came up on deck with Poston, who had replaced Kilburnie as the navigational assistant. Montgomery looked closely at Kilburnie and smiled, trying unsuccessfully to hide it in his beard. "Shave too close?" he asked.

Kilburnie grinned. "Walked into a stanchion."

The master screwed up his beard again, obviously now trying not to laugh. "Funny, that's what the gunner said, too. Only I think he walked into a bigger one. There must be a lot of new stanchions down there."

After breakfast Captain Burbage came on deck and paced the quarter-deck slowly, occasionally flexing his injured leg. On one pass, he looked closely at Kilburnie's face but said nothing.

At exactly 8 A.M., when the hour glass was turned by the quartermaster, he turned to the master. "Master, change course to head for Portsmouth. My orders are to end our patrol at 8 A.M. today."

Montgomery grinned knowingly. "Aye, aye, sir. We've been out a long time. We all need a little rest, and the gunner needs a lot more than most."

The next two years went by quickly as Fergus gained experience as a lieu-tenant. When the *Athena* arrived at Plymouth on the Devon coast of Eng-land on January 15, 1797, after a routine patrol she began immediately to provision and load ammunition.

Fergus found himself heavily engaged in ordering, inspecting, and stowing under Kittrelle's direction the steady stream of boxes, butts of water and beer, barrels of lime juice, and equipment of every kind that came aboard.

On the third day in port a messenger arrived with a note from the senior commanding officer of the ships in port, the captain of a large ship of the line. The harbor was a flurry of activity as four other frigates were busy pro-visioning and loading ammunition. Burbage read the note and turned to Kittrelle. "Conference of all commanding officers," he said. "I'm off to see what this is about."

Kittrelle watched him walk up the wharf, his gait slightly askew because of his leg wound, before turning to Fergus. "Kilburnie, let's get on with this provisioning and try to finish before the captain gets back. I think we'll be leaving soon and we want to be completely loaded."

"Where do you think we'll be going?" Kilburnie asked. "Back on patrol?"

"I don't know for sure, but you can bet your farm that it will be some-where the French and maybe the Spanish are gathered to do us harm. This won't be just individual patrolling. It will be a war game on a large scale."

The captain was back in an hour, his face set in a frown. As he crossed the quarterdeck, he looked at Lieutenant Kittrelle, and his face relaxed some-what. "Come below, and I'll tell you what's going to happen."

Kittrelle opened his mouth to speak, but closed it again without saying anything and followed Burbage below. In the cabin Burbage invited Kit-trelle to sit down and ordered his steward to bring a bottle of his best brandy and two glasses. "I have a feeling we're going to need this," he said.

Burbage dismissed the steward, who seemed to be a bit put out at having to leave. After an unusually large gulp of the brown liquid, he began. "First, we're leaving as soon as possible. I hope we're fully provisioned and full of ammunition."

Kittrelle nodded knowingly. "I thought so, and I speeded up the provisioning. Young Kilburnie is working the rear ends off the crew up there."

Burbage took another swallow. "Explaining why we're leaving so soon is much more difficult. I never thought much of our intelligence service, but this time I think they've come through. They say they have it on good authority that the Spanish fleet is preparing to leave its ports in southern France and to pass through the Straits of Gibraltar and out into the Atlantic Ocean."

Kittrelle's glass stopped in midair, and he turned toward the captain. "Whatever for, sir?"

"The French and Spanish are plotting to join forces and invade Ireland."

Kittrelle took a huge swallow. "My God! What a farce that would be! They'll never succeed at anything so daring. They don't operate well together either. Never have. They'll fight more with each other than they will with us. How many troops do they have? How many stands of arms? And is Ireland rife with rebellion?"

"I don't know the answers to those questions and it isn't my business to know. I agree with you about their differences, but the Admiralty doesn't intend giving them a chance. Admiral Jervis is now lying off the southern tip of Portugal with orders to be ready to intercept the Spanish fleet before it can join the French fleet in French ports along the Atlantic coast."

"But if they elude Jervis and join forces he will surely be outnumbered two to one by their combined forces."

"Jervis will want to take them on separately before they can join forces, although I sometimes think that they would be easier to beat after they had joined. They would sink each other faster than we could. But if Jervis wants to take them on that way, that's where we come in. Six of us will leave to join him. Six ships added to his fleet won't make much overall difference, but five frigates will. He needs our speed to scout for him and find the Spanish fleet before it can join the French.

"The five of us will form a scouting line and sweep down their most probable direction of advance. We will also take two fast dispatch sloops with us to carry messages back to the admiral as to what we have found. It will be an important task, and our success or failure will be very important. We will be his eyes and ears."

Kittrelle grinned expansively. "I can hardly wait. I'll go on deck and hurry Kilburnie along."

The next morning, January 19, the ship of the line moored nearby led the British contingent out of the harbor through its protected entrance. The *Athena,* since Burbage was the senior frigate captain, led the frigates out ahead of the ship of the line and formed a column ahead of the massive but still graceful battleship.

Burbage took pity on the ships following the *Athena* the next day and ordered the frigates to form a line abreast at two-mile intervals. That way they could practice their assigned future mission to act as scouts. Also, keeping station at night was much safer.

The wind was from the west, and the ships managed to make about six knots, or about one hundred and fifty nautical miles a day. The one thousand miles from England to southern Portugal took eight days, and on the ninth the lookouts reported, "Many sail dead ahead."

In a few hours Jervis's fleet lay in front of them. This was the first time Fergus had seen that many warships in one place. But he knew the French and Spanish ships were just as big as the British, and in some cases bigger. The difference in the battle would come to depend on the crews who manned the guns. Men were what would make the difference, and traditionally the British had men who had never been beaten. Long odds only seemed to make them fight harder.

Few sails were set on the British ships, as the admiral obviously intended maintaining his geographical position while he sent scouts south toward Gibraltar. The ships of the line were making only enough way to keep approximate stations. When the reinforcing group approached, a series of flag hoists went up, fluttered briefly, and were swiftly hauled down. The ship of the line was ordered to join the battle line, and Burbage, as the senior frigate captain, was ordered to report aboard the flagship.

The master brought the *Athena* close aboard the *Victory,* Admiral John Jervis's flagship, and turned to parallel its course. Both ships backed their sails to kill their way and make it easy to lower a boat, and soon Burbage was in his gig and being rowed to the waiting flagship.

While he was gone, Kilburnie came on deck and stood watching the large ships of the line. Their open gun ports bristled with the guns clearly visible through them. They were what his grandfather had told him were the backbone of the navy. "Always shoot on the up roll," his grandfather had said. "That will cause the most damage to the sails and rigging."

"Why?" Fergus had asked.

"We don't want to waste shots on their hulls. That won't make them want to surrender. Disabling her sails and rigging will enable us to overtake her sooner, board her, and take her quicker."

"Are the French so different?"

"Yes. They fire before the up roll. It gives more hits in the hull, and we don't care about that, except for the gun crews on the lower decks. All in all they sail faster and we shoot better."

An hour later Burbage was back. Kittrelle met him as he came over the side, saluted, and made his way through the saluting side boys. Burbage was pensive. "Come below to my cabin," he said soberly.

When they were in the cabin, this time with the officers, the captain said, "I'm to take the five frigates toward Gibraltar and set up a scouting line to look for the Spanish fleet. I'm also to send the fast sloops back to our fleet, one at a time and twice each day, and even a frigate if necessary, to keep the admiral informed."

"If you find the Spanish fleet?"

"And even if we don't. Negative intelligence is also valuable. The admiral seems to be convinced they are out there." He paused and his face changed into a tight smile. "Call it an admiral's intuition."

"As sharp as a lady's?" Essex asked.

The officers laughed.

"I see," Burbage said. He stood up and chuckled. "Aye, and as fickle, I'll wager."

The officers laughed louder.

"The gig must have been hoisted by now. Let's go to the quarterdeck. We'll go southeast when the frigates are ready and form a scouting line. I want to get to the east as fast as we can."

A day later the scouting line had been set up and had swept a twenty-mile-wide path fifty miles to the east of the fleet. Burbage reserved the northernmost scouting station for himself, thinking it was the most likely point of contact with the enemy. Until the thirteenth, Burbage sent either a sloop or a frigate back to Admiral Jervis twice a day to keep the admiral informed that nothing had been sighted.

On February 12, a heavy fog descended over the area, and the adjacent ships in the scouting line disappeared in the wet, gray mist. Burbage increased his already doubled lookouts but nothing was sighted through the heavy gray blanket. Burbage paced the quarterdeck angrily, frequently waving his arms about as if trying to disperse the fog. With the fog came an eerie silence that magnified the sounds made on the *Athena,* the creaks of the rigging, the splashes of the bow waves. The men moved slowly and spoke in hushed tones as if afraid of breaking a spell.

Fergus peered into the murk, straining to hear anything that might indicate a ship ahead. He knew the crews could become confused in the fog, and although he knew there was no danger of piling on some rocks he didn't fancy the idea of a collision.

Kittrelle came up to him, moisture glistening on his hat and uniform. "Damn this weather!" he muttered bitterly and acted as if the bow itself was becoming soggy in the mist. "We could sail right by the damned Dons and not even know it."

"Do you think they're there?" Fergus asked.

"Doesn't matter what I think, Kilburnie. The captain thinks the Spanish are close." He shook his head. "Damn me, but he's acting more like an admiral every day."

Fergus glanced up ahead again. "Will we turn back soon?"

Kittrelle fixed him with a hard look. "Kilburnie, we'll turn back when the captain is ready. Stop asking foolish questions."

Before Fergus could reply, the sound of a cannon shot was heard. No one could tell which direction it came from. Men began to talk excitedly. "Someone's found the Spaniards! Maybe someone's on a rock! She's signaling for help."

"Silence!" the captain thundered from the quarterdeck. "The next man who talks will be flogged until his back is raw."

The cacophony died down immediately and soon the only sounds were from the rigging and waves alongside. A few seconds dragged by. Then minutes. Still nothing. Then another shot, closer, but still the bearing couldn't be determined. A buzz of voices rose.

"Quiet, damn you!" Kittrelle snapped.

"Sir," Fergus whispered hoarsely, "could that be the Spanish signaling something?"

Kittrelle's eyebrows shot up. "Exactly!" He drove a fist into an open palm.

"The Dons fire signal guns in the fog." He patted Kilburnie's shoulder. "Go tell the captain."

Fergus trotted quickly to the quarterdeck, touching his hat in salute. "Sir, Mister Kittrelle believes the guns are Spanish signals."

The captain clasped his hands behind his back and lowered his head for a moment. "Hmmm," he said and raised his face to Fergus. "He might be right, Kilburnie, and if he is, the Dons could be close. Tell him to clear the decks for action. I'll not be caught blundering into Spanish ships with my guns not loaded." He held up a cautionary finger. "But tell him to be quiet. I don't want the *Furias* panicked and shooting at me."

The crew rushed to their stations. Kilburnie walked behind his guns, checking the loading of the weapons and quietly talking to the crews.

"Reckon it's the Spanish?" one gun captain asked.

Fergus merely shrugged.

The *Athena* crept ahead, all hands straining to pierce the thick fog. Another gun fired, and this time it seemed to be dead ahead, but how far away, Fergus wondered. He glanced at the captain, who stood passively on the quarterdeck, speaking quietly with Kittrelle.

Suddenly the wind picked up from ahead. Just as suddenly the fog lifted, and Burbage's heart sank. There, dead ahead about five hundred yards, was the Spanish line of battle, gleaming in the sunshine coming through holes in the heavy overcast. It was headed northwest, all sails set. Their crews were not at quarters, and the sailors appeared to be lounging around the decks. At least five heavy ships had the *Athena* within easy gun range.

Burbage came to life. "Good God! Wear ship!" he yelled. "Commence firing!"

Montgomery bawled out the orders. "Hurry, damn you!"

The crew raced madly to their masts and yards and began hauling furiously at their lines and sheets. The gun crews left their stations to tend to the sails and their sheets.

The remaining gun crews scrambled to get their guns aimed and ready, and as the ship began to swing the starboard battery began to fire a ragged salvo, but it was too late and a useless exercise. There were just too many targets.

Fergus tried to pick out the Spanish ships he thought would be the most dangerous to them, and the rate of fire improved as he ran up and down behind the battery shouting advice and encouragement and designating certain targets he felt would be most dangerous.

They had a few minutes of grace as the surprised Spanish crews ran to their stations, but soon the Spanish ships began to fire at the outgunned *Athena*. Shots whistled overhead through the rigging and sails. Thirty-two-pound balls crashed against the heavy oak sides, but a frigate was never built to withstand thirty two-pounders. Some easily penetrated the frigate's relatively thin sides. One hit at the waterline and rattled inside the hull, banging loudly against the bulkhead. Others swept the quarterdeck.

Fergus was riveted to the deck, watching the unfolding scene with an odd sense of detachment as the *Athena*'s rate of swing increased slowly. Maybe, he thought, we'll get away with this yet to report to the admiral.

Shouts and yells rose about him. He heard Burbage shouting to Montgomery, "Bear a hand." And then he heard Kittrelle calling his name.

He turned toward the quarterdeck. Kittrelle shouted, "Keep firing, for God's sake!"

Fergus looked about his battery and then toward the Spanish ships. His battery would still bear and they were sure to hit something. "Now!" he shouted. "Fire!"

The guns belched fire and smoke and the stench of burned gunpowder wreathed the deck. When it was clear Fergus could see that the *Athena* had almost completed her turn. All they needed now was a few minutes of grace. He also realized that their luck was running out and the men about him paused to glance at the Spanish as they reloaded their guns.

Suddenly there was what seemed to be a fluttering motion along the side of the nearest Spanish ship. It was the gun ports snapping open. For a moment the gun crews stared into the gaping holes in the side, and then snouts of the cannon moved slowly as their straining crewmen winched them out. Everyone knew what was coming. A man near Fergus began to pray and a Latin sailor crossed himself. Still another spat at the Spanish ship and cursed loudly.

Then came a flash of lights and puffs of smoke. As the metal hurtled toward the helpless ship through the thick, moist air there came a groan from the crew.

And then, it seemed to Fergus, the world fell in on him.

8
AFTERMATH

The *Athena* staggered under the hail of thirty-two-pound balls that hit her. Fergus reeled and was thrown to the deck, which quivered and shook beneath him as if the ship were a living thing. Crashes and snaps mixed with the yells, screams, and curses as the metal plowed through wood, hemp, and flesh. At first the *Athena* seemed to be in her death throes, but as suddenly as the storm of metal had broken it abated as the fog closed in again.

Fergus stood up shakily and looked aloft. The sails and rigging were a shambles. Most of the sails had rents and holes, and many halyards and sheets had been cut and were flapping in the wind. The upper deck was a charnel house, covered with dead and wounded bodies. At least half of the guns on the quarterdeck and forecastle were heavily damaged or overturned. The ship was still swinging in obedience to Burbage's last command to wear ship. Now the stern was pointed to the Spanish battle line.

The next broadside came through a break in the fog, and more damage resulted. A yard fell forward, taking a sail with it. More men fell. Miraculously Fergus survived again. He looked forward to see where the fog bank was, and for the first time in many years he prayed they would reach it completely before the Spaniards could reload. Somehow his prayers were answered, and the view of the ominous Spanish battle line dimmed slowly as the *Athena* crept into the heavier fog. A few scattered shots followed in a few seconds, but they only produced geysers of saltwater that rose harmlessly in the fog.

Fergus looked aft toward the quarterdeck. To his horror, it seemed that no one there had survived the carnage. He began to make his way aft. He saw the body of a marine with both legs smashed to pulp. As he stepped over him the man's eyes fluttered open and he clutched at Fergus's legs. The man tried to impart a message to Fergus, but as he opened his mouth his eyes glazed and his hands fell away.

Fergus staggered to the wheel. Pools of blood and body parts were everywhere. Find the captain, he thought. He'll know what to do.

But as soon as he saw Burbage he knew the captain was dead. His body was splayed in a grotesque manner, and his eyes were unseeing.

A wave of nausea swept over Fergus. It was not just the blood and parts of bodies, it was the sadness of seeing his captain. He sagged against the wheel and tried to vomit.

"Kilburnie!" a voice laden with pain rasped nearby. Fergus looked around wildly.

"Here! Kilburnie!"

Fergus stared at the body of the dead helmsman, which seemed to move a bit.

"Damn it, Kilburnie! Come over here." Suddenly the body of the helmsman rolled over and Kilburnie could see that Kittrelle had pushed him aside.

Fergus sprang to the obviously wounded lieutenant. He tried to haul Kittrelle to his feet, but Kittrelle fainted and Fergus lowered his body to the bloody deck. Kittrelle's leg was bent at an odd angle. As soon as he regained consciousness, Fergus said, "Your leg, sir."

Kittrelle raised himself on his elbows and looked down. "Damn," he hissed, "that's worse than getting the pox."

When Fergus tried to straighten his leg, Kittrelle's face turned into a mask of pain. "My God!" he cried, balling his fists until the knuckles were white. A guttural, animal-like cry came from his clenched lips. "The ship," he sobbed, "the ship."

Fergus didn't understand at first. Then he realized that no one was at the wheel. They could be running broadside to the Spanish. He moved to the wheel and spun it. When he felt the resistance of the rudder he knew it was intact.

"I'll take her," said Poston, who materialized suddenly from a pile of bodies.

Seeing the surprised look on Fergus's face Poston grinned. "Just had the wind knocked out of me." He took his position at the wheel.

"Steer northwest," Fergus ordered. When Poston did not repeat the order, Fergus looked at him inquiringly.

Poston could not hear yet, but he nodded and spun the heavy wheel.

Fergus went forward along the upper deck, surveying the heavy damage. He estimated the ship could still make a few knots if the damaged sails could be cut away. The wind was from the southwest and would ease the strain on any repairs they could make on the rigging and masts. Further forward he ran into the sailmaker, who was already directing a group of uninjured seamen in the splicing of lines and the rigging of replacement sails. Men from the guns below on the gun deck were coming up topside. The gun crews below decks had been relatively uninjured.

Fergus asked a gun captain coming up the ladder, "How is it down there?"

"Sir, we took two shots through the side, but they didn't do much. We lost four men, though."

Fergus asked the sailmaker, "What can you do to give us a few knots so we can get out of here?"

The sailmaker was glum. "Not too much. The mainmast is beyond repair. The fore and mizzenmasts should both hold up, but we're short of replacement yards. Whatever we do will be makeshift. I can get us home, but we can't fight much without a lot of time in a large repair yard."

The carpenter came up from below and joined Fergus and the sailmaker. Fergus turned to him. "How's it below, Chips?"

The carpenter shook his head. "Six two-foot-diameter holes in the hull from thirty-two pounders. I can patch them temporarily, but the whole hull has been weakened because the shots did a lot of internal damage as they bounced around. The worst damage is a large hole in the hull at the waterline. The gunner has a group of strong-backed marines on the pumps. My mates are trying to patch the hole even though the water is pouring in hard."

Fergus shook his head. "I asked a gun captain if there was much damage from the balls we took. He said no."

The carpenter snorted. "Ha! He doesn't have to fix it. Believe me, it's bad."

"How much water have we taken?"

"About three feet. We can't pump it out fast enough until we plug the holes. It will get to the magazines before we can stop it. Without dry powder we won't be able to fire the guns."

Fergus frowned. "Well, you two have convinced me. We'll have to head for England."

The carpenter shook his head doubtfully. "Not just for England. We've got to get to a large repair yard on the Thames. Portsmouth couldn't fix us."

Fergus went below to see for himself how things were. After the gun captain's erroneous report he didn't want to take any chances. Furthermore, he had to find Essex, who was the next senior lieutenant to Kittrelle.

He stopped a passing loblolly boy. "Have you seen Lieutenant Essex?"

The man nodded, "He's with the surgeon."

"Is he all right?"

"He might lose an arm."

Damn, thought Fergus, I can't do all this alone. He pushed the loblolly boy aside and made his way to the surgeon's post on the orlop deck.

As he passed through the gun deck, he saw it wasn't as bad as the upper deck. Sunlight streamed through a few holes, illuminating a few overturned guns. In spite of the blood the men weren't standing about in shock. Some of the gun captains were trying to right the guns, make small repairs, and sort the dead bodies. Still, they seemed anxious, as well they should. The ship was leaking like a sieve, all the powder was wet, and the Spanish fleet was between them and home. Fergus tried to cheer the men as he passed on toward the orlop deck below. There the dead, dying, and wounded were scattered about awaiting treatment from the overworked surgeon.

Pollitt was hunched over a table, his back to Fergus. The man on it was obviously in intense pain. His eyes were tightly closed, the cords stood out on his forearms as he clutched the sides of the table. His lips moved over his teeth, but other than a few sharp intakes of breath he made no sound.

"Hold still!" snapped Pollitt, who was working quickly. He grabbed a lancet and began to probe.

"Aagh!" came a sharp scream from the patient as he fainted.

"Quick! Get what you can." One of Pollitt's assistants plucked out something and cast it on the bloody deck. Fergus moved around to see what was happening, and what he saw caused bile to rise in his throat. The sailor's leg was a mess, sticking out from his bloody trousers. The surgeon was busy yanking out six-inch splinters. They were so jagged flesh came out with them.

"Hello, Kilburnie," the surgeon said without looking up from his grisly task.

Fergus was amazed at his calmness. "Where is Mr. Essex?" Fergus asked, averting his gaze from the doctor's work. "A man said he might be losing his arm."

"Oh, no, Essex is fine." The man's leg quivered. "Damn! He's waking up." Pollitt reached down with a pair of forceps and pulled out a large splinter. It came out without a pointed end. He turned to Kilburnie. "Hold this wound open while I get this out."

Fergus swallowed hard and reached for the leg.

"No, no," Pollitt said, "Get on the other side."

The surgeon's apron was covered with blood in various stages of drying and his hands were bright red. His sharp features seemed strangely incongruous on his young face. He was actually the same age as Kilburnie. "No," said the surgeon, gesturing with his hands, "spread the skin this way." He made a move parallel to the man's body.

Fergus reached down gingerly.

"Come on, Kilburnie, open it up for me." He selected two fingers of Kilburnie's hands and plunged them into the wound. The man moaned and his eyes fluttered open. The doctor told his assistant to hold the patient down and plunged his forceps into the hole.

A strangled cry came from the patient, "Don't take my leg!"

"Hold him down!" Pollitt glared at his assistant. He glanced at Kilburnie, "Don't even think of going anywhere." He probed deeper. The man sobbed from the pain. "Keep quiet!" Pollitt ordered. Finally a look of satisfaction crossed his face as he produced the end of the splinter. "There!" He smiled and dropped it on the deck. Then he nodded at his assistant, who produced a bucket of water and splashed some on the leg.

The man screamed again. Pollitt looked at the oozing wound. "Damn!" he muttered. "Too much bleeding."

He turned to a charcoal brazier near the table's end. With a cloth protecting his hand, he fished out an iron glowing cherry-red. He put it back in and produced another that was orange. "Better," he said. "Kilburnie, remove your hands."

As soon as Kilburnie withdrew his fingers, Pollitt pried the wound open slightly and thrust the iron into it. Instantly the air was filled with the smell of burning blood, hair, and flesh—the same sickly sweet smell that had greeted Kilburnie earlier. The sound of sizzling flesh and the man's screams filled the orlop. Kilburnie blanched and the surgeon stared at him. "Kilburnie, get a grip on yourself, I'll wager you've seen worse on the farm."

Pollitt returned the iron to the fire. "Here, take him away and bandage him." He reached under the table and pulled out a bottle. After a long pull he said, "You were looking for Essex." He pointed a bloody finger to a corner. "Over there."

Fergus found Essex seated on an overturned bucket with a man bandaging his head. He had his hat in one hand and a metal cup in the other. There was no sign of a wound. He looked up at Fergus and smiled. "One moment I'm running to my battery and the next moment something hits me on the head and I find myself under a pile of dead men." He drank from the cup. "What is it, Kilburnie?"

Fergus stared at him. "Your arm. Someone told me you had lost it."

Essex laughed. "Don't worry, I'm fine." His eyes searched Kilburnie's face. "What is it?"

"The captain is dead," muttered Fergus in an anguished tone.

Essex's eyes widened. "Where is Kittrelle?"

"Wounded." Fergus's voice was filled with emotion. "His leg is bad."

"Good Lord, Kilburnie!" Essex yelled. He turned to the man bandaging his head. "Hurry!" he snarled.

"Yes, Mr. Essex, I'm done now."

Essex sprang and to his feet. "Come on, Kilburnie, follow me."

They broke through knots of men around the ladder and climbed to the quarterdeck, where Montgomery stood with Poston at the wheel.

"Montgomery," Essex called out, "where are the Spanish?"

The master pointed over the stern. "Thereabouts. How far back, I don't know."

Essex rubbed his hands. "Good, Montgomery," he said excitedly. "Steer a reverse course to the one we were on when we bumped into the Dons." He glanced at the rigging. "As soon as we can make sail."

Montgomery strode off, yelling at the men who were chopping at the mizzenmast. "Work faster or you'll feel a rope end!"

By the time night fell the holes in the hull were patched, and the exhausted marines reduced the level of water to two feet. Aloft new sails were rigged on hastily spliced yards on the fore and mizzenmasts.

Essex had one of the midshipmen cast the log. "Three knots," the midshipman reported.

Again the lookouts reported single guns being fired in the distance. Fergus listened carefully to the explosions and their reverberations and ordered the course changed one point to starboard. When Poston reported steadied on the new course, Fergus said to Essex, "We want to stay in contact. We can scout even if we can't fight."

Essex turned to the senior midshipman. "Call the sloop alongside and tell him to find Admiral Jervis and report the Spanish fleet on course toward Cape St. Vincent. Probable time of arrival dawn on the fourteenth. Also tell him to report to the admiral that the *Athena* inadvertently engaged the Spanish fleet, and her captain has been killed. She is badly damaged, but is capable of carrying out her mission without any help."

At dawn the swirling gray fog suddenly lifted. Where there had been a thick gray blanket, now the sun shone through a high overcast.

The lookouts shouted down and those on the quarterdeck could see a single ship heading for them.

Essex struck the rail with his fist, "This damned light! I can't make her out. Mr. Montgomery, can you tell?"

Montgomery stepped to the rail, taking Essex's glass. After a moment, he said, "She looks British, a sloop." He lowered the glass. "Maybe one of ours sent to look for us," he said in a hopeful tone.

The approaching ship fired a gun to windward and hoisted the white ensign.

A ragged cheer went up from the crew on deck, more in a mood of relief than exhilaration. Fergus let out his breath. "Well, at least I won't be spending time in a Spanish prison hulk."

Poston grinned. "Mister Kilburnie, you won't be shoved into some dank hull. You're an officer now. I'll die of fever, and you'll be free as a bird, strutting about somewhere on parole."

The sloop approached and rounded up under *Athena*'s counter.

"Hello, *Athena*!" called the *Lively*'s captain.

"Hello, *Lively*," replied Essex.

"Do I have the honor of addressing Captain Burbage?"

"No, sir, Captain Burbage is dead. The first lieutenant is wounded and I am acting captain."

There was a pause. "I am sorry to hear that, sir," the *Lively*'s captain replied in a flat voice. He seemed affected by the news. "What is the condition of your ship, sir?"

"The *Athena* has a holed hull with leaking plugs. No mizzenmast, half a mainmast, and a weakened foremast. More than half of our guns are disabled and all of our powder is wet, save that in the marine's cartridges and the officer's pistols." Essex laughed shortly. "Our condition, sir? Splendid! We'll take on any Spaniard, even the *Santissimo Trinidad* herself. We'll use cutlass and pike. Just give us time to catch her."

The *Athena*'s crew laughed and then cheered at Essex's answer.

The *Lively*'s crew returned the cheer and Fergus heard at least one man call out, "Good old *Athena*!" The captain of the *Lively* swept his hat off and bowed deeply.

Essex returned the gesture and the crews of both ships erupted in even louder cheers. Fergus felt his throat tighten, in memory of Captain Burbage and also in pride for his ship.

The captain of the *Lively*, a lieutenant of about forty years of age and probably thirty years of service, was named Hanson. "We will stand by you," he assured the *Athena*.

Hanson was rowed over in his gig, accompanied by two bottles of his best port. Later that evening in the great cabin that still bore the scars of Spanish cannonballs that had entered through the gallery's windows and had gone on forward to wreak havoc on the gun deck, Essex, Fergus, and Hanson had as convivial an evening as they could on the eve of a fleet action.

"Damned bad luck running into that Spanish three-decker like you did," Hanson said, sipping port from one of the few remaining unbroken glasses in the cabin.

Essex nodded curtly. "Indeed," was his clipped response. His attention, Fergus noted, was directed toward the sound of far-off guns.

"So, Kilburnie, you're a Scot."

"Yes," said Kilburnie, bristling. "I hope I'm not in for more humor at my expense."

Hanson held up his hand and chuckled. "Go easy, lad. T'was merely an observation. Oh, that fierce Celtic pride!" He laughed, harsh in tone but hearty in spirit. "I say that, Kilburnie, because you might be fighting a kinsman soon. Maybe one shot at you this morning." Hanson broke into a huge smile and looked at Essex. "The lad doesn't understand."

Essex returned the smile. "And I'll admit, sir, neither do I."

Hanson reached for the port and poured himself another glass. "Why, the Stuarts, of course." He looked at both officers and upon seeing only confusion in their faces launched into an explanation. "Some Jacobite officers, Scottish and Irish mostly, but some Englishmen, still serve the Spanish crown. Faithful to both the Pope and the crown of England they are." He took a huge swallow of port, obviously enjoying playing the role of schoolmaster. "Many command ships in the Spanish navy. In fact, Commodore Nelson captured a ship coming out recently and her captain was named Stuart. A relative of the pretenders he was."

Essex winked at Kilburnie and leaned forward. "You speak of Nelson. What of him? His name seems to come up often."

Hanson paused and rubbed a hand over his chin thoughtfully. His eyes showed the huge amount of port he had consumed. "Well connected," he said. "An uncle or something on his mother's side. I believe his father is a country parson."

He drained his glass and reached for the bottle again. "Lieutenant at nineteen, post captain at twenty, and now a commodore." He glanced down at his uniform and snorted. "Small, even delicate like a woman." He drained his glass again and slammed an open hand on the hastily repaired table, making the other glasses jump.

"But he fights like a lion! Like a lion!" Hanson's eyes blazed. "Damn!" he said. "He and Johnny Jervis will do for the Dons!"

Suddenly he was self-conscious and leaned back in his chair. "Aye," he said, his calm restored. "He'll fight like hell."

As he looked down at the glass in his hand, a cannon shot reverberated in the distance, causing all the officers to look in the distance through the gallery ports.

"Will it ever be day?" Essex said quietly.

"Eh?" Hanson inquired hazily, the port finally having an effect.

Essex smiled and waved his hand airily. "Nothing, sir, merely a line from Shakespeare, *Henry V.*"

"I see," Hanson mumbled, who obviously didn't see.

Later, as Fergus stood next to Essex watching Hanson being rowed back to the *Lively,* Fergus said, "He's cheery enough."

"He certainly is," chuckled Essex. "He's a wonderful combination, full of gossip and ready to share it and his excellent port."

Kilburnie sighed. "Yes indeed. I hope he's assigned to escort us home. We could sample whatever else he has in the way of something to drink. The surgeon is saving all we have for his patients."

Far off a signal gun boomed. The fog was rolling in again. Fergus saw Essex's jaw tighten and then relax. Essex began drumming on the rail. "Kilburnie."

"Yes?"

"This is frustrating. I'd rather be on one of the ships of the line, getting ready to fight the Dons."

For a moment Fergus pondered the thought, but before he could say how he liked his ship Essex went on. "But of course that is something we can't control. Luck, influence, their lordships' arbitrary decisions determine our lots." Essex struck the rail lightly. "Listen to me, a regular philosopher. But that port was good."

Fergus belched slightly and sighed.

Essex said, "Kilburnie, you should rest now. Tomorrow will be quite a day."

As Fergus turned to leave, Essex said, "I'd like you to stop by to see Kittrelle."

Fergus went to his stateroom, took up a candle, and, without knocking, entered Kittrelle's stateroom. As soon as he closed the door, Kittrelle's voice came, clear and unencumbered with sleep. "Who's there?" he demanded from his cot.

"Kilburnie, sir," replied Fergus, somewhat surprised to find Kittrelle awake.

"Well, Hanson's finally away, eh?"

"Yes, sir," Kilburnie said somewhat tentatively.

"Come closer, Kilburnie," growled Kittrelle. "I'll not bite."

Fergus came to where he could look directly down at Kittrelle. The surgeon had not taken Kittrelle's leg. He had merely declared it "broken" and set it to mend. Still, Kittrelle was in pain, as Kilburnie could tell in the flickering candlelight.

"Damn it, Kilburnie. Stop moving around and sit down. I'll not have you looming over me."

Fergus sat on a stool, placing the candle on a shelf.

Kittrelle moved about a bit, wincing as he did so. "Damn!" he muttered and sank back with a sigh. "So, what's the news and where are the Dons?"

"Well, sir, the ship still isn't fit to fight, but I think she'll be able to get home." Kittrelle grunted in acknowledgment. Fergus continued. "The Spanish are somewhere close by."

"I can still hear, Kilburnie."

"Yes, sir," Fergus guessed Kittrelle wanted more details. "They seem to be off to the northeast."

"Well, let's hope Admiral Jervis hasn't missed them."

"Lieutenant Hanson seems to think they will all meet soon, maybe tomorrow." Fergus paused for a moment. "Could Jervis's fifteen ships of the line defeat the Spanish fleet of about twenty-three ships?"

"What troubles you?"

"It's the odds, sir. They have nearly two to our one."

Kittrelle cut him off fiercely. "That makes no difference to our navy. The Spanish line we saw, if only briefly, was a gaggle. If Jervis maintains a tight formation and goes right at the Dons he'll scatter them. Even if the Dons try to pull themselves into a reasonable line, he'll scatter it."

"But if he can't?"

"He's no fool. He'll live to fight another day."

Kilburnie said, "I remember Burbage's courage and coolness against the French and against odds."

"Good, then. Now pour me a large measure of rum. Pollitt said my leg would hurt like the devil. I hate to admit it, but the man was correct."

Fergus poured some rum in a glass and brought it to him. After Kittrelle finished it, he sighed and smiled. "God awful! But it's good for what ails me. Now I must sleep or that old hen Pollitt will be clucking at me."

"Sir, any messages for Essex?"

"No, I'm a passenger for now and will probably be for the trip home. He's captain for now anyway." Kittrelle patted Kilburnie's arm. "Now you rest, too, hot work tomorrow."

Early on the fourteenth the fog suddenly lifted, replaced by the sun shining through a high overcast and a haze on the horizon.

The horizon was empty. Long swells strained the complaining timbers and stretching lines. Below Kerry exhorted another shift of men to pump out the water that had collected in the bilges and elsewhere.

The *Lively* capered about, trying to stay within supporting distance.

Fergus went below to shave and attend to his uniform. He was running a razor over a particularly stubborn area of his beard when he heard a loud cry and then the running of feet and more voices. He dressed hurriedly and ran to the quarterdeck. What he saw stunned him for it was at once spectacular and terrible.

Two miles to starboard, just out of gun range, the Spanish fleet was sailing northeast. In the fog it had gotten somewhat disarrayed, but it still presented a powerful force. One or two ships straggled two miles to the rear.

Fergus looked ahead. There was Admiral Jervis's fleet, closing from the west on a northeasterly course under full sail.

Fergus gasped. He would get to see a full-scale naval battle in minutes. The outcome would decide who would rule the Atlantic Ocean. Jervis would have a heavy task. Fail it, and Great Britain would suffer grievously. Ireland might even be occupied. Succeed, and Great Britain would continue to be able to rule the sea for decades to come.

As he watched the two fleets prepare to engage, Fergus counted the number of ships in each formation. Admiral Jervis had only fifteen capital ships and only two carried as many as a hundred guns. Fergus could see twenty-seven Spanish ships. Seven were giant three-deckers, and one, the *Santissimo Trinidad,* carrying one hundred and thirty guns, was a four-decker, the largest warship in the world.

Jervis stood on implacably. Fergus marveled at his courage and integrity of purpose as his ships swung into line behind and in front of his flagship, the hundred-gun *Victory.* The Spanish fleet struggled to concentrate its two groups, eight to the east of Jervis's approaching group and seventeen to the west of it. Admiral Jervis had seen the weakness in their battle line, seemingly unmindful of the danger of being caught between the two forces, and he headed for it on a northeasterly course. Soon he had split the Spanish fleet, and the heavy ships of each side began to fire at each other. Flashes stabbed out from the sides of the ships and clouds of dingy smoke began to roll up in the sky, accompanied by the reports of the heavy guns. Just before the ships opened fire, Fergus could hear a loud cheer from their large ships. Soon smoke obscured some of the ships, but Fergus could see the heavy damage being done, particularly to the Spanish ships near the middle of their broken line.

As the British ships passed through the gap in the Spanish line, Jervis ordered them to reverse course again in succession. Kilburnie, his long glass glued to the action, read off the signals, and Poston looked up the meanings of the groups of flags. Again the British ships pounded the Spanish ships from both sides, whereas the Spanish could only fire on one side.

Fergus could see one of the smaller British ships veer out of line and sail across the bow of a large Spanish ship. "Jesus!" Fergus muttered. "He's violated their standing battle instructions. He'll catch hell!"

Entranced by the bold action, he grabbed a long glass again and tried to identify the culprit. Others saw it, too. "Damn! that's Nelson," yelled Essex. It was the *Captain,* Commodore Nelson's flagship. He shrugged. "Whatever he does seems to turn out all right. His reputation has spread throughout the British fleet."

As soon as the *Captain* moved past the last ship in the British line, that ship swung in behind and followed her. The *Captain* and her followers charged at the Dons, and Nelson placed them across the line of the segment of the Spanish fleet he had cut off.

This position was gained at a terrible price, for the large ships, which included the *Santissimo Trinidad,* began to pound the smaller *Captain.* Fergus shuddered to think of the punishment being meted out to Nelson and his crew.

When the smoke cleared, Fergus could see the *Captain* going alongside one of the large Spanish ships. Kilburnie watched its movements intently. Commodore Nelson was clearly visible on the quarterdeck of his flagship. The *Captain* was firing every gun, but the Spanish ship had more and bigger guns and was tearing the *Captain* apart, devastating her topside. Nelson's flag captain continued to bring his ship alongside the towering monster. Fergus could read *San Nicolas* on the counter of the ship.

Ahead of the *Captain* the other seventy-four that had turned with Nelson now ran across the bows of numerous Spanish ships, blazing furiously at a two-decker, then a three-decker.

Behind these leading Spanish ships, others began to bunch up, allowing Jervis's other ships to pour murderous fire at them. Fergus could see masts toppling, spars falling, and yards and rigging flying in all directions.

"Nelson is mad!" cried Essex, bringing Fergus's attention back to the *Captain.* He swept the topside of the *Captain* again with his long glass. Her foretopmast was down and not a sail was left aloft, but Nelson had managed to run under the stern of the *San Nicolas.* Still the Spanish ship wasn't beaten, sweeping the quarterdeck and smashing the wheel.

Yet Commodore Nelson and his flag captain were alive. Kilburnie could see the flag captain wave at the crew to throw grapnels over to the *San Nicolas.* The two ships became locked together and the two officers led a boarding party that climbed up the stern of the Spanish ship, breaking the windows out of the after structure. Another officer led a party up the side, their cutlasses gleaming in the soft light.

As the ships swung, still drawn tightly together, Kilburnie could see the quarterdeck of the *San Nicolas*. Commodore Nelson broke out of the after structure onto the quarterdeck and there was a brief scuffle with a few men still there. Then it was over, and the Spanish captain handed his sword to Nelson.

Then a second ship, the *San Josef,* out of control and almost as damaged as the *Captain,* crashed into the *San Nicolas.* Kilburnie could see Nelson and the boarding party move over to the quarterdeck of the *San Josef.* After a brief struggle it was over, and Kilburnie could see the Spanish captain handing his sword to Nelson.

"My God!" he said. "He's captured both of them!"

The midshipman standing next to Fergus said derisively, "Impossible! Even Commodore Nelson couldn't have captured them both."

"I'm sure. He's done it!"

The remaining Spanish ships milled around in confusion, not responding to the orders of their admiral. The division created by Commodore Nelson transformed the Spanish fleet from an organization into a collection of individual ships seeking to escape from the carnage.

In an hour the battle was over, and Jervis's flagship came to the west to clear the area in the failing light. The Spanish fleet had left behind four captured capital ships, and the remainder had fled in the direction of Cadiz. The change of course brought the *Victory* close to the laboring *Athena*.

Suddenly Poston, who had been relieved on the wheel and was observing the action, shouted, "She's hoisted our call."

"See to a response," Essex said calmly.

Poston ran to the signal bag and hoisted their call numbers, fifty-six, in answer. Then he manned a long glass again. He began to read off a group of numbers. Fergus committed them to memory and then pulled the weighted signal book out of the binnacle. He ran his finger down the pages until he found the correct numbers. "Well done," he read from the signal book.

Poston laughed exultantly. "Then the signal means, 'Well done, *Athena*.'"

With a somewhat puzzled voice, Essex said, "Answer it."

The *Victory* and her followers stood on, and as they crossed the *Athena*'s bow, Fergus found himself admiring the splendid but damaged ships. Britain would now rule the seas for decades more, and Ireland was safe.

An hour later the *Athena* was ordered to leave the fleet. Fergus was pensive, thinking how much Burbage would have liked to know of the signal. After all, he had been the one responsible for the *Athena*'s accomplishments.

Poston guessed what he was thinking about. "Sir, he'll know about it wherever he is. You might want to tell Lieutenant Kittrelle about the signal, though."

Fergus realized how thoughtless he had been not even to suggest that Kittrelle be informed, and he turned and looked at Poston. For the first time he noted that Poston's shirt was bloodstained. "My God! You're wounded. Why didn't you say something?"

Poston shrugged and tried his arm. "I can still spin the wheel."

"I'll take the wheel. Go below and see the surgeon. While you're there, tell Lieutenant Kittrelle all about what has happened."

Poston left, and Fergus took over the wheel. After a few minutes he realized he had new responsibilities now and he couldn't afford to be distracted by the task of steering.

Essex looked at him and shook his head. "Get someone to relieve you."

Kilburnie called over a likely looking young seaman from a nearby gun crew who were trying to right an overturned gun. "What's your name?" he asked.

"Spicer, sir."

"Do you know anything about steering a ship?"

"No, sir."

"Well, you are about to learn. Take the wheel. When I want you to change the rudder, I'll hold up my hand. Left hand, move the wheel to port, right hand to starboard. One finger, one spoke; three fingers, three spokes, and so forth."

After a few minutes, Spicer seemed to have learned the first step. Fergus came up behind him. "See that small black line in front of the compass card? It's called a lubber's line. It's fixed and indicates the ship's heading. Actually it turns as the ship turns. The compass card is what is really fixed. Can you read?"

"Yes, sir. I see the big letters on the compass card. N, SE, and so forth."

"Those are called the points of the compass. When I tell you to steer by one of them, turn the wheel to bring the point against the lubber's line. When it's there, put the rudder amidships again."

"Sir, how will I know the rudder is amidships?"

"There's a black ring around one of the spokes. When that's up, you've got it."

Spicer smiled. "Sir, this isn't too bad. I think I can do it all right."

"If you would like, I'll speak to Mr. Montgomery about making you a quartermaster's mate."

Spicer grinned even more broadly. "And that will mean no more holystoning?"

"That's right."

"Sir, I'll do it."

For ten days the *Athena* plodded north toward England. The crew, particularly the sailmaker and the carpenter and their mates, did their best to make repairs, but the task was daunting. Fergus, who knew they would be in a shipyard soon, didn't press them. They had been through hell and needed some time off from the daily routine. Occasionally sails were sighted. Most of them were of much smaller ships that scurried away from what they thought was a large frigate.

Fergus watched them, regretting that they did not have the ability to chase and take them.

On the first of March the *Athena* sailed slowly up the Solent, through St. Helen's Roads, and past the Horse Tail. They anchored off Spithead.

"I hope the commanders of the forts will not be angry at my failure to salute," said Essex, running a telescope over such places as Monkton Fort, Southsea Castle, and massive Cumberland Fort.

As soon as the anchor was down, a pinnace arrived alongside, and a yard supervisor clambered aboard. He stood at the top of the sea ladder, looked around with wide eyes, and shook his head. "A hellish mess," he said.

9

THE EXAMINATION

hen the yard supervisor had finished his inspection of the *Athena,* he turned to Essex and said, "Just like I suspected from what we've heard about you. We'll have to get you alongside right away." With that he tipped his hat and almost slid down the ladder.

Not much later another small boat bobbed up. Essex gave permission to come aboard, and a small, sharp-featured man clad in black scampered up the ladder. He strode over to Essex, purposefully extending his hand. "Good is my name," he said. "Pilot. I'm to take your ship in." He pumped Essex's hand once and strode to the wheel, lightly touching it. Then he grabbed it firmly and turned it a few times. "Hmm," he said cocking his head. "You have rudder damage?"

Poston took umbrage to the suggestion, but deferred to an expert. "Steers fine," he said as evenly as he could.

The pilot pursed his lips. "As you say." He turned to Essex. "Sir, prepare to raise your anchor and give me some sail."

"Mr. Montgomery will assist you," said Essex, indicating the sailing master who was standing next to the binnacle.

"A good day to you," said Good, in his plain clipped tone. "Shall we bring her in?"

Montgomery nodded and began to issue orders to the crew. Soon all was ready and Good began his task.

As soon as the anchor was up, the ship began to move under a gentle breeze toward the ships to the left side of the Portsmouth Great Basin. With almost delicate movements of the wheel Good brought the ship around the various jetties and into a slip. Men waited on the pier for lines to be thrown from the bow.

Good shouted more commands and then ordered the bow lines out. After some heaving and pulling on board and ashore, the *Athena* was snug on her berth.

Within the hour the wounded were brought off the ship and dispatched to a hospital at Haslar. Essex ordered the men to continue the work they had begun to repair the ship. "The faster we put her to rights, the faster we can turn her over to the dockyard, and the faster we can get back to sea," he told the men.

He confided another concern to Fergus. "The faster we get to sea the fewer men we'll lose to desertion," he said. "Furthermore, there'll be less chance of the crew being parceled out to other ships."

But such was not to be, for orders soon arrived. Essex and Kilburnie were ordered to report to the Admiralty and the crew was ordered to receiving ships to provide replacements to other ships. As Fergus guessed, when the crew was mustered the day after being told of their fate, a great many men had gone missing. To Fergus's amazement Essex was strangely unconcerned. "Most have probably gone off to find other ships of their choice rather than risk going to a floating hell. Some will try to get home. Because of the press most of them won't get beyond Portsdown Hill. No, I'd say the king won't lose more than the services of a handful."

On the day the crew was marched off to the receiving ships and the officers, warrant officers, and midshipmen dispersed, many men shook Kilburnie's hand and expressed a hope to serve with him again. As Fergus came down the brow for the last time, he turned to look at her. Essex, leaving last, strode slowly down the brow, clutching a parcel under his arm. He joined Fergus at gazing at the *Athena*.

After a minute of silence, he clapped Fergus on the shoulder. "Come, Kilburnie, off to London." His cheerfulness was forced, and with that the two officers turned away and left their ship to the tender mercies of the shipwrights.

As expected, Fergus's coach trip to London was bumpy, wet, and uncomfortable, but his reception at his uncle's house was warm, friendly, and loving. His aunt smothered him with kisses and then stood for a long time gazing at him in his uniform, occasionally dabbing her eyes with a handkerchief and saying over and over "how much of a man" he looked. She sent a servant to inform Jeris of Fergus's return and then bustled to the kitchen to supervise the preparation of a huge celebratory dinner. Fergus barely had time to change his shirt when he heard the door flung open and his uncle calling his name.

Fergus came downstairs quickly, almost colliding with his uncle.

"Well," Jeris said, "*Lieutenant* Kilburnie!" The satisfaction was as evident in his voice as it was on his face. Fergus started to protest that it was only a temporary commission, but his uncle was already pulling him into the parlor. "No talk until we toast you properly." Jeris poured two large brandies and shoved one into Fergus's hand. "There, boy." He raised his glass. "To you."

Fergus smiled. "To Captain Burbage," he said.

After one of Aunt Martha's grand dinners filled with food and battle stories Fergus and Jeris moved to the parlor for drinks.

Sunk in a chair in front of the warm fire, Fergus grew contemplative. "To the *Athena*," he intoned solemnly.

"Aye," replied his uncle softly, "and to your good captain's memory." Both men drank quietly for a long moment, each borne away by private thoughts.

Jeris broke the almost meditative silence. "Well, lad, how was your journey from Portsmouth?"

"Not much better than the one from Scotland, but, thankfully, it was only a couple of days long. Still," he sipped his rum, "the bumping and rattling did not bother me as much. I was too busy looking at the land to give them much notice."

"The land?" Jeris asked.

"Yes, I could not take my eyes off the fields, the trees, the grass and I couldn't hear enough birds—proper birds, I mean, not those damned gulls and terns. It seemed so beautiful, I forgot for a moment it wasn't Scotland."

Jeris smiled knowingly. "Spoken like a real sailor!" Fergus gave a quizzical look that made Jeris smile all the broader. "Bless my soul, lad, but any good sailor longs for the land when he is at sea. Why do you think whenever an admiral or captain strikes it rich he buys a country house and surrounds himself with sleek cattle, fast horses, and fat fields? Damn me, on the *Fervent*, the captain could talk of nothing but his pigs in Ireland, County Meath it was!" He chuckled at the thought. "The sea is a trackless waste, but it's our trade." He looked at his empty sleeve. "Damned hard trade, too." He took a gulp of rum and pursed his lips. "Damned hard. But so far you've come through not too badly scarred, eh?"

"Yes, Uncle," Fergus replied, lightly touching a scar on his forehead, "not too badly scarred." He then turned the conversation to what was truly foremost on his mind. "Uncle, what of the *Athena*? What news of her?"

"You know more than I, Fergus," his uncle replied looking pointedly into the fire.

Fergus felt ready to burst. "Uncle Jeris, at the battle! The battle!"

Giving a sly smile, Uncle Jeris settled back in his chair. "Well, Admiral Jervis—who, I am told, will receive a peerage, perhaps an earldom—gave your ship a mention in his report. Nothing much, mind you, but he was impressed that she was saved after running afoul of a couple of Spanish three-deckers."

"Oh," said Fergus in a disappointed tone.

"You weren't expecting an earldom, too?!"

Fergus flushed in embarrassment. "No, but. . . ."

"Come now, lad, it was our greatest victory since '94," he said, referring to Lord Howe's defeat of the French in June 1794, "and God knows this country needed one. Don't feel yourself slighted if Jervis is made an earl and that Nelson fellow is proclaimed the hero of the hour. Ballads are being sung in their praise and taverns are being named for them from Aberdeen to Belfast to Plymouth, I'd wager."

"But Nelson deserves it! I saw him take those two ships!"

"Certainly, but what of Collingwood in the *Excellent* who followed Nelson and raked the head of that Spanish line? Or Troubridge in the *Culloden* who tacked so brilliantly? Mentioned in Jervis's dispatch, yes, but I doubt any boy is now hawking sheets of some foolish song about either of those two men." He cocked an eyebrow. "So, then, how do the actions of the *Athena* and her mere survival compare to the *Excellent*'s or the *Culloden*'s?"

Crestfallen, Fergus stared into the fire. "Not very well."

Uncle Jeris leaned back in his chair. "Ambition is fine, Fergus, but to realize it, you need two things—skill and luck. That day, Nelson, roughly equal in skill to any other captain, was simply luckier than most." As Fergus sat mulling over his uncle's observations, Jeris rose and poured himself another measure of rum. "Now, then, what are your plans?"

"I don't understand, Uncle. My plans for what?"

"For the navy. You are a temporary lieutenant or, more precisely, were a lieutenant. But, from the way you talk I think you wouldn't mind wearing that coat again."

"You're right but, Uncle, you better than anyone know the regulations. If I'm to make lieutenant from the lower deck, I must first be a master's mate. Even if I were appointed midshipman it would be five or six years before I could . . ."

" . . . take the examination for lieutenant." Jeris held up a hand. "Thank you, but I do know all this. Yet, you seem to have forgotten I am a fairly senior Admiralty clerk. Do you not think I have thought this through?" He leaned forward. "Remember, as I did with your brother, when you were old enough I booked you on a ship as a midshipman so that if you were appointed a midshipman, you could take the examination in a year. But, as there is a war on, I think the navy will not be as particular as they were in the past about how it gets its officers." Now, a great satisfied smile crept across Jeris's face. "Especially if those men have letters testifying to their courage, as you do, Fergus." Catching his nephew's surprised expression, Jeris continued, "Yes, Fergus, Burbage wrote me of your actions against the French boarding party."

Although pleased by that information, Fergus had another concern. "But what of the examination? I cannot avoid that."

"Indeed, so, that is why for the next month you shall study for it here, in my house. I'll be your tutor, if necessary."

"Why the next month?" Fergus was becoming quite confused by the rapid turn of events.

"Because, my boy, a month from tomorrow, you will be examined."

Fergus was dumbstruck for a moment, but quickly found his tongue. "I cannot be ready by then!"

"Nonsense! You will be. I'll see to it." He drained his glass. "Now, Fergus, when did you last write to your family?"

Fergus cleared his throat nervously. "Well, I. . . ."

Jeris clucked his tongue. "As I thought. Now, before you head off to bed, write your family a letter and tell them what you have decided to do." He stood and brushed off his coat. "I'll see you in the morning."

The next morning Fergus came down to a huge breakfast, a large pile of books, and a stern lecture from Uncle Jeris admonishing him to study hard and not be idle. Looking at the teetering stack of books, Fergus wondered if he would not have been better off in the Army after all.

A day passed, then a week and then two as Fergus studied by day and was drilled and tutored by Uncle Jeris by night. Still, it was not all work; he found time to wander London, marveling at the sights and feeling the enormous energy of the great city, and in the evenings Uncle Jeris would relate the latest gossip from the Admiralty or entertain guests—sometimes officers, sometimes fellow Scots—who had their own stocks of tales.

On the Tuesday of the third week, as Fergus sat studying, a knock came at the front door. Fergus heard the maid answer the door, speak to someone—a man by the sound of it—and then came a gentle tapping on the library door.

Fergus opened the door. "A man to see you, sir," said the maid and then added in a loud whisper, "He's in livery."

Intrigued by the idea of a liveried servant calling for him, Fergus went into the hall. There he found a man dressed in a bottle-green coat faced with red and decorated with silver buttons and lace. The man extended a hand in which there was a letter sealed with red wax.

"Thank you," said Fergus, taking the letter.

"I am to await your response, sir," announced the servant tonelessly.

Fergus nodded in acknowledgment and opened the letter. His eyes immediately went to the signature. It was from Essex!

Kilburnie—

I hope this note finds you well. I am staying at my family's house in London while I await my orders. I have hopes of getting my own ship—a cutter, perhaps—but, as we all do, I serve at their lordships' pleasure.

Please dine with me tomorrow. My coach will call for you at two o'clock.

Essex

"Please tell Lieutenant Essex I accept his invitation." He hoped his tone wasn't too lordly.

"Yes, sir," replied the servant impassively. With that—and no more—he departed.

The next day Fergus dressed simply in a blue suit his uncle had demanded he have made and for which his uncle had paid. His linen was clean and his shoes were blacked properly as well.

Promptly at two o'clock there came a knock at the door and the same servant stood there, as impassive as before. "Mr. Kilburnie, sir?" he asked, bowing ever so slightly.

You jolly well know who I am, Fergus thought, but he played his role. "Yes."

"Very good, sir, please come with me." He gestured Fergus to a waiting coach. It was a magnificent affair of dark polished wood and metal fixtures burnished to a bright shine. The horses were obviously well bred and matched, all black, and their harnesses shone with frequent polishing as well.

The servant opened the carriage door with a murmured "Allow me, sir," and Fergus climbed in. He found himself in a rich interior that carried the heavy aroma of tobacco smoke mixed with some tantalizing traces of perfume. It was in such surroundings that he made his way through the streets of London to a magnificent house on what was obviously a fashionable street.

Fergus descended from the carriage, clutching his hat. He moved to knock on the huge door but before he could do so, it swung open noiselessly and another man in livery greeted him. "Mr. Kilburnie, sir?"

Again, there was a role to be played. "Yes."

"Please follow me, sir. His Lordship and Mr. Essex are waiting."

Fergus entered a hallway into which a large part of his family's farmhouse in Scotland could have fit. The walls were painted a delicate robin-egg blue and plaster moldings and other decorative devices decorated the ceilings and walls. At the end of the hall, a grand staircase swept up and then split into two wings that soared around a huge window through which light poured in. Paintings and statuary were in abundance and a huge, yet delicate glass chandelier loomed above him. Fergus followed the servant into a high-ceiled room painted a vivid red. A few candles and a cheery fire were all that illuminated the room.

"Ah! Fergus," Essex called happily, rising from a chair. He came forward, his hand extended. He and Fergus shook hands. "How good of you to come—and on such short notice." He grabbed Fergus's arm firmly and steered him toward the fireplace, where, sitting in another chair, was the man, Fergus guessed, the servant had referred to as "his lordship."

In the style of people used to others waiting for them, his lordship slowly rose. He was a large, heavyset man, dressed richly, but not extravagantly, in a wine-colored suit. The ruddy face seemed open and friendly enough, but around the mouth and eyes were etched lines that bespoke cares of no little weight. His hair was dark, but heavily flecked with gray. Under dark eyebrows dark blue eyes—neither friendly nor hostile—quickly ran over Fergus.

"Father, may I present Mr. Fergus Kilburnie, late of Ulster, Scotland, and His Majesty's Ship *Athena,*" Essex said somewhat grandly. "Fergus, my father, the earl of Satterfield."

Fergus bowed. "My lord," he said, hoping his voice did not betray his nervousness.

The earl of Satterfield obviously didn't hold with reserved behavior, for he burst like a summer thunderstorm on the young Scotsman. "Kilburnie!" he boomed. "A pleasure, sir, a pleasure!" He shook Fergus's hand forcefully. For his part, Fergus was amazed to feel what seemed like callouses on his lordship's hands. "My son tells me much about you and all of it good." He laughed heartily, deep in his broad chest. "Not that I believe him, mind you. He was always making up stories about everything. Perfect sailor, eh?" Essex blushed and gave a shy smile.

"For me, it was the Army—the American War—as it was for all my family until this young scoundrel," to Essex's obvious embarrassment, he tousled his son's hair, "told me he wanted to join the Navy." He gazed at his son fondly. "Ha! Serves me right letting him read about a lot of damned Greeks blundering about the Mediterranean looking for some damned sheepskin!"

"Father, it was your school," protested Essex mildly.

"Yes, but when I was at school, I spent my time learning useful things rather than listening to some master prattle on in Greek."

"What were they, sir?" asked Fergus, curious to learn what this nobleman considered useful.

"Eh? Useful, you mean?" responded Lord Satterfield. Fergus nodded. "Cudgeling and rat-catching, sir," the earl said firmly. "Cudgeling and rat-catching."

At that moment a servant materialized in the doorway and announced that dinner was served. "'Bout time, too," grumbled Lord Satterfield. "I am damned hungry—and I have to sit today." Fergus shot Essex a questioning glance which Lord Satterfield caught. "Sit," his lordship said, "in Lords."

Fergus thought he caught on. "The House of Lords, sir?"

"Good God, yes, the House of Lords! Where do you think I meant?!"

Essex interrupted. "Father, perhaps Kilburnie is somewhat confused. A Scottish peer can sit in Commons."

"Damned queer practice, it is, too," grumbled his father.

"Indeed, Father, indeed."

Seemingly satisfied by his son's explanation, the earl shifted conversation back to nonpolitical topics. "I hope your appetite hasn't waned any, Kilburnie, stuck as you are in this godforsaken city. The country is the place for a man, away from lawyers, stock jobbers, Jacobin mobs, and bankers. A pack of rogues, the lot! No, give me the country—industrious tenants, stout yeomen, honest artisans, and companionable clergymen like we have in Berkshire."

Fergus looked about as Lord Satterfield led them into the magnificent dining room in which sideboards and the table groaned under the weight of plate and fine crystal. Surrounded by such luxury, Fergus thought, would make living in this "godforsaken city" quite tolerable.

Three servants ushered the three men into chairs at the head of the deeply polished table. Almost immediately, the first course was served: oysters, a dozen a man. By each man was then placed a silver tankard.

"Ah," said the earl and tucked in with relish. After he had eaten three oysters, the earl drank deeply from his tankard. "Kilburnie," he declared, "there is nothing like porter with oysters." Fergus would have agreed had he not been busy eating.

The next course was a creamy soup in which swam enormous chunks of lobster and which itself was accompanied by sherry. "Some considered lobster to be worthless, Kilburnie," said his lordship with an air of triumph, "but my cook can do wonders with it!" This course, too, was eaten in silence, save for the click of spoons on china and the pouring of more sherry into glasses by the servants.

The soup bowls were cleared and each man was then presented with a brace of what appeared to be small ducks. "Ducks all right," said Satterfield as he took up his knife and fork and attacked the birds vigorously. "Sea ducks from Norfolk. Damned fine." A red wine was poured into a glass by each man. The earl took his up and drank a large swallow. "Claret," he said with no fear of contradiction and no little enjoyment.

Essex was too busy carving his own ducks to disagree, but it was obvious by the way he drank deeply that he shared his father's taste for wine. Fergus lifted the glass tentatively to his lips, the bouquet coaxing him as he did. When the wine touched his tongue, he was pleased by its complex flavors. His next sip was in fact a swallow and Lord Satterfield beamed at him in approval.

As the men were finishing the ducks, a servant entered carrying a platter on which rested a large roast of beef. Placing it down near the earl, the man began to carve off thick slices of meat. "Excellent!" exclaimed his lordship as the deep pink, almost red interior of the beef was exposed. He watched with unconcealed delight as the man placed several slices on his plate. Fergus watched in amazement as Essex's plate was then piled high with juicy beef. In a few moments he too was presented with heaps of meat.

Other servants entered with dishes filled with all sorts of vegetables. Following the examples of Lord Satterfield and Essex, Fergus helped himself when they were offered. As he looked down at his plate, piled high with food, he wondered if he could finish everything. Soon, however, he found himself keeping up quite well with both his dining companions in terms of wine drunk and food eaten. Lord Satterfield smiled at Fergus's heroic efforts to eat the food presented him; clearly, he appreciated any fellow trencherman.

After more helpings of beef and several more glasses of claret, his lordship sat back in his chair and wiped his mouth with an enormous napkin. "Splendid," he declared. "Now, let's have some cheese." A servant cleared the plates and glasses while another fetched a huge wheel of Stilton cheese. Still another presented a bowl of apples and another a bowl of nuts. These were followed by a decanter of port.

Lord Satterfield cut a huge piece of cheese from the wheel and deposited it on his plate. He then selected an apple and expertly peeled and dissected it. The port was poured, passed to the left, and soon all three men were munching contentedly. After a few bites of cheese, his lordship obviously decided that it was time for conversation because he began to ask questions of Fergus. "So, Kilburnie, what of you and the navy? My son is refusing to leave; says he likes it now more than ever."

Essex gave a tight smile.

"Well, sir," Fergus answered, "I too plan to stay in the navy. My uncle has scheduled my examination for lieutenant next week."

Lord Satterfield cracked a walnut and dug out the meat. "Lieutenant? Next week, eh?" He paused with the meat near his mouth. "If what my son says is true, you should have little trouble." He popped the meat in his mouth. Fergus was tempted to ask the earl just what he meant by that, but decided not to pursue it.

Lord Satterfield was not finished with his questions. "Tell me, Kilburnie, do you pay much attention to politics?"

"No, sir," the Scotsman answered honestly. "Well, around election time, I notice because it always seems great sport—what with all the speeches and drinking—and, in Ireland, the occasion for a brawl or two between factions, but politics seems more of a gentleman's occupation. I'm the son of an estate agent."

"Well, there's always a fight to be found during an English election, too. The Irish have no exclusive rights to such things." Satterfield's eyes took on a wistful look. Fergus immediately understood why his lordship had found cudgeling so useful a subject for study as young man. It prepared him for the often violent nature of English elections.

"People seem to like it though when an election is a good hard fight, lets 'em know the mettle of their leaders," continued Satterfield. "In that way it is like sport. It is blasted expensive sport, though. It cost me more to keep the two of my sons who are interested in politics," he raised his voice slightly and glared momentarily at Essex, "in Parliament during the last elections than it did to keep my entire racing stable last year."

At the mention of horses, Fergus brightened. Noticing this, Essex took the opportunity to steer talk away from politics and informed his father of Fergus's experience with racing.

"Blast it, boy," Satterfield chided his son, "why did you not tell me this before?!" He immediately barraged Fergus with questions about horseracing in Ireland. Soon, all three men were talking about all manner of things equestrian quite happily. All went well until Satterfield asked who owned the stables in which Fergus had gained all this experience.

"Lord Inver, sir."

"Hmm . . . I believe I know of him. Irish peer, but his people originally came from, now let me see, Nottinghamshire? Or was it Lincolnshire?"

"I thought he was Irish," stated Fergus.

"Oh, he damned well is. Some ancestor went over around the time of James I and carved himself off a nice piece of Irish land, but all the marriages have been with the Irish. So after a few centuries he hasn't much English blood. I hope he doesn't go about saying he does." He gave a gruff laugh and took a sip of port. "Now that I think of it, he married his daughter well, your Lord Inver did."

Whether it was the surprise at hearing mention of her or the fact that he had drunk quite a bit of porter, sherry, claret, and port, he didn't know, but suddenly Fergus blurted, "Shannon! Is she well?"

Lord Satterfield almost immediately began to laugh and Essex stared at him in amazement at the outburst. Fergus felt his face go beet red. "I just . . . ah . . . I knew . . . ," he stammered in embarrassment. He cleared his throat and said as nonchalantly as he could, "You were saying she is married, sir?"

This did not have the effect Fergus wanted. Lord Satterfield laughed again and this time Essex joined him.

When both had calmed sufficiently to be able to speak, Lord Satterfield patted Fergus's arm. "I am sorry, sir, but such an outburst, well." He smiled kindly at Fergus. "I understand why you had such a reaction; Lady Malin makes quite an impression on all men who see her." He drank some more port. "Yes, she married Lord Malin, another Irish peer, but with far more land and far more money than Inver. He also has extensive interests in England; in fact, he might receive an English title if he continues his service to the government. Quite a catch for, ahem, 'Shannon' and her father." Satterfield lifted a cautionary finger. "Still, he must watch himself. He often is rumored to be a supporter of Catholic emancipation and that does not sit well at all with the king."

To Fergus these were only tantalizing clues. He wanted to know how Shannon was faring, but to display too much curiosity might be more than a little unseemly. He turned the conversation back to horses, a subject to which Lord Satterfield and his son were more than happy to return.

When the light had changed to that of late afternoon the butler appeared in the doorway. "M'lord, may I suggest it is time to depart for the House?"

"Damn!" muttered Satterfield, heaving himself to his feet. "My country calls." With a resigned look on his face, he extended his hand to Kilburnie. "It was grand to meet you at last, Kilburnie. Please accept my best wishes for luck with your examination."

Fergus bowed. "Thank you, my lord."

Satterfield gestured to his son. "Walk me to the carriage, my boy. I so rarely see you now." Essex nodded and the two left Fergus alone for some time.

When Essex returned, his face bore a pensive expression. "Father says you may stay as long as you wish, but," he raised a cautionary finger in the same manner as his father, "he did suggest you might need to return home to study."

As much as he wanted to stay with his friend and speak to him in this magnificent house, Fergus admitted it was time to go.

"Well, then," replied Essex, "I shall accompany you in the carriage for I am meeting Father later at his club."

As they rode back to Jeris's house, Fergus asked Essex if he had any news related to his next assignment. "No, but I fear now that I may not get the cutter I wanted. Still, as first lieutenant on a brig or a sloop, I will probably see action and, I hope, advancement. So I shall either be dead or a commander within a couple of years." He smiled at his friend. "What are your hopes, Fergus?"

"I need to pass my lieutenant's examination first. Then I would like to return to the *Athena*."

Essex shook his head vigorously. "No, Fergus, that would not do. There are men like Kerry, you know, who would resent your promotion and that includes men on the lower deck. Think, too, of the seemingly innocent stories about you that might make you the object of ridicule among the crew. You might be accused by other officers of playing favorites with your old friends in the crew. No, you need to go to a new ship."

Fergus was somewhat amazed at his friend's analysis of his situation. "I am curious, Essex, have you been thinking about my future much?"

"No," admitted Essex, "but that's what Father told me before he left."

Fergus sank back in the seat. Clearly, Lord Satterfield was shrewd, almost as shrewd as Uncle Jeris. Maybe, Fergus thought, even more.

After much studying and drilling, the day for Fergus's examination arrived. Despite his uncle's warnings of a long day ahead and his aunt's usual urgings to eat, Fergus could do no more than drink some tea and nibble at some toast.

"Come, come, Fergus," coaxed his aunt, "have some food."

"Ah, no, Aunt Martha, my stomach is too nervous."

"Come now, Fergus," said Uncle Jeris soothingly, "you're no more nervous than I was when I took my examination and I ate like a horse that day. It won't do for your stomach to start growling during the examination." Fergus tried to eat some more food, but could only manage a couple of bites before giving up and merely drinking his tea.

At the appointed hour Uncle Jeris led Fergus out the door and to a waiting carriage. During the trip to the Admiralty, Fergus did not speak; he merely stared out the window, although he really didn't see anything.

At the entrance to the Admiralty, Uncle Jeris alighted and Fergus followed. The doorman tipped his hat to Uncle Jeris who soon was navigating the building's halls with his nephew in tow. When they arrived outside of the examination room, Uncle Jeris looked Fergus in the eyes and clapped him lightly on his shoulder. "Now, lad, the man in charge of this board is a Captain James Fallows; he's called 'Black Jim' and you'll soon see why. He's a hard man, but not unfair. I do not know who the other officers are, but count on it that they will be watchful of your every move. Don't fidget. Don't panic when you cannot think of an answer immediately; the important thing is the correct answer. But don't dawdle, either." Fergus responded with a short nod. "And watch your temper!"

Fergus looked at his uncle with unfeigned surprise. "Aye, Captain Burbage mentioned your problems as well as your courage." Jeris quickly looked over Fergus's shoulder, then back into his eyes. His voice dropped to a low tone. "You have faced much worse than the men in that room, Frenchmen coming over the side, Spanish three-deckers, the death of your captain, to say nothing of the sea itself. You shall do well, of that I am certain." He grabbed his nephew's shoulder tightly. "Now, kiss me, boy, and I'll be gone."

Fergus did as his uncle bid and as soon as Uncle Jeris departed he sat down in a chair outside the room. With Fergus were six other men, all midshipmen, all but one of whom looked older than Fergus. As one man turned his head, gray hairs caught the light.

The door of the examination room suddenly swung open and a red-faced clerk in a disheveled suit stomped out of the room. Through spectacles perched on an enormous, almost purple nose, his bulging brown eyes surveyed those who were waiting with barely disguised contempt. He cleared his throat and announced, "Midshipman Brush! Mi . . ."

The clerk was barely past the first syllable when one midshipman sprang from his chair. "Here I am!" said a sharp-featured man in his early twenties. He tucked his hat under his arm and advanced rapidly for the door, accelerating all the time. Had the clerk not blocked his passage, Fergus thought, the midshipman would have entered the room at a dead run.

The clerk glared at Midshipman Brush. "Eager, aren't you, Mr. Brush?" Brush shrank back some. The clerk sighed. "Come with me now." He turned and led the young man into the room. Mr. Brush was announced by the clerk and then the door closed firmly.

After what seemed like an eternity, the door opened and Brush emerged with a look of ill-concealed joy on his face.

The clerk called another name—"Mr. Carleton!"—and a handsome young man with sandy hair calmly stood and crossed the room to the waiting clerk. He gave the man an easy smile and said softly, "I am Mr. Carleton." The clerk, although clearly vexed at this man's unperturbed air, said nothing in direct reply, but the curt tone he used to announce Carleton spoke volumes of displeasure.

Fergus studied his partners who awaited their bureaucratic judgment. One man fidgeted with his uniform, brushing away imaginary flecks of dust from his hat, his coat, and his breeches, in that order, over and over again. A man with a fierce glint in his eyes and a forcefully set jaw sat staring at the wall opposite him, softly drumming his fists on his thighs. The man with gray hair (Fergus did see it correctly!) seemed relaxed, almost resigned as he slumped in his chair, his hat down over his eyes. A younger, stout man paced the floor, his hands behind his back, his nervousness an almost tangible presence. As he walked, he muttered to himself. A prayer? Fergus wondered. Or maybe a snatch of information he was afraid he would forget.

The door boomed open and all heads turned toward it. Carleton emerged, his unworried, unhurried demeanor intact, as if all that had happened was expected, even planned. To the clerk he gave a tolerant, almost taunting smile; to the other men he flashed a conspiratorial grin. He then moved down the hall.

Plainly agitated by Carleton's nonchalance, the clerk snapped out the next name, to which the stout man responded. The clerk brusquely hurried him into the room and closed the door with more than the required force. The gray-haired man stirred long enough to lift his hat, peer at the door, and mutter something about "the rudeness of some people," and return to his rest.

After a short while, Fergus heard laughter, which after a pause grew even louder. He hoped the young man had not made such an error that it caused this gale of hilarity. Silence again descended on the room until the door creaked open and the midshipman came out, his hat under his arm. He was tight-lipped, but only for a moment, for as soon as Fergus caught his eye he winked and broke into a huge smile. Leaving, he began whistling loudly and practically skipped down the hall.

So it went until, by the sun, Fergus judged it to be early afternoon. Finally, the gray-haired midshipman was called. As he walked up to the clerk, he muttered to no one in particular, "Let's hope this does it." The time he was behind the door seemed to stretch for an eternity. Fergus tried to listen, but the voices were muffled, although at times he detected a sharpness to some of them. When the midshipman emerged, followed by the clerk, Fergus came quickly to his feet.

"No, not yet," the clerk said forcefully, holding up his hand. He then returned to the room, shutting the door behind him. The gray-haired man looked first at Fergus, then at the closed door, and then, cocking an eyebrow, back at Fergus. "Hmmm," he said, shifting his gaze to his hat.

"What do you think they are doing in there?" asked Fergus, made anxious by the change in routine.

"I don't know," the man said laconically, "but I suspect you will know soon enough."

Fergus's eye flickered toward the door. "How did you fare?" he inquired, though more out of his desire for useful knowledge than genuine curiosity.

"Well enough, I suppose," said the man noncommittally. He placed his hat under his arm. "Funny thing about war."

"What?"

"It is damned hard work and adds yet another item to the list of ways a man can be killed at sea. Does wonders for promotion, though." With that thought he brightened, winked at Fergus, and with a cheery "Good luck!" was on his way.

Now thoroughly perplexed, Fergus watched the midshipman walk down the hall. What was that all about? The rattle of the doorknob startled Fergus. He barely had time to assume a posture of earnest anticipation before the door opened.

The clerk surveyed him coldly. "Come," he barked, and Fergus followed.

The room was simply laid out. At a long table facing the door sat four officers, all post captains. At a smaller table to the left was a pile of papers, an ink pot, and pens, the clerk's perch. In front of the long table, dead center and about six feet from it, was a lone chair. "Mr. Kilburnie," the clerk said with palpable distaste.

When the clerk was seated, a dark-haired officer in the chair second from Fergus's right said, "Please sit down, Mr. Kilburnie." It had to be "Black Jim." He had a dark, almost olive complexion that gave him the look of a Spaniard, and his brown eyes were almost black.

To Black Jim's right sat a portly man whose flushed face, Fergus surmised, almost certainly came from his attention to the joys of claret and port, not any recent physical exertion. The fact that he seemed ready to burst out of his uniform seemed to confirm Fergus's suspicions. Yet his eyes were not befuddled, but as cold and gray as a winter sea, indicating canniness and, perhaps, ruthlessness.

The officer farthest to Captain Fallows's right was bald, his head a huge expanse of shiny pink scalp about the fringes of which ranged wisps of white hair. Watery blue eyes set closely near an aquiline nose examined Fergus openly. To the left of Fallows was a man with a weathered face and unruly brown hair that was going gray at the temples. His hazel eyes seemed friendly; indeed, the man exuded a heartiness and goodwill that Fergus found most appealing.

Fallows cleared his throat loudly. "Mr. Kilburnie, you present us with an interesting case." He glanced down at his folded hands. "You were made a temporary lieutenant by the late Captain Burbage. Now, prior to that you were . . . ?"

"A quartermaster's mate and a gun captain, sir."

"Ah, just quite," replied Fallows gazing intently at Fergus. "Now, promotions from the lower deck to the commissioned ranks are not altogether rare. . . ."

"Breadfruit Bligh," stated the bald man, "confounded idiot. Caused a mutiny, lost his ship."

"Cook," countered the man with the weathered face, "damned good man. Best navigator we've ever had. Given three ships, didn't lose one."

The fat captain had no comment, but shook his head wearily.

"Thank you, gentlemen," said Fallows sharply. He returned to the subject at hand. "As I was saying, not altogether rare, but scarce enough to demand that any man who stands for such a promotion receives close scrutiny." He paused and looked at Fergus meaningfully. "Do you understand, Kilburnie?"

"Yes, sir. I understand, sir."

"Good. Now, Kilburnie, these men," he gestured down the table in both directions, "will ask you questions testing your knowledge and other attributes crucial to a proper naval officer." He folded his hands again. "Captain Gilbert, please begin."

The bald man leaned forward, reminding Fergus of an eagle swooping down on its prey. "Kilburnie, tack your ship."

No time wasted with niceties, thought Fergus. He immediately began to try to dredge from his memory the sequence of orders for such a task. First

. . . what? Wait! Something was missing from the question! Gilbert had laid a trap for him and he had almost fallen into it. He looked as innocently as possible at Gilbert and asked politely, "Please, sir, what direction is the wind coming from?"

"Ha! He found you out, Gilbert!" merrily burst out the officer to Fallows's left. He slapped the table loudly with his right hand. "Good for you, lad!"

"Captain Howell! If you please, sir!" barked Fallows. Howell said no more, but his expression was gleeful.

If Gilbert's omission was intentional, his face betrayed nothing at Fergus's question. "From the port, sir," he said dryly, putting his fingertips together and resting the index fingers on his lower lip.

Fergus thought for a moment, closing his eyes, trying to picture the *Athena* and hear Montgomery's commands. He opened his eyes, looked at Gilbert, and began with what he hoped was confidence. "Sir, the first command is 'Ready about.' That is followed by 'Helm's alee'—telling all the maneuver is about to be performed." He licked his lips. "Then, 'Left full rudder,' 'Ease the headsail sheets,' and 'Haul the spanker boom amidships.' Next, the main must be braced. So, it is 'Rise tacks and sheets' and then as soon as the weather edges of the mainsails begin backing, 'Mainsail haul.'"

Fergus gripped his chair hard. "'Shift the headsail sheets,' for the foremast and 'Ease the spanker' for the mizzen; that should get her head into the wind. Once on the new tack, but only when the mainsails begin to fill, 'Let go and haul' to the foremast and then 'Set the mainsail.' I believe my ship is tacked, sir."

Gilbert pulled his fingers away from his mouth. "I believe it to be as well, sir."

"Any more questions, Captain Gilbert?" asked Fallows. He received a slight shake of the head in reply. "Captain Hall, sir, are you ready to examine Mr. Kilburnie?"

"No tricks like Gilbert clumsily tried, the oaf," cracked Captain Howell. "Kilburnie here is clever."

Fallows rolled his eyes and Gilbert, his face reddening, glared at Howell. Fergus noticed that Hall obviously decided to pay no attention to Howell's prodding, probably because he realized it was aimed at Gilbert, not him. "Thank you, Captain Fallows, I am ready." He sat back in his chair and folded his hands across his wide midsection. "Sir, please inform me of the proper sequence for loading a gun." A ghost of a grin ran across his lips. "It doesn't matter from which side the wind is coming." Howell chuckled loudly and Gilbert went crimson. Fergus quickly rattled off the necessary commands.

A slight nod from Captain Hall. "Now make it fast for heavy weather." Again, the answer came swiftly as did another nod. "All right, sir, please tell me how much powder should be used to fire a thirty-two-pounder."

Fergus had never fired a thirty-two-pounder on the *Athena* and Kerry, jealous of his position, had never instructed him. So he tried to remember how many pounds of powder were used in the smaller guns and extrapolate from that. "Well, as best as I can figure, the charge to fire a ball from a thirty-two-pounder should be roughly fifteen pounds of powder."

Hall gave another, almost imperceptible nod. He followed it with a dismissive flick of the wrist. "I have no more questions."

Fallows looked down the table at the final questioner. "Captain Howell," he said in some relief.

Howell leaned forward. "Kilburnie, here's an important question. What's the proper grog—five water or three water?"

Fergus knew that some captains preferred to mix five parts of water to one part of rum, but remembered the *Athena*'s grog was always a three-to-one mixture. The crew had been unanimous that five-water grog was "like a cotton shirt, too thin to keep out the cold."

"Three water, sir," he responded firmly.

Howell smiled broadly, new creases spreading across his already lined face from the corners of his eyes and mouth. "Now, suppose you are in command of an armed transport and a French brig hauls up close and demands your surrender! What do you do, sir?" Howell came to his feet, his fists resting on the table in front of him. "Come, sir! You have seconds to decide!"

Fergus looked over at the other men. Gilbert's face bore an expression of amusement. Fallows gazed intently at him. Howell did not change his expression, although there seemed to be a trace of a smile. Fergus shifted his gaze to meet Howell's eyes.

"I would wait, sir, until the French drew near enough. Fire what guns I had and then grapple her. My next command would be 'Boarders away,' and I'd take her by cutlass!"

Howell gave a short bark of a laugh and pressed his point home. "But you are outmanned, sir. Why not strike instead of board her?"

"I'd trust in surprise, sir, the unexpected."

"It is a risk, however!"

"Better to take that chance than end up for sure in a French prison hulk!" Fergus declared.

Howell said nothing for a moment, but only tapped the table lightly with his fists. He sat down slowly and unballed his fists, his palms flat on the highly polished surface. He turned his head to Captain Fallows. "He'll do!" he declared loudly.

Fallows seemed distressed at this declaration. "Please, sir," he said quietly, but firmly, "there must be no discussion of our impressions of Midshi . . . ah, Mr. Kilburnie while he is in our presence."

Howell shrugged. Looking back at the other members of the board, Fallows asked if there were any questions. None was forthcoming.

Fallows returned to Fergus. "Mr. Kilburnie, as I stated at the beginning of this examination, to move from the lower deck to a commission is a rare thing in the navy. This board might have the unpleasant duty to recommend that you be retained as a master's mate or, should you wish, discharged from the service altogether. Do you understand?"

Fergus fought an urge to spring to his feet and declare it was the navy or nothing, but he remembered his uncle's advice. He held his tongue and merely said, "Yes, sir."

Fallows nodded. "You are dismissed then, Kilburnie." He turned to the clerk. "Mr. Bartholomew, please see Mr. Kilburnie out."

Fergus rose and made for the door, which the clerk opened for him—the only courtesy the man had shown all day to anyone. Stepping into the anteroom, he realized that he felt none of the self-confidence the other men had displayed. It was confusing. Captain Howell seemed pleased and he had answered all the other questions satisfactorily. Why then had Captain Fallows been so intent on dampening things? As he walked to Uncle Jeris's office, another thought struck him: The questions had not been that difficult at all and Captain Fallows hadn't asked a single one. Now, why did that happen?

Still puzzling over the entire episode, he knocked at the door to his uncle's office. "Yes!" his uncle called and Fergus entered. Jeris was poised over a thick document, making a notation with a pen. A cheery fire blazed in the grate, fighting against the damp chill of the room. Seeing his nephew, he put down the pen and stood up. "Well then, how did you fare?"

"It was odd, Uncle. I thought the examination would take hours, but they asked me all of six questions and only one gave me any trouble. One of the officers—a Captain Howell—even said, 'He'll do' to one of my answers. But at the end and at the beginning Captain Fallows lectured me about how rare it is for officers to come from the lower deck and then said the board might recommend that I be retained as a master's mate or discharged from the navy." He sank down in a chair. "What am I to think?" he said in a mixture of anger and rising despair.

Jeris stood up, walked to the window, and looked out for a bit, absentmindedly rubbing his stump. "Lad, we all have to accept the fact that our plans don't always come to the end we'd wish. A period of peace ended your grandfather's days in the navy—that and one man's blind prejudice. A French cannonball in the American War ended mine. If the decision is made that you would best serve the king as a master's mate then that is your lot." His tone became more forceful. "You tolerate your lot until such time as it can be changed." He turned from the window and his eye bore into Fergus. "Do you take my meaning?"

"Yes, Uncle, I do," replied a chastened Fergus.

"Even if you leave the navy, your life is just beginning. You know horses; that is a talent prized by many men. If you wish I might be able to get you a position at an Admiralty dockyard. God knows we need honest men in those places. If the sea is where you'd like to make your trade, there is no shame in the post office packets or the customs cutters, not to mention the East India Company or any merchantman."

"I understand what you're saying, Uncle. Even if my commission is lost, all is not lost. Still, my country is at war and I want to serve her the best way I can and that, to my mind, is in the navy."

"Admirable thoughts, my boy, but even patriotic fervor cannot always overcome the habits of peacetime." Jeris looked at his desk and pulled a face. "I have had enough of that," he said dismissively. "Let us repair to a tavern of my acquaintance and console ourselves with strong drink."

Throughout the rest of that week, Fergus waited for news of his examination. Every night when Uncle Jeris came home, Fergus would greet him at the door. Jeris would frown, shake his head, and say, "No news, lad." The disheartening routine continued through the next week. Uncle Jeris's words of encouragement failed to raise his spirits as it became increasingly obvious to Fergus that he would have to forgo the navy and look for a new career. Maybe, he thought, chasing smugglers wouldn't be so bad after all. There always was the chance of action against a French privateer or two.

By the third week Fergus stopped going downstairs to greet his uncle and merely waited to see him in the evening. On that Wednesday, a particularly dismal day, Fergus was writing a letter to his parents when he heard the door slam and his uncle call for him in his best quarterdeck voice. "Fergus! Fergus! Damn it, lad, where are you?!"

So insistent was his uncle's tone that Fergus dashed out of his room and down the stairs, almost colliding with his uncle coming up. The rest of the household had heard Jeris's homecoming and were gathered in the hall, their faces showing both curiosity and anxiety.

"Jeris Fairlie!" Aunt Martha scolded. "What is the meaning of this?"

Jeris pulled Fergus down into the hall and produced a folded paper from his pocket. "What is it?" he boomed. "God's teeth, woman! What has Fergus been waiting for these past three weeks?" Fergus still did not comprehend just what his uncle was talking about. "Your commission, Lieutenant Kilburnie!"

Aunt Martha, the maid, and cook were the first to realize what the exact nature of Uncle Jeris's news was.

"Oh, dear," said Aunt Martha, tears coming to her eyes.

"Oh, sir," said the other two women, dabbing their eyes with the corner of their aprons.

Suddenly, it all burst in on Fergus. He immediately embraced his uncle, knocking the man's hat off his head. "What? When?" Words came out in a jumble. "Commission!"

Jeris struggled against his nephew's embrace. "Unhand me, boy!" Fergus broke his embrace and grabbed the paper Jeris offered. "It's all flowery Admiralty language," Jeris said, "but the point is made, eventually, that you, along with dozens of other men of allegedly honorable conduct, have been gazetted to the rank of lieutenant, Royal Navy."

Suddenly Fergus felt lightheaded and sat down on the stairs. "So that is it, then?"

"No, it is not," replied Uncle Jeris firmly. "You now need to find the proper ship, too."

"I'd like to return to the *Athena*," Fergus said wistfully.

"No, that won't do. You'd do better to get yourself on a small ship, a cutter or a brig. There's always a chance of action there—special services, chasing privateers or French raiders—and that is what is needed to be noticed by the Admiralty. Fortune favors the brave, after all. Just look at Nelson, knighted for that damn fool action at Cape St. Vincent. He's now an admiral and talked about for a major command in the Mediterranean." Jeris smacked the railing with his palm. "Good God! We have not yet toasted your good fortune."

Moments later, Uncle Jeris had herded everyone into the parlor. Although he wanted everyone to have rum, Aunt Martha flatly declined, choosing sherry instead for herself and the servants.

Fergus said, "Uncle Jeris, Aunt Martha, I owe you both so very much."

"Nonsense, lad," replied Jeris with mock severity. He raised his glass. "To Lieutenant Fergus Kilburnie, Royal Navy." Fergus raised the glass to his lips. "No, boy," bellowed Jeris, "never do that!"

"Do what?!"

"Drink to yourself. Damn, but I must take it upon myself to teach you to comport yourself properly in a wardroom before you embarrass yourself." He shook his head. "Now, Aunt Martha and I and the girls will toast you, then you may drink the bottle dry if you so wish." After the small ceremony was complete, Aunt Martha shooed the servants out and excused herself to preside over the kitchen.

Alone now, Fergus and Jeris settled into chairs by the fire. "Fergus, you must know that you owe a great deal to people other than me for your good fortune. As an Admiralty clerk, I have a measure of influence, but it is puny relative to other men's. I cannot grant the type of favors that gain the allegiance of powerful men; I can only bring matters to their attention and hope it is enough. Often it is not. There are dozens, if not hundreds of men, who can foil even my most carefully made plans."

"Which means . . . ?"

"Which means, lad, that you have had more patrons than you realize." He paused for a moment. "Most important, Essex and his father, Lord Satterfield."

"But they said nothing to me," protested Fergus.

Jeris rolled his eyes. "Damnation, boy, how did you think you came by such an easy and short examination? Fallows is well connected to Lord Satterfield and he made sure to pick officers so that a majority would not be too hard on you. He called you last because he knew that Captain Hall would be getting hungry and that Captain Howell would have baited Captain Gilbert mercilessly all day. The two are known rivals; I'm surprised they didn't come to sword points in that room. He knew the men would be ready to leave quickly."

Jeris got up and poured himself another measure of rum. "Furthermore, your social station being what it is—son of a Scottish estate agent, well, now a Scottish strong farmer—there was some objection to your promotion. Lord Satterfield's name was enough to make those who objected see sense."

Fergus sat silent for a moment. "Uncle, do you know why Lord Satterfield decided to help me?"

"Certainly, lad. You can thank Essex. He is a true friend to you. He came to see me at the Admiralty and asked what he could do in your favor. Knowing his father's status, I immediately told him you would need a far more powerful patron than me if you were to advance in the navy. So Essex persuaded his father to meet you and arranged the dinner. He asked his father that if you were to Lord Satterfield's liking, his lordship would assist you."

"I take it I was to Lord Satterfield's liking."

"Oh, yes, quite. Essex told me his father admired your appetite, love of claret, knowledge of horses, and lack of political opinions."

Fergus laughed. "I should write to Essex and Lord Satterfield and express my thanks."

"Immediately," agreed Jeris. "However, you might not receive a quick reply from Lieutenant Essex."

Fergus noticed his uncle was trying not to smile. "And why is that, Uncle Jeris?"

"It is because your friend is currently on his way to Plymouth to take command of His Majesty's Cutter *Hardy*, a trim little ship, quite fetching, I'm told."

"You had something to do with this?" asked Fergus. He knew in an instant the question was superfluous; the satisfaction was evident on his uncle's face.

Jeris smiled into his glass. "Let's just say Lord Satterfield now knows that our humble family can make good on its debts."

For Fergus, the next few weeks were a whirl of activity. Uniforms had to be purchased as did dozens of items that Uncle Jeris swore were necessary for an officer. Fergus tried to maintain a hold on his spending, but the cost of even the most basic items dazzled him. "Uncle, these prices," he said one day in near despair. "I'll be ruined."

"Don't worry," replied Jeris. "Your share of prize money from that French frigate should arrive soon and then you'll have money to pay for everything.

Should that prize money not come in, well, lad, I've never known a man who could be thrown into debtors' prison when he is still at sea."

But more than the expense of outfitting himself, what truly worried Fergus was his next ship. He had seen too many officers vainly petition the Admiralty for positions on ships and knew of others who haunted taverns in Plymouth, Portsmouth, Dover, wherever there were king's ships, hoping to meet captains who needed officers. Still, he hoped he would not have to settle for just any ship. The prospect of being an officer on some huge creaking hundred-gun ship of the line, tied like a dog on a lead to some admiral's flagship and waiting for a great battle that might never come, did not appeal to him. Then there was the bottom of the rung: a hired ship in which he could labor for years in obscurity and soul-deadening routine. No, he was determined to find a frigate or a smaller ship. Soon, however, his problem was resolved and, not surprisingly, it was through his uncle's good offices.

As his uncle explained, "Remember the Irish captain I told you about, the man who had the *Fervent*. Well, it seems his nephew, a Fitzjames, recommended a friend of his, a Commander Morris, to me for advice. Morris seems a good man and has seen his share of action. As it is, he was on the *Culloden* with Troubridge at Cape St. Vincent. Anyway, Morris tells me he has need of an officer on his ship, a sloop out of Plymouth, the *Swallow*, fourteen guns, a bit small but a fine ship, and would I know of a worthy young lieutenant ready to sail with him? Not bad for a half hour's work, eh?"

"Who will be first lieutenant?"

"You shall be, Fergus."

Fergus was somewhat surprised because he knew that as a newly minted lieutenant he could count on being junior to just about every other lieutenant. "How did you manage that, Uncle? Or do I have Lord Satterfield to thank for this?"

"You have no one to thank for this, boy. The reason for your seniority is quite simple: you shall be the *Swallow*'s only lieutenant."

"The only one?" gasped Fergus.

Uncle Jeris looked quizzically at his nephew. "Yes, the only one." His voice took on an exasperated tone. "I told you she only had fourteen guns. You didn't expect to lord it over a wardroom of adoring lieutenants and a gunroom full of dozens of snotties, did you?"

Fergus managed a self-conscious laugh. "No, I suppose not, but. . . ."

"But nothing, just be happy you have a sailing master. Otherwise you and Morris would be stuck doing the navigation."

Clearing his throat, Fergus looked at his uncle. "Uncle Jeris, are you sure I am ready for such a posting? I mean to say. . . ."

An incredulous look came to Jeris's face. "Well, well, you mean to say that you want to wait for a better ship. There are good men with much more experience than you, good men who sit onshore mouldering away on the half-pay list who would sell their souls for a chance like this! And you don't want it?"

A wave of shame washed over Fergus as he watched his uncle's anger mount. "Uncle," he protested, "I'm not being ungrateful. I'm just surprised at, well, so much responsibility, so soon."

"Fergus, the navy is at war and cannot afford to run a school for young lieutenants. By being confident enough to take the examination for lieutenant, you told me—and the rest of the navy, for that matter—that you are ready for whatever the Service decided to give you. I did not misjudge you, did I?"

"No, Uncle, you did not. It's all just sinking in now."

"It will really sink in when you're the only surviving officer, your command is a dismasted hulk, and the glass is dropping." Jeris gave a heavy sigh. "Fergus, if you say you're not ready, I'll put you on the half-pay list. No disgrace. I'd rather have you mucking about in some stable, happy to be up to your knees in horseshit, than making an ass of yourself on a quarterdeck. There are already enough fools in the navy, thanks to jobbery. I'll not knowingly put another one into an officer's uniform."

Fergus shot to his feet. "I'm ready, Uncle," he said as forcefully as he could. "I'll do you and the family proud."

Jeris nodded gravely. "See that you do."

10
THE SWALLOW

ne week later Fergus was in a jolly boat, being rowed through Plymouth Harbor and the anchorage to His Majesty's Sloop *Swallow*. Peering around his baggage, he could see the ship. At first glance, she seemed fairly ordinary, brig-rigged with her sides pierced for fourteen guns. There was no noticeable quarterdeck, but on ships of her size that was fairly common.

A second glance—and that was all it took, a glance—Fergus could see that she was different. She seemed to sit lightly on the water as if her anchor was all that kept her from rising into the air and floating away; her masts were set at a slight, but noticeable angle. Delicate, that's it, he thought, she seems delicate.

As his boat came nearer, he could see figures moving about the deck, a few casting a look his way. A man toward the stern peered in his direction and then barked out what Fergus thought were orders. The words were indecipherable, but the tone was unmistakable.

When the jolly boat bumped against the side, the boatman grumbled, "We're here," clearly nervous to be near a navy ship. Fergus took a look at the old man's face. Perhaps, he thought, his concerns about impressment weren't altogether ill-founded. The navy had an insatiable appetite for men and anyone who even looked like a seaman could count on the unwelcome attention of the dreaded press gangs.

"Comin' up, sir?" a voice called from above. Fergus looked up to see a gaunt man in the blue coat of a warrant officer, the sailing master maybe.

Fergus nodded and clambered up the side. Two men stood by and the bosun pipe trilled. The sailing master touched his hat. "Welcome aboard, sir."

Fergus returned the salute. "Thank you." He held out his hand. "You are . . . ?"

The man shook Fergus's hand briefly but firmly. "Peck, sir, sailing master." He ran a hand down his coat. "Ah, but that's obvious."

He then motioned to a burly man also wearing the coat of a warrant officer, who was standing by the mizzenmast. The man clomped over and saluted halfheartedly, a slight touch to the hat. "This here's Jones, Bosun," Peck said by way of introduction.

"How do you do, Mr. Jones?" said Fergus in a manner he hoped seemed friendly and extended his hand.

Jones eyes widened slightly and he shot a glance at Peck that bespoke surprise, but at what Fergus couldn't tell. He hoped it was his friendly tone, not his Scottish burr.

Jones's huge, calloused paw enveloped Fergus's not small hand. "I'm well, sir." An undiluted Welsh accent.

"Good," replied Fergus. Jones began shifting his feet nervously. "What is it, Jones?"

"Ah, nothing, sir."

Fergus sensed Jones was uncomfortable in his presence. "Jones, please attend to my baggage; the boatman is worried about being pressed and undoubtedly wants to be away."

The Welshman's face loosened somewhat, but no smile came. "We've no pressed men on the *Swallow,* sir," he protested proudly. Peck sharply nudged him. "Aye, aye, sir." Jones stomped away.

"Well, Mr. Peck, shall we examine the ship?"

Peck gestured with his right hand toward the bow. "Yes, sir, from stem to stern."

A gust of laughter came from below. It bore a distinct feminine tone. "Are there women on board, Peck?"

"'Course, sir. We're in port, ain't we?" Peck explained. "Men's wives, at least so they claim, and a few doxies. Most go back to shore at night."

"Most?"

"Is there a problem, sir?"

"No, I'm just curious. Where do you put them in so small a ship?"

Peck laid a finger aside of his nose. "Lots of room in them hammocks, sir."

Standing by the binnacle with Peck a few hours later, Fergus decided he liked what he had seen. True, the quarters were quite cramped forward, but that was to be expected with eighty men and twenty marines on board, not counting the three warrant officers, the marines' lieutenant, the surgeon, Fergus, and the captain. Still, nothing seemed out of place.

Then there was the *Swallow* herself. "She's not like any sloop I've seen before," Fergus declared to Peck.

"She's rare, all right. In our navy, at least," the sailing master replied. "That's 'cause she's French." He patted a bulwark lovingly and smiled as though at a pleasant inner thought. "She's Toulon-built of Adriatic oak. Best the Frogs could afford."

"When was she captured?"

"Little more than three years ago in the Channel, coming out of Brest. She ran into two frigates and had to strike."

"How does she sail?"

"Just beautifully, sir. She skips along in light air that would leave other boats becalmed; with a good wind behind her—even a heavy wind— she runs like a thoroughbred. And a light touch is all that's needed on the helm."

Fergus was impressed quite favorably with the men as well. They seemed at ease with each other and their ship and, if Jones was to be believed, all were volunteers. That counted for a lot, he figured. Yet whenever Fergus came close to any of the men, he detected a wariness, a reserve.

Another remarkable thing was the large number of blacks among the crew. Certainly, the *Athena* had a good number, as did just about every large ship in the navy, but not counting the gunner, called "Jamaica Sam," there were ten other black men, a large number in crew that numbered no more than ninety.

When Fergus mentioned his observation to Peck, the sailing master gave a sly smile. "Well, sir, up until, oh, about a year ago, the *Swallow* was in the West Indies and a more feverish, sickly hell on earth you can't imagine. We had lost more than a few men. So, we got the idea that Jamaica Sam could help us get some men in Kingston."

An alarming thought hit Fergus immediately. "You pressed slaves?"

"Bless me, no, sir. They were provided the opportunity to volunteer for a good ship, to live the life of a sailor, and they took it."

"I'm not sure exactly what you mean."

"Well, sir, Jamaica Sam goes ashore, meets some men who are working around boats. Likely recruits, you might say. They agree to take the king's shilling. They come out in boats like they're delivering victuals and, quick as you please, we have ten new shipmates." He cleared his throat meaningfully. "'Course we had to keep them below deck for a while, just 'til we cleared Kingston the next morning."

"So they were slaves."

"Well, they might have been slaves, sir, but the captain didn't ask many questions. Now they are as free as any other British man-o-war's man."

Fergus wondered if a West Indian planter would arrive at the same conclusion, but kept these thoughts to himself.

"I'll go see about your baggage, sir." Peck saluted and turned away.

Almost immediately, Fergus heard Jones's heavy footfalls. "Good day to ye, sir," said Jones brightly. "You find the *Swallow* to your liking?"

"Why, yes, Jones, I do. She's a far cry from my last ship."

"And what ship was that, sir?"

"The *Athena,* thirty-six-gun frigate."

"A good ship?"

"Yes, quite. What I meant is that the *Swallow* is much smaller than the *Athena* and with far fewer men, although the *Swallow* seems a bit more crowded. The *Athena* was a fine ship." Fergus decided to try to do some fishing of his own. "And the *Swallow,* Jones, how do you like her?"

"She's a good home and you might say a happy ship. We've a small crew that's been together for a long time, about three years. Why, sir, I was on her prize crew." He took a long puff on his pipe. "I'll say this, sir, and you can take it as you will. Sailors aren't much different than other men when it comes to their home; they don't like changes in it."

Fergus took the point immediately. "Jones, you know it is not up to me as to any changes that might be made. That will be Captain Morris's decision and about all I know of him is that he is well recommended and was with Troubridge on the *Culloden* at Cape St. Vincent."

"Ah, a big-ship man," Jones shook his head discontentedly. Was a thirty-six-gun frigate considered to be a big ship?

Fergus decided on a change of tack. "By the way, Jones, what is it the *Swallow* does?"

"You do not know, sir?" Jones sounded surprised, almost hurt, by Fergus's ignorance. "Well, sir, it is our duty to chase French privateers, 'the Wolves of the Channel' as they style themselves."

"Have you had much success?"

"Some. We caught two brigs out of Brest, a chausée-marée from L'Orient, and two cutters out of there, too." He smiled and rolled up on the balls of his feet. "It's like being privateers ourselves, sir, seeing as the prize money is divided up between so few men. Jamaica Sam says he'll soon have enough to buy himself a tavern, Peck's always talkin' about helpin' an old uncle run a brewery, and, as for me, I'll go back to Milford Haven, open a ship's chandlery, and buy shares in whaling voyages." Jones sighed contentedly. "Ah, yes, the *Swallow* is a good provider as well as a good home."

So informed, Fergus left Jones to his dreams of Milford Haven and went below to see about his baggage. He found Peck directing one of the black seamen as he stowed Fergus's sea chest and other gear into the tiny stateroom. "Well, sir, you've come well equipped," muttered Peck.

"Thank you, Peck," Fergus cheerfully replied. Peck threw him a look of such obvious exasperation that Fergus almost laughed. Deciding he had had his fun, Fergus told Peck he would stow his baggage.

"Good luck to you, sir," a relieved Peck muttered and motioned for the seaman to follow. Fergus stepped back into the passageway. "Peck, what is this man's name?" he asked as the black man drew abreast of him.

"Him? Oh, he's Ben Coffee."

"Hello, Coffee."

The man looked him dead in the eye, frankly assessing him. "Hello, sir," he replied in a peculiar accent, the "sir" sounding like a soft "sah" or "surh."

Fergus held the man's gaze for a long time. "Thank you, Coffee, for handling my baggage."

Coffee blinked and glanced at Peck. "Yes, sir."

"Well, good day to you, Coffee."

"Yes, sir."

"Come on, Ben," said Peck and the two moved off down the passageway.

As Fergus unpacked his sea chest and stowed his gear, he considered his situation. Good ship, well built and with a good record, but it was the crew that impressed him more.

Clearly, the *Swallow*'s men were not a cowed lot. In that, they reminded Fergus of the fishermen with whom he had sailed: independent-minded, but close enough to read each other's thoughts and anticipate almost any order and experienced enough to appreciate the need for instant obedience. Tough and high-spirited, they would be sternly resolute in battle. Now, he thought, I understand Jones's concern about a "big-ship man"; he and probably all of the crew are scared of the type of discipline they have come to expect on ships of the line—arbitrary and occasionally harsh. That type of discipline had about as much place on this ship and with these men as it would on an Aberdeen fishing smack.

Somewhere forward a fiddle began to play. Fergus paused to listen. Another fiddle struck up the same tune. He recognized it immediately, "The Last Time I Came O'er the Moor." Someone knew Scottish songs, probably some Scotsmen in the crew. Maybe some of the fishermen I knew, he thought. A woman's voice, high and clear, joined the fiddles. Fergus began whistling as he stored his gear. Whether by accident or by design, Uncle Jeris seemed to have put him in a good ship. With these men and a good captain like Morris, the *Swallow* would be an excellent place to learn the trade of officer.

The next day dawned bright and clear, matching Fergus's spirits. The crew, too, seemed cheerful. They know, he thought, they'll be leaving soon. That's the way it was with sailors, they anticipated leaving as much as they did coming home.

"Mr. Kilburnie, sir." A voice interrupted Fergus's thoughts.

Fergus turned and there was . . . damn! . . . the name was lost on him. "Ah, yes, ah. . . ."

"Green, sir, able seaman," the heavily bearded man said.

"Ah, yes, Green." Fergus felt himself flush. Were his expressions so easy to read? "Yes, Green, what is it?"

"Boat approaching, sir. Looks official, says Mr. Jones."

Fergus looked out over the rail. Sure enough, there came a boat, propelled by two oarsmen and bearing one sour-faced civilian. Dismissing Green, he made for the ladder.

Within minutes, the boat bumped against the side and the civilian made his way up the ladder. He made straight for Fergus. "You senior man?" he asked curtly. When Fergus indicated he was, the man thrust a packet of letters into his hand. "Them's for the ship and there's one for a Mr. Kilburnie."

Before Fergus could thank the man, the civilian was down the ladder and the boat was moving away.

Fergus glanced down at the letters. One bore the name of the ship and the words "senior officer" in fine handwriting; the other was addressed to him in a familiar hand, that of Uncle Jeris. Walking back toward the binnacle, he hurriedly opened the letter from his uncle. It was short, but its contents were weighty.

> *Fergus:*
>
> *News of a sad nature has reached me. Your captain—Morris—was riding point-to-point in some damn fool place in Surrey last week. His horse failed to take a fence and threw Morris, who broke a leg and will not be fit for duty for some time. This means the* Swallow *will have a new commander. Regrettably, the decision is now in the hands of the local admiral and I am unaware of who he might choose.*
>
> *Whomever the captain is, you must remember it is your responsibility to support him.*
>
> *Good luck to you, my boy.*
> *Uncle Jeris.*

Fergus heard a footfall behind him. "Bad news, sir?" Peck asked.

"It could be, Peck. I don't kn— . . ." As he had turned to face Peck, he saw that many of the crew were gathered in knots about the deck. Obviously, they understood the letters' possible import. Fergus cleared his throat and continued. "It could be, Peck. I've just been told by private letter that Commander Morris has had an accident and the *Swallow* is to have a new captain." Peck gave an inquiring look. "But I do not know who it is to be," Fergus said in response to the look.

"Er, sir, the other letter might tell us more," the master replied, gesturing to the other document that Fergus held.

Without an answer, Fergus broke the seal and read it quickly. It, too, was short—written in the crisp, yet mildly floral style favored by navy clerks. Indeed, Peck was right; it did relate news of their captain.

"Peck," said Fergus, not looking up, "please assemble the crew."

Peck whirled about. "All hands lay aft!" On a small ship like the *Swallow,* it took only moments for the crew to assemble near the binnacle where Fergus stood.

"According to this letter, men, our new captain will arrive tomorrow." He glanced down at the letter. "He is James Waterbury." Looking back up at the crew, he saw no face register recognition. Fergus lowered the letter. "When the captain arrives tomorrow, he will receive all proper honors as is his right and our duty. He also certainly will expect a well-turned-out ship and crew." He caught a glance between Peck and Jones. "But, after seeing this ship yesterday, not much will need to be done. Eh, Mr. Jones?"

Jones puffed up with delight. "Correct, Mr. Kilburnie, sir."

Peck smiled as well.

"Good then," said Fergus. "Mr. Peck, dismiss the crew."

Peck ordered the crew dismissed and they went off to their duties, the buzz of their conversations starting immediately.

"Peck," Fergus called softly.

"Sir."

"I think it is time to get rid of the women, too. I don't think a new captain will want to hear their giggles when he comes aboard—and he might surprise us by being here at first light."

Peck rubbed his chin contemplatively. "Aye, makes sense. I'll have them on shore right away, sir."

"And Peck," Fergus said, before the master could move away to attend to his duties.

"Sir?"

"No long good-byes."

Peck shot him a wink. "I understand, sir."

Throughout the day, the men worked on the ship, making it presentable for their new captain. Yet, as Fergus had assumed, not much work needed to be done on such a well-kept ship. Fergus busied himself by examining the stores, the magazine, the shot room, and the navigation instruments. After grog and dinner, the men turned to again, but it was soon clear to Fergus that the *Swallow* could pass an admiral's inspection in its current state. At three o'clock, therefore, he called Jones to his side.

"Jones, pipe all hands to make and mend."

"Aye, aye, sir." Jones was plainly pleased with the order, which officially directed the men to attend to their clothes, but in essence actually allowed them to do as they pleased. Soon the call was piped, and not soon after that all gear was stowed and the ship was quiet, except for those hands who gathered in groups, most smoking, some playing cards, others actually repairing clothes. The low murmur of conversation was sometimes punctuated by laughter at some joke or a derisive retort to some claim of accomplishment, either nautical or sexual.

Looking at this tableau of a happy ship and a good crew, Fergus knew he should feel elated. He knew, however, he was still a stranger on the *Swallow* and would not be embraced as a full-fledged member of this tight little band until he had proved himself in some way. Furthermore, until stepping on this ship, he had not fully realized the gulf that existed—and must be maintained—between officers and sailors. Inasmuch as he wanted to sit among the men, he knew it was not right to do so.

Instead, he turned to the binnacle, where Jamaica Sam, Peck, and Jones stood smoking and staring out over the rail toward Plymouth. All three casually touched their hats at his approach. "Good afternoon, sir," they chorused.

"Good afternoon." Fergus noticed the three men eying him somewhat warily. Well, he thought, this is my first full day and there's a new captain tomorrow. "We must make sure the men get plenty of rest tonight."

Nods of affirmation and a couple of grunted "Yes, sirs" was all he got in reply. "Well, ahem . . ." He realized that he was trying far too hard to make conversation. I'm in the wardroom, but I'm not yet of it—yet. He tried to think of way to break off the conversation, but he couldn't. It was merciful then what the three warrant officers did. "I must go and attend to the boats, sir," said Jones, pipe stem clenched in his teeth.

"Of course, Jones." Fergus said gratefully. Off went Jones.

"I must excuse myself as well, sir," piped up Peck. "I promised Jamaica Sam I'd beat him at cribbage." Sam nodded in silent agreement.

"Yes, by all means." Peck and Sam moved off, too.

Fergus was alone, but at least he didn't feel quite so lonely.

Early the next morning, the lieutenant of marines and the surgeon appeared, arriving in the same boat. The marine took the salute in an almost off-handed manner, his eyes already taking in Fergus. Almost immediately he strode up to Fergus and extended a hand. "Well, new lieutenant, eh? Welcome to our happy ship. I am Malcolm Browne, that's Browne with an *e*. Lieutenant Malcolm Pelham Browne, Royal Marines, to be precise. I am here to protect you from the pirates who make up this crew—especially those scoundrels Peck and Jones." He gave a short bark of a laugh.

Fergus introduced himself.

"Oh, a Scotsman, eh? Well, well, you'll be disappointed then. The cook doesn't know how to make haggis, but the plum duff is passable. So there's some comfort for you." He paused and fixed Fergus with a hopeful look, "Hmm, perhaps you brought some of that good Highland whiskey? Ah, no, I can tell by the look. Ah, well, thank God I brought enough claret and porter then."

As Browne rattled on, Fergus had time to take a full measure of his wardroom mate. His hair was almost completely grey, but the broad, round face was smooth and uncreased. Large blue eyes under sleepy lids flanked a sharp, rather long nose. The mouth was thin-lipped, but not cruel. Browne had a broad torso that seemed precariously balanced on thin legs and his arms seemed a little short for his body and his hands were small. Yet, what struck Fergus the most was Browne's accent: Irish, perhaps Dublin.

"You're an Irishman?" Fergus blurted, almost before he knew what he was saying, and as he said it he blushed in embarrassment.

Browne laughed heartily. "Ah, the young lieutenant will not mistake me for a Frenchman. I take this to portend well for my safety during a boarding action." He smiled broadly; apparently, all was forgiven. "Now, it is even worse than that. Not only am I an Irishman, I also am a Dubliner, though the family has a country seat in King's County." He gazed intently at Fergus. "You are familiar with Ireland, Kilburnie?"

"I, ah, my family spent some time in Ulster."

"Up there amongst your kith and kin, holding the plantations for old King Billy against the Stuarts and the Papists, eh?" This was said in a jolly enough tone, but Fergus detected a slight edge.

"No, not exactly. My father runs, I should say, ran Lord Inver's estate."

"Ah, Donegal, then," observed Browne. "I have cousins there, you see," he said in way of explanation. "Good horse country. I've seen some excellent hunters from there; ridden a few, too. Still, shooting is more my sport. Some excellent shooting in Ireland, eh?"

Fergus was a little confused by Browne's rapid speech. "What?"

"Shooting. Ever done any?"

"Not in Ireland. Just at sea and then only Frenchmen."

"Oh, say, very good! Our new lieutenant is a fire-eater. 'Only Frenchmen.' Very good." Browne chortled at the jest. He slapped Fergus on the back lightly. "It is time for me to oversee my baggage as well as see to the idle lot known as my men." He smiled again. "But first let me introduce you to the surgeon."

Browne then turned to the thin man who stood by the bulwark, overseeing the loading of various items of baggage. "Bailey, the men can handle your claret without breaking it!" he called. "Come and meet our new lieutenant!"

Bailey turned, but not before exhorting the assembled sailors to "be damned careful!" Bailey was younger than Fergus expected; in fact, he did not seem much older than Essex. He had a longish oval face in which were set a long nose that the generous would call aquiline, the less generous sharp; hazel eyes; and a small, but full-lipped mouth. His hair was dark, almost black and, all told, the effect was to make him almost delicate looking. "Ah," he said brightly, extending a small, long-fingered hand, "welcome to our happy home." Fergus murmured his thanks, to which Bailey brightened. "Oh, you're a Scot. How nice to hear again that accent," he chirped merrily. "I took my medical training in Edinburgh and I must say I enjoyed it immensely." He gave a longing sigh. "A marvelous city, the Athens of Britain."

"Well, I must admit I don't know much of Edinburgh except that some cousins are there and my parents often told me of their dreams that I attend the university."

Bailey chuckled, "Ah, but the lure of the sea, eh?"

"Well, yes, something like that," said Fergus, relieved that Bailey had provided him an easy way of explaining his odyssey from Ireland to the *Swallow.*

"As for me, when the war came, I figured that with my luck if I joined the army I would be sent to the West Indies to rot on some feverish island. So I joined the navy—and was sent to some feverish island." A short high laugh came forth. "At least we're home now." Before Fergus could make a comment, Bailey continued, "Time to stow my baggage in that overgrown hatbox known as my stateroom before our new captain arrives." And with that he left Fergus.

Browne looked after the surgeon with a smile. "You'll find he brightens up the wardroom considerably. And he drives the crew mad with his advanced ideas. Always goading them to keep the ship clean and let in fresh air." He shook his head. "Has this notion that bleeding might not be the best cure for yellow fever." Browne shrugged, "Well, he is adept at setting broken limbs. So he makes for a good ship's surgeon." He touched his hat. "Off to see to my men. My sergeant must be below, either getting drunk or relieving some poor tar of his tobacco money." He gave a wink and went below.

Fergus turned and looked toward shore. Still no sign of the captain.

Early that afternoon, not too long after the men had finished their grog, the cry went up, "Boats approaching!" Fergus trained a long glass at the watercraft. There were two. In the first were two men; in the stern sat a man in commander's uniform, his arms crossed across his chest and his jaw firmly set—the new master and commander of the *Swallow.* Toward the bow sat another, larger man but with the look of seaman. The captain's coxswain, no doubt, thought Fergus.

The second boat lagged behind. It was laden with all sorts of sea chests, boxes, and cases and one man who looked distinctly uncomfortable sitting in such a small boat. Making matters worse, the man continually fussed with the luggage, making minute adjustments and nudging things to and fro. Each time he would do so, the boatman would stop rowing and shake his fist at the man.

Fergus wondered if Peck, Jones, and the rest of the *Swallow's* men would consider the captain's style of arrival to be a "big-ship" affectation or any captain's just due. He didn't have much time to wonder as Captain Waterbury's boat, unburdened as it was by a small mountain of baggage, a blustering passenger, and a quarrelsome boatman, made its way quickly toward the *Swallow.*

Snapping the long glass closed and tucking it under his arm, Fergus turned inboard. The men who had craned their necks initially to take a glance at the new captain were taking great pleasure at his servant's less than dignified progress toward their ship. Some cackled with laughter; others shook their heads with wry smiles on their faces. Others offered opinions of their new shipmate. "Damn, he's madder than a wet hen." "'E's no sailor, that one." "Aye, no seaman would rock a boat like that." "I'll be damned if the boatman doesn't heave him into the sea." It was plain to Fergus that baiting the captain's servant would soon be a favorite activity on the *Swallow.* But now there was the proper ceremony.

"Man the side! Muster the crew!" The bosun pipes trilled and men fell into their assigned places to greet their new captain. Captain Waterbury's boat bumped alongside; he climbed the ladder and soon appeared at the bulwark. The pipes trilled again, side boys saluted, the marines raised their muskets in salute, and the officers whipped off their hats.

Doffing his hat in recognition of the salutes, Captain Waterbury walked down the lines of side boys to where Fergus awaited him. As he approached Fergus, his face—framed by dark, thinning hair—bore no expression, although the eyes were in almost constant movement. He stopped in front of Fergus and clapped his hat back on his head. He was a man of somewhat sharp features; his nose was aquiline and his long chin seemed to come down to a point. His mouth was small, the thin lips almost colorless. Yet, his complexion showed he had spent time at sea. It was lined and still bore a shadow of color. His eyes were deep blue and the skin around them was deeply grooved from squinting at sparkling water.

"Welcome aboard the *Swallow*, sir."

"Yes," came the toneless response. "Yes, quite." Waterbury looked around slowly, his nose wrinkling in obvious distaste. He pulled a kerchief out of his sleeve and sniffed at it. An odor of cologne wafted across the quarterdeck.

Fergus, still standing at attention, looked around the deck to find the smell that seemed to be irritating the captain.

"Something is wrong with this ship," Waterbury said in a hoarse whisper. "This ship stinks to high heaven. Get this pigpen cleaned up if it takes all night."

Kilburnie tried to change the subject. "Would you like to inspect the crew, sir?"

Again, the flat voice responded, neither pleased nor displeased. "Yes, Kilburnie, and please stay downwind of me."

"Yes, sir," Fergus said, gesturing to where the crew was mustered.

Without a word, Captain Waterbury turned toward the crew. With Fergus in tow he walked slowly down the ranks of sailors. He looked every man up and down carefully. The only man he spoke to was Ben Coffee. "Where are you from?" he inquired.

"Kingston, sah!" came Coffee's cheerful response.

Upon hearing Coffee's accent, Waterbury's eyes widened momentarily. He then glanced back at Fergus with an questioning look and a cocked eyebrow. Fergus said nothing, thinking a word or two of explanation later on in the privacy of the captain's cabin would suffice.

After inspecting the men, Waterbury ordered Fergus to assemble the men aft. There, standing by the binnacle, he produced his official orders from the local admiral that he was to assume the position of "Master and Commander" of HMS *Swallow* and read them aloud. The deed was done. James Waterbury was now the undisputed lord and master of one ship, one lieutenant, three warrant officers, fourteen guns, and eighty men.

Waterbury turned to Kilburnie, "My servant will be following me in another boat with my baggage and victuals. See that they are sent to my cabin when they arrive."

He ignored Kilburnie's salute and strode to the ladder leading to his cabin.

Fergus followed him closely. "Sir, let me escort you to your cabin."

Waterbury turned abruptly, his nose wrinkling again. "You smell like the ship."

II

Disappointments

s Fergus learned almost immediately, Captain Waterbury was a stickler for just about everything. After he visited his cabin, he had the crew go to their stations and then he embarked on an inspection of his new command, working his way down the length of the ship.

Not satisfied with that, Waterbury made his way up the masts and then went below, poking into every compartment. Everywhere he went he asked probing questions and seemed displeased when the answers were not immediately forthcoming.

When he finished, he motioned to Fergus. "Mr. Kilburnie, you shall dine with me this evening." He looked him dead in his eye. "We have much to discuss," he said meaningfully.

At the appointed hour, Fergus went to the captain's cabin. He rapped gently on the door. "Yes?" came a voice, not the captain's.

"Lieutenant Kilburnie," Fergus felt more than a little self-conscious. "The captain invited me to dine. . . ."

The captain's servant—Alden by name—opened the door. Alden had quickly become a butt of jokes in his few hours on the *Swallow*. By the time he stepped on deck he had ended his quarrel with the boatman and almost immediately started one with Jones and Jamaica Sam by perfunctorily ordering men about. The two had informed him, in no uncertain terms, that only the captain and Mr. Kilburnie were to give them orders. Reluctantly, they detailed some men to help stow the captain's baggage and Alden had clucked and fussed until all of it was put away in what he considered proper fashion. Some of the men had taken to calling him the "Mother Hen"; others were content to make clucking noises whenever he drew near. Plainly still smarting from his reception, Alden's disapproving glance was so obvious that Fergus almost boxed his ears for impudence.

"It's Lieutenant Kilburnie, sir," he announced in a loud voice. Fergus was perplexed as to why he did so because the captain sat at a table less than ten feet from him and was looking him square in the face.

"Come in, Kilburnie," said the captain. He gestured to a seat across from him. "Please sit down." Fergus did as he was bid. "Wine?" Fergus nodded and Alden poured.

Fergus waited until the captain drank before he picked up his glass. It was a red wine, much like Lord Satterfield's claret in color, but to Fergus's tongue distinctly inferior in flavor. "Very nice, sir," he said. Well, it was *good* and, since this was only his second experience with claret, perhaps he shouldn't air an opinion lest he be queried on the extent of his experience and found wanting. Alden bustled about self-importantly, refilling the glasses and inquiring as to anything else the captain should want.

"No, thank you, Alden," the captain replied firmly. "You may attend to the food." Alden set the bottle of wine on the table, perhaps with a little too much force, and picked up a basket before leaving the cabin for the galley.

"Alden has been with me for many years," Waterbury said in way of explanation, "but I don't think he has ever become accustomed to navy life." He shook his head. "More wine, Kilburnie?" Fergus assented readily. "Now, Kilburnie, since we're the only two commissioned navy officers on this ship, I thought it would be pleasant for us to share a meal and discuss the *Swallow*."

And, for a time, it was. Alden soon reappeared with an excellent dish of duck in a sauce of wine and vegetables. In between bites of food and sips of wine, the two officers engaged in small talk. Waterbury dominated the conversation, speaking of time in London—the plays he had seen and gaming houses he had visited—as well as his trip to Plymouth and the difficulty he had securing the proper provisions for the voyage. Fergus didn't say much, although he burned to ask about their orders.

After Alden cleared the plates, he produced a decanter of port and two glasses. Waterbury poured a measure for Fergus first and then filled his glass. He then raised his glass and an eyebrow. "Kilburnie?"

Although it was clear something was expected of him, Fergus was at a loss as to what to do for a second but then remembered one of Uncle Jeris's lessons in wardroom protocol. He snatched up his glass. "His Majesty the King," he said solemnly.

"The king," replied Waterbury. They both drank.

Waterbury leaned back in his chair. "Now, Kilburnie, before we talk about the *Swallow,* I'd like to know something about you. When did you receive your commission?"

"Well, sir, you might say I'm freshly caught as a lieutenant."

"Ah, but you were in the navy for some time before that?"

"Yes, sir, I was on the *Athena* with Captain Burbage for several years."

"As a midshipman?"

Fergus cleared his throat and felt his cheeks growing hot. "No, sir, I started as a. . . ." He cleared his throat again. "I started as a seaman, sir," he said flatly.

For a long moment Waterbury said nothing. Then a corner of his mouth turned up and, as it did, Fergus realized that Waterbury had known this all along. "Really?" said the captain with evident satisfaction at a trap well sprung. "Well, that's not something to be ashamed of, is it?" he said, somewhat disarmingly.

"I suppose not, sir," Fergus said, a bit nervously.

"And a lieutenant so quickly? How did you manage that?" asked Waterbury smoothly.

"Well, I had been appointed a mate for a time by Captain Burbage and then I was made a temporary lieutenant when we needed officers. The others had been killed or wounded, sir."

"Yes, that seemed to happen a lot with the *Athena.* People being killed and the ship being cut to pieces, that is." Something unpleasant had crept into Waterbury's tone. A strong hint of superiority was it? Was Fergus being baited?

"We saw quite a bit of action, sir," Fergus tried to explain.

"Yes, yes." Waterbury waved a dismissive hand. "But we're not here to talk about our old ships, but our new one, the *Swallow.*" He sipped some port. "Now, Kilburnie. What are your thoughts about her?"

Relieved to have moved to a topic in which both men had a mutual interest, Fergus began speaking rapidly. "Well, sir, I have only been on her since yesterday, but the ship is a real beauty. Mr. Peck says she handles splend— . . ." Fergus stopped in midsentence when the captain held up his hand.

"Please, Kilburnie, I can easily see the nature of this ship. I have, after all, served on more than a few ships myself." He smiled. "She'll do well in almost any kind of weather. We can chase any sail and if what we find is too big for us, well, then, catch me who can." He leaned forward and lowered his voice. "What I am interested in is the crew."

Fergus was perplexed by Waterbury's sudden confidential air. "The crew, sir?" In order to gain some time, he sipped some port. "Well, sir, Mr. Peck, Mr. Jones, and Jamaica Sam seem to have things well in hand. The ship is neat and tidy, no loose lines or halyards. The crew . . . well, sir, they seem to be more of a family, although that's too strong a word, than a crew. They like their ship and her ways and don't seem to like the idea of being turned into a miniature version of an admiral's flagship."

Instantly, Waterbury's eyes turned grey and surveyed Fergus coldly. Fergus knew instantly he had said too much. When Waterbury spoke, his voice betrayed a barely restrained anger. "Well, Mr. Kilburnie, it seems I have a lot of work to do and you have a lot to learn." He struck the table with his fist. "I'll not have anyone tell me how to run my ship—not you, not Peck or Jones or Jamaica Sam." His voice rose. "Damn it, I am captain and the *Swallow* will bear my mark." He took a large gulp of port. "You, sir, are young and it shows. You shall learn all too well about the true nature of the men under you. Only a weak-willed captain will let his mates have their heads and only a fool will take their word for anything."

Fergus realized he had just been insulted—perhaps unwittingly, perhaps not—twice, but he held his tongue except to say quietly, "I see, sir."

Waterbury sneered. "I doubt you do, Kilburnie; you're still bedazzled by your new uniform. But a week or so at sea and you'll be able to see what I mean by making the *Swallow* bear my mark." He finished his port. "That is all for now, Mr. Kilburnie. I expect to leave when the tide ebbs in the morning."

Fergus stood up. "Yes, sir. Good evening, sir."

"Good evening, Kilburnie."

Fergus turned to leave, but Waterbury's voice stopped him. "Kilburnie."

"Yes, sir."

Waterbury's tone softened as suddenly as it had hardened. "If what I've said, about the crew, I mean, surprises you, I can understand it. Any young officer has much to learn," he continued soothingly. "As you come from the lower deck, you also must become accustomed to looking at things in a different way."

"Yes, sir."

"I have much to teach you, Kilburnie, but you must be willing to learn."

"I am, sir," Fergus replied truthfully.

Waterbury flashed a small smile. "Good, good. Now, the sooner we get to sea, the better off we shall all be."

"Yes, sir. Good evening, sir."

Waterbury waved his hand dismissively and gave another smile. "A good evening to you, Kilburnie."

Moments later in his stateroom, Fergus pondered his dinner with Captain Waterbury. On one hand he did not like being talked about like he was some animal—"the men who serve under you," as Captain Waterbury said—nor could he believe the *Swallow*'s former captain had been "weak-willed." Whoever the captain had been, he seemed to have created a capable crew who loved the *Swallow*.

But, he told himself, perhaps Captain Waterbury was right. After all, Fergus had been on the *Swallow* only a few hours longer than the captain. It could be that Peck, Jones, and Jamaica Sam were tricking him, the newly caught lieutenant, and laughing behind his back. His sense of exclusion the day before then wasn't something he dreamed up. Were they playing him for a fool? Waterbury was experienced and he did seem well meaning enough. True, he was a bit blunt and prone to bad temper, but many other officers were; he thought of Grandfather, Uncle Jeris, and Captain Burbage. Finally, Uncle Jeris had written him that "whomever the captain is, you must remember it is your responsibility to support him." Well, that settled it; he was bound to deal with the vagaries of the captain's character and hope for the best. Maybe, he thought, the *Swallow* will make its mark on Captain Waterbury instead of the other way around.

The next day, the sun came up into a milky sky which, throughout the morning, became darker and darker. By the time the tide had begun to ebb, there were dark grey clouds scudding low and the wind was blowing hard from the northwest.

Captain Waterbury stood all morning at the stern, quietly watching the preparations for sailing. His eyes were restless, never resting for long on any one activity. As Fergus moved about the deck that morning, he was conscious of Waterbury's gaze resting upon him every now and then, but tried to take no mind of it. He also tried not to interfere with Peck and Jones, who obviously needed none of his help to get the *Swallow* ready for sea. It was an uncomfortable position. If he poked his nose into the business of the master and bosun, he could expect hostility, but if he merely watched, Captain Waterbury was certain to think less of him.

In the end, therefore, he was relieved when Peck told him the ship was ready for sea. At last, he would have something—even if largely ceremonial—to do. He walked up to Captain Waterbury and touched his hat. "Sir, the *Swallow* is ready for sea."

Waterbury nodded. "Thank you, Mr. Kilburnie." He looked about the deck and up into the masts. "Time to take her out," he announced. He stepped forward to the binnacle. "Helmsman!" barked Waterbury.

"Yes, sir," quietly replied Packer, a wizened former fisherman from Hull.

"I shall give the orders directly to you. Do you understand, Packer?"

Packer's raised his eyebrows and exchanged momentary glances with Peck and Jones before softly replying, "Aye, sir."

If Captain Waterbury caught the brief hesitation, he did not comment upon it. Instead, he turned to the master's mate and the bosun who stood close by. "Mr. Peck and Mr. Jones," he snapped.

"Yes, sir," they chorused.

"I am in the habit of giving orders rapidly as well as seeing them carried out promptly and smartly." The captain fixed them with a frosty gaze. "Like any crew, the *Swallow*'s men probably have grown a little soft from their time in port. Today, we shall see if we can't reacquaint them with the sea." He looked at the dark sky, from which a few cold, wind-driven drops of rain now fell. "And what better weather in which to do it." Waterbury smiled mirthlessly. "Mr. Kilburnie!"

"Yes, sir," replied Fergus.

"You, sir, shall stand close by me. I want you to watch," Waterbury paused for effect, "and learn."

"Yes, sir."

"Good." He returned his attention to Peck and Jones. "Let us be off then."

With that Jones's whistle twirled and Peck began to bark out orders. Soon, the *Swallow*'s anchor was up and she was moving through the anchorage, responding to Packer's light touch on the wheel. As Peck had told Fergus, with the strong wind behind her, the *Swallow* gathered way quickly and soon was moving fast through the anchorage. As the deck heeled under his feet, Fergus spread his feet to brace himself.

Soon the harbor was behind them and the Channel was before them, wild and white-capped in the strong wind. Wind whistling through her rigging, the *Swallow* took a large wave and the spray traveled the length of the deck. Fergus looked at Waterbury, who stood with his arms crossed and a look of grim satisfaction on his face. Occasionally, he would run his gaze over the ship and up into the rigging and give a quiet order to Packer, who moved the wheel in response. Every now and then, he would bark an order at Peck, who would relay it to Jones who, in turn, would get the crew climbing into the rigging. Throughout, the captain's feet remained firm on the deck although his knees flexed instinctively to the ship's movements.

For her part, the *Swallow* rode the seas well, although she kicked up more than enough spray. Her timbers creaked and her masts groaned, but overall she seemed, well, playful. Fergus was pleased with the feel of the ship even in this somewhat heavy weather.

Hours later, when they were well out into the Channel, the weather cleared somewhat. The clouds thinned enough to allow shafts of sunlight to hit the sea, making the grey water glitter as it was tossed by the winds. The waves died down a bit, as did the wind, but hardly to what one would call calm. The captain called Fergus to his side. "Mr. Kilburnie, I shall now see how well the crew truly responds to my commands." He gave a tight smile. "As I said, watch and learn."

For the crew, the next few hours were ones of almost constant motion. Waterbury tacked the ship, wore the ship, crowded on sail until she heeled alarmingly in the still strong wind, had the sails close reefed, and then crowded on sail again. Then he wore the ship, tacked her, tacked her again, and wore her again. All the while, he stood almost motionless by the binnacle; his head swiveling as he took in sail, crew, sea, and sky seemed to provide the only movement.

The sky was rapidly darkening when Captain Waterbury put an end to the day's work and ordered Fergus to set the watches for the evening. He made no more comment beyond saying, "We shall see how far the *Swallow* takes us tonight," and then disappeared below.

Fergus summoned Peck and Jones to his side. To their questioning looks, he merely repeated the captain's parting words.

Peck muttered something under his breath. "Begging your pardon, sir, but was that all he said?" Fergus nodded, to which Peck shook his head. "Damned queer."

Jones nodded in agreement and his face took on a perplexed look. "He's a good seaman, that much I can tell." His look softened somewhat. "He took to the *Swallow* quick enough."

"Um, aye," replied Peck a bit halfheartedly, "that much he did."

Fergus was at a loss for words. He was somewhat surprised that the captain did not say anything in the way of encouragement to the crew or, at least, to Peck and Jones. Captain Burbage would have said something and probably called for a tot, too, he reflected. Yet Fergus remained mute, not wanting to say anything that might be considered critical of the captain. "Well, every captain has his own ways. Perhaps he'll tell us more in the morning."

Peck and Jones made noncommittal noises and took their leave. Thus, Fergus was left alone to consider Waterbury's words: "Watch and learn."

The next day was much like the previous one. As the *Swallow* felt the first ocean swells, Waterbury ran her and the crew through the same demanding paces: tacking, wearing, sails up, sails down, wearing, tacking, and more tacking. By noon, the crew was bone tired, but if Waterbury took notice of it he gave no indication.

Before Fergus went down to the tiny wardroom for his dinner, Waterbury summoned him to his side. "As soon as you finish dinner and," he looked up at the sky, "work out the noon sight, report to me. I want to start some gunnery drill."

For a moment, Fergus thought to mention that the crew had been working furiously since breakfast, but he caught himself. Captain Waterbury is not Captain Burbage, he thought. And if he makes the ship efficient, do I have grounds to complain? "Yes, sir, I shall tell Jamaica Sam as well."

"Mr. Kilburnie, you shall not tell Jamaica Sam anything," Waterbury snapped.

"Sir?" Fergus could not hide his surprise.

Waterbury's face flushed a bit. "I wish to see how well the crew reacts to surprises. You don't think a French frigate would give us much warning, do you?"

"No, sir. Of course not, sir."

"Very well, then, Kilburnie. Not a word." Waterbury said, his tone much less harsh. "Now, go and have your dinner, but don't be long."

Fergus took his leave and went quickly below to the tiny wardroom. Peck, Jones, and Jamaica Sam were there already, bolting food and washing it down with large swallows of beer. The mood was not pleasant.

"Damn me, Kilburnie," said Peck, "but all morning, up and down the rigging, tack and wear. And then what's he say? Nothing! Not if he likes it! Not if he doesn't! Not a word!" Peck reached for a tumbler of rum and almost drained it in one gulp. "Damn," he muttered to no one in particular.

Jones and Jamaica Sam murmured their agreement into their tankards.

Fergus felt compelled to offer some form of defense of the captain. "Perhaps he is waiting until he has a few days on board to get a feel of the men and the ship before he says anything. He always tells me, 'watch and learn.'"

Jones rolled his eyes in response. Peck snorted and finished his rum. "It is as plain as day that the *Swallow* is a good ship with a good crew, and any man who can't see it right away is a fo— . . ." Peck caught himself before he uttered anything that might be construed to be disrespectful of the captain. He frowned. "Well, at least he speaks to someone." He rose from the table, wiped his mouth, and left with a muttered, "See you on deck."

Jamaica Sam then spoke up. "Mr. Kilburnie, what does he say about the guns? Perhaps soon he'll see us at work there. Maybe that'll loosen his tongue."

Fergus did not reply immediately, but quickly reached for his beer, hoping his face betrayed nothing. He drank and then said with as much conviction as he could muster, "Well, Sam, that's up to the captain."

Sam raised an eyebrow and looked at Jones, who responded with a shrug. Suddenly Sam's face broke into a wide smile. "I best go see to the guns then." He shoved his plate forward and rose. "See you on deck, Mr. Kilburnie," he said happily and shot Fergus a wink. Fergus's heart sank; clearly, guile was not his strong suit.

Jones leaned back and toyed with the tumbler in front of him. "Has the captain said anything else to you, Mr. Kilburnie?"

"No," replied Fergus flatly.

Jones pursed his lips and then smiled. "Well, I'll be off then, too." His eyes twinkling, he rose and said, "Jamaica Sam will need some help getting the guns ready." He gave a chuckle and laid a finger on the side of his nose.

"Don't worry, Mr. Kilburnie. The captain will never know that we knew." He bustled out the door. Fergus wished he could be as confident as Jones that Captain Waterbury would not detect some amount of advanced warning.

No too long after he and Peck had worked out the *Swallow*'s position, Fergus reported to Captain Waterbury, who stood at his customary place by the binnacle. Alden, the captain's servant, was standing by him, a decanter of wine in his hand. Fergus waited until Alden had refreshed the captain's glass before he approached.

"The noon sight is complete, sir."

Waterbury gave a slight nod and took a sip of wine. "Thank you, Kilburnie." He took another sip of wine. "Have you dined yet, Kilburnie?"

Dining seemed a grandiose way to describe a rushed meal accompanied by beer and rum. "Yes, sir."

"Ah, good." He paused meaningfully. "Mr. Kilburnie, would you please tell me why the gunner is bustling about the guns like a hen after her chicks."

Fergus felt himself blush. "Well, sir, during dinner, Jamaica Sam asked if you had any intention of exercising the guns. . . ."

Waterbury cut him off, "And you replied . . . ?"

"I told him it was your decision, sir."

"I see. Was this done with various winks and nods?"

"No, sir," said Fergus, sensing the captain was about to spring another trap.

"So, Lieutenant Kilburnie," asked the captain, rising anger evident in his voice, "how then did Jamaica Sam know? Some form of African magic? Hmm?"

Fergus considered many answers, none of which sounded good. Still, he had to say something. "Perhaps, he just guessed, sir," he suggested meekly.

Waterbury held up a hand. "Spare me your excuses, Kilburnie. You either warned Jamaica Sam about my plans or you are so simple that you cannot keep a secret."

"I . . . I," Fergus wanted to protest, but he did not know exactly what to say to such accusations.

Waterbury didn't wait for an answer. Instead, he rounded on Fergus, bringing his face, now tight-jawed and purple with rage, within inches of the young Scotsman's. An accusatory finger shot up and wagged under his nose. "You, sir, either are a liar or a damned idiot," he hissed. "Do you actually think that you, a freshly caught lieutenant who climbed in by the hawse pipe, can somehow fool me? Do you?"

Fergus felt his face flush with anger and the same feeling as when he brawled with Kerry on the *Athena* came over him. Yet, somehow, he managed to control it. He swallowed. "Sir, I did not tell Jamaica Sam of your plans, sir." He fought to keep himself from yelling. "He asked if there were plans to exercise the guns and I replied it was your decision."

"With many winks and nods, I'd wager," Waterbury sneered.

"No, sir, none."

Waterbury stepped back, his face no longer purple and tight. The storm apparently had passed. He drew himself up and rested his hand upon the pommel of his sword. "Mr. Kilburnie," he snapped, "clear the decks for action."

"Yes, sir," said Fergus in as neutral a voice as he could muster. He turned to Peck. "Mr. Peck, clear the ship for action."

Peck immediately bellowed out the order and the marine drummer began to beat the ship to quarters. Perhaps it was the warning that certainly had been passed by Jamaica Sam or perhaps the crew was eager to show their new captain what they could do; whatever it was, the decks were cleared and the guns were manned and ready in a twinkling. Fergus was somewhat amazed at the speed, even the *Athena's* men would have been beaten.

A satisfied look on his face, Peck walked up to Fergus. "The decks are cleared, sir. The ship is ready for action." Fergus turned and formally reported what Waterbury could already see.

Waterbury was consulting a watch when Fergus approached. He waited a moment before snapping the lid closed and looking at Fergus. "Seven and a half minutes, Mr. Kilburnie, seven and a half minutes," the captain quietly, yet pointedly, observed. "Not as good as it should be on a ship this size." He frowned and returned the watch to its pocket. "We shall have to work on this."

"Yes, sir," Fergus acknowledged, careful to maintain a bland tone.

Still frowning, Waterbury announced, "Well, let's see what our guns can do."

Fergus was thankful because gunnery put him in charge of the starboard battery in the waist of the ship (Jamaica Sam in charge of the larboard) and gave him a little distance from the captain. "Starboard battery!" he ordered. "Load and run out!" Jamaica Sam echoed Fergus's order and gun crews moved smartly about their tasks.

Peck had had three empty barrels lashed together and heaved over the side when the call came to clear the decks for action and they now bobbed in the wake of the *Swallow.* Captain Waterbury gave the orders to the helmsman for the ship to be brought about and soon the barrel was coming to bear on the starboard side maybe three hundred yards away.

"Fire as you bear, Mr. Kilburnie!" ordered the captain.

Fergus acknowledged the orders. "All right, boys," he said in an encouraging tone, "fire as you bear." In response, the gun captains crouched behind their guns, four-pounders that to Fergus seemed almost toy-like compared to the *Athena*'s, and handled the lanyards attached to the flintlocks.

Waterbury had brought the ship around so that Fergus's battery would fire first. Looking over the short bulwark, Fergus could see the barrels floating on top of the swells about one hundred and fifty yards away. Out of the corner of his eye, he saw the gun captain at the most forward gun lean down to sight along his gun's barrel. Seemingly satisfied, he stepped back a little and yanked the lanyard. The process of firing a gun this size was not different from any larger gun. What was different, however, was the sound the gun made when it fired, more of a crack than anything that seemed to stab at Fergus's ears.

Trying to ignore the sound, Fergus looked toward the target. The ball did not take long to cover so short a distance. A small geyser of water rose beyond the target. Had there been a ship there, the ball would have hit. As the *Swallow* went past the barrels, the guns fired in succession. Three of the seven fired low, one ball skipping off the water and sailing over the target; the other four passed either over the barrels or close enough by to be considered hits against a ship.

Not bad at all, thought Fergus. He glanced toward Captain Waterbury, who stood in his customary pose by the binnacle—arms crossed, chin jutting out—looking toward the target. "Should I reload, sir?" he called to Captain Waterbury.

Waterbury seemed surprised by Fergus's request, but said nothing in response, giving instead a curt nod. Fergus gave the order to reload.

The *Swallow* went well beyond the barrels and then came back on them, this time exposing the larboard battery to the target. Fergus turned to look at the other guns' work and was more than a little satisfied to see the target actually struck once and all the other shots land close by. The *Swallow*'s gun crews obviously knew what they were doing. As soon as the final gun was fired, Jamaica Sam ordered them reloaded and the men went briskly about their tasks. And so it went for almost two hours, the *Swallow* nimbly dancing about the target while her four-pounders cracked away as soon as they were in range.

Through it all, Waterbury stood almost motionless, his face betraying not a single emotion. As soon as he called for an end to practice, however, he called harshly to Jamaica Sam and Fergus. "Mr. Kilburnie! Gunner! Come here!"

Now it was Jamaica Sam's turn to look surprised. Obviously, he was not accustomed to being addressed in such a manner. He exchanged a concerned glance with Fergus and made his way aft to the binnacle as did Fergus.

It was evident something was bothering the captain for he went right into a litany of complaints. "I was not pleased by this practice at all. The gunnery seems accurate enough, but the rate of fire was much too slow, as was the pace of reloading." He looked directly at Jamaica Sam. "Which gun was slowest in your battery, Gunner?"

Jamaica Sam blinked in amazement. "I don't know, sir," he responded. "I never think of things like that. The guns were ready to fire when we came into range."

The captain's face flushed with anger. "And you, Kilburnie, which of your gun crews was the slowest?"

Fergus hesitated; he honestly didn't know. Moreover, to his eye, the crews moved quickly enough; no one seemed to slack off their tasks. Yet, he knew that the captain would be displeased with such an answer. Still, he would not damn any crew to whatever punishment Waterbury seemed to be devising. Why else ask for the slowest crews? "I don't know, sir. The men seemed to move quickly."

Clearly, this was not what Captain Waterbury wanted to hear. He flushed purple and wagged that same accusatory finger at Fergus and Jamaica Sam. "Good God," he hissed, "how did you two make it this far in the navy?" He fairly quaked with anger. "I saw the problems with my own eyes and I have been on this ship for less than a week. Less than a week!" The captain was now yelling and the men had stopped in their tracks, watching the outburst.

"I shall tell you what guns were slow!" he bellowed. His finger went to Jamaica Sam. "The second gun from the bow." The finger moved back to Kilburnie. "The very middle gun! The gun right under your nose!" The finger came down and the captain's cheeks lost some of their color. "Mr. Jones!"

he snapped harshly. Jones came forward, a pained expression on his face; he did not want to be brought anywhere close to the captain's wrath. "Stop the grog for the men on those guns for a week."

"Yes, sir," Jones replied quietly.

The captain expelled a breath and rested his hands on his hips. His cheeks returned to their normal color. "And Mr. Jones?"

"Yes, sir."

"Why do you not carry a rope end?"

"I never had need of one, sir. Not on the *Swallow*."

The captain turned to the bosun. His jaw was set firmly and his eyes blazed. "Mr. Jones," he said coldly, "I suggest you start carrying one and I expect to see you use it." A malicious smile came over his face. "You and your mates."

Jones looked pleadingly at Fergus.

"Mr. Jones," the captain said in a low, ominous tone. It was a warning.

Jones glanced down at the deck and then back at the captain. "Yes, sir."

Waterbury look triumphantly at Fergus. "There, Kilburnie," he said mirthlessly.

Stopping a man's grog could be a cruel punishment, Fergus knew. Very few things in the navy were given freely and without charge. Rum was one of them. It was warmth against the cold or a moment of camaraderie with shipmates. For some men it dulled the sharp edges of shipboard life, making tolerable at least the stench, the bad food, the lash, and the always present prospect of death. Many sailors viewed it as a right, not a privilege, and many of them would prefer to be denied food rather than their tot.

Fergus also was mindful of the ways around the stoppage of grog. "Sippers" were the most popular. A sympathetic shipmate would allow a man being punished to take a sip of his grog. Some men actually would buy another man's tot. Another much more risky way about the punishment was to find a way to break into wherever the spirits were stored and tap a barrel.

What truly concerned Fergus, however, was what Waterbury might do if he saw a man denied grog drinking "sippers." Obviously, his temper could be volcanic, and in the midst of his anger he could order a savage punishment. Later that day over supper in the wardroom, Fergus confessed his concerns to Jones, Browne, Jamaica Sam, and Bailey. Peck was on watch. All agreed that what could happen would be ugly and to pass word among the crew to be careful not to try anyway around the captain's orders.

"My sergeant will keep my boys in line," Lieutenant Browne assured Fergus. Recalling Sergeant Turing's leather lungs, huge fists, and massive physique, Fergus knew Browne's men wouldn't transgress any such unofficial order because they knew if the captain's punishment didn't kill them, Sergeant Turing's probably would.

Jones looked particularly glum. "Me and my mates with rope ends. You should have seen the looks when I told them to make 'em." Jones sighed heavily. "And use 'em."

Bailey pursued his lips. "I suppose I shall have to prepare to tend to wounds incurred when lashed." He turned to Jones. "I do not envy you your probable duty."

Jones sighed again and nodded. "I'll not have my mates do it. It is my duty." He looked directly at Fergus with pleading eyes. "And what shall you say to the captain if he starts flogging the crew at the drop of a hat?"

It was a question that, in a way, Fergus knew was coming. Still, he would rather not have to answer it, at least not now. He had his hopes and decided to share them with these men. "First, there is not much I can say to the captain. You know that he is God on this ship and he can do whatever he wants to do. Also, I am not at all certain he would appreciate any advice." He looked pointedly to each man. "From any of us." He paused and sipped some wine. "Still, I am hopeful that as soon as we capture a prize or two that he shall be much happier." The men about the table nodded.

The next day brought the opportunity Fergus was hoping for: a strange sail appeared on the horizon. "Sail, ho!" shouted down the lookout, who thrust his arm out toward the larboard stern quarter.

Fergus sprang into the rigging with a telescope and trained the glass toward the horizon. It appeared to be rigged as a brig; he could make out two masts. Well, it might be a merchantman plodding for home or a French warship or a privateer manned by hardy sailors from Brest, Normandy, and Poitou. But the *Swallow* could outrun anything she couldn't outfight, of that he was sure. As close as he could figure, the ship's course was roughly parallel to the *Swallow*'s. If the wind stayed up, he figured, they could crowd on sail and intercept.

He made his way down the rigging and presented himself to the captain who had emerged on deck. He told the captain what he had seen, closing his description by saying, "Sir, I'm sure we could catch her."

Waterbury said nothing. He bit his lip in thought and then flicked his eyes to the horizon. "Very well, Mr. Kilburnie. Let's get a look at your ship."

He gave orders to hoist more sails and bring the *Swallow* toward the unidentified sail. "You realize, of course, that she'll show us her heels as soon as we come over the horizon."

"Maybe not, sir. After all, the *Swallow* is French-built; if they are Frenchmen, they may think we're friendly." He smiled. "And then we'll have them!"

Waterbury nodded silently, but not enthusiastically.

"Shall I clear the decks for action, sir?"

Waterbury shook his head. "No, Mr. Kilburnie. Let's see what your Frenchman does."

Kilburnie took his leave and walked over to where Peck and Jones stood looking expectantly at the horizon. As more and more of the sails could be seen from the deck, they leaned forward in anticipation. "She's French, all right," declared Peck, slapping his hand on the rail.

Jones nodded in agreement. "Damned right." He smiled in obvious satisfaction. "If all goes well, we'll have her in an hour or two." He looked at Fergus and winked. "Your first prize, Mr. Kilburnie?"

"No, Jones," said Fergus, "we caught our share on the *Athena*. And we still don't have this one. So don't count your prize money yet."

Jones grinned. "Ah, but I have a feeling. Call it Welsh magic." Peck rolled his eyes. Jones caught the gesture. "Have I not been right about the other ones?" he insisted.

Peck laughed. "Yes, and if you keep talking about your 'gift,' you'll be burned at the stake back in Plymouth."

Fergus looked back at the horizon. The ship was larger now and some of her hull could be seen. She didn't look too much like a warship, and he could not see any gunports that might indicate a privateer, even when he ran the telescope over it. By now Browne had sauntered over. Fergus expected him to be giddy with anticipation of a fight; Browne, after all, was both Irish and a marine. Fergus was prepared to make a joke touching on that point, but Browne's serious expression stopped him.

Browne gently tugged on his sleeve, moving him away from Peck and Jones who were gazing intently at the approaching ship. "Have you noticed our captain, Mr. Kilburnie?" Browne inquired quietly. Fergus shook his head. Browne cast his eyes toward Waterbury slowly, as if not to draw attention to himself, but insistently all the same.

Fergus looked quickly at the captain. Rather than standing rock-still by the binnacle as he usually did, the captain was pacing nervously in his traditional domain, the leeward side of the quarterdeck. His hands were clasped behind his back and he had his head down, not even looking at the horizon.

When Fergus brought his eyes back to Browne, the marine officer raised an eyebrow.

"Well, we're about to go into action and it's his first action as a master and commander," Fergus said. "I'd be a little nervous, too."

Browne gave a slight, somewhat mocking smile and a quick nod of the head. "Just as I thought." He then turned and walked down the deck.

Fergus's defense of the captain had been intuitive, but now as he slyly watched Waterbury pace the deck the contrast between this behavior and Waterbury's usual confidence was obvious. His mind conjured up an image of Captain Burbage coolly drinking wine before his first battle. No, he thought, he just has a lot on his mind. I would, too.

Tradition dictated that the captain almost never be disturbed when in the quarterdeck sanctum. Yet now, Fergus debated whether or not he should do so before the *Swallow*'s quarry came too close and surprise was lost. He recalled Essex's stern admonition of notions in the heads of the Lords of the Admiralty. He could not allow Captain Waterbury, indeed all of the men of the *Swallow,* to be thought as anything less than brave in the face of the enemy.

He looked toward the unknown ship. She did have a French look to her all right and, if all went well, it would not be long before the ship would be in range of the *Swallow*'s guns. Then it would be a matter of hoisting the colors, firing a warning shot, and demanding her surrender. Of course, Fergus scolded himself, at sea even the most carefully drawn plans had a way of going dreadfully wrong. He looked back at the captain. Waterbury was still pacing the deck, his eyes still cast downward.

"Damn!" a sailor exclaimed.

Fergus fixed his telescope on the ship. He could see clearly a burst of activity on the ship. A knot of men clustered around the stern. Something flashed in the weak sun; obviously someone was running a telescope over the *Swallow.* Fergus could make out much gesturing among the men at the unknown ship's stern, the name of which he could not make out quite yet. He examined her lines; she could be fast, if her bottom were clean, and with a good head start she might even outrun the *Swallow.*

Now was the time for being careful. *They are suspicious of us—and rightly so—but anything too obvious might spook this ship into turning tail* and running, Fergus thought. Careful or not, however, plans had to be made. Fergus made up his mind; he had to get orders from the captain.

Waterbury was still pacing the deck, sparing only an occasional glance at the French ship from his constant gaze at the deck. Fergus approached gingerly and cleared his throat. The captain's head swiveled up at him, the eyes reproachful. Fergus steeled himself for a blast of abuse, but, oddly, it never came.

Instead, the captain sighed impatiently as if he had had his dinner interrupted by some mere trifle. "Yes, Mr. Kilburnie."

"Sir, the men on the French ship are becoming concerned by our presence." He cleared his throat. "Do you have any orders?"

Waterbury looked past Fergus at the French ship. A sarcastic grin came over his face. "Orders for the Frenchmen?"

Fergus felt himself flush. "No, sir," he carefully replied, "for the *Swallow.*"

The captain clenched his teeth and inhaled sharply. He then fixed a most unfriendly gaze at Fergus. "Mr. Kilburnie," he said coldly, "I intend to give my orders whenever I am ready to do so and not be prodded by my first lieutenant into doing so a moment sooner." A humorless smile flitted across his face. "I trust I make myself clear."

"Yes, sir." Fergus's tone was a chastened one.

"Very well, then." The captain waved a hand dismissively. "Keep me informed."

Fergus returned to the rail and looked at the Frenchman. The *Swallow* was making steady progress in her pursuit of the . . . he scanned the stern with his glass . . . yes, there it was . . . the *Etienne.* A nice, quiet name for what Fergus hoped would be a nice, quiet merchantman. Then, what looked like gunports on her starboard side came into his sight. He counted four. Damn! That might mean a fight or it might mean that a tight-fisted shipowner had sent his ship to sea with few, if any, guns for those gunports. Well, we'll know soon enough.

Fergus moved the telescope back to the group of men at the stern. He started as he realized he was looking staring straight down another man's telescope. The man holding the telescope lowered it quickly and said something to a man near him. The man broke off and began clambering up the rigging of the stern mast, a telescope dangling from his shoulder. He climbed the rigging and stopped just before he reached the first crosstree. He then steadied himself and aimed his telescope directly toward the *Swallow.* After a moment or two, the man shouted something down to the men by the stern. A few seconds went by and the group of men broke up swiftly, some making extravagant gestures. The French, it seemed, were preparing to fight or readying themselves to run; either way, it did not bode well for the *Swallow.*

Fergus immediately made his way to the captain. Other men had seen the burst of motion on the French ship and crowded the rail, offering their opinions and voicing their concerns. "She rides too high for a merchantman." "Could be a coaster, coming back in ballast." "Aye, or she could be a warship out looking for us." All of these ideas could be correct, Fergus thought as he moved toward the quarterdeck, but only one man's opinion mattered: the captain's.

Waterbury had noticed the commotion on the *Etienne* and was craning his neck to look at the French when Fergus approached. "Kilburnie," he said with a slight air of exasperation, "what is going on on that Frenchman?"

"Sir, the ship is the *Etienne.* She might be armed."

"Might be?"

"Yes, sir, she has gunports, but I figure French shipowners might be very much like British shipowners and. . . ."

"And might decide it is more profitable to ship cargo instead of powder, shot, and cannons." Waterbury seemed pleased to have finished Fergus's sentence for him.

"Yes, sir."

"Now, to my original question: what is happening on the *Etienne*?"

"It appears they have an idea as to our true nature—or, at least, part of it—and are preparing to run or fight."

Waterbury frowned. "Well, if she runs now, there's not much we could do."

"Well, sir, if we get on her larboard quarter and keep pushing her in that direction, she'll lose the wind from the starboard quarter and maybe even be forced to tack. If it comes to that, the *Swallow* can catch her."

A disdainful look was Fergus's reward. "Oh, you think so?" asked Waterbury archly. Before Fergus could answer, Waterbury clasped his hands behind his back and rolled up on the balls of his feet. Settling back down, he sighed. "Well, Mr. Kilburnie, I suppose we should clear for action in any case." He began to stride toward the binnacle. "Whenever you are ready, Mr. Kilburnie."

Fergus turned immediately and called to Jones. "Mr. Jones, clear the ship for action." The cry was repeated and, already anticipating a fight, the *Swallow*'s crew sprang into action. The marine drummer began the long roll and soon that sound was joined by the others of a ship preparing for action—the thud of feet on decks, protesting blocks, the hammering and banging from below, and a cacophony of shouts, most urging speed in some task. Some of Browne's marines climbed into the tiny platforms that passed for fighting tops on the *Swallow;* others took their places along the rail. A few even took a place in gun crews, their red coats providing a dash of bright color. Fergus also noticed that Jones and his mates carried rope ends.

As soon as the decks were cleared and the guns manned and loaded, Fergus turned to the captain. To his amazement, Waterbury was consulting his watch. Fergus decided not to make mention of this fact as he reported the ship was ready for action.

"That took nearly eight minutes, Mr. Kilburnie. Even slower than in practice." He slowly closed the watch and put it back into his waistcoat pocket. The captain had begun to open his mouth when Peck shouted, "She's turning, sir."

A bare eight hundred yards away, the *Etienne* had swung to the larboard until the wind was coming almost directly over her stern. Her captain then must have ordered a sharp turn to the starboard for she swung to that side, presenting her starboard side to the *Swallow*'s bow, albeit at a shallow angle. Suddenly, her gunports flew open (five on each side) and the black snouts of iron cannon poked out. Well, now, we know she is armed, thought Fergus. A streak of color caught Fergus's eye as what looked like a small bundle rose near the trailing edge of the spanker. As it hit the yard, the wind caught it and a French tricolor streamed out.

As the range dropped to no more than four hundred yards, the side of the *Etienne* erupted in a gout of flame and dirty smoke. The battle, it seemed, was joined. The five balls from the French whistled through the sails and rigging, holing sails and cutting lines. One ball struck the foremast with a hard knock, audible throughout the ship.

Captain Waterbury ordered the ensign to be broken out and soon the flag was flying from the spanker. Yet accepting the *Etienne*'s challenge was about all the *Swallow* could do at the moment. As the *Etienne* had come close to crossing the *Swallow*'s bow, none of the latter's guns could bear. Furthermore, no sooner than had the guns been fired when the gunports snapped shut and the Frenchman's bow swung back toward the larboard, putting her stern to the wind. She gathered way quickly and began to open the distance from the *Swallow*.

"Damn me, but he's a cunning bastard," cried Peck in a voice that mixed personal frustration and professional admiration. "He'll keep doing what he is doing, making a shallow turn to starboard or larboard, firing at us, and then running. He's trying to slow us down by picking our rigging to pieces and when he gets a big enough lead, he'll run." He scanned aloft and scowled. "Damn you, Mr. Jones! Let's not make it easy for him! Get some men aloft and try and fix some of that."

Jones soon was bawling out orders and some men made a mad dash up the rigging, trying to make good some of the damage the French had already done. Some of it, though, would obviously have to wait until another time.

"There he goes again." The *Etienne* went into a shallow turn to the starboard and lost a little speed in doing so, but came around sharply to port, her larboard battery ready. Her cannon boomed again.

"Look out!" Jones yelled to the men aloft. "Some of that's chain shot!" Chain shot, Fergus knew, was two small balls between which was a length of chain. It was purposefully designed to wreck rigging, yards, and spars and performed that task quite well. Of course, it mangled flesh and bone as well as it tore rope, wood, and canvas. The shot came in high, and with a low moan it ripped through the *Swallow's* rigging. The topgallant of the foremast was snapped off and crashed to the deck; a foremast yard cracked and hung drunkenly by a few lines; and the sound of rending canvas was all around. But of all the sounds, the most piercing were the screams of the men aloft who were hit by the chain shot.

A marine and a sailor plunged from the mainmast, hitting the deck with a sickening thud. The men closest rushed over to help their stricken shipmates. The marine's right arm was almost torn off, white bone showing through the flesh and blood; he might have survived that wound but his neck was twisted into an odd angle.

The sailor lay face down in an expanding pool of blood, his legs at a crazy angle from his torso. It was one of the black sailors, that much Fergus could see. A man rolled him over. A strangled cry came up, followed by the sound of retching. Then one man shrieked, "Oh, God, Ben Coffee! They got Ben Coffee!" The voice cracked and broke down into sobs. Coffee had been torn almost in two by the chain shot at about waist level and his guts were oozing out through the wound on to the deck.

Turning away from the horrible sight, Fergus looked about the deck. Men were staring back at the two dead men, dumbfounded and seemingly paralyzed. Then a voice from the fighting top howled, "Whoresons!" and a musket cracked. Fergus looked up. A marine had fired his musket at the *Etienne*. At four hundred yards there was almost no chance the ball would find its mark; therefore, it seemed more an act of personal defiance.

The shot seemed to galvanize the men. With an angry roar, they rushed back to their guns. Two shipmates had been killed and they wanted blood. Jamaica Sam ran to the forwardmost gun of his battery, snatched up a handspike, and muscled the gun around to where it was practically parallel with the hull. Sighting down the barrel, he adjusted the elevation and jerked the lanyard. The gun jumped back crazily, almost falling over. The men watched transfixed as the ball sailed toward the *Etienne*. Jamaica Sam had aimed well, but the range, now being rapidly opened by the French, was too long. The shot splashed short by about fifty yards.

Sam ordered the men to reload and, shaking the handspike at the French, yelled, "Come back and fight, you frogeaters!" The men cheered and began to hustle what guns could be brought to bear even slightly to fire at the French. The marines in the top began firing away as well, the hollow booms of their muskets mixing with the creak of complaining lines and the grunts of sailors.

"Stop it!" came a voice from by the binnacle. "Stop that damned useless noise." It was Captain Waterbury who came forward, his eyes blazing with anger. "Stop it!"

Lieutenant Browne, who already was poised to yell up to the men in tops, obviously thought the order pertained to his marines. "Damn you, stop firing! You're wasting powder! You heard the captain!"

The captain brushed by Browne and came up to Fergus. "All of you," he screamed, his face purple with rage and spittle on his lips, "cease firing! Now!" To a man, the crew turned and looked in wide-eyed amazement at the captain. He didn't seem to notice, however. "I said cease firing!" He balled up his fists and stomped his feet. "Stop it!"

Fergus was at once angry and ashamed at the captain's behavior. Angry because the captain didn't need to yell, not at this crew. Ashamed for the captain; this tantrum would not go down well with the men. Yet he knew he had to do something to put as good a face as possible on the captain's anger. "Captain's right, lads!" he shouted, looking away from the captain. "We have to catch them before we can shoot them!" He looked around to find Peck and Jones. "Mr. Peck! Mr. Jones! We can catch the Frenchman by nightfall.

Get some men aloft. Jama— . . ." Suddenly, Fergus felt himself being jerked around by his left shoulder and whirled to see the captain's face inches from his.

"Silence! Damn you! Silence!" he screamed. Captain Waterbury's face was a contorted mask of rage. "You don't give orders on my ship, you impertinent pup! You are insolent, sir," he shrieked. "Insolent!" Captain Waterbury looked about wildly, his chest heaving. All was quiet, except for the noises of the *Swallow;* the men were transfixed. He turned back to Fergus. "I am captain and I say the chase is over! I shall not risk my ship because your damned," he swallowed, "your damned blood is up!" His chest rose as he drew in an enormous breath. He again thrust his face into Fergus's and roared, "I command this ship! Do you understand me, you whelp?"

Fergus felt the blood rush to his ears. Involuntarily, his right hand went down to the pommel of his sword and his left hand clenched into a fist. He fought two urges: the first, to punch the captain and send him sprawling, the second, to scream right back at the captain, to tell him he had been trying to make him look better in front of the crew. He was about to lose those battles when Browne's voice cut the heavy silence. "Kilburnie," the marine said softly and laid a hand firmly on his shoulder. "Kilburnie."

Fergus felt the anger drain out of him, and as it did his body seemed to sag a bit. He shook his head to clear it, took a breath, and looked at the captain, who still had his face thrust close to Fergus. "Yes, sir, I understand my position on this ship." Although he was somewhat relaxed, his voice still quivered with anger. "I was only. . . ." No, he thought, explanations were useless. "I understand my position quite well, sir."

Waterbury drew back with a look of triumph on his face. "It is well you do, Kilburnie," he sneered. "Such is not often the case with officers who are sons of farmers." The pain Fergus felt at this remark was almost physical. It was not only a taunt and an insult, but a deliberate attempt to lower his standing with the crew. Fergus felt his face grow red. For his part, Captain Waterbury seemed delighted with his parting shot, for he turned on his heel and strode back toward the quarterdeck. "I shall be in my cabin," he called breezily over his shoulder. "Return to our original course, Mr. Kilburnie."

Fergus said nothing, nor did he look at the captain. He stared at the deck for a moment. Quite suddenly, he felt as if he was going to cry, but he knew he couldn't. Not now, not here. He raised his head, inhaled deeply, and exhaled audibly. Spying Peck, he quietly said, "Mr. Peck, please return to our original course." He cleared his throat and raised his voice a bit. "And please ask Mr. Jones to attend to repairs as best he can." He turned around to Lieutenant Browne. "Mr. Browne, would you please prepare the two men for burial. I shall ask the captain when he would like to perform the service."

The gunner was still standing at the gun he had labored to fire at the escaping French. "Jamaica Sam," he called, "please attend to the guns. Make sure the powder is stored properly." Jamaica Sam met his eyes and gave a silent nod. Fergus looked about at the men who were still clustered around the bodies, although they were no longer staring at them. "Well, *Swallow*s," he said, trying to sound encouraging, "we'll get the next Frenchman we come across." He looked out at the fast-disappearing sail and many heads turned to follow his gaze. "But for now, let's get the *Swallow* back together." With a murmur of assent, the men turned to their tasks.

The tension over the next two days was almost palpable. The burial ceremony, conducted around sunset on the day of the deaths, should have been a way for the captain to bring the crew together, almost as a family, in their grief at losing two shipmates.

But Captain Waterbury raced through the ceremony, reading tonelessly from the prayer book. As soon as the canvas-wrapped bodies were slid into the sea and the final prayer said, he closed the book and curtly told Fergus to dismiss the crew. He had said nothing about the two dead men nor did he ask anyone else to do so. "Dumped over the side like a load of bad beef," one man muttered as the crew moved back to their duties.

For the rest of the time, the captain divided his time between his customary stance at the binnacle and his cabin. He said little except to give orders in a peevish tone and snap at Alden, his servant. Even the captain's coxswain came in for a tongue-lashing for a trifling manner.

Fergus noticed some men giving him sidelong glances as he went about his duties. It was not the glances so much as the unknown reasons behind them that concerned Fergus. Was it some lower-deck gossip, perhaps started by the captain's coxswain, about his former lowly status? He recalled Essex warning him that some sailors disliked officers who were drawn from their ranks. Maybe his failure to stand up to the captain that day was what prompted the glances and whispers.

In the wardroom, everyone was careful to maintain an air of normality and not to say anything about the incident—at least whenever Fergus was present. Yet, often Browne would give Fergus a pat on the back and look coolly at him as if to ask if he was all right. Fergus would nod and give a small smile as if to say, "Yes, I am fine." He was happy Browne never pressed the matter because he would have said that his mind was consumed by dire thoughts about his future on the *Swallow,* his future in the navy.

On the evening of the second day after the battle, Fergus was summoned to Captain Waterbury's cabin. The more Fergus pondered the captain's character, the more Waterbury appeared to be the type of man who would derive pleasure out of making men's lives miserable and justify it because he was the captain and, therefore, could do so with impunity. Why else the vindictive statement about Fergus's background? He might write a damning letter to the Admiralty that might sit in a file for years—until it came time for Fergus to be considered for promotion. Then the damage would be done, for Fergus would have no way of countering what was said in the paper. In his mind's eye, he could see the raised eyebrows, the pursed lips, and the silent shaking of heads as it was passed around. Or Waterbury might start talking to other officers about him. Nothing outlandish because nothing outlandish was needed. A whisper, a hesitation when asked about "your old lieutenant, Kilburnie," or an arch comment about the "son of a farmer." And, of course, who would not take the word of a commander or post captain they knew? As Essex had observed, in the navy, once an idea entered people's minds it was difficult to remove.

On the third day after Captain Waterbury's tantrum, the cry of "Sail ho!" again went up. The crew crowded to the rail and peered toward the horizon. Soon enough, the topsails of what appeared to be a brig broke over the horizon. Immediately, there was a buzz of conversation as those who fancied themselves experts (and there were not a few) on the subject argued whether the rig was French, British, Dutch, Spanish, or American. One man loudly fancied the approaching ship actually Portuguese, but he was quickly hooted down. Some began to wager how fast it would take the *Swallow* to overtake the ship and, after much consultation with the winds, those wagers were taken.

Fergus stepped up to the captain who was standing by the binnacle. "Sir, should I set a course to intercept?" he asked brightly. Here, he hoped, was the opportunity to put things right.

Waterbury furrowed his brow and looked at the far-off sails. "Please hand me a glass, Mr. Kilburnie." Fergus did as he was bid and the captain raised the telescope to his eye. After a few minutes of studying the ship, he snapped the telescope shut. "No, Kilburnie, no. Whatever she is, she definitely is not French." Waterbury turned to the helmsman. "Maintain present course."

The helmsman sang out in reply, repeating the order in such a way that the men around him heard. Immediately, a babble of voices went up and faded just as quickly. A couple of men cast dark looks in the captain's direction as they wandered back to their tasks. Fergus just watched in frustration as the ship slowly dipped back under the horizon. Damn, he thought, we should have at least looked.

Later that day, "Up spirits" was piped and the men moved gratefully up to the grog tub for their daily tot. As always, the men joked and talked as they were issued their rum and then moved away to sit and enjoy it. The last few men were waiting for their grog when Fergus heard the captain bawl his name.

"Kilburnie!"

Fergus made his way as quickly as possible to binnacle where the captain stood, a furious expression on his face. "Yes, sir?"

"Mr. Kilburnie," he said, loudly and contemptuously, "am I the only man with eyes on this ship?"

Confused, Fergus hesitated to answer. "No, sir."

"Then, please tell me, sir, why I am the only one who can see that the man whose grog I stopped for a week is drinking?" The captain's voice had raised to a shout by the time he had finished his question.

Fergus looked about the knots of men clustered around the deck, seeking the face of the man—Barton, by name—who was denied rum. He could not see him, but he could see that the crew was looking at the captain.

"There!" the captain screamed, his finger pointing down the deck. It was then Fergus saw the man, sitting by a gun in the starboard battery, his eyes wide with fear. A cold feeling came over Fergus; whatever was about to happen would not be pretty. "Come with me, Mr. Kilburnie!" the captain barked and strode purposefully down the deck toward the bow, Fergus in tow. He stopped directly before the man who had come to his feet.

With one look, Fergus knew the man had been drinking; against orders, official and otherwise, someone had given him sippers. Hmm, by the smell of it, Fergus thought, he had taken the entire tot.

"Good God, man," the captain yelled at the quaking sailor. "Did you think you could defy my orders and not be punished for it? Answer me!"

The man swallowed hard, but said nothing, for which Fergus was thankful. Anything he would have offered as an excuse probably would be a transparent lie and that, in turn, would send the captain's anger to new heights. Better to take what was coming anyway and not make it worse. Yes, Fergus thought, Barton would be triced in the rigging for a day or maybe even two.

The captain's voice interrupted Fergus's thoughts. "Ten lashes!" the captain barked.

Fergus was startled. "Ten lashes, sir?"

"What did you say, Mr. Kilburnie?" asked the captain coldly.

Fergus realized that he had made a great mistake. He scrambled for an explanation. "Ten lashes. Yes, sir. When would you like punishment to occur, sir?" There. Correct and formal.

"No, Mr. Kilburnie. You said 'Ten lashes' as if it was a surprising punishment for the infraction."

Fergus was trapped—and the captain knew it. "Well, sir, I have never been in this position before. As first lieutenant, that is, and. . . ."

A malicious grin came across the captain's face. "You're correct, Mr. Kilburnie, you never have. So, in order for you to learn properly," the captain looked at Barton, "make it fifteen." Confused, the sailor's eyes flicked nervously between Fergus and the captain. The captain rubbed his hands together gleefully. "There, my man," he said to Barton, "five more lashes with the cat on your back so Mr. Kilburnie can learn how to hold his tongue. You don't mind, do you?" The man merely shook his head. "Good. Didn't think you would," Waterbury clucked.

Fergus was desperate to spare the man any further pain. "Ah, sir, I . . ."

Waterbury cut him off with a savage look. "You question my judgment one more time or say one more thing about this man's punishment, Kilburnie—one more!—and I'll double it to thirty lashes."

Drawing himself up, Fergus touched his hat. "Fifteen lashes, sir. When would you like to have the punishment executed, sir?"

Waterbury consulted his watch. "As soon as the men return to duty. The sooner the better."

"Yes, sir," Fergus said flatly.

"Good," the captain clasped his hands behind his back and bounced up and down on the balls of his feet. "I shall be in my cabin, Mr. Kilburnie," he announced. He then turned around and began to walk aft, but then stopped and turned slightly so he looked at Fergus over his shoulder. "That is, if you'd like to discuss this man's punishment any further." Giving a smirk, he resumed his walk aft.

Fergus turned to the sailor. "I am sorry. I didn't mean to, ah, cause you any further. . . ." God, what to say to this man?

"Aye, I know you meant well, Mr. Kilburnie," Barton said. "Truth is, it's my fault for asking for sippers. But," he shrugged, "it's not the first time I've been on the bad end of the cat."

Despite Barton's words, Fergus didn't feel any better; in fact, he felt even worse.

At the appointed time, the men were assembled aft "to witness punishment." In two files by the starboard rail, the marines were under arms with bayonets fixed. Three paces in front of the mainmast stood the officers, and the captain a pace in front of them. The crew was about ten paces in front of the officers. On the larboard rail was where Barton would be flogged; his hands would be tied to the rigging and then Jones would execute the punishment.

Fergus studied the faces of the men. Some stared straight ahead; others glared sullenly at the captain. A few looked down at the deck. Most, however, bore expressions of resignation.

When all was ready, Fergus ordered, "Hats off," and all of the sailors removed their hats. Two bosun mates hustled Barton forward to the rail. Barton silently stripped himself to the waist. Fergus could see the scars of a previous flogging crisscrossed on Barton's back. He then held his hands up and the two mates tied his wrists securely to the rigging.

"Bosun," said the captain, "the punishment is fifteen lashes well laid on." Jones stepped forward, the baize bag holding the cat-o'-nine tails tucked under his left arm. "Bosun, do your duty."

Jones removed the cat from the bag and shook out the nine pieces of thin line that gave the device its name. The small knot tied toward the end of each line, however, was what made the cat such a fearsome instrument for they were what laid open a man's back with an intense burning pain.

Taking his position near Barton, Jones hefted the cat and nodded at the marine drummer, who stood with his sticks poised. During a flogging, the roll of the drum would muffle a man's cries of pain. The drummer began the roll and Jones brought down the cat for the first lash. Barton clenched his teeth, but no sound passed his lips. Indeed, it was not until the sixth stroke that he cried out, but it was more of a gasp than anything and the drum's sound almost drowned it out. At the tenth lash, however, Barton gave a strangled cry as the cat bit deeply into his back.

Grunting with effort, Jones lashed faster, obviously trying to end the torment as soon as he could. Twelve . . . thirteen . . . fourteen . . . fifteen. All was silent. The drummer stopped the long roll. Jones stood behind Barton, his brow wet with exertion and the now bloody cat hanging limply by his side. The two bosun mates came forward, untied Barton's wrists, and gently lowered him face down to the deck. The surgeon bustled forward and a bucket of sea water and then a bucket of fresh water was poured over Barton's bloody back. Fergus winced as Barton quivered in pain. The surgeon ordered Barton carried below and the men parted ranks as the two mates did so.

The captain stood silent for a moment, casting his eyes about the crew, as if daring someone to say something. "Mr. Kilburnie!" Fergus came forward and saluted. "Dismiss the crew."

Fergus again saluted and turned. "Crew dismissed." Silently, the men broke away, their conversations a low buzz.

"Mr. Kilburnie," Captain Waterbury called.

"Yes, sir."

A taunting smile played across the captain's lips. "I trust you found that edifying."

Yes, damn you, Fergus thought, I learned never to flog a man just to make a point. But he also had learned, as Captain Waterbury had wished, to hold his tongue. So, in reply, he merely said, "Yes, sir, most edifying."

12
TRANSFERRED

In the aftermath of Barton's flogging, life on the *Swallow* took a definite turn for the worse. Captain Waterbury let more ships slip by, offering such excuses for his failure to investigate as "She's too big for us." "No, too fast." "Too far away." "No, no, British, definitely."

The men grew restive and frustrated at the sight of so much prize money sailing away unmolested. The frustration began to erode the camaraderie among the crew. Small mistakes that would have been joked about before were criticized with scathing insults. Minor arguments turned into major ones and then into fights. Jones sometimes had to use his rope end to break the men apart. If he failed to do so swiftly enough, Captain Waterbury would have a man flogged.

The crew's frustration was shared by many in the wardroom but only occasionally was it expressed and then only in an oblique manner. "Damn me," said Peck, after one particularly tempting ship was allowed to scamper away, "the men were madder than wet hens to see that little French ship run away. We could have caught her, too."

Jones nodded in agreement, but said no more, although Fergus could guess that whenever the warrant officers were alone, the captain's lack of aggressiveness was discussed much more openly.

Yet, within the wardroom—and, more important, in front of the men—the officers and warrant officers kept their opinions about the captain to themselves. They all knew that once lost, discipline was hard to recover.

For his part, the captain remained keenly sensitive to any affront to his authority and dignity—real or imagined. Any officer or warrant officer who seemed to do as much as hesitate to relay out an order was severely chastised, more often than not in front of the men. To suggest another course of action, even on minor matters, was to invite a display of the captain's ugly temper or a round of cutting insults, again often in front of the crew.

In a private meeting in the captain's cabin, Fergus urged him to reduce his use of the cat, saying that the men needed a fight, not flogging, to restore their spirits and make things right. The captain listened to him, that much was true, but his response was to look down his nose and contemptuously say, "You are dismissed, Mr. Kilburnie."

The next day Waterbury had two men flogged for piddling offenses. Twenty lashes a piece. After punishment, he snarled at Fergus, "Any further opinions on my discipline, Mr. Kilburnie?" Fergus offered no more.

The captain also enjoyed baiting Browne and his marines. Many times when Browne was in earshot, he would openly and venomously describe the marines as "an idle lot" and a "burden on the navy." It was Fergus's experiences that the bootnecks were often the butt of sailors' jokes, but it was never his experience that an officer actually shared in seriousness what sailors said in jest.

Captain Waterbury also had an extremely low opinion of the Irish; so Browne had to bear hearing the captain's notions of his race as well as his service. "Papist blackguards" was one of Waterbury's favorite phrases for describing all Irishmen, despite the fact that Browne belonged to the Church of Ireland.

Browne bore this abuse with remarkable equanimity. Once the captain described the Irish as "wild and undisciplined, totally addicted to strong drink, horseracing, gambling, and fighting." Browne had laughed and replied that the captain might be right, although he never had much of a taste for horseracing.

. . .

And so it went for two weeks. One evening the captain called the officers and warrant officers to his cabin and announced that the *Swallow* was heading home. "Our provisions are running low and I'm none too confident about the repairs performed after our . . . ," he paused, seeking the correct word, "action against the *Etienne* should we meet a storm." Fergus could see Peck's and Jones's jaws tighten at the last remark. He leaned back in his chair. "When we return to Plymouth, along with proper repairs, I might be prepared to make a few other changes as well."

"Do you mean the rigging, sir?" asked Peck dryly. "For I have a few ideas that might give us the speed you seem to think we need."

Waterbury reddened at Peck's dig. "No, I mean among the crew," he paused purposefully, "and the officers."

There was a deep silence. The captain had issued a threat. Out of the corner of his eye, Fergus saw Browne's face go red. "Just what is that supposed to mean, sir?" Browne asked coldly. Browne's voice had the same menacing quality of a sword being drawn slowly yet purposefully from its scabbard. The Irishman's temper, so long held in check, seemed to be slipping its traces.

At first, Captain Waterbury seemed surprised at Browne's tone. He leaned forward, his eyes blinking rapidly. "Did you say something, Mr. Browne?"

"Yes, sir," Browne's voice was controlled, but there was a distinct edge to it. "I merely asked just what you meant by changes among the officers." Fergus immediately recognized the tone from his days in Ireland. It was the last chance for a man to retract a statement or offer an explanation, no matter how flimsy, and thus avoid a challenge to "a meeting." Yet, challenging a superior officer was unheard of; therefore, Browne was treading on extremely dangerous ground. But then, mused Fergus, so was Captain Waterbury.

"What I meant, Mr. Browne," the captain said smugly, "is that I find the performance of some of the officers and warrant officers to be, well, lacking." He toyed with the pen in front of him and smiled. "And I intend to make some changes, as is my prerogative as captain." The smile broadened as he said it. Now the captain's look became obviously malicious and he moved his gaze from man to man. "Also, among my prerogatives—no, one of my duties—as captain is to inform the Admiralty of my reasons for replacing any of my officers. Reasons that are, for the good of the Service, best communicated in private letter."

Waterbury gave a thin, malevolent smile and continued. "Now, I probably shall withhold any decisions until I discover if there are to be any inquiries regarding our action with the *Etienne*." He again looked from man to man, raising an eyebrow expectantly.

There it was, Fergus thought, as plain as day: Captain Waterbury was concerned about reports of his conduct in that encounter and was trying to using an exceptionally heavy hand to keep people quiet. Fergus was somewhat surprised at this approach for it truly wasn't needed. In his report the captain would state—as he did in the log—that the French ship had so damaged his rigging that he had to break off the action and heave to to make repairs. It probably would end there. The *Swallow* was not a frigate, after all; therefore, very few would care about one small abortive action. Furthermore, he was master and commander of one of His Majesty's warships and the Admiralty tended not to second-guess captains' decisions—unless, of course, they lost warships.

An unfounded accusation of incompetence or cowardice would ruin the career of the man who made such a charge and, doubtlessly, Waterbury could hide behind his cherished "captain's prerogatives" and a court of inquiry would be more than willing to believe him. Yet Waterbury chose the route of exceptionally clumsy blackmailing.

Fergus and the other men stood motionless and silent. Did the captain want them to say they would keep the *Etienne* episode quiet? That would be a foolish request; the crew was bound to talk, of course.

Browne broke the silence by clearing his throat. "Sir?"

"Yes, Mr. Browne?" Waterbury folded his hands on the table and turned his eyes toward the Marine.

"I, for one, respectfully request an immediate transfer to another ship upon our arrival in Plymouth." Again, Browne's tone was completely correct, but clipped.

"And why would you want to leave us, Mr. Browne?" asked the captain, his voice betraying a broad hint of displeasure. He spread his hands. "Whatever can be the problem?"

"Sir, I cannot think of a better ship than the *Swallow* as well as a better crew, but I believe the time has come for me to leave her."

As so often happened, Waterbury's temper got the better of him. He sprang to his feet. "You mean the time has come for you to leave me! You cannot stand that I have shown you to be an inefficient officer! You refuse to learn from me, you mollycoddle your men when it's obvious that more than a few could use a dozen lashes or so!" He slammed his fist down on the table. "Damn you, sir! I have no use for an insolent officer, especially a damned marine. You shall have your transfer immediately, Mr. Browne. In fact, I want you off my ship as soon as we drop anchor in Plymouth! If you're aboard more than a minute after the anchor is dropped, I'll have you arrested for disobeying an order!" The captain's face was now flushed a deep purple. He gestured extravagantly toward the door of his cabin. "Now, sir, get out of my sight, you insolent Irish blackguard," he thundered.

Browne calmly bowed and then murmured, "As you wish, sir." He turned and exited the captain's cabin.

During the captain's outburst, Fergus had tried hard not to look directly at the captain, fearing he would then be subjected to a torrent of invective. He hoped that, as usual, the captain's temper would quickly abate and when it did he and the other men would be dismissed. This time, however, the encounter with Browne had brought the captain's temper to a fevered pitch.

"So," he sneered, "which one of you wants to join Mr. Browne on the beach in Plymouth, wandering the streets and grog shops begging for a ship?" No one spoke and the silence laid heavy on the men in the cabin. "Well, speak up! Who?" Waterbury's voice began to raise in volume. Still, there was no response. Waterbury began to scan the faces of the officers intently. "Come now, aren't there any of you men who wish to leave my ship, leave because I make you work, because I flog your damned precious sailors? Hmm?" Again, no response, but the captain's eyes continued to run over the men, a thin smile creeping onto his face.

Damn, thought Fergus, he is enjoying this, like a cat toying with a mouse—except, of course, what the cat did was ultimately useful. He said nothing and tried not to meet the captain's gaze, but it fell upon him all the same.

"Kilburnie," Waterbury hissed, "what about you? You were a friend of Browne's, were you not?"

Fergus replied, "I am a friend of Mr. Browne's, sir."

A sharp intake of breath by the captain and Fergus regretted the response instantly. "Oh, you are," said the captain in a mocking tone, "you are." The captain leaned forward over the desk and shook a finger at Fergus. "Well then," said Waterbury in a voice quaking with anger, "you may join your friend. . . ." The captain took a deep breath and exploded, *"Off my ship, you insolent whelp!"* The tone became hysterical, "Get out of my cabin! Get out now, you Scotch fool!" Fergus took a step back and began to bow. "Now, damn your eyes! Get out, now!" Fergus made for the door, but the captain continued to rant. "All of you, get out! Immediately! Leave me!"

Days later, the *Swallow* made her way into Plymouth Harbor. For any normal ship, this would have been a happy occasion, a safe return to home port, but the men of the *Swallow* were not thinking of the homecoming but of the hellish time the trip home had been. Waterbury had been in a particularly sour mood and he meted out punishments—stoppage of grog, tricing to the rigging, and, of course, flogging—every day. The men seethed with resentment, performing their duties slowly and sullenly; some even spoke back to the warrant officers, themselves in no mood to brook anything that might bring the captain's wrath down on them. Jones used his rope end ruthlessly on men with whom he had joked mere weeks before; with one blow Jamaica Sam flattened one man who had complained about gunnery drill. Fights among the crew broke out with even more frequency and their causes were increasingly petty. In short, the *Swallow*'s crew was coming apart.

That morning Fergus arose and finished packing. He was torn about leaving the *Swallow*. Waterbury was intolerable and clearly did not want Fergus on his ship, but still Fergus felt guilty about leaving. Leaving the men to the mercies (such as they were) of Captain Waterbury did not appeal to him. Was he somehow failing them? Still, the captain was not about to accept Fergus's advice on anything and, actually, Waterbury seemed to take out his anger against Fergus on the men. No, it probably was best he leave.

What to tell Uncle Jeris, Father, Mother, Essex, and Lord Satterfield? Fergus sighed heavily as he contemplated informing them that he had been thrown off his first ship and perhaps would never go to sea again, but rot ashore on the half-pay list. Perhaps he could explain to Uncle Jeris what had happened; perhaps Uncle Jeris already knew Waterbury by reputation. Then, again, Waterbury could have patrons even more powerful than Lord Satterfield and, of course, there was no way to prevent him from whispering in the ear of anyone he encountered.

A soft knock came on the door. "Mr. Kilburnie, sir?" It was Peck, coming to collect his baggage.

"Yes, Peck, come in."

Peck entered, his brow furrowed with concern. "Captain's compliments, sir, but he said that you and Mr. Browne are not to leave the ship immediately upon anchoring, as he has been called ashore to visit upon the admiral."

Fergus nodded. "Has the captain left already?" He then heard a bosun's pipe sound and the distinct thud of marines' boots stomping on the deck. "Ah," he smiled, "he's just gone then?"

Peck gave Fergus a sly smile. "So it appears, sir."

"Peck, what bothers you? You came into the cabin looking as if all the world's cares rested upon your shoulders."

"Well, sir," Peck shrugged, "you never know mischief that . . . ," he cleared his throat and grinned, "that type of signal portends. Usually, a captain isn't summoned for quite some time."

"Ah," scoffed Fergus gently, "anything that disrupts what's familiar is something sailors don't like. Maybe there's a new admiral and he just likes to make captains jump."

"Aye, perhaps." It was obvious that Peck's opinion that the demand for the immediate appearance of the captain did not bode well was a firm one.

Some hours later Fergus was on deck. His baggage, along with that of Browne, had been brought up and a longboat swung out to take the two officers ashore. Looking about the harbor, Fergus could detect nothing out of the ordinary. "Captain's boat approaching!" called the lookout.

Peck waited until the boat was near until he called out, "Man the side!" A bosun's mate and two marines materialized and Captain Waterbury was welcomed back with all appropriate ceremony. Something obviously troubled him, for he barely acknowledged the salutes and began casting his eyes about as soon as he stepped on the deck. "Mr. Peck, assemble all the officers in my cabin immediately." He shot an angry gaze at Fergus and Browne. "That includes Lieutenant Kilburnie and Mr. Browne."

Moments later the officers were crowded into the captain's cabin. He did not waste time. "I have been informed by the admiral of grave news." Waterbury paused and pressed his hands to his temples momentarily. "There has been a mutiny at Spithead, and not in just one ship but a large number of ships." The captain was clearly worried. "There are reports that men in the pay of the French incited the mutinies in hopes of leaving the southern coast undefended."

"Invasion, sir?" asked Jones incredulously. "There's to be a French invasion?"

Waterbury's eyes widened at the word as if he had not even dared contemplate them, lest the idea be borne out. "No, Mr. Jones, we don't know of one yet." He glanced nervously out the cabin's windows. "But one never knows."

Browne cleared his throat to gain the captain's attention. "Sir, has there been any bloodshed? Officers killed?"

Waterbury's eyes shifted to Browne. "Oddly enough, only in one instance." He snorted. "And the mutineers claim to be loyal to the king, interested only in improving pay and conditions in the fleet." He clenched his fist. "By God, if I were in command at Spithead, there'd be men hanged for treason by now."

More likely the entire fleet would be in a state of mutiny, thought Fergus.

"Sir, what are we to do?" asked Jamaica Sam.

"A good question," said Waterbury. "The admiral has told me he wants this ship to be revictualed and back to sea within twenty-four hours. We are to patrol near Brest and keep an eye on the French, just in case they try to exploit the mutiny and invade." He tapped his fist lightly on the desk. "So, prepare to move the ship to the dockside. But," he held up a cautionary finger, "on no account tell the men about why we are leaving so quickly. They must not know."

"About the French, sir?" asked Peck.

"No, no, about the mutiny. If news gets out, it might give some men ideas. And in no case shall the men be allowed ashore. The French might have agents in Plymouth just waiting for an opportunity to spread the mutiny throughout the fleet. Also, watch who they speak to on the dockside, who knows what rumors are about in this damned town."

Browne again cleared his throat. "Will Mr. Kilburnie and I be staying on board the *Swallow*, sir?"

The captain scowled. "No, you shall not." He looked at the other men. "Mr. Peck, as I said, prepare the ship to move to the dockside." He shifted his gaze back to Browne and Fergus and gave a triumphant smile. "We shall shift position after Messrs. Browne and Kilburnie leave." The smile broadened. "Which shall be soon after I have a word with them in private." He waved a dismissive hand. "Thank you. Now attend to your duties."

The captain waited until the others had left before he spoke to Fergus and Browne. "Well, gentlemen," he said happily, "our last meeting." Again, the triumphant smile. "I must admit that this mutiny business makes it all the more important that you two leave the *Swallow* now. I'll be free of your interference with my discipline, the type of discipline that guarantees mutiny doesn't happen on a ship. These men won't dare to even think of mutiny because they know I shall be firm." He nodded in obvious self-satisfaction.

"As to your future, Mr. Browne, because of my meeting with the admiral, I was unable to do much more than tell the ranking marine officer here that you would be joining him and his other idlers until such time as he needs to send a detachment to sea." Browne merely nodded in reply.

Waterbury leaned forward in his chair and looked directly at Fergus with a look of utter malicious delight. "As for you, Kilburnie, I was fortunate enough to make the acquaintance with the captain of the *Aberdeen* while awaiting the admiral's attention. Captain Leeks is a kindly sort and in need of a first lieutenant. So, since the admiral was kind enough to assign me a new first lieutenant, I was more than happy to tell Captain Leeks of your ability to fill his vacancy. He accepted immediately and expects you today."

Waterbury folded his hands in front of him. "You don't seem all that enthusiastic, Kilburnie. I thought you would be happy to being placed on a ship named after a city in your backward country." Fergus did not rise to the bait, so Waterbury continued. "Furthermore, the *Aberdeen,* the captain assures me, is a most commodious ship and one engaged on the most important of duties."

Fergus sensed, no, he knew, that Waterbury had offered him to this Captain Leeks because Waterbury considered a post on the *Aberdeen* to be even worse than sending him ashore. The ship probably was in fact a cramped hulk assigned to a most dull duty. Again, however, he said nothing. What did it matter now?

Waterbury paused for a moment, looking back and forth between the two men. "I do believe it is time for you to go, gentlemen. You are no longer officers of this ship and I have no room for passengers." He gestured toward the door.

About ten minutes later Fergus and Browne stood by the bulwark, watching the longboat being loaded with their baggage. Browne had taken leave of his men in an informal manner; they had clustered around him as soon as he emerged on deck. Many said they looked forward to serving with him again and Fergus heard many seemingly heartfelt farewells and thought he even saw a tear glisten in the eyes of some extremely hard men.

As for Fergus, he had never really become one of these men, he thought, and so did not expect any farewells. So he was amazed when Peck, Jones, and Jamaica Sam came up and offered him their hands. "We're sorry you have to leave us so soon, sir," said Jones when it was his turn. "We know you'd have fit right in given the right . . . well, circumstances, sir."

"Aye," said Peck and Jamaica Sam in affirmative chorus.

Fergus suddenly felt his throat tighten. "Ah, thank you, I wish the circumstances had better as well, but . . . ," he shrugged and left the statement unfinished.

Waterbury's voice broke in, "Come, gentlemen, be off. We have work to do." He moved to the rail and gestured purposefully.

Browne gestured to Fergus. "You first." Fergus stepped to the ladder and saluted Waterbury as a bosun's pipe sounded his departure. Waterbury returned the salute, adding his by now familiar grin of triumph. I hope you rot in hell, too, thought Fergus as he moved to his seat in the longboat. Turning to the right he looked up to see what was keeping Browne. Browne was standing at the rail, talking quietly to the captain. Suddenly, the captain stiffened and stepped back, his face white. Browne then took his own step back, swiftly saluted, and, to the bosun pipe's squealing, slowly made his way down to the boat.

As the boat moved away from the *Swallow,* Fergus noticed that many men stood at the bulwark, some even raised a hand in a farewell wave. Yet, his eyes kept going back to the figure of the captain glaring after them. "What did you say to him, Browne?" asked Fergus quietly.

Browne kept looking back at the *Swallow* and said plainly and quite forcefully, "I told him that wherever I saw him next I would demand satisfaction and if I did not get it, everyone would soon know the coward he is." Browne glanced briefly at Fergus. "And his rank be damned." He then returned to gazing at the *Swallow.* Fergus knew enough about Browne to realize that the marine meant every word.

13
THE ABERDEEN

fter hiring a couple of old wharfingers to carry their baggage, Fergus and Browne parted ways at the dockside. "Well, Kilburnie, I wish you all the best on your new ship," said Browne cheerily as he shook Fergus's hand vigorously.

"Well, I'm sure that Captain Waterbury got me that ship because he thinks it a greater punishment than no ship at all," replied a downcast Fergus.

"Come now, cheer up, Kilburnie. We are at war and war has its own peculiar ways of dealing out fortune. Who knows? You might blunder into some Spanish treasure galleon or a rich fat prize of another sort. Then you can return to Scotland, rich and renowned, the stuff of tavern ballads."

Fergus admitted to himself that such was a chance, but a remote one at best. "I hope you're right, Browne, about good fortune, but I have my doubts right now."

Browne laughed, "Damn me, Kilburnie, but you are a typical dour Scot." He took Fergus's hand and shook it again. "There," he said, "there's some good old Irish luck for you." He then clapped Kilburnie on the shoulder. "Keep well, Kilburnie. You have the mark of a fine officer—for a sailor— and you should go far if you stay alive. So avoid tropical climates and the beds of married women, at least those with jealous husbands." With that Browne winked and strode off, followed by his hired men.

Fergus's man was enterprising enough to secure them a cart for, as he said in an almost indecipherable West Country accent, "It's a long way to where the *Aberdeen* is docked, sir."

As they made their way through the base, Fergus was so consumed with thoughts about his new ship and his future in the navy that he barely noticed the bustle of the place, the port from which Drake had sailed to defeat the Spanish Armada, the breeding ground of so many of England's great sailors.

Thoughts of disgrace and, worse still, explaining that disgrace to his family and friends crowded out the cacophonous din—the screech of sea birds, the rattle of heavily laden wagons, and the babble of hundreds of voices. So immersed was Fergus in his own thoughts that it took three tries for the man hauling his baggage to get his attention, "Sir, this here's your ship, the *Aberdeen*."

"Oh, yes," said Fergus absentmindedly and dug into his pocket for a coin to pay the man. "Just take them on board."

The man gave a smile that displayed a few gaps and shook his head slowly. "No, sir, but thankee, I served in His Majesty's Navy many years ago and know that, during a war, the navy doesn't much care what its sailors look like as long as it gets enough of them." With that he unloaded Fergus's baggage on the ground. "I'll keep watch over your things, sir, until you get your welcome."

For the first time Fergus got a look at his new home. Inwardly he groaned; she was a seventy-four-gun ship of the line, too big to be used as a frigate and too small to be anywhere but the tail of a battle line. Waterbury had chosen a floating purgatory for Fergus, for in a ship like this there was little or no chance of the action that drew the attention of their lordships and, therefore, a negligible chance for Fergus to advance. Damn!

With a heavy heart, he walked up the brow and took the salute of two sailors, a bosun's mate, and a midshipman. The midshipman was a mere sprite of a boy, about fifteen or sixteen with blond hair and fair skin; yet he seemed at home in his uniform and on a ship. "Welcome aboard His Majesty's Transport *Aberdeen*, sir. I take it, sir, that you are Lieutenant Kilburnie."

"Yes, I am," replied Fergus.

The boy smiled, "Very good, sir, the captain asked that you see him immediately upon arriving. If you'll follow Hankins here, sir," the midshipman gestured toward the bosun's mate, "he'll take you to the captain."

"Yes, certainly, but first, Mr. . . ."

"Brooke, sir."

"Yes, Mr. Brooke, please see that my baggage is stored in my stateroom and that the man who brought it gets this." Fergus produced a coin and extended it to the midshipman.

"I shall indeed, sir," the midshipman said brightly and touched his hat in salute.

As Fergus followed Hankins toward the stern, he looked about the gun deck. Something seemed strange; there weren't any guns near the bow or the stern and the ones that were clustered amidships seemed smaller than they should have been. Furthermore, a ship this size should have been teeming with men; there seemed to be hardly any on the *Aberdeen*. Had she just come out of ordinary? Was she the victim of Admiralty bungling and sat here waiting for a proper complement of men and guns? Then he remembered Brooke's greeting. "His Majesty's Transport!" Dear God, Fergus thought, a transport! This is worse than I thought. His heart sank what seemed another couple of fathoms. Yet it could be even worse, depending on what she carried as her usual cargo. Well, no time like the present to find out. "Uh, Hankins . . ."

"Yes, sir?"

"What exactly is it we transport on the *Aberdeen*?"

"Oh, all sorts of things, sir," replied the bosun's mate in a noncommittal voice.

"Ah, yes, like?"

Hankins stopped before a door. "Here we are, sir." He cracked a smile. "I suppose the captain can answer all your questions." Hankins knocked, and when he heard "Yes?" opened the door and walked in. "Our new lieutenant, Mr. Kilburnie, sir."

Fergus stepped into the room, his hat tucked under his arm. After the dark of the passageway, he blinked in the bright light that a row of windows behind the captain let stream into the cabin. "Lieutenant Fergus Kilburnie, reporting, sir," he said in his best quarterdeck voice.

Captain Leeks was an older man, in his late fifties or early sixties, with a bald head about the edges of which hung wispy white hair that tumbled down to his collar. His face was thin, as were his long-fingered hands. He was a post captain, that much Fergus could see by his uniform. Leeks waved Fergus into a chair and gestured to his steward. "Let us welcome our new lieutenant aboard properly," he said when the man came near. "A good bottle of sherry, I should think." He looked at Fergus, "You will take a glass with me, Kilburnie?"

"Of course, sir," replied Fergus. Any request to drink with a captain was in fact an order to do so. Soon the steward appeared with the bottle and poured two glasses, handing the first to the captain and the second to Fergus. He took a tentative sniff. A familiar scent filled his nostrils and he smiled.

"You seem to know this sherry, Kilburnie," said the captain.

Fergus blushed. "Yes, sir, a family I knew in Ireland drank quite a bit, as did our local vicar."

A sharp, short laugh came from Leeks. "Smuggled a fair bit of it, too, I'd wager." He lifted the glass slightly. "Well, welcome aboard, young man. The *Aberdeen* isn't much, but she's home." With that he tipped the glass up and drained it. The steward immediately came forward and refilled the glass.

"Thank you, sir," said Fergus and took a sip of the sherry, savoring its complex flavors. "I'm . . ."

Leeks paused with his glass almost at his lips and gazed intently at Fergus. "Yes?" Fergus said nothing, a bit taken aback by the interruption. "You weren't about to say you were glad to be here, were you?" said the captain in an amused tone. Fergus felt himself flush. "I thought so," chuckled Leeks. He took a sip of sherry and looked for a moment at Fergus, a trace of a smile on his lips.

"Young man, you know why you are here as do I. Your captain took a dislike to you or you took a dislike to him or perhaps both. Am I wrong?" Fergus shook his head and fidgeted with his hat a bit. Odd, but the cabin seemed to be getting warmer. "Yes, so I thought. Your captain, Waterbury, saw an opportunity to fob you off on me and pick up a new officer, one more to his liking." Leeks sipped the sherry again. "There I was, good old doddering Captain Leeks, the captain of a transport, a man obviously with little influence. Reeking of drink, too. Oh ho, Waterbury thought, Kilburnie shall either fade into obscurity or meet a deserved drowning on this man's ship."

Yes, thought Fergus, that is probably the way Waterbury thought; honestly, it was the way I thought.

Leeks cleared his throat. "Of course, although I am old and would have been put out to pasture years ago were it not for the belligerence of the French, I am not completely befuddled." He smiled, but not in a completely friendly manner. "Do I seem befuddled to you, Kilburnie?"

Fergus swallowed hard. "No, sir," he said in a tight voice. He felt a bead of sweat roll down his right temple.

"Good," he said, "it always is a great comfort to have the confidence of one's officers." He turned to the steward. "Open some windows. Mr. Kilburnie seems to be a trifle warm." He turned back to Fergus with a devilish grin on his face; he was quite plainly relishing this interview. "Now, Kilburnie, do you know why you are here, on the *Aberdeen?*"

"No sir, well, yes sir, well. . . ." What was the right answer in this case?

Leeks chuckled. "You are partly right whatever answer you give, Kilburnie. But, at its root, the reason why you are on the *Aberdeen* is luck. Had your former captain met any other officer in the admiral's anteroom you would now be walking the streets of Plymouth, wondering how quickly you might be able to find a ship or get to Dover or Portsmouth where the pickings might, just might, be better. But Providence or luck or whatever thrust me into his path."

He finished his sherry, but waved the steward away. "I knew what he was about and what he thought I was about and, honestly, Kilburnie, I didn't like the man. His first command and already he pictures himself an Admiral of the Red, pacing the deck of a hundred-gunner while a staff of flunkies flutters about loudly discussing what rank in the peerage he should receive from a grateful nation." There was no small amount of bitterness in Leeks's tone. "So, old befuddled Captain Leeks thinks perhaps Waterbury has done this young man a disservice, has failed to size him up properly."

Leeks's voice grew loud. "Quite possibly, I think, Waterbury is incapable of knowing how to help a young officer, maybe he doesn't know what makes a good officer, because it is so damned obvious that he shall never be one!" He slammed a fist on the table, causing the glass to jump. Leeks remained still for a moment, his eyes burning with a fierce light. He then slowly loosened his fist and sighed. "So, Kilburnie," he continued in a quiet tone, "I decided to take a chance on a man I had never met and bring you on board."

Fergus said nothing for a moment, somewhat shocked by the captain's outburst. Then he realized just what Captain Leeks was offering him—a second chance—and a great wave of relief swept over him, so great that he almost sobbed. "Thank you, sir," he said quietly. "I shall try not to let you down."

Leeks smiled, this time with genuine warmth. "Very good, Kilburnie," he said in a friendly tone. He then gestured for the steward. "Let's have a drink on that."

About an hour later, Fergus stood in his stateroom, marveling at its spaciousness relative to the one he had on the *Swallow,* and musing on the conversation he had had with Captain Leeks.

Fergus learned that he was to be first lieutenant again because, as a favor to some old friends, Captain Leeks had taken on two newly commissioned lieutenants. "They are nice lads, saw them both grow up. But their fathers and their uncles think they need some more—shall we say?—seasoning before they are ready for a sloop or frigate. I agreed."

The midshipmen, Fergus learned, were on board as well for the same reason: old friends, former shipmates of Captain Leeks, asked him to take these lads under his wing. "You see, Kilburnie," the captain explained, "besides her official duties, the *Aberdeen* is something of a floating schoolhouse, although there are many who would claim I am running but a hedge school. But in the main I give these lads a bit of experience so when the time comes for them to step onto another ship, they have a notion of what to expect and, perhaps more important, what is expected of them." Fergus considered that Captain Leeks and Uncle Jeris might find some grounds for disagreement on that point—he remembered Uncle Jeris's stern admonishment that taking a king's commission meant you were ready for anything the navy threw at you.

Fergus was relieved somewhat when Captain Leeks described the *Aberdeen*'s duties to him. "As you can tell just by smelling, we do not carry horses or men," the captain said. "If we did, we would never be tied up dockside." The *Aberdeen*'s task was to take supplies to ships in the Mediterranean fleet, the type of things the Royal Navy could not get or did not want to get in the Mediterranean. Masts, spars, yards, cordage, guns, shot, and other necessities for a large fleet were carried back and forth to Gibraltar and other British bases in the Mediterranean.

As to the *Aberdeen* herself, the captain explained that she had been a ship of the line, built a mere eight years before in a private dockyard. As was the case with many ships so built, the builders were trying to squeeze as much profit as possible from the contract and so did not build her "exactly to Admiralty standards." In a few years, therefore, she was declared unfit for service in the battle line. The outbreak of war prevented her from being sent to the breakers, however. Armed transports were needed and quickly; so the *Aberdeen* had landed all of her guns—except for eight twenty-four-pounders on the upper deck, two twelve-pounders on the forecastle, and two twelve-pounders on the quarterdeck—and been pressed into service.

When Fergus remarked on this relatively light armament, Captain Leeks assured him that smaller ships would leave the *Aberdeen* alone because they thought she'd "blow them to hell with a single broadside" and if she ran into larger ships "we would deserve whatever we got for blundering into an enemy battle fleet."

As far as her sailing qualities were concerned, the captain admitted, "She isn't what she once was; besides, her design is such that she's a bit broader in the beam than newer ships. Which means," he looked quizzically at Fergus, "what, Mr. Kilburnie?"

"She's a few knots slower than the newer ships, sir."

"Very good, Mr. Kilburnie," Leeks replied with apparent approval.

Fergus did not admit his misgivings about the crew—if the navy saw the *Aberdeen* as fit only to haul supplies, were her sailors castoffs from other ships, just like him?—but the captain again seemed to read his mind. "I'm sure you'll find the crew just as good as the *Swallow*'s or the *Athena*'s. Sailors don't much care about chasing the French and fighting them because, unlike officers, they have little desire for promotion and glory. As for danger, well, their lot is dangerous enough, as you know. I'm proud to say that most of the *Aberdeen*'s men have been with her for quite awhile. After all, we aren't in action, are we? The crew seems content with its lot and so whenever I need a couple of men I can count on the crew to do my recruiting." His face darkened for a moment. "I have, I must admit, received a few Lord Mayor's men in my time, however."

Fergus knew that "Lord Mayor's men" were men, usually guilty of petty crimes, who were cleaned out of London prisons and sent to the fleet. Many times they were more trouble than they were worth. "Were they satisfactory, sir?" he cautiously asked.

Leeks shrugged. "Some yes, some no. The ones who were grateful to be out of the filth of the jails usually learned to like it on the *Aberdeen*—although a few of them needed the close attention of my master and bosun to drive home the lesson." Fergus smiled at the captain's euphemism for what probably was a harsh beating or two. "Then there were some fellows who were quite unwilling to learn their new trade, to do their duty for the king."

"What happened to them?" Fergus had visions of incessant flogging.

"They were given every opportunity to desert," Leeks said flatly. The shock Fergus felt at that statement must have been obvious, for Captain Leeks had laughed out loud. "Perhaps I should explain myself before you think me mad, Kilburnie. You see, I made sure these men were allowed to get off the ship in those ports in which there was a red-hot press." He grinned hugely. "A press gang can pick a man with even a day's time on a ship out of any crowd. Those men, therefore, were swept up in a twinkling and deposited on other king's ships, probably with captains who flogged their backs raw. So, while these men and their services were lost to the *Aberdeen,* they were retained by their lordships and His Majesty. If any escaped the press, they probably ran afoul of the law again—and had their necks stretched in due time."

After that exchange, Captain Leeks took Fergus about the ship. "Not much difference from any ship, except, of course, in size." The captain was correct in a sense, except Fergus had a little difficulty getting used to the seeming abundance of space produced by gun decks entirely empty of guns and largely empty of men. When he remarked on this, the captain laughed. "As commodious as it seems now, when we're carrying a full load of supplies you'll feel cramped, I assure you."

There wasn't time to meet all of the crew, but the captain did take the time to introduce Fergus to the sailing master and the bosun. The master was a Scot, Duncan MacGregor, ironically enough from Aberdeen itself and, to Fergus's further amazement, a former fisherman. Tall, lean, and rawboned, he had a weathered face, his brown eyes peered out from under thin eyebrows, and his dark hair was a wild mass of curls, flecked with red; the overall effect was that of an English artist's impression of "a wild Highlander." To say MacGregor was taciturn would have been an understatement. He greeted Fergus with something best described as a grunt, and when the captain asked him if all was ready for sailing he answered with a gruff, "Aye, sir. She's ready." It was quite easy to imagine MacGregor meting out a rough, sea-going justice on the gun deck.

The bosun was a little pot-bellied Englishman from Newcastle named Danbury. He was balding, his black hair in full retreat from his forehead, but his eyebrows were thick and bushy and seemed to run as one above his brooding brown eyes. His eyebrows went up a bit upon hearing Fergus's voice. Fergus smiled at the reaction; like most Englishmen from the border areas Danbury probably was brought up on tales of battles against marauding bands of Scots (just as Scots from the border were weaned on stories of fights against savage bands of Englishmen).

The number of midshipmen (six in all) might have seemed a trifle large at first, but keeping in mind Leeks's desire to do numerous "favors" for old friends and shipmates, Fergus considered the number about right. The boys seemed older than the midshipmen Fergus had seen on the *Athena;* the youngest was almost fifteen and the oldest was twenty. Perhaps, Fergus thought, Leeks took them on to give them the polish and experience they needed to pass their examinations and get the ship of their dreams; perhaps, too, their families had despaired of their ever getting their commission and so dispatched them to Leeks in hopes of salvaging their naval careers.

Whatever the reason for their presence on the *Aberdeen,* the gun room seemed a happy place and the midshipmen a cheerful lot. Even more important, the oldest midshipman—the twenty-year-old Adams— did not have the hard mouth and cold eyes of a bully; instead, his demeanor was that of an older and presumably wiser elder brother. "I'll expect you to handle some of the midshipmen's education, Kilburnie," the captain advised him when they left the gunroom. "It'll be none too demanding, however; Danbury, MacGregor, and I shall continue our lessons, but you shall endeavor to drill the basics of gunnery into them."

"Why gunnery, sir?" Fergus had asked, amazed that Leeks had surmised his interests so well.

"Quite simple, Kilburnie. Your former captain said of you, to quote him exactly, 'Kilburnie styles himself a gunner.'" He shrugged. "Let us see if there is anything to that."

As for the crew, Fergus knew it would take some time to know their names, but they seemed competent enough and comfortable with their lot. As the captain had said, they had no thirst for glory or promotion— although he knew that the occasional dose of prize money was always welcome. He asked the captain about the mutiny stories, which the captain largely confirmed—although he said he doubted the French were behind them. "The men asked for more pay, not surprising as the cheeseparers at the Admiralty haven't increased the rate of pay since, oh, I believe, a Stuart was Lord High Admiral. For all the nation's alleged love for its tars, Kilburnie, the government has an odd way of showing it."

Fergus agreed with the sentiment in general, although he was certain that Uncle Jeris did not fall under the category of "cheeseparer."

That night brought a pleasant dinner and equally pleasant after-dinner conversation with the captain. The captain had a wealth of stories about the navy and not a few prominent officers were mentioned—not all of them in the best of lights—although the overall tone was good-natured. Leeks also had an excellent cellar, the contents of which—like his stock of tales—he was not reluctant to share. "Voyages back and forth to the Mediterranean have their advantages," he said, winking at Fergus. "Especially as the excise men never bother a king's ship."

Before he dismissed Fergus for the night, the captain told him that stores and supplies would be loaded the next morning. When Fergus asked what his duties were, the captain had said it would be best to watch the crew at work. "Get an eyeful before you give anyone an earful," Captain Leeks had advised him in a friendly tone. Although Fergus bristled somewhat at the suggestion—it reminded him far too much of Captain Waterbury's frequent admonishments to "watch and learn"—but a sneaking feeling that Captain Leeks probably was not in the business of giving unsound advice prevented him from objecting.

Work started early indeed the next morning. Before breakfast Danbury had men rigging lifts for hauling aboard the supplies expected that day. Not long after breakfast, wagon after wagon began rolling up to the dockside and soon the scene was a jumble of creaking lines, squealing tackles, stamping horses, cursing teamsters, sweating wharfingers, and yelling sailors. The captain was true to his word about what the *Aberdeen* carried: spars, yards, parts of masts, anchors, gun carriages, hundreds of yards of coiled lines of all thicknesses, casks of rum, barrels of beer and biscuits, shot of all sizes, and dozens of other items. From below decks, the sounds of heavy objects being manhandled into place rumbled and the decks shivered with the activity.

Danbury moved with a speed and agility that surprised Fergus; indeed, he seemed as nimble as the boys the captain had set to hauling buckets of porter to the laboring men. Danbury was everywhere, on the main deck, below decks, speaking with the captain, bellowing at the men on the lines, and cursing the teamsters as "a gang of pox-ridden lubbers."

For his part, the captain strolled slowly about, observing the work quietly, offering an occasional word of encouragement, always addressing the men by name, or conferring quietly with MacGregor or Danbury. If content with the work, he would sit in a chair brought up from his cabin and refresh himself with a glass of porter.

Dinner was piped at the usual time, as was grog, and then work began again in earnest. Fergus watched the work intently, trying to glean what he could about the crew from a relatively distant perspective. He would have felt better had he been in the hold or on the dockside, working or just doing something that would prevent him from looking like a spectator. About mid-afternoon he got his chance.

One of the midshipman scampered up to him. "Sir, the captain sends his compliments and would you please check the wagon of salt horse that is on the wharf." "Salt horse" was the navy's term for the salted beef that was often a staple on warships and almost always despised by the sailors.

"Does the captain think there is something wrong with it?"

"The captain said that the man from which it comes would steal the coins off a dead man's eyes."

Indeed, thought Fergus. From what Uncle Jeris told him and what he had seen with his own eyes, a great many of the men who supplied the navy's victuals fell into that category. After he dismissed the midshipman, he made his way off the ship and over to the wagon in question. A huge teamster stood by the wagon, puffing on a pipe, which, Fergus reasoned, he did in a vain battle against the reek of brine. Another man, slightly better dressed and slightly smaller, was adjusting the harness on one of the draught horses.

When Fergus announced he was here to examine the casks, the better-dressed man smiled brightly and said, "Certainly, sir." He then turned to the teamster. "Hey! Get a barrel down so the officer may examine it."

The man nodded and mounted the wagon; he then began to heft one of the barrels down. "Here, then," he called, "give me some help." The smaller man scowled and muttered something under his breath. The two managed to get the barrel to the ground without breaking it, although it hit the stone pavement with a heavy thud. "As you can see, sir, all nice and tightly sealed," the smaller man chirped.

"All right, then," said Fergus. "Open it."

"Of course, sir," the smaller man said easily. He nodded to the larger man, who fetched a bar and quickly pried open the top, releasing the brackish aroma of the meat. The smaller man grinned at Fergus. "There, sir, as you can see, filled to the top and the meat's still good."

"Let's see a piece then."

The man immediately reached in and grabbed a slab of the meat; the larger man put the barrel's top back on and the smaller man deposited the dripping beef on top of it. "There, sir, only the best for the navy."

Although Fergus disliked the man's obviously false earnestness, he did have to admit that the beef looked good. Still, he wanted to check again. "Bring out another piece, from closer to the bottom this time."

"Of course, sir, can't be too careful." After the large teamster pulled the lid away, the smaller man took off his coat, rolled up a shirtsleeve and plunged his arm into the barrel. He fished out another piece of meat and dropped it on top of the other one. "Again, sir, all right and proper."

Fergus bent down to look closely. Yes, it did look fine; in fact, that was the best piece of salt beef he had ever seen. He straightened up and looked at the small man, who was now beaming with satisfaction. Even the large man was grinning. It suddenly struck Fergus that something was wrong. It was a small feeling, but it was there. He shot back a wide smile at the smaller man. "That indeed does look good. You may close the barrel."

The small man picked up the beef, tossed it back in, and directed the teamster to close the barrel. He then wiped his wet hand on his breeches and began to roll down his sleeve, whistling softly.

"Now I'll pick a barrel to examine," Fergus announced in a light, friendly tone.

The man froze and then looked wide-eyed at Fergus. The teamster stopped in mid-hammering, the maul inches from the barrel's top. The smaller man shot a look at the teamster and then back at Fergus, his friendly composure recovered. "Why would you want to do that now, sir?" He wiped his brow theatrically. "It's such a hot day and we've been at it since before the cock crowed."

"As have the men of this ship and all of the honest laboring men on the docks," Fergus said flatly. "I want to see another barrel. Now."

The man gave a peevish look and the friendliness evaporated. "Well, then, you take it down yourself. I'm not one of your damned tars."

Fergus stepped close to the man and smiled. "Well, now, you seem like a strong, spry man, as does this man here." He gestured to the teamster. "My captain might take a long look at you and your friend and decide that you are just the men we need on our crew—especially for our long voyage in the West Indies."

The man gulped and Fergus saw the teamster's eyes go wide. Both men knew he could impress them in a moment and, being from a port town, they knew, by way of story, that the West Indies were a dreaded destination where sailors died in droves from deadly fevers.

The man's shoulders sagged. "All right then," he said resignedly, shaking his head. "Which one?"

Walking around the wagon, Fergus's eye fell on a barrel, in the third row from the top, that was dripping brine. He pointed to it. "This one, here." The two men groaned in anticipation of the heavy lifting they would have to do, but the threat of impressment was enough to overcome any objections they had.

Eventually, amidst muttered curses and dirty looks, the barrel was lowered to the ground. It appeared old, but there was nothing wrong with that; barrels were used over and over again. Yet there was a layer of dried salt near the seams and brine dripped freely from the top and bottom. Fergus gestured to the teamster. "Open it," he ordered. The man hesitated. "Open it, I said," Fergus barked. The man shrugged and pried the top open. As soon as it was open, an extremely foul odor came out; the meat inside was obviously putrid. "Only the best for the navy, eh?" Fergus snapped at the small man who shrank back against the wagon. Not waiting for a response, he strode over to one of the barrels that had been hauled down earlier. He shook it; it seemed quite light. He stabbed a finger at the top. "This one, too."

The teamster did as he was told, quickly this time. This time a cloud of flies came out along with the strong smell of rotten meat. Peering into the barrel, Fergus could see that most of the brine was gone, exposing the meat, over which now crawled hundreds of flies and maggots. He rounded on the small man, his fists clenched. "You thieving bastard!" he hissed. "I'll see you hanged for this."

Amazingly, the man gave a smile. "Now, sir," he said smoothly, reaching into his pocket and drawing near, "before you make a mistake, sir." Something was pressed into Fergus's hand. "There, now, sir." Fergus looked down at his hand; in it was a small leather bag. He squeezed it and felt coins through the leather. Stunned by this attempt to bribe him, he looked back up at the small man in amazement. The man winked. "All's well that ends well, eh?"

Fergus clenched his fist around the bag, drew back, and struck the man in the face as hard as he could. The man gave a strangled cry and dropped to the ground like a sack of meal. He then scrambled back, holding his hands to his face, blood streaming from his nose.

Fergus stepped up to the first barrel and gave it a vicious kick; the putrid meat and brine spilled out, swamping the small man and causing the teamster to jump back in disgust. "Take this garbage," Fergus pointed at the man on the ground, "and that garbage—and get out of my sight." He then turned and marched over to the barrel that contained equal parts of rotted beef, brine, maggots, and flies. He opened the bag and held it over the barrel. The eyes of the teamster and the small man looked pleadingly at him. Fergus smiled cruelly and upended the bag. The coins tumbled in and disappeared into the fetid morass. He tossed the bag at the teamster and said cheerfully. "All's well that end's well, eh?" He then turned and stalked back toward the ship.

As he did, he became conscious of dozens of eyes on him. He glanced about and saw that the little comedy he had just played with the two men had become the center of attention on the *Aberdeen* and on the dock. Men had stopped working and watched it unfold. Now they were staring at him; he flushed in embarrassment. Someone began to laugh and the laughter began to spread. Certain he was the center of this humor, he felt his cheeks go a deeper red and looked around in order to find the swiftest way back onto the ship. Then he noticed that everybody was looking not in his direction, but in that of the wagon. He turned about and saw an amazing tableau. The small man, soaked in rancid brine, was loudly urging the teamster to fish about in the barrel in which Fergus had dropped the bribe. The teamster stood with his arms crossed, resolutely refusing to do so.

Captain Leeks was in exceptionally good humor when Fergus reported and gave him his account of the events. "Damn me, Kilburnie, if you don't like salt horse, you just should have said so!" With that, he clapped Fergus on the back and called to his steward for wine. "We must toast such a feat for in rejecting that beef you probably saved the lives of hundreds of Britons. Such a service is demanding of an immediate promotion to admiral, wouldn't you say?"

Fergus smiled sheepishly. "Well, sir, I don't know about the promotion. But I would be willing to wager that whoever sold that beef to the navy has killed more men than the French."

The captain laughed uproariously. "Undoubtedly, Kilburnie! Undoubtedly!" He paused while the steward brought the wine up to the captain and poured two glasses. The captain took one and thrust it into Fergus's hand and took one for himself. Leeks raised his glass. "To you, Kilburnie. A worthy addition to the *Aberdeen:* an honest man who can hit hard and straight."

The work of loading was completed by the light provided by lanterns, the moon, and the stars. "No time like the present," said Captain Leeks sternly when Fergus asked if work should continue. "Besides, I wish to be off with tomorrow afternoon's ebb."

In port the midshipmen were entrusted with the watch, and so Fergus was able to sleep uninterrupted. Alas, the silence of his stateroom became almost as oppressive as the din of the day's work and for what seemed to be hours he swung slowly in his cot, thinking about his lot in the navy. For the first time in many months his thoughts drifted to Shannon.

Shannon. Her face, her hair, her eyes—everything came back to him clearly. He sighed loudly as he thought of that day in the churchyard. Perhaps he would have been shot dead or run through by her father had he pursued matters, but, perhaps, he mused, I should have tried. Then, he reproached himself for thinking of her for it had been . . . what now? . . . five years (that long?) since he had left Ireland. Married to a big lord with an Irish title and a English one in the offing, she probably had given birth to a few children. If she was still alive—and childbirth took ladies as well as the low-born—she would be busy being a lady of grand estates and, undoubtedly, a huge townhouse in Dublin or London without the time to dwell on thoughts of a boy she had known in Ireland.

The idea of finding a girl and becoming married now teased him. He laughed at the thought. On the lower deck marriage was out of the question (unless you counted those women who would become your "wife" for whatever time your ship was in port). For officers, although there was frolicking with doxies for those who didn't mind bought women—and plenty of officers didn't—there was barely enough time ashore to find a decent dinner and bed, let alone find a woman suitable for marriage and court her.

He would have to wait. Until when? When the war was over? Already this conflict was in its fifth year with no signs of stopping. And when the war was over, there was a very real chance that he would be sent ashore as a lieutenant on half-pay. Not exactly a good prospect for a girl of marriageable age and decent fortunes. Maybe he would have to wait until he was retired—because of age, wounds, or exhaustion. With a fair amount of prize money it was possible to live a comfortable retirement. Then he smiled as he remembered the plans of the men of the *Swallow,* simple, honest men looking to live simple, honest lives after the navy. Well, that is me exactly, he thought. I have no dreams of an admiral's barge, although a post captain's gig would not be unwelcome.

But that was a long way off. For now, he began to recall the tales that men on the *Athena* had told of the women of Spain and Italy. Maybe he could find some "diversion" in Gibraltar or on Minorca? He sighed contentedly and drifted off to sleep, his mind still conjuring up images of dark-eyed girls with raven-colored hair and flashing white teeth.

The next morning one of the ship's boys bustled into his stateroom, announcing loudly that he would fetch hot water for shaving. He grabbed the pitcher and set off. Fergus struggled out of his cot and stretched. When his head didn't strike anything, he thought for a moment that perhaps life on a ship of the line would not be so bad after all—if you could stand the boredom. A short knock came at the door, and before Fergus could answer the boy came in with the pitcher, announcing, again in a loud voice, that he had indeed brought hot water for Fergus.

"You don't have to shout," Fergus said as the boy put the pitcher down. "I'm not in the maintop; I'm only a few feet away from you."

"Mr. MacGregor said you was a gunner," replied the boy matter of factly.

"What's that have to do with anything?" asked Fergus sharply. Truly, the *Aberdeen* was becoming a more and more eccentric place.

"Well, he said that all the gunners he knows is deaf; so he said you had better shout if Mr. Kilburnie was to hear you!" The boy's voice increased in volume as he spoke.

"I can hear just fine!" Fergus yelled back. Then he shut his mouth tightly as he realized what he had just done. "Get out, you rogue!" he snapped. A confused look on his face, the boy made a hasty exit. Now, Fergus fumed, he probably thinks that all gunners are mad as well as deaf.

After shaving and dressing, he went to the wardroom, a brightly painted cheery place, for his breakfast.

"Good morning, Kilburnie!" boomed Danbury.

"Oh, God, not you, too!" Fergus exclaimed. "I'm not deaf!"

"Nonsense," replied Danbury in a loud voice. "All gunners are deaf!"

Fergus shook his head in exasperation and attended to his breakfast.

The door opened and MacGregor came in and plopped down into his seat. He shook his head and muttered something about the weather.

"What? Did you say something, MacGregor?" asked Fergus.

"Kilburnie asked a question," Danbury observed in a loud voice.

"Damn ye, but there's no need to rant so," barked MacGregor. "I'm not deaf; you daft bugger. Kilburnie is!"

"I am *not* deaf!" shouted Fergus at the two men.

"Nonsense!" they chorused. "All gunners are deaf!"

Fergus leaped to his feet and shot a finger at the two men. "Now, you see here, you. . . ." He stopped in mid-sentence as he noticed that the two men were barely concealing laughter. "Oh, by God, you bastards. . . ." MacGregor and Danbury now let go and laughed hugely. Fergus sat down, his face beet-red. He had been hooked expertly and landed in style.

"Come now, Kilburnie," said Danbury as soon as he had regained control of himself. "You must admit that was done well."

Fergus's anger dissipated almost immediately when he realized the teasing was in good fun. "I am assuming you and MacGregor frequent more than a few chalk streams."

"Ah, no," responded MacGregor. "Salmon's my fish." His face pulled together in a wry grin. "Good Scottish salmon."

"Yes," replied Fergus, "I know the type you like—fresh caught lieutenant!" The two mates laughed.

"Now," said Danbury, raising a finger in warning. "What we did is nothing compared to the surgeon."

"The surgeon? I didn't know we had one."

"Oh, yes, Chandler is his name. A great lumbering oaf of a man with hands like hams and marlinspikes for fingers," Danbury said. "Does a passable job setting limbs, though." MacGregor nodded in agreement. "He is a great one for the jokes, though."

"Aye," said MacGregor, reverting to his usual taciturn self.

"I'll watch myself around him then," said Fergus with great firmness.

Danbury smiled. "See that you do. He'll see you as a challenge."

After quarters the crew busied themselves by seeing that everything was right and ready for putting to sea. Danbury checked lines and yards and MacGregor turned a keen eye to just about every part of the ship. One quartermaster's mate was put to work polishing the binnacle to a bright shine; another was making the wheel glow. "Even a dowager duchess attends to her looks," Captain Leeks had said when ordering the work performed.

At about ten o'clock, three officers appeared at the brow, an older rotund man in a somewhat disreputable coat of a military cut and two young lieutenants in what looked like new uniforms. The carriage in which they had arrived was piled high with luggage of all sorts and behind it was a small wagon on which rested crates and barrels of various sizes, but which all bore the marks of distillers, brews, and wine merchants. At the sight of these men, Captain Leeks rubbed his hands together gleefully. "Ah, excellent, I see Chandler has made the proper stops."

"What are those, sir?" asked Fergus.

"He has made sure my lieutenants have come to me on the day of the ship's sailing and that we shall not go thirsty on our long voyage." Before Fergus could ask which the captain would have been content to sail without, Captain Leeks gestured toward the brow. "Go and greet your new colleagues, Kilburnie. The *Aberdeen* is a friendly ship. I shall await their respectful approach in stately splendor."

Fergus went to the brow as ordered and greeted the three men. The lieutenants—Starr, a sandy-haired thin fellow with bright blue eyes, and Worthington, a plump chap with large, soft brown eyes and dark hair—were visibly nervous when they met Fergus, their first lieutenant (if they only knew, he thought). Chandler was all bonhomie and slaps on the back and his heavy ruddy face lit up when he saw that he had another potential victim for his humor. "Ah, Kilburnie, is it?" he said as he shook Fergus's hand, his eyes sizing the Scotsman up as a cat would a mouse. "Very good," he clucked.

Fergus informed the lieutenants that the captain awaited them and pointed them in Leeks's direction. The two men walked off in some distress.

Chandler had men haul the lieutenants' baggage up the brow and down to their staterooms and was paying the coachman. Danbury had a sling rigged and some men trotted down to the wagon and began to load the precious cargo into a net. He yelled, "Any of your men break so much as one bottle and I'll have their backs flogged raw!"

Chandler turned to Fergus. "So, Kilburnie, welcome to our ship. I must question, however, the reason you ended up here, for almost no officer comes aboard such a ship by choice." Fergus cleared his throat to respond, but Chandler held up a hand. "No, please, I can tell by your face that I have brought up a painful episode. And me, a surgeon. What is it the Greeks say, 'First do no harm'?" He bowed slightly. "I take your leave, Kilburnie. I must confer with the captain about acquiring some lemons when we reach Gibraltar." He touched his hat and moved back toward the quarterdeck.

As the captain wished, the *Aberdeen* sailed from Plymouth with the ebb of the tide and made her way out toward the Atlantic—and out of the reach, it was hoped, of marauding French privateers. After a few days, the *Aberdeen* settled into the routine of a ship at sea and Fergus grew accustomed to her peculiar rhythms. As heavily laden as she was, her speed was slow, although Captain Leeks preferred to say "she has a regal tread" whenever Fergus showed him the distance covered each day. The crew seemed content and the young lieutenants were eager to learn and to please (just like me, Fergus thought). Soon the wardroom had a happy atmosphere, made almost farcical at times by Chandler's incessant jokes, practical and otherwise. One day everyone's dinner had a cloying sweetness to it and the cook was at a loss to explain why. MacGregor was ready to thrash the man until Lieutenant Worthington tasted the contents of the salt cellar—sugar. In the face of such evidence, Chandler admitted he was the culprit.

The training of the midshipmen at the guns took up a large part of Fergus's time. Gunnery, Fergus had to admit, was nothing close to the science and art that navigation was. It was more a matter of having a good eye and, of course, speed. In a ship-to-ship fight an opponent had to be pounded into submission and, since his purpose was the same, the victor usually was the ship that fired faster. So, the gun crew had to work like a well-oiled machine, the men doing their tasks instinctively, intuitively, and quickly.

For the midshipmen's training, therefore, he had them serve at different positions at a gun. When they had mastered the tasks associated with them, he changed their positions again. Fergus didn't use any powder until he thought they were ready to take any position at the gun. Captain Leeks then allowed Fergus to fire some charges and, finally, a couple of balls at a floating barrel. The next drill at the gun, Fergus received the captain's permission to let the midshipmen fire the gun as they would during a fight—fifteen rounds fired as quickly as they could be at a floating target. At the end of the exercise, the midshipmen were exhausted and begrimed with smoke, but the target was battered to matchsticks, and the crew, who had gathered to witness the practice, cheered heartily.

That night Fergus told the captain that he didn't think that more training on the guns would be of much use to the midshipmen. "There is not much more I can teach them about gunnery, sir. They can serve at all positions and fire and reload and fire again quickly. These men shall be officers, not members of a gun crew. I cannot see the merit in any more of this type of work."

"You surprise me, Kilburnie," the captain said after a moment of thought. "There is, of course, the practical side to what you have them do. On their next ships, these men shall be able to train raw men into an efficient gun crew and run a battery well, careful to pick out the small mistakes that can mean the difference between victory and defeat. Such abilities, I think, shall be prized by any captain." He took a sip of sherry. "But they are gaining much more than mere knowledge of gunnery: they are gaining confidence in their abilities. You see, these lads were sent to me because they lacked something, call it the spirit, the fire, needed in an officer. Why any one of them lacked it, I can't tell. Perhaps, some are by nature shy; others may come into their own later in life than others. Yet, in our navy, well, let me say that it does seem odd—has for some time, in fact—that the determination of a man's worth is all too often made when he is a mere boy. But the present system has served the navy well and as some learned man once said, 'If it is not necessary to change, it is necessary not to change.'" He shrugged. "Still, in my waning years, I do a little to help those the Service might currently overlook." Leeks smiled. "I seem to have rambled again, Kilburnie, but that is one of the privileges of a captain, eh? I hope the point I was making about why the gunnery practice is important was clear."

"Yes, sir, quite clear." And, in fact, it was.

On the fifteenth day of the voyage, seabirds began to circle overhead and some of the older men swore they could smell land. Fergus felt a little wrench for he knew that miles over the horizon to the port was Cape St. Vincent and the waters where Captain Burbage had died and the *Athena* received her brutal pounding at the hands of the Spanish. Damn, it was little more than a year ago, but it felt like a lifetime to him. He smiled ruefully as he asked himself if his fortunes had indeed improved in that time. Well, I do have the king's commission, at least.

The next morning, the southern coast of Spain hove into view and by sunset the tip of the Rock of Gibraltar poked over the horizon. Just before sunset of the next day, the *Aberdeen* dropped anchor in the large and crowded harbor. Captain Leeks was rowed ashore in his gig almost immediately. A few hours later, he returned, clutching two bottles in one hand and a sheaf of papers in the other.

Anxious to learn the content of the papers Fergus met Captain Leeks at the brow. Leeks first held up the bottles. "Here, Kilburnie, take one of these for the wardroom. It's good French brandy." Fergus took the bottle, murmured his thanks but, as he did, looked purposefully at the papers in Leeks's other hand. The captain chuckled. "My, Kilburnie, you are straining at the traces like a hound. Remember, my boy, the *Aberdeen* is a transport, not a thirty-six-gun frigate." He smiled benevolently. "Well, I know what is in the orders. So come to my cabin and we'll sample my bottle of brandy while I tell you about them."

A few minutes later the captain and Fergus were seated, glasses of brandy in their hands. The captain took a large swallow and smiled widely. "Ah, wonderful stuff, isn't it, Kilburnie?"

Fergus had taken only a small sip, but had to admit it was good, quite unlike the raw whiskey he had drunk in Ireland and Scotland. "Yes, sir, quite good."

Leeks nodded in approval, took another swallow, and opened the sealed envelope. After a moment of reading he grunted and flicked the paper toward Fergus. "As you shall soon see, Kilburnie, the admiral has given us orders that correspond almost exactly with what he told me over a couple of glasses of his excellent brandy. No mean feat, I assure you." Leeks folded his hands over his stomach and sighed. "After we unload some supplies that are needed by some of the ships here, we are to wait here until we can rendezvous with a rather powerful squadron of ships that are being detached from Lord St. Vincent's fleet. We shall travel in their company—as long as we can, that is—until we meet Rear Admiral Nelson's squadron." Another swallow of brandy. Leeks then leaned forward. "The admiral tells me that some peacock of a French general is rumored to be sailing from Toulon, though where is unknown. Some say Naples; others to capture Lisbon and deny Lord St. Vincent a base from which blockade the Spanish at Cadiz— and then on to Ireland." He shook his head in amazement. "Really, these rumors! Anyway, Nelson is set to see what the French are up to; I can't see him doing more than that with three seventy-fours and a few frigates. So their lordships decided it might be better to stop the French rather than just follow them; hence, this squadron is to be dispatched."

Fergus's ears pricked up when he heard a familiar name. "Is that the same Nelson who commanded the *Excellent* at last year's battle? I didn't know he had been promoted."

Captain Leeks nodded, "The very same Nelson. Losing an arm didn't slow him down at all." He rubbed his chin thoughtfully. "Nelson's an odd sort of fellow, I'm told. Some have told me he has a woman's vanity and that to many upon meeting him he seems a complete fool. Still, there are others who say he is possessed of a keen intelligence and no little charm, although perhaps that is the wrong word. Whatever he is truly like, there is no discounting his bravery or his dash. He does seem to like to run right at the Frogs and the Dons whenever he meets them."

"After the battle, I met one man who was quite taken with Nelson—in a way I have never seen before," Fergus recalled.

"Well, there are many men who change in temper whenever they catch a whiff of gunpowder; some for the better, some of the worse. Maybe Nelson is one of those who changes for the better."

A few weeks later the ships detached from Lord St. Vincent's fleet made their appearance and for Fergus it was none too soon. Gibraltar was an exotic place; many of the women—the Spanish ones, at least—were all that he had dreamed of and, although he could not speak a word of Spanish, things went well enough.

Carlita, however, did speak excellent English and had a view of love and romance decidedly different from what he had encountered in Britain or Ireland. They met while Fergus was walking one day in town and had stopped into a dressmaking shop. He had done so because Captain Leeks recommended that he buy lace for his mother, but all thoughts of his family in Scotland were driven from his mind at the sight of Carlita. He thought she was one of the seamstresses, but later discovered she owned the shop and lived upstairs. Two days later he was sharing her bed and did so for the next seven nights. It all had to end, he knew, but with the sharp light of the Spanish sun, the deep blue of the Mediterranean, and the scent of flowers, time seemed to pass slowly and gloriously. Captain Leeks had been quite understanding when he asked for a few days off the ship. "By all means, Kilburnie. Enjoy yourself—that is, as much as your Scotch conscience shall let you. Things are different in this part of the world; you should get to know how."

The morning of the day before the *Aberdeen* had to leave, he and Carlita were lying together, listening to the church bells calling the faithful to Mass or Morning Prayer. Fergus was trying to decide just what to tell this beautiful, passionate woman about his leaving when she gave a sigh and embraced him. "I love you British sailors," she said. "We enjoy ourselves for a week or two—and then you leave before you bore me with talk of your horses, your dogs, your shooting, and your wives." She laughed, "So much better than the goddamned soldiers!"

"What if I come back to Gibraltar and want to see you again?" Fergus asked playfully. "Or want to marry you and take you back to Scotland?" With other women he never would have dared speak of marriage—lest they take it seriously—but somehow he knew Carlita would take the mention as he meant it—in jest.

She laughed again, light and lilting, her eyes bright. "Oh, you are mad, Fergus. I could never live in Scotland. Too cold and too wet. Besides, who would keep me company when you were at sea?"

"By 'keeping you company' you mean . . . ?" asked Fergus. Even after a week of her intense passion he could still be surprised by her frankness.

"Exactly! I could not abide one of your vicars, all somber and prayerful. And were I to take up with a neighbor of yours, you soon would have to kill him in a duel. Your Celtic honor would demand it!"

If you were my wife, Fergus thought, I'd be mad to take a mistress. Or, at least, too tired. "How do you know so much about Celtic honor? This is Spain, not Scotland."

"Fergus, many of the Irish—how do you call them? 'the Wild Geese'— came to Spain to live. Even some of your Scotsmen who could not live under your . . . ah, what do you call. . . ."

"The Kirk?"

"Yes, your kirk." She smiled slyly, "And your German king." She giggled as Fergus shot her a cross look. "Besides their loyalty to the faith and their king, they also brought their Irish and Scottish ways." She chuckled. "And that includes fighting for their precious honor."

"Well," said Fergus defensively, "the Spanish are known for their pride as well."

"Ha! Why do you think these Irish and Scots prospered in Spain? The only thing different was the language and the weather!"

"You seem to know a lot about the Irish, Carlita. How do you come by the knowledge?"

She looked into his eyes. "My mother's father was an Irish soldier who first served a Stuart and then came to Spain to offer his sword to a Catholic prince, rather than your Protestant Dutch king." She kissed him lightly. "So I know something of this Celtic honor."

Damn, thought Fergus, even in Spain I cannot escape the Irish. "You haven't answered my first question," he teased.

She kissed him again. "I would see you again, Fergus, and we might— how do you English say it?—'have a gallop,' too. That is, if I have a lover then. If not, well, you are always welcome to stay, but not too long." It was a view of sexual relations that the Kirk in Scotland would consider purely diabolical. Of course, the past week's activities, especially in a room deco-rated with what Fergus knew to be graven images favored by Papists—a crucifix and a small statuette of Mary—would be considered sufficient by some in the Kirk to consign him to Hell's fires. But, Fergus thought hap-pily, I'm not in Scotland.

Carlita noticed the smile and gave a mock pout. "See? You are already thinking about your wife. Soon, you shall speak of her—and I shall be bored."

Fergus again protested that he was not married. She replied by kissing him deeply. When he tried to hold her tighter, she wriggled from his grasp and climbed out of bed. Naked, she walked to the shuttered window and peered out. She then turned back to face him. "You are leaving soon, yes?" Fergus paused for a moment and then nodded. "Tomorrow," he responded quietly.

Carlita grinned. "I knew it! I could read it in your eyes last night." She walked over to a wardrobe, opened it, and began to take out clothes. "I must go then."

"Why? Where are you going?" Fergus asked incredulously as she dressed quickly. Usually, they—well, she had said it—"had a gallop" in the morning.

She smiled broadly. "I am not off to see a French spy and tell him of your plans. The whole town knows of them by now, anyway." She had finished dressing and now went to a small table over which was a tiny mirror and began to brush her hair. "I have much more important things to do." Her tone was now somewhat serious.

"Business?" asked Fergus, somewhat surprised by her shift in tone.

She arranged her hair and fetched a shawl from a chair. She then opened the drawer of the small table and pulled out what looked like a long necklace of silver beads with a cross dangling from it. From Ireland, Fergus knew it was the rosary, what was known as "the beads"—another Popish device he had been warned about as a child. "Yes, Fergus, you could call it that." She came over to the bed, leaned down and kissed him lightly on the lips. "I need to hear Mass and then say a rosary and light a candle for you."

She brushed his cheeks with the back of her hand and let her fingertips linger on his lips. "Now, be gone, my British sailor, when I return. I find long goodbyes as boring as long talks about dogs and shooting." A kiss on his forehead. "Vaya con Dios," she said huskily. She must have caught his puzzled look for she laughed brightly again. "Go with God, you fool." Shaking her head, she walked to the door, turned and blew him a kiss. He blinked and she was gone, her footsteps dulcet on the stairs.

Fergus stayed in bed for a while, but how long exactly he did not know—nor did he care to know. He just lay there and listened to the sounds of the day—the birds' merry songs, the people milling about on the street—and thought of Carlita. No, it wasn't love, he chided himself, but yet there was something about her, a spark—damn me, he thought, remembering their nights and mornings together, a raging inferno at times—she carried that he had never encountered before in a woman, even in Shannon.

He sat up and let his legs dangle over the side of the bed for a moment. He then rose and walked across the floor to the chair over which he had laid his clothes. After throwing some water on his face, he shaved quickly in the tepid water and then pulled on his uniform. He peered in the mirror and ran his fingers through his hair, hoping he looked presentable, not like a man who had just spent a week in a house in Gibraltar in the arms of a beautiful woman. He smiled back at his image. "So what if I did?" he said aloud and laughed when he caught himself.

Although Carlita did not like long goodbyes, he still wanted to write a note; however, a search of the room revealed no paper. Fergus sighed and sat down on the bed. Well, perhaps he could send a note from the ship. He looked about the room one more time, gathered the few things he had brought, and walked to the door. Before he shut the door, he turned back to look one more time and sighed. "Go with God," he whispered to the empty room and, closing the door, began the long trip back to the *Aberdeen*.

14
UNDER ADMIRAL NELSON

he next morning the *Aberdeen* joined the procession of ships that sailed off to join Nelson's relatively small force. Captain Leeks and Fergus stood by the binnacle and discussed the ships around them.

"A fine force," said Captain Leeks firmly as he swept the horizon with his arm. "Ten line-of-battle ships, seventy-fours, and a few frigates. All good ships captained by good men. Unless we run afoul of the entire French fleet we'll have a fighting chance."

"More than that, I think, sir," answered Fergus. "On the *Athena* I saw some of these ships in action." He pointed at the ship in the van. "Captain Troubridge and the *Culloden*. Damn me, sir, seeing her go after the Dons was a sight to behold—and one I hope I never forget."

"I know what you mean, Kilburnie," said the captain. "I was with the fleet at the Battle of the Saintes." Unconsciously, he rolled up on the balls of his feet and smiled. "I can still see it now. Dozens of ships, hundreds of sails, and thousands of guns. What a spectacle! Then, a French four-decker, the *Villa de Paris,* I recall, blew up. Gad, I'll not soon forget that day."

Fergus turned back and looked at the other men-of-war about the *Aberdeen.* He wondered if the Spanish sailors at the Cape St. Vincent battle and the

French matelots at that battle in the Caribbean fight during the American war wanted to forget those days; or was the impression of such a battle—any battle—such that it would never leave their memories? Unbidden, the image of the Spanish ships' gunports snapping open came to him and filled him with a cold dread. He then remembered Captain Burbage's sightless eyes and the man screaming on the surgeon's table on the orlop deck. Involuntarily, he sucked his breath in sharply. He wouldn't soon forget that day.

"Eh, you say something, Kilburnie?" asked the captain.

"No, sir, just recalling an . . . ah . . . event."

The captain grinned and rubbed his hands together. "Ah, that Spanish girl, I'd wager."

Fergus merely smiled. Just the mention of Carlita pushed the ghastly images of war out of his mind and replaced it with the magnificent memory of Carlita. For a moment he thought he could smell the lavender scent she wore—and made, he had discovered—and hear her effervescent laughter.

"Kilburnie," the captain said cheerily. "Don't think of her too much. We still have a ship to run and I don't fancy doing all the work."

"Yes, sir," Fergus replied, but not thinking of Carlita would be a difficult— if not impossible—task.

It was one thing for their lordships to gather a force of ships and send it off to help Nelson. It was quite another for that force to find the man they were to support. A small ship, the *Mutine,* had been sent to find Nelson and bring him word of the reinforcement. The fleet groped through the Mediterranean toward Toulon, hoping that Nelson was not conducting a close blockade with the few ships he had or that he had not blundered into the entire French fleet and been crushed in an uneven fight. It was with great relief, therefore, that the force rendezvoused with Nelson on June 7 off Toulon.

"Splendid. Now, we'll see some action," declared Chandler that night at dinner. "This Nelson is a fire-eater." Worthington and Starr seemed delighted at the prospect of crossing swords with the French, as did Danbury and MacGregor. Captain Leeks, however, took care to dampen their enthusiasms. "Let's not have any dreaming about prize money and promotions, gentlemen. Please remember the *Aberdeen* is an armed transport and, as such, does not belong in the line of battle."

"I'll be sure to tell that to the captain of a French three-decker when he decides to fire a broadside at us," replied Chandler sardonically.

Leeks nodded. "Well, that is a chance we take looking the way we do, but I'm sure Kilburnie here and his midshipmen will be able to give a good account of themselves on the guns." There were chuckles around the table. The captain raised a cautionary finger. "Furthermore, our good surgeon seems to have forgotten one important thing when it comes to engaging the enemy. Anyone care to venture a guess as to what it is?"

The men about the table looked at each other warily and then back to the captain. It was Starr who piped up first. "Sir, I believe I know the answer."

"Yes, Mr. Starr," said the captain, "please illuminate us."

"Well, sir, don't we have to find him first?"

Captain Leeks smiled broadly. "Ah, Mr. Starr has got it on the first try."

Chandler cleared his throat and lifted his glass in toast. "My dear Mr. Starr, you are indeed correct."

A few days later, the *Aberdeen* found Nelson in his flagship *Vanguard* anchored in the lee of San Pietro. As they drew near, Fergus was astounded by the appearance of the flagship. Two masts were completely gone, and others were heavily damaged. Fergus picked up a long glass and examined the ship carefully, wondering what he should do. Then he noticed a flurry of activity on the flagship's upper decks. They were lowering a boat.

The boat pulled to the ship's ladder, took aboard an officer, and headed for the *Aberdeen.* A senior officer came aboard. He introduced himself as the first lieutenant of the *Vanguard.* "I hope you have what we need," he said. "If you don't, we may have to bring you alongside and dismantle your masts."

"We have a big cargo of mast parts, spars, and rigging, and sails. From what I can see from here, you can use most of them," Captain Leeks said.

Fergus interrupted. "What happened to you?" he asked. "You look like you've been in battle."

The officer whistled soundlessly. "The biggest and longest storm I've ever been in. It came on us suddenly before we could get the sails in and the upper masts down. You see what happened. If the *Alexander* hadn't been able to tow us, we'd still be there. Several other ships were badly damaged, but they were able to repair themselves."

"What can we do?" Leeks asked.

"Come right alongside to starboard. The *Alexander* is on the other side. We can rig a series of lifts from her masts and yours and step the lower masts directly into the flagship. The upper sections of the masts are lighter and should be easier to hoist aboard and rig."

After they were alongside, Fergus marveled at the skill of the boatswains and their mates as they swarmed aloft, hauling after them large lines and tackles. The skilled petty officers, augmented by several dozen seamen, worked every day from dawn until it was too dark to go aloft.

On the fourth day, as the job was being finished, a dark, lean officer leaned over the side of the flagship and spoke to Fergus. "Aren't you Lieutenant Kilburnie, recently of the *Athena*?"

Fergus closed his slightly opened mouth as he recognized Admiral Nelson. "Ah, yes, sir."

"I am honored to meet you. The *Athena* did a superb job, and Admiral Jervis was very appreciative of it. I understand you suffered for it and lost your captain."

"Thank you, sir."

"Tell your captain to get under way when I do and follow me east. Stay within signal distance, but don't get in the way, and stay to leeward of us if we run into the French fleet. Good luck."

The slim figure disappeared, and Fergus went below to inform the captain of their orders.

For the next seven weeks, Nelson, flying his flag in HMS *Vanguard,* led his ships on a merry chase across the Mediterranean in search of the French. A ship from Tunis told of a French fleet bound toward Sicily. While that meant that the rumors about Ireland and Portugal probably were untrue, it did not make the task of guessing where the French were heading all that much easier. Fearing a French invasion of the Kingdom of Two Sicilies, the fleet had run as quickly as possible to that country's capital, Naples, and anchored outside of the Bay of Naples on June 17. There were no French ships or armies to be found.

Nelson sent Captain Thomas Hardy ashore to glean any information from the British ambassador, Sir William Hamilton, secure supplies and, most important, to try to secure the services of the Neapolitan navy's frigates for scouting and reconnaissance. Supplies were gladly given, but the British were denied use of the frigates and Captain Hardy received precious little information from Sir William—beyond that the French were headed for Malta. Almost immediately the fleet sailed toward the island that had long been a Christian fortress in an Ottoman sea. On the twenty-second, a brig was encountered and the fleet learned that Malta had indeed been captured by the French. As Nelson mulled this news over, some sails were sighted to the southeast and some ships dispatched to discern their identity. But no sooner were they on their way when Nelson recalled them and ordered a new course to be set—for Egypt.

Again, because of the want of frigates, Captain Hardy and the *Mutine* were sent racing ahead of the main fleet. In this case his task was to see if the French had made their appearance in Egypt.

The other ships and the *Aberdeen* made their way as best they could, which to Fergus's surprise was fairly quickly. Captain Leeks, on the other hand, was not at all surprised. "These ships have crack crews, Kilburnie, and fine men in command. Furthermore, the knowledge of a French fleet somewhere out there," he swept his hand over the horizon, "is enough to make any man get a few extra knots out of the slowest ship."

"I truly expected, sir, that we would be told to wait somewhere in Sicily or wherever."

Leeks shook his head. "Nelson doesn't know where the French are—no one does, except the French themselves. So he needs to keep us close in case we run into any heavy weather," he paused meaningfully, "or heavy fighting."

And close to Nelson was how the *Aberdeen* spent the next few weeks as Nelson led his force in search of the French. First, the ships swept up by Palestine and Syria, then by Cyprus and the Turkish coast. After that, they beat back to Sicily—Syracuse, to be precise—for water and another peek around the southern coast of Italy, just in case. On July 23, they sailed away from Sicily, bound for the Greek islands.

When at supper the night they left Sicily, Fergus wondered aloud why a search was mounted in this direction. It was Chandler who shrugged his shoulders and said, "Well, it is the one place in this godforsaken ocean we have not yet looked."

"Damn me," Fergus protested, "the French could be halfway to Ireland by now or even have taken Lisbon."

Chandler shook his head. "No, we probably would have heard some news if the French had been by this way again. My guess is they are back at Malta trying to decide what to do next." The other men displayed agreement with silent nods.

So the fleet sailed toward the Greek islands under a bright sun and on seas of an amazing blue. The crew began to grumble about this wild-goose chase about the Mediterranean, although the brilliance of the scenery had done much to abate the usual grousing. Captain Leeks did his best to keep the crew's spirits up. He arranged for a hornpipe contest as well as for music to be played as often as possible. Worthington, it turned out, was a fair flute player and the surgeon was quite handy with a violin, playing with equal ease the elegant music of Italian and German composers and the rollicking tunes of home. For it all, however, the men seemed content to ply the Mediterranean Sea in the familiar surroundings of their good ship. As Danbury remarked one evening, "One of the lads said to me, he says, 'Mr. Danbury, this is much better than blockade duty off of Brest in February.'"

"Aye," responded MacGregor laconically, "he does have a point."

"He damned well does!" exclaimed Chandler.

To which Captain Leeks raised a glass. "The British sailor is a most perceptive fellow. God bless him!"

On July 28 the fleet put into Koroni in the Gulf of Messenia and Captain Troubridge of the *Culloden* was sent ashore to meet with the Turkish governor, both as a courtesy and as a way of gathering intelligence. The crew lolled about the decks and the officers gathered about the binnacle; everyone was trying to think of something to say that would put a good face on the matter—or at least one that would be better than saying that Nelson had again misjudged the French admiral's intentions.

Fergus noticed Captain Troubridge's boat's return to *Vanguard,* but, as it was hardly extraordinary, he took scant notice of it. He was more interested in the work being done by some men on a mainmast yard. It was with some irritation, therefore, that he noticed the men in the yards looking at the flagship. "MacGregor! Danbury!" he called. "What are those men doing up there?"

"Signal from the flagship!" went up the call from the midshipman who had the deck watch.

Fergus turned to see flags fluttering up on the *Vanguard*'s yards and he marched back toward the quarterdeck for a glass, muttering about unnecessary signals meaning more work for an already hard-pressed first lieutenant. By the time he arrived Captain Leeks already was on deck and was peering at the signal flags. He turned to Fergus as he approached. His face was broken by a wide smile. "All captains report, Kilburnie! Something is afoot!" He smacked a fist into his palm. "I can feel it!"

Fergus decided to say nothing about the captain's recent admonishments about the *Aberdeen*'s status as an armed transport. "I'll call your gig away immediately, sir, and tell the steward to fetch your best coat."

"Yes, yes," said the captain, clearly distracted by thoughts of whatever it was he felt was afoot.

The meeting with Admiral Nelson did not take long and soon Captain Leeks's gig bumped alongside. Standing at the brow with the welcoming party, Fergus was astounded by Leeks's rapid ascent up the ladder and the gleeful look on his face. The bosun's pipe's notes had scarcely faded away when the captain announced, "Egypt!"

Inwardly, Fergus moaned. Were they now all to go back to Egypt? For what? To find another empty harbor? Yet form must be maintained, so he allowed himself a brief response, "Egypt, sir?"

"Yes, Kilburnie, Egypt! The French fleet was sighted, sailing toward Egypt!"

This was the news for which every man in the fleet had waited for weeks. "Are they sure, sir?"

Leeks threw up his hands in a gesture of exasperation. "Damn me, Kilburnie. This is not a time for questions! This is the first scent we've had of the French for almost two months!"

Fergus knew enough about fox-hunting to know that even with a strong scent in their nostrils hounds were often outwitted by the fox. But he decided not to mention this fact to the captain. "Any orders, sir?"

Now, it was Leeks's time to be astounded. "Of course! Prepare to make sail. We are leaving immediately! The admiral's blood is up!" So, too, it seemed, was the captain's.

By the glass and by the calendar, it was not an exceptionally long passage to Alexandria, Egypt, nor as the crow flies was it a very great distance. Nevertheless, to Fergus, the hours and days dragged by. He had tried to steel himself against disappointment by keeping in mind that the Turkish governor might have been incorrect about the French fleet or even in the pay of the French to offer misleading information. Who knows? he said to himself. The fleet that was reported sailing to Egypt might have been us. After all, how could a Greek or Cypriot fisherman tell the difference between a French fleet and a British one?

But the captain's enthusiastic certainty was infectious and after a few days he too was convinced that, as the captain has said, "something was afoot." But something nagged at him. Just what was afoot? It probably was too late to stop the French army and its Corsican general, although catching the transports would be a nice prize. It was the French fleet that was the real prize, for by crippling or destroying it not only would the invasion force wither on the vine but the Royal Navy would gain unquestioned control over the Mediterranean Sea and so prevent any further French adventures— by sea, at least—in the Mediterranean and the Atlantic. But would it be there in Egypt? That question, Fergus knew, was on the mind of every man in the fleet, from Admiral Nelson to the lowliest seaman in the most humble ship. So straining eyes scanned the horizon, looking of the slightest hint of a topsail that might betray a frigate that might betray the French fleet.

15

BATTLE ⊙ OF THE
ΠILE

n the morning of July 31, the British force was approaching
the coast of Egypt. Signals were hoisted on the *Vanguard*
and soon the *Swiftsure* and the *Alexander* went ahead to see
what was in Alexandria Harbor. Lookouts high in the
Aberdeen's masts soon called down to say that could see many masts in the harbor, but were unable to say if they were warships. The men gathered wherever
they could get a good view, shifting their gaze from the two ships that had
been sent ahead to the horizon and back again. The excitement, the anticipation seemed to have a physical presence; there was constant low murmuring as the men spoke either to shipmates or themselves.

Captain Leeks stood on the quarterdeck, a telescope pressed to his eye.
Unconsciously, he shifted back and forth on either foot. "Kilburnie!" he called.

"Sir?"

"Get one of the midshipmen in the rigging with a glass," he said in a
voice taut with emotion. "I want to know what signals the *Swiftsure* or the
Alexander sends *immediately.*"

"Yes, sir," said Fergus. He turned and ordered one of the midshipmen
to do as the captain said. The lad moved off at something close to a dead run
and scampered up the mainmast's rigging.

The captain lowered the glass a bit from his eye and cast a sideways glance at the climbing midshipman. "Hmm, that is the fastest I have seen that young man move, outside of responding to the call for dinner." He winked at Fergus. "Ah, youth."

"Sir!" called down the midshipman. "The *Swiftsure* is signaling, sir."

"Very good," replied Captain Leeks, cupping his hands to his mouth as he spoke to the midshipman. "What are the signals?"

"I can see into the harbor, too, sir!"

"Damn me, Kilburnie," said the captain as an aside to Fergus, his tone one of mild exasperation. He turned his attention back to the midshipman. "Very good, Mr. Puller. Now, please tell me what signals the *Swiftsure* is flying."

"I don't see any men-of war in harbor, sir!" Puller yelled, his voice quavering with excitement.

Fergus had had enough. "Puller! The captain wants to kn— . . . !"

"Kilburnie, quiet, please!" interrupted the captain. "What was that, Puller?"

"No men-of-war, sir. In the harbor, sir!"

"Are you sure, Puller?"

Puller scanned the harbor again with his telescope. "I can't see any, sir."

Leeks paused and looked through his telescope. "God, Puller's right. The *Swiftsure* is signaling that there are no enemy warships in the harbor." He snapped the telescope closed. "French whoresons!" he said angrily. "Where the devil are they?" He breathed deeply and exhaled a great sigh. "All right, Mr. Kilburnie, call Mr. Puller back to earth and keep a close eye on the *Vanguard* for any signals."

The captain turned to walk away, but paused. "Mr. Kilburnie, when reminding Mr. Puller of the necessity to answer a captain's questions, please do not be too harsh. After all, we all have been waiting for seven weeks for a glimpse of the French fleet."

As the *Swiftsure* and the *Alexander* made it back to the fleet, Admiral Nelson continued the move to the east. To scout ahead, he sent the *Zealous* and the *Goliath* toward Aboukir Bay, a body of water roughly fifteen miles from Alexandria. The *Aberdeen* sailed along with the rest of the fleet, the mood on board decidedly glum.

Dinner was piped about half-past one. In the wardroom, the meal was taken largely in gloomy silence, save for requests for the salt or more to drink and Danbury's occasional mutterings of "Damn frogeaters" to no one in particular and MacGregor's usual reply, "Aye."

Fergus was concerned. After seven weeks of racing about the Mediterranean in search of an enemy that might not be there, even the best crew of the finest warship could become difficult and quarrelsome. Denied the opportunity to take their frustrations out on the enemy, the men might start brawling among themselves or, worse, become less prone to take ship's discipline. He reminded himself to ask the captain about this problem and ways it might be handled. The meal was soon finished, but, as unwilling as the men about the table seemed to talk, they seemed equally reluctant to return to their duties.

Above their heads feet thudded on the deck. MacGregor looked up and scowled. "What is all that runnin' for?"

Voices, high with excitement, were soon added to the sound of running. Danbury rolled his eyes. "Damn, there's a fight." He moved to get up from the table. Then came cheers, closely followed by the sound of a man walking swiftly in the direction of the captain's cabin and an insistent rapping on the door.

Fergus tossed down his napkin and drank what was left of his wine. "I'll see what this is all about," he said firmly. Damn, he thought, what is happening? He entered the passageway and turned to walk toward Captain Leeks's cabin—and almost collided with the captain. "Oh, uh, sorry, sir. I heard. . . ."

Captain Leeks's eyes were bright and his expression gleeful. "Come, Kilburnie, Mr. Starr has brought me the most wonderful news!" He pushed by Fergus, who was then almost run down by a breathless Starr.

"Oh, my apologies, Mr. Kilburnie, but I must get back on deck," said Starr, who barely slowed down.

"Starr!" said Fergus, exasperated. "What is happening, by God?"

Starr looked over his shoulder and smiled broadly. "The French fleet, Mr. Kilburnie. We've found them!"

Fergus was momentarily dumbstruck, but was shaken from it by tumultuous shouting and a stampede of men from the wardroom, everyone making for the deck.

Coming out onto the deck, Fergus could see the men were in the rigging and any other position that afforded them a view of the enemy. He looked about for the captain, in vain, it seemed as he was nowhere to be seen. He caught Danbury's eye. "The captain?" he asked. Danbury gave his head a little toss toward the foremast. Fergus looked up in the rigging and spied the captain at the first crosstree, peering through a telescope. He looked back at Danbury, who shrugged his shoulders and winked.

Well, Fergus thought, might as well see for myself. He strode forward and climbed the rigging until he came to the captain's perch. "Ah, welcome, Mr. Kilburnie, to my aerie," the captain greeted him. He held out the telescope. "Well, we have finally run them to ground. Here, take a look."

Bracing himself in the rigging, Fergus took the telescope and scanned the scene before him. The bay itself was a magnificent anchorage; from the west it had the shape of a fishhook, with the coast to the northeast forming the shaft and a long sandy arm curving through south and west and almost back to north. And, like a fishhook, there was a barb at the end. A massive, low-lying structure—probably bristling with artillery, he thought, at the end. It dominated a narrow passage between three small islands in this shadow and another shoal-surrounded island. Any ship trying to force that entrance would be severely punished for trying. Even the impetuous Nelson would not attempt it.

He shifted his glass to the western arm of the bay. Most of it was sand, but in the middle, due west of the middle of the French battle line, was a massive but low-lying structure, known as Aboukir Castle. He could see the heavy guns protruding from the stone embrasure. Circling the French shore defenses to get at the anchored French ships would be very difficult. Nevertheless, he could see Nelson's fleet passing from the west at full sail. He shifted his gaze toward the French ships and carefully counted them. There were thirteen line-of-battle ships anchored in a slightly bowed line, bow to stern; the entire line pointed to the west. A few frigates were anchored inside and roughly parallel to this line of ships, and a collection of smaller ships were in the windward end of the bay. Looking back at the French ships, he noticed that the ships were roughly the same size as Nelson's—seventy-fours or close to it—although the seventh ship in the line was a massive three-decker of the type that Fergus had seen at the battle of Cape St. Vincent. She probably carried at least one hundred guns, maybe more, and was undoubtedly the admiral's flagship.

He lowered the telescope and handed it back to the captain. "Sir, the French are at anchor and cannot maneuver. Certainly, we have the advantage."

The captain thought a moment before replying. "Perhaps. A line of anchored ships can be a strong position, Kilburnie, especially if the admiral has been wise enough to set out extra anchors in order to allow the ships to be moved by pulling in or letting out the cable." He scanned the French line again. "And I cannot tell if the French admiral has ordered them to do so."

"What does that mean for us?"

"Us, Kilburnie?" A wry smile danced on Leeks's lips.

"Well, the rest of the fleet, sir."

"If Admiral Nelson was a prudent, cautious man, he would order a withdrawal to the east and then a morning attack with the sun in the Frogs' eyes." He glanced around and frowned. "But for that to succeed, the wind would have to change or we would have to beat back in the morning and then make a run back down the starboard side of the French line." He shook his head as if dismissing the idea. "Or the French might decide to up anchor and come after us in the morning or even run and hide again. No, I'm sure Admiral Nelson's general intention is as firm as it was the last time I was on board the *Vanguard.*"

Fergus searched his memory for what Captain Leeks had said of that visit a couple of weeks ago. "Please pardon me, sir, but I cannot recall what Admiral Nelson said to you."

"He said that should we meet the French we should sail right at them. I do believe Admiral Nelson intends that we should fight all of the French right now while we still have some light."

"But, sir, that might mean a night action. I mean to say, the wind shall drop somewhat at sunset and the ships' speed would be cut."

The captain shrugged. "Few men have the stomach for a night action and that includes the French. Furthermore, that French admiral probably thinks we shall call upon him in the morning. Although, knowing the French as I do, a great many of his captains probably want to come after us now or probably urged the admiral to attack us once we were spotted off of Alexandria." He slowly closed the telescope. "Attacking now would give us the advantage of surprise."

A signal soared up on the *Vanguard.* "Ah," said Leeks, peering at it through his telescope, "there is your answer, Mr. Kilburnie. We are told by the admiral to clear decks for action." Cheers rang from the men below as they did from the ships close by. The captain looked about and turned back to Fergus, a sheepish grin on this face. "Come, Kilburnie. I should be down on the quarterdeck, comporting myself with proper dignity." With that he winked and made his way down the rigging.

Fergus stayed long enough to take a last glance at the tableau before him. The proud line of the seventy-fours and the fifty-gun *Leander,* the *Vanguard* toward the van, and the French ships at anchor, all bathed in the bright light of late afternoon. He spied the *Culloden* and remembered her at Cape St. Vincent. "Oh, to be on her now," he breathed and made his way to the deck.

The fleet made slow but steady progress toward the arm of the bay. The excitement in the air was electric; the men's eyes had a glint and they moved purposefully about the ship. Noticeable, too, was their relative quiet. The men spoke in hushed tones, as if the French ships were but the product of some great collective dream, a specter that would vanish upon awakening. Worthington and Starr looked longingly at the advancing fleet; they knew that men they knew would have the chance to demonstrate themselves under fire tomorrow and, although that opportunity bore the very real chance of death or dismemberment, they envied their friends for it.

Momentarily, Fergus cast a look at the *Aberdeen*'s puny armament and allowed himself a dream of what would happen if, say, one of the French frigates or brigs tried to attack. He saw himself sighting down a cannon and ordering it fired, leading a boarding party and. . . . He gave a short laugh. Stop it, he told himself. The smaller French ships wouldn't dare come near the *Aberdeen* in fear of being blown to atoms with one broadside and larger ships certainly weren't going to leave their marvelous defensive position and chase a seventy-four-gun ship of the line, no matter how far behind she lagged.

At about 5:30, the fleet was roughly abreast of the island and Admiral Nelson ordered the fleet to form a battle line. The *Vanguard* hove to in order to let some of the other ships pass the flagship, putting Admiral Nelson roughly in the middle of the line. The light took on a softer feel as the sun dipped lower and lower toward the horizon. Yet it remained bright enough to expose every detail and sharpen the edges of everything. Each ship hoisted a huge white ensign as it bore down toward the end of Aboukir Island and the entrance into the bay. Through a telescope Fergus could see some activity on the French ships and in the fort, but none of the ships seemed to be making preparations to sail.

A half hour later, the lead ships had come close or indeed had passed the tip of the arm of the bay. Now, Fergus thought, was the moment of truth: Would the admiral lead the ships in an attack right now or, after reconsidering the situation, wait for tomorrow? At the van, movement caught his eye, the lead ships began to make a turn—to the starboard. The issue had been decided and the battle was about to be joined. Signals fluttered in the *Vanguard*'s rigging: "Engage the enemy's van and center."

"Just 6:00," said the captain, examining his watch. He peered intently at the French line. "Hmm, well, it appears the French have just realized what is in store for them. They are lowering boats." Indeed, boats were lowered and the men in them were apparently trying to run cables between the anchored ships, although to what end Fergus couldn't imagine. It was, he knew, too late to do much but make sure there was plenty of shot and powder ready. Damn! he thought, just to be on the *Leander* instead of the *Aberdeen* which was relegated to standing off the bay, ready to assist any ship that might be damaged and drifting.

"Look!" cried Worthington, pointing at the French line. "One of them is trying to get sail up!" The ship immediately before the huge flagship was indeed trying to make sail. Perhaps the French admiral had indeed decided to take his chances outside of the bay. But to do so now would mean he would lose any semblance of command, his fleet would be thrown into utter confusion, easy pickings for the coordinated British attack. No, thought Fergus, this is no time to change his mind.

The British ships came on relentlessly, seemingly oblivious to the activities in the French ships as they prepared for action. To Fergus the silence was maddening. The whole scene seemed somehow unreal.

"Good God," cried the captain, "look at Foley!" By "Foley," Captain Leeks meant Captain Foley who commanded the *Goliath*. What had gained the captain's attention was that Foley was trying to take the *Goliath* to the head of the line, a position held at that moment by the *Zealous,* captained by "Sam" Hood. The *Zealous* was living up to her name and seemed reluctant to relinquish the van. "Oh, ho!" cried the captain. "Hood shall not give up too easily!" And for some minutes it appeared that Foley and Hood were equally determined to enter the bay abreast of one another if necessary. Then Hood's ship dropped back a bit and the *Goliath* moved ahead.

A few minutes later, the battery on the island open fire and shot splashed near the *Goliath*. Then the first two French ships began firing as well. Fergus knew the weight of metal those ships could throw. I'd wager Captain Foley isn't so pleased to be in the van now, he thought. Yet the *Goliath* and the *Zealous* appeared unscathed as they moved toward the French van and Fergus wondered if the French were so surprised by the attack that it threw off their aim. He felt his stomach tighten, however, when he saw Foley's ship working toward the bow of the lead ship in the French line. He looked over at Captain Leeks, whose eyes met his. Leeks merely raised an eyebrow and resumed looking through his telescope. It appeared that Foley planned to take the *Goliath* across the bow of the French ship and then move down the landward side— and that the *Zealous* and a few other ships might follow.

The basic idea made sense—engage the enemy ships on both sides. In this situation, however, there was grave danger of running aground and becoming a sitting duck for cannon ashore and afloat. Fergus knew that accurate charts of this coast were few and far between so Captain Foley would have to work through carefully, placing men in the chains to take soundings, but that also meant exposing his ship longer to fire from the battery ashore. Yet there was little evidence of apprehension; indeed, it appeared that the *Goliath* was picking up speed. About ten minutes after the commencement of the firing the *Goliath* swung round the bow of the lead French ship and fired a thunderous broadside as she did.

The men on the *Aberdeen* cheered as the *Goliath* moved by the French ship and made a port turn, running down the line. "Foley has the luck of the devil," cried Danbury as the *Goliath* ran past the first French ship and began hammering at the second. She then began to slow and, to Fergus, it appeared she had dropped anchor but with the fading light and the billowing clouds of powder smoke—which became thicker and thicker as the other French ships took up the fight—it was rapidly becoming difficult to see the battle. The French frigate near the head of the French line opened fire at the *Goliath* and the British man-of-war replied, although not as vigorously since it was pounding the second ship in the French line.

Captain Hood had his ship pour another raking broadside into the first French ship and then the *Zealous* took position abreast her and began to play a heavy fire upon her. Next, the *Orion* swept by the *Zealous*'s starboard and moved between the *Goliath* and the French frigate. The air reverberated as if from a thunderclap as the *Orion* unleashed a broadside. The French frigate seemed to shake and then come apart under the wall of shot thrown at it. Like most of the ships of the line, the *Orion* mounted carronades as well as its rated guns and the weight of metal in a single broadside was immense.

A flicker of movement caught Fergus's eye and he turned the telescope to the head of the French line where the foremast of the first ship was just going over the side. Well, Fergus thought, that was heartening.

Another ship—with all the smoke and the increasing darkness he could no longer tell which—went by the head of the French line, hammering the lead ship again. The next one, however, made her way to a gap between the first and second ship and began pounding the already heavily punished ships.

"Kilburnie!" called Captain Leeks, "Can you see the *Vanguard*?" He took the telescope from his eye. "Damn this smoke! I can barely see a thing."

Fergus strained his eyes as he peered into the gloom. There was something, a ship of the line was moving down the seaward side of the French line, firing as she went. Furthermore, it appeared that the other ships were following her. The head and center of the French lines were therefore trapped between two lines of British ships. But what about the ships to the rear of the French line? Fergus tried to examine the line, but in the descending night and the thick smoke he could make out few details. Still, it appeared that there was some activity on the end ships but whether to get under way or prepare for action or both he couldn't tell.

He snapped the telescope shut. Damn, he'd know if he was on the *Culloden* or the *Leander*. He muttered a curse under his breath at his bad luck. "Sir, I cannot make out many details, although it did appear that the *Vanguard* was leading the other ships down the other side of the line."

"And the French, Kilburnie?"

Fergus didn't think the captain wanted to know if the French were fighting. The flashes of the guns could be plainly seen even through the murk and the reports could be felt, indeed, the very air seemed to shake with them.

"The ships at the end of the line, sir, were bustling about a bit, but why, I couldn't tell."

The captain digested the news for a moment and then looked up at Fergus, his devilish look turning to sadness. "Well, then, Mr. Kilburnie, we must remain in this position—as Admiral Nelson ordered." He looked toward the battle and shook his head. Then he opened his mouth as if to speak, but then closed it firmly, again shaking his head.

Fergus approached closely. "Is there something wrong, sir?"

Leeks sighed heavily. "For a moment, Kilburnie, I thought about heading into the end of the French line and causing some mischief." He waved a hand at the *Aberdeen*. "But it would be neither wise nor proper to ask the men to endure a pounding for my sake," he said resignedly. "Still," he said lightly, "I'm glad to know that I still have the stomach for a fight." He rubbed his hands together gleefully. "Assemble the crew."

"Very good, sir," replied Fergus and dispatched two midshipmen to have all hands lay aft.

As most were already on deck, they gathered quickly. By the light of lanterns Captain Leeks addressed them. "Men, we all know that the fleet is engaged in a sharp fight with the French. Before we had our view blocked by the night and the smoke, it looked like our ships were getting the best of the French, but war is a fickle thing and, for all we know, that French monster in the center might be beating the *Vanguard* and any other ship that comes near into a mastless hulk."

There was some murmuring among the men. "Don't think it can't happen, lads. Whatever attributes the French may lack, it has been my experience that courage is not one of them. And, with a little luck, even a Frenchman can get off the odd good shot or two." Some of the men chuckled. "But I do not think that is the case, for we had surprise and dash on our side. Furthermore, Mr. Kilburnie saw activity on the French ships at the rear of their line. I believe they have no stomach for a meal of grape and chain shot." Some laughter. "And therefore, might try to run under cover of darkness." He paused and then added sternly. "If the French come this way, we must be prepared to do our part."

Fergus was flabbergasted. Leeks knew the *Aberdeen* would be hard-pressed to beat a ten-gun brig in a stand-up fight, let alone best a French two-decker or, God forbid, that three-decked behemoth. Now he was talking about doing just such a thing.

Captain Leeks continued, as if he had read Fergus's mind. "Now some of you are no doubt thinking that I intend to engage that monster of a three-decker, given half a chance. Well, be assured, men, that although we have been under a hot sun for almost two months I have not yet lost my mind." There was some laughter. "Still, if a French ship comes upon us as he tries to escape, he may be so frightened by our great bulk, looming ahead in the darkness, that he might surrender or run himself aground in order to avoid being pounded like his friends back in the bay." Captain Leeks took on a stern look. "So keep a sharp eye out, men. We need to have an idea of just what we might be fighting before I'll lay the *Aberdeen* close alongside any ship."

For the rest of the night, the *Aberdeen* tacked and wore east of the bay. The sounds of the battle shook the ship and the smell of gunpowder and burning wood permeated the air. Toward the center of the French line a fire began at a little after 9:00, the glow reflected on the smoke and fog. Clearly, a large ship was ablaze. The fire grew brighter and brighter until there seemed to be a tower of flame in the middle of the bay. The firing seemed to slacken a bit, as if all had stopped to watch the spectacular conflagration. Suddenly, a brilliant flash lit up the scene as would the brightest sunlight; seconds later it was followed by a huge rumble and then a roar.

Transfixed by the spectacle, no one said anything. After a few minutes, Fergus moved to the stern rail where the captain stood, gazing toward the battle. "God's teeth, Kilburnie, the magazines must have exploded!" he said when Fergus came close.

Indeed, Fergus thought, but which ship's magazines? And what about any ships that were alongside?

The captain made his way to the stern rail and Fergus followed. "Kilburnie, inspect the ship. After an explosion that big you never know what has shaken loose. Take the carpenter with you and make sure to check below. I'll have Mr. MacGregor see to the masts and sails."

Fergus nodded and, after finding the carpenter and a lantern, went below decks to inspect the ship. All was well, but the inspection took longer than he wanted because any man who had been below wanted to know what had happened and barraged Fergus with questions. When he emerged back on deck, Fergus was immediately struck by something peculiar: silence. When he reported to Captain Leeks by the stern rail he made mention of it.

"Funny thing, eh?" replied the captain. "I did not notice it myself for a couple of minutes. Maybe the explosion stunned everybody or all the French have struck." A rumble of gunfire came across the water to them. "Apparently not." He turned to Fergus. "How is the ship?"

"I could find nothing wrong," replied Fergus. He looked over the captain's shoulder toward the interior of the bay. He could see almost nothing, except for a few stabs of light he took for gun flashes and the much subsided glow of the enormous fire.

"Mr. MacGregor could find nothing wrong either." The captain also turned and looked across the water. The rate of fire had increased somewhat now. Unbidden, the captain remarked, "If Nelson wins tonight and lives, he'll be made a peer."

"What if he is killed?"

"If the battle is lost and Nelson falls, it shall give the navy someone to blame. If the battle is won, then his death at the moment of triumph shall give the navy and the nation a hero, a legend perhaps."

The next morning, dawn broke at 4:44 A.M. and Captain Leeks gave orders for the *Aberdeen* to make her way into the bay. As the ship approached the bay, the men were able to make out, slowly at first because of the still weak light, the aftermath of the fight. Smoke from the smoldering hulks, wood, canvas, and cordage hung over the water, drifting slowly back to the *Aberdeen;* however, it did not obscure the view into the bay.

The first detail to come into view was a cluster of French ships at the eastern end of the bay—three frigates and five ships of the line, completely dismasted, holed in many places, their upper decks a shambles. Amazingly, though, men still milled about the guns and a tricolor flag was nailed on top of the stump of her mizzen. It was a brave sight, made all the more so because of the apparent timidity of her consorts.

In the western end of the bay was a loose jumble of ships, many dismasted and all showing damage of one sort or another. Fergus searched in vain for the enormous three-decker, but couldn't find her. It was she that had exploded so spectacularly. Other French ships that had struck their colors were hemmed in by British ships of the line that had their colors flying proudly; at least six ships had surrendered and a seventh, the *Alexander,* was a floating wreck, useless without extensive repairs. At the far western end of the bay was a forlorn sight: the British ship of the line Troubridge's *Culloden* apparently aground and being tended to by the *Mutine.* She looked undamaged; apparently she had never been in the fight last night.

Yet, even with the evidence of defeat in front of their eyes, some of the French showed they still had some fight in them, for a moment at least. A little after dawn some of the French ships had tried to mount an attack against the *Alexander* and the *Majestic,* which had lost her mainmast and mizzenmast. The attack, however, came to the attention of the other British ships and the *Goliath* and the *Theseus* came to the rescue. The French ships beat a retreat immediately and one frigate ran aground and surrendered (although the striking crew set the ship alight). In their haste to get away from the approaching threat, two ships of the line also ran aground in the inner recesses of the bay and struck.

Yet, the men of the *Aberdeen* mainly directed their attention toward the sight just as brave as that of the wrecked French ship: the dismasted British seventy-four, which was either aground or anchored at the extreme eastern end of the bay. Her colors still flew and men still swarmed over the ship, attempting to make right the immense damage wrought by French guns. In any other fight she would have been made a prize, her crew prisoners, and been sent to serve her captors, perhaps against the men who built her. But here in Aboukir Bay she was probably more in danger of sinking or holing herself than being taken by a French man-of-war.

The captain summoned Fergus to where he stood on the quarterdeck. "Kilburnie, we'll pass as close as possible to the *Bellerophon* and hail her. If she needs our help immediately, we shall attend to her before rejoining the rest of the fleet. I'm sure Admiral Nelson would approve."

Fergus acknowledged the order and moved over to the binnacle to discuss with MacGregor the best manner, the safest manner to approach within hailing distance of the *Bellerophon*. MacGregor was looking at the lay of the land and rubbing his chin in thought when Danbury walked up nonchalantly. "Here," he said gruffly, pointing toward the bay. "What's that French bastard doing?"

Fergus and MacGregor looked over at the gathering of French ships. A French frigate had broken away and apparently was making for open water. MacGregor gave a contemptuous snort. "He's running from his fleet."

"No, he's not," said Danbury after a minute. "He's making for the *Bellerophon*."

MacGregor fixed Danbury with a look of utter amazement. "You're mad. What would that frog captain do with the *Bellerophon*, eh? Tow her home?"

Fergus did not pay much attention to the two men and their argument, but instead watched the French frigate carefully. She could be making for open water and safety, but wouldn't it be safer to move when the surviving line-of-battle ships did so as well? Still, MacGregor had a point, what would the French captain do with a dismasted seventy-four if he captured her? What, then, was he doing?

The argument between MacGregor and Danbury grew louder until Danbury tried to draw Fergus into it. "Here, we'll ask Mr. Kilburnie. Mr. Kilburnie, is the French bastard trying to run or is he making for the *Bellerophon*?"

Shrugging his shoulders, Fergus answered truthfully. "I can't really tell. He could turn either way, and until he gets closer we won't really know."

Danbury rolled his eyes, and MacGregor shook his head in a displeased manner. Both men turned back toward each other and prepared to resume the argument when MacGregor peered again at the French frigate. He rubbed his chin as he was wont to do when thinking. "You know, Danbury,

I'm beginning to think you were right about that French frigate and the *Bellerophon*."

"Of course, I am damned right, ya Scotch fool," barked Danbury.

By now the captain had joined the small crowd looking at the French frigate. "I do believe Mr. Danbury is correct about the French frigate. And even if he's not, I don't want him to get any ideas about firing at the *Bellerophon* when he passes her." He grinned broadly and his eyes twinkled. "Well, Mr. Kilburnie, there is only one thing to be done then."

Fergus felt his heart beat faster, and a marvelous feeling came over him. He knew what the captain wanted to do, but he decided to let Leeks have his fun. "And what is that, then?" he asked barely suppressing a smile.

"Your guns are still primed and loaded, Mr. Kilburnie?"

"Why, yes, sir, they are."

Leeks rubbed his hands together. "Then have them manned and let's see what they can do against that frog frigate."

Fergus touched his hat. "Very good, sir." He turned to Danbury and MacGregor. "Prepare for action!"

The two men whooped with glee and began bawling out orders. The men knew what to do, however, and some were already into preparations for battle when the orders came. In a twinkling, therefore, the *Aberdeen* was ready for action.

Before Fergus moved down to the guns, Captain Leeks called him aside. "I'll try to give one battery a few shots at him, a strong whiff of powder will do the men's spirits a world of good. But," he raised a cautionary finger, "don't fire if there's a chance of hitting the *Bellerophon*. I shall not have our ship gaining a reputation for poor gunnery or poor eyesight."

By the time Fergus reached the guns, the French frigate had moved closer still to the battered *Bellerophon*. The men stood, looking as best they could over the bulwarks at the French ship. They were eager for action, Fergus could tell, eager to participate, even in a small way, in the great battle they had only witnessed. Saving another ship would give the crew the right to swagger a bit in Portsmouth or Plymouth or wherever the *Aberdeen* next dropped anchor. Dammit, thought Fergus, I'll be able to swagger a bit, too. He had already dreaded telling Uncle Jeris that he had merely watched the battle from afar in this broken-down armed transport.

A clear young voice called down to the captain; the *Vanguard* had hoisted a signal and a sharp-eyed midshipman had spotted it. "It is to the *Zealous*, sir." Captain Leeks asked for the signal number and, after receiving it, consulted the book. After a moment, he closed the book and clasped his hands behind his back, saying nothing. Fergus looked toward the British ships and noticed that one of the seventy-fours, which had been near the center of the bay, had begun to move toward the French frigate and the *Bellerophon*. Well, he thought, at least we weren't warned to stay away.

It seemed like an eternity, but soon the *Aberdeen* was close to the *Bellerophon,* having beaten the French frigate and the *Zealous* there. As the *Aberdeen* moved past the dismasted ship, Captain Leeks ordered the men to give three cheers for the ship and its crew, and the crew cheered lustily. What was left of the seventy-four's crew cheered back. The captain of the *Bellerophon,* or the senior surviving officer, Fergus thought grimly, doffed his hat in salute to the *Aberdeen* as she went by and Captain Leeks returned it in kind. Even with action imminent, Fergus still felt a twinge of regret that he had not been on such a ship last night in the middle of the great battle.

A midshipman came walking up. "Captain's compliments, Mr. Kilburnie," he said in a voice quavering with excitement. "He says that when we pass the *Bellerophon* he shall give an order to raise the gun ports and run out the guns. If you think you have a chance of hitting the Frenchman, he asks you to give the order to fire directly."

I'll be damned sure to do so, thought Fergus and sent the midshipman on his way. Fergus told Lieutenant Starr, who commanded the port battery, of the captain's intentions. Starr was obviously delighted. "My brother is on the *Culloden;* he will be absolutely mad with envy," he said, enormously satisfied.

"Now," said Fergus, who could not help but smile at Starr's delight, "tell the men to be ready to elevate their guns quickly. The range is quite long."

Starr acknowledged the order and strode happily back to his guns, moving from crew to crew telling them what to do. Fergus was pleased to see the confidence with which the lieutenant carried out his duties. True, it wasn't the gun deck of a seventy-four, a thirty-six, or even a cutter, but the young lieutenant acted as if he was striding the deck of the *Vanguard* herself.

The French frigate had been moving rapidly toward the *Bellerophon* but now, with the *Aberdeen* coming around her and the *Zealous* bearing down from the west, the seventy-four must have no longer seemed such a tempting target, for the ship seemed to hesitate, and then, imperceptibly at first, started to turn away.

Some of the men gave howls of frustration, but these cries were barely out of their mouths when the captain called out, "Now, if you please, Mr. Kilburnie!"

Fergus bowed slightly to the captain and gestured to Lieutenant Starr. "Mr. Starr," he said.

Starr quickly touched his hat and gave the orders for the gun ports to be opened and the guns to be run out. The men gave a half yell, half cheer as they heaved on the lines and wheeled the guns forward. The gun captains crouched behind the guns, their hands on the quoins, and peered down the gun barrels.

Impulsively, Fergus crouched behind a gun and looked out the gunport at the fleeing Frenchman. Not maximum elevation, he thought, but close to it. Starr also bent down and looked through a gun port toward the enemy. "Take the quoins out a couple of notches, lads." His tone was firm, confident. The gun captains did as they were bid, and the barrels of the guns sloped up toward the sky. Starr moved down to his left to the first gun of the battery and took a position a few paces back from it. He raised his arm. "Gun number one." He dropped his arm. "Fire."

The gun captain yanked the lanyard and there almost immediately came the whoosh of the powder in the touch hole, followed by the explosion of the main charge, in the case of these smaller guns more of a crack than a roar. The men looked over the bulwarks, craning their necks to see the fall of the shot. A few seconds later, the ball splashed into the water, slightly left of the Frenchman and slightly over.

Starr scuttled back to the second gun. "Gun number two, fire!"

The cannon barked and this time the ball fell a little short of the Frenchman, but not far from the center. Starr smacked his fist against his thigh. "Gun number three, increase elevation by one notch." The gun captain adjusted the elevation and Starr moved over to the gun. "Now, lads, we wait just a moment for the Frenchman to turn and show us his sides."

And after a few excruciating moments, the Frenchman did just that. "Gun number three, fire!" Again the crack and again the wait for the ball to hit. Suddenly one of the French frigate's mainsails jerked crazily and some lines went loose. A cheer went up from the crew. They had found the range.

Starr stood back. "All guns fire!" The remainder of the broadside belched smoke and flame at the Frenchman who was now starting to complete her turn. The men of the *Aberdeen* were rewarded by a few more hits on the rigging of the Frenchman and one that gouged her bulwark deeply. The men cheered even more heartily. Starr stood back and smiled broadly at Fergus. His brother's insanity was all but assured, thought Fergus.

Later that night, Fergus sank into his bunk exhausted. It had been a long day, and in some sense a little frustrating. Not long after the frigate went scuttling back to the company of larger ships, whoever commanded the remainder of the French fleet decided to make for the open seas. The last French ships of the line and two frigates (one of which had attempted to attack the *Bellerophon*) made sail and tried to make good an escape. But again, misfortune struck the French; in tacking one of the French ships of the line ran aground. Yet, the French admiral did not linger and the four ships left hastily. Of all the British ships, only the *Zealous* had engaged, but then she was recalled by Admiral Nelson, and the French ships were soon over the horizon.

The rest of the day had been one of backbreaking labor. The *Aberdeen* was ordered to make for the dismasted *Majestic* and lend assistance to her. As the ship moved through the bay, she did so through immense amounts of debris and hundreds of bodies.

Many bodies were mangled beyond recognition; others had arms or legs missing. A good number were scorched and Fergus guessed these men had been from the exploding French flagship. He found he couldn't take his eyes off the ghastly sight of corpses swirling in the wake of *Aberdeen*. Everywhere dead men.

The shock he felt at such a sight must have been plain because the captain left a conversation with Danbury and MacGregor and came to him with a look of concern on his face. "Are you well, Mr. Kilburnie?" he asked. "Perhaps you should see the surgeon."

Fergus shook his head. "I'm all right now, sir. It is just that I'm . . ." He paused; he wanted to lie, to say it was the sun, but he couldn't do it—not to this man. "It was the sight of all the corpses, sir. I've been in action before and seen dead men by the score. I've tossed still-twitching bodies over the side." He had glanced down at his hands. "But . . ."

"The sight of so many, Mr. Kilburnie?"

"Yes, sir. It just struck me so heavily."

"It should. It is a terrible thing to see these poor wretches, many of them ours, dead." The captain sighed and extended his hands in a gesture of resignation. "But it is part of our trade."

"And a damned hard trade it is," Fergus said.

It was only now, however, in his bunk, as sleep came over him, that Fergus realized that he had echoed the words of his uncle. He drew some comfort from the fact that at least he could tell his uncle about this great victory—and rightly say he had a role in it, although a small one.

The *Aberdeen* was busy for the next two days, bustling from damaged ship to damaged ship. Supplies were hauled out of the hold in a seemingly constant stream, and many times the *Aberdeen* crew would lend a hand, plugging shot holes or mending rigging and sails. Chandler assisted the surgeons on other ships and did a fair amount of work on the wounded French captives. Work went on well into the night, especially on many of the French ships that had been deemed as having potential to join the Royal Navy.

Moving from ship to ship as they did, the officers and men of the *Aberdeen* picked up stories about the battle from both sides. At night they would exchange the tales. Worthington was markedly impressed by the French and said so forthrightly one night when the officers gathered in the captain's cabin.

"I was weaned on stories and broadsides of the cowardly Frogs and how they would shrink before our steel." He lightly hit the table with his fist. "What nonsense! The courage of some of these men was amazing. One ship, the *Franklin,* fought for hours with just three guns in action and more than half of her crew dead. It was her captain or the admiral on her who started getting up sail when we attacked." He continued, the admiration plain in his voice. "The *Tonnant,* a ship of the line, was dismasted but not before she did the same thing to the *Majestic.* Her captain had an arm shot off but refused to leave his deck. They placed him in a tub of bran to stem the bleeding and he died there, giving orders to the last. The captain was correct; the French do not lack for courage."

Chandler nodded. "The French admiral was almost cut in half by a cannonball and he too refused to go below. He said a French admiral should die upon his own quarterdeck." He poured himself another measure of port.

"They are a brave race," added Captain Leeks, "and deserve better than the fools who lead them from the desks in Paris and the bumpkins they put on these ships and call sailors."

"What do you mean?" asked Starr.

The captain looked for a moment at his glass. "Please, gentlemen, don't take what I am about to say as somehow treasonous or disloyal. I say it only because you need to know what happened in their navy in order to be better officers in our navy." He took a sip of port and then continued. "Had the French admiral done what I am told the *Franklin*'s captain or admiral wanted to do—which was to meet us at sea—the French could have done great execution among us. They had heavier ships—a three-decker and two eighty-gunners—and all excellent sailors; that is to say, the French sail ships well. If the greater part of the French line had got under way and stood out when they had a chance, the mischief they could have done would have been substantial. I dare say, Mr. Starr, then your brother would have been dead or a prisoner of the French this very day." He shrugged. "Perhaps they might have defeated us piecemeal." He gave a thin smile. "Happily, we'll never know.

"I am of the opinion that the French admiral decided to remain in a defensive line because he thought he had to." He looked directly at Fergus. "Any thoughts as to why, Mr. Kilburnie?"

Fergus admitted that he had none.

The captain leaned forward. "It is quite simple, gentlemen. Look at the sailors of the French fleet and at some of your counterparts, the lieutenants. Most of these men are as out of place as a beggar at a nobleman's levee. They simply don't belong at sea." He took a sip of port and looked quizzically at Fergus as if bidding him to speak.

Fergus thought for a moment and then cautiously replied, "What you seem to be saying, sir, is that if the French officers were better seamen and more of the French seamen were actual seamen, the French admiral probably would have taken the chance at an open engagement."

"Yes," piped up Worthington. "Many of the experienced French officers were driven out of the navy or murdered because they were noblemen or simply had prospered in the old navy. In fact, some of these men are now fighting with us."

It was Starr's turn. "So, if the French were as competent at sea as they once were . . ."

"And had a turn of luck or two," loudly interrupted MacGregor.

"And had a turn of luck or two," echoed Starr, "they could well, sir, they could sweep the seas."

"I don't know about that, Mr. Starr," the captain replied.

The other men laughed and Starr blushed a bit. "However, during the American war, they needed only one victory at sea to inflict the final defeat on us on land." Leeks's face took on a look of satisfaction. "Well, gentlemen, I am beginning to think you might make decent officers yet," he joked. He looked over at MacGregor. "Eh, MacGregor?"

"Possible, sir," MacGregor said, chuckling.

"But, sir," said Starr. "You said something about this lesson about the French applying to our navy."

"Indeed, Mr. Starr." He cast a look about the men in his cabin. "Here's the part their lordships might not like to hear. When we have a war, the navy develops an insatiable appetite for men. Impressing seamen is one thing; they understand the demands of life on a ship and what it means to be a shipmate. Not so with a motley collection of thieves, drunkards, runaway apprentices, and fever-wracked wretches scraped out of workhouses, jails, and the gutter by comfortable constables, sheriffs, and judges eager to rid their counties of such people." He looked about the room. "The same reason—differing only in degree—why the French admiral didn't weigh anchor and come at us at sea is probably the same reason why their lordships took pains to send some of Lord Vincent's ships from the fleet blockading Cadiz to Admiral Nelson instead of sending channel fleet ships off to Admiral Nelson directly. Quite simply, gentlemen, they were concerned about the ability of the crews to function in an efficient manner, or at least not to be mutinous."

"Aye," added MacGregor.

"Aye, indeed," Leeks said sharply. "Be careful, gentlemen, that the navy doesn't need to turn to the ships with untrained crews and incompetent officers in an hour of great national need, like the French had to do in this campaign." He set his glass down firmly. "God's blood, but this evening has become far too morose. After all, a great *Aberdeen* victory for the navy and the nation took place only a couple of days ago." His eyes lit up. "Ah, we need music. Chandler, fetch your fiddle and give us a tune. And make sure it is a jolly one."

A few days later, the *Aberdeen*'s holds were emptied of all manner of supplies. The admiral had already sent the *Leander* and the *Mutine* with dispatches describing his great victory. It would have been a great honor to have carried them as well but, as Captain Leeks told Fergus, such work was best carried out by "fast ships, well-armed ships, or fast, well-armed ships and the *Aberdeen* fits none of those descriptions." The men were becoming restless. Their work was done here. To them, and to Leeks and to Fergus, it was time to leave this damnable climate and head back home or at least to familiar waters.

On August 5 a signal was hoisted in the *Vanguard* requesting the presence of Captain Leeks. His gig was swung out and he was rowed to the flagship. When he returned about two hours later, he carried two large canvas bags and two bottles. After he received his appropriate honors, he called to Fergus in a happy tone. "Assemble the men aft, Kilburnie! Immediately!"

Kilburnie did as he was bid and soon the men were crowded below the quarterdeck. The captain was clearly excited. He walked back and forth while he waited for the men to gather. "Men! I have just spoken to Admiral Nelson. He asks that I convey his best wishes and his thanks to officers and men of the *Aberdeen* for, as he said, 'such an admirable role in the victory God has seen fit to grant our arms.'" The men seemed pleased at the news.

"He also ordered the *Aberdeen* to carry another set of dispatches describing the victory home to England." At this news the men cheered wildly. When they had quieted down, the captain beamed at his crew. "Such praise and such news calls, I think, for an extra measure of grog." He pointed at MacGregor, "What say you, Mr. MacGregor, to that?"

"Aye!" cried MacGregor with as much emotion as Fergus had ever seen him display. The crew roared its approval. Captain Leeks turned to Fergus, "Dismiss the men, Mr. Kilburnie, and then come and see me in my cabin."

Minutes later, Fergus knocked at the captain's door. The captain was clearly excited; his eyes were bright and his cheeks were flushed as he sat at his desk fidgeting with a pen. "Well, Kilburnie," he said cheerily, "it was a most satisfactory visit to the flagship."

"So it seems, sir. The men are quite happy to be going home and, of course, the extra measure of grog always is welcome."

"Oh, Kilburnie, it was much more than the news we would be going home that made the visit satisfactory. It was Admiral Nelson's words of praise for this ship. Nothing grandiose, mind you, just a few quiet words and then," a look of utter delight came to the captain's face, "he asked my opinion of matters pertaining to the battle, the conduct of the French, and the navy."

"Did you tell him what you told us the other night?" Fergus asked. Admirals, he thought, rarely liked to be lectured to—on any topic—and he was eager to see what Nelson's response was to Captain Leeks's ideas.

"Why, yes, Kilburnie, I did," the captain answered firmly. "It was a conversation conducted more man to man, no, sailor to sailor, than admiral of a fleet to captain of a lowly armed transport." He raised an eyebrow. "You didn't think I would play the flunky—all flattery and smiles—did you, Kilburnie?"

Fergus felt himself blush. "No, sir." He changed the subject as quickly as he could. "What did Admiral Nelson say exactly, sir? About your ideas, that is?"

"He did not say much—odd in itself for an admiral—but listened sincerely. He was not thinking of prize money or honors and pretending to listen to me. He gave me his full attention. When I gave him my opinion about the efficiency of the French crews and our need to avoid such a situation with our ships, he smiled and said he was glad to hear that he was not alone in his opinion." He laughed softly. "Mr. Starr shall be happy to know that the admiral shares his admiration for the courage of the French. He agrees that if well officered and well manned their ships would be formidable foes."

Captain Leeks held a smile for a moment, but a more serious thought must have intruded for he suddenly took on a serious expression.

"What is it, sir?"

"Kilburnie, the admiral also told me that ours is somewhat a dangerous mission. We have no way of knowing what French ships may be out there and where. He hopes that our size shall be sufficient to scare away all but the largest French ships and that even a large French ship will want to avoid an action."

He dropped the pen with which he had been fidgeting and folded his hands in front of him. "The admiral tells me that some of the French ships he saw in Alexandria Harbor have made their escape already. Now, the admiral says, the dispatches must get to England, but there is a chance that French generals or high government officials are on these ships. So if we run across one, we should consider taking her."

"Consider, sir?"

"Why, yes, Kilburnie, consider. I'll not attack a French transport laden with soldiers. If the French brought the issue to a boarding action, we'd be defeated for sure."

He tapped the table and stood. "Prepare to sail, Kilburnie. I wish to leave on the next tide."

16
FÍRST PRÍZE

hile the *Aberdeen* was finishing unloading, Fergus found out that the British casualties were about two hundred men and no ships lost. The captain of the *Vanguard* estimated that the French fleet had lost their flagship, the *Orient,* six ships, their admiral, and about two thousand men.

When Fergus relayed that information to the captain, he invited Fergus down to his cabin and had his steward break out a bottle of his best brandy. With glass in hand, he offered a toast. "To King George the Third, the Royal Navy, Admiral Nelson, and the British seaman."

Fergus emptied his glass. "Thank you, Captain, and now I should get back up on deck and finish up."

When the unloading was completed, Captain Leeks reported by signal that their cargo was completely unloaded. Back came a signal, "Return to base. A boat is on its way to you with dispatches that you are to deliver to the Admiralty without delay."

As the *Aberdeen* threaded her way between the anchored wounded ships of both navies, Fergus noted that hundreds of British seamen and marines were gathered on the *Vanguard*'s weather decks where divine services were being held. The hymns welling from hundreds of throats could be heard for miles and plainly on the quarterdeck. After rounding the battered point and sailing out the entrance to the harbor, the *Aberdeen* was soon on course for Gibraltar. No sails were in sight, but Fergus confirmed what they had guessed: in the darkness, four French ships, two ships of the line and two frigates, had escaped to the east and when last seen were on course for the southern French ports.

Captain Leeks did not seem to be perturbed. "They'll be well ahead of us," he said.

For a week the *Aberdeen* sailed west, making good time, and Fergus gradually relaxed, hoping the French ships would be on a more northerly course toward the southern coast of France and would not choose to go south around Corsica. Captain Leeks was below most of the time, lost in an alcoholic fog.

On the seventh night the sky became heavily overcast and thick rain cut visibility to a hundred yards. Captain Leeks insisted that they keep as much sail on as possible as long as the wind was tolerable.

At dawn, a lookout shouted down, "We're in the middle of four ships!"

Fergus grabbed his long glass, but it wasn't necessary. The ships were so close he could see them plainly as French, and they were all in gun range. Apparently they were not expecting the *Aberdeen* or any other ship. Fergus could hear shouting coming from the decks of the ships as gun crews ran to their guns.

"Wear ship! Right full rudder!" Fergus shouted. "Commence firing when ready!" He sent a midshipman below to call the captain.

It seemed to take forever for the *Aberdeen* to make her turn. Captain Leeks had always made it a habit for the ship to be at quarters before each dawn, and the *Aberdeen* was able to open fire as soon as she settled on course and the gunners could lay their guns. The nearest French ship still did not have her gun ports open.

For a while Fergus thought they might get out of gun range before the French could open fire, but they were not that lucky. Large guns began to boom, and Fergus knew the French ships of the line had a long range. Some of the shots were short, but the longer-range guns sent splashes high on both sides of the fleeing ship. A few even whistled through the rigging, bringing one sail down.

Captain Leeks burst on deck, pulling on his jacket, his gray hair flying in all directions. "What's going on?" he shouted.

Before Fergus could tell him, a shot caught the captain waist high. His body fell in two parts, and blood flooded out of it. He was dead instantly.

Fergus turned to a nearby gun crew. "Get him below!" he yelled.

Soon the firing fell off and then stopped altogether as the *Aberdeen* raced downwind. The French, obviously in a hurry to get home, let her go. Fergus heaved a sigh of relief, but kept an eye astern on the heavy rain clouds.

An hour later the blood had been washed from the quarterdeck. Fergus regained his aplomb, but he was sorry to lose the captain. Leeks had let Kilburnie have his head, and the experience had been rewarding. Now Kilburnie had to figure out how to get the *Aberdeen* home. Most of the French fleet in the Mediterranean was still in Aboukir Bay but Fergus knew there were still four undamaged ships to the west. He had to hope they were bound for home port and were not interested in a lone British transport.

After an hour of moving downwind, Fergus decided to move to the south for several hours before resuming a westerly course. The decision was sound, and for the next week the *Aberdeen* sailed on undisturbed. Each morning as the lookouts above anxiously scanned the lightening horizon Fergus paced the quarterdeck. Each time the lookouts reported the horizon clear, Fergus was relieved. At the end of the week the Rock of Gibraltar loomed ahead.

While watering and provisioning at the port of Gibraltar, Kilburnie was called to the office of the admiral of the port. When he got back he said to the master, "We've been ordered to take on thirty marines and fifty sailors from a shipwrecked frigate. I've also arranged to load eight twelve-pounders and their carriages."

MacGregor shrugged. "Well, I guess that's what a transport is for. Have you seen the guns?"

"Yes. They're a little old-fashioned in design and shape, but sturdy and well cast. They'll need a little cleaning up and some pieces of wood in the carriages."

The master said, "Well, the yard can take care of all that when we get there."

"Oh, no. We'll do it."

"What for, sir?"

"We might find a use for them."

A week later, just south of Beachy Head, a lookout reported a sail. Fergus went aloft and when he got back on deck, he said, "It's a French frigate, at least thirty-six guns."

"Jesus!" the master said. "Let's get out of here."

"No," Fergus said. "We can take her on."

MacGregor shook his head. "You must be mad."

Fergus laughed. "No, I'm not mad, and I have a plan."

A month later the *Aberdeen* stood in to the anchorage at Plymouth Harbor on the south coast of England. Kilburnie paced the quarterdeck watching the seamen aloft moving along the yardarm with their feet braced along the foot lines rigged below the yards. The master reduced the sails slowly, and the ship crept toward its assigned anchorage.

It was the first time he had brought a ship to anchor while serving as its captain, and he was nervous. Although he was concerned, he still felt very confident, and he was determined to do well. He realized the maneuver was not very complicated. As the ship moved slowly toward its assigned berth, he could see the captains of several first-line ships pacing up and down with their hands behind their backs and watching him from their quarterdecks, and he did not want to give them a chance to criticize him.

As the *Aberdeen* passed close aboard an impressive hundred-gun ship, the *Orestes,* her signalmen made a hoist that was addressed to the *Aberdeen.* "What does it mean?" Kilburnie asked a midshipman standing near him.

The midshipman broke out the signal book and ran a finger down the pages. "Sir, it means 'Well done.'"

"Ah," Kilburnie said. "I should have remembered that number. I heard it before on the *Athena.*"

Kilburnie was puzzled. How could they know that the French frigate slowly following them and flying British colors was the prize of a lowly transport?

He turned his attention to the task of getting to his assigned anchorage, and when the sailing master nodded to him, he ordered, "Let go!"

The anchor rumbled down toward the muddy harbor bottom, followed by several fathoms of thick hemp cable. Soon the boatswain looked aft and reported in his peculiar northern accent, "Cable up and down, sir."

Puller looked over the side, studying the movement of water alongside. "Way's off!" he shouted.

"Very well," Kilburnie said. "Stop off the cable."

When the business of securing the ship from sea was well in hand, Kilburnie walked over to the starboard side where he could see the Royal Navy boat landing. A midshipman on watch carrying a brass long glass was scanning the water toward the landing.

"What do you see?" Kilburnie asked.

"Sir, there's a boat headed this way. There's a civilian in the stern."

When the boat was closer, the midshipman said, "Sir, the passenger in the stern sheets has a patch on one eye and only one arm, and it ain't Admiral Nelson."

Kilburnie laughed, but he was stunned. "Must be my Uncle Jeris," he said.

"What, sir?" the midshipman asked.

"Never mind. Man the side with the boatswain and six side boys."

It was indeed Jeris, and he climbed slowly up the side, using his one arm carefully to grab the lines rigged alongside the steps leading to the gangway. When he was aboard and on the quarterdeck, he smiled broadly at Fergus and said, "Permission to come aboard, sir. I'm beginning to like these side boys."

Kilburnie laughed. "Of course, Uncle, you're my first important visitor. Come down to my cabin."

In the cabin Jeris looked around carefully. "Od's blood! This cabin is fit for an admiral."

Kilburnie laughed again. "And once it was occupied by one. Now that the old *Aberdeen* has been made into a transport, her official status has been lowered, but her appointments remain the same. Now, Uncle, sit down and join me in some refreshments. There isn't much liquor or wine left. Ah, er, the last captain seems to have used up most of the supply, but I have some real coffee. Tell me why you are here and how you knew I was entering port today."

Jeris nodded. "I'd like some coffee. The last question first. A fast packet came in three days ago with the report of your action and an inventory of your prize. I've read it, of course, in great detail."

"But how did the other captains know? One of them sent me a message when I was standing in."

Jeris snorted. "They know everything within hours. Nothing is secret in the navy."

Kilburnie shifted in his chair. "Yes, I sent a copy of my report with a fast packet I ran across a few miles south of Land's End a few days ago."

Jeris adjusted his eyepatch. "The rest follows. From your inventory, I knew your prize was going to be very valuable, and I didn't want the local prize court to divert any part of it from you. I'll follow their deliberations and actions closely. Now for the most important issue at hand. I read your report, but tell me again how you won this remarkable action. A poorly armed transport isn't supposed to be able to best a thirty-six-gun frigate, even if it is a Frenchman."

Kilburnie grinned. "It wasn't all that hard. I had stopped at Gibraltar to discharge the last of my cargo and to make a few repairs and take on provisions and water. The admiral of the port directed that I take aboard thirty marines and fifty seamen from a ship-wrecked brig, and I persuaded him to load aboard eight twelve-pounders and their carriages taken from a salvaged ship. They were a little old-fashioned and battered, but we made them usable.

"I put them below on what used to be my gun deck and freed up all the gun ports on both sides. Then I rigged all of the guns for easy change from side to side, if you consider it easy to haul one of those big hogs across the deck and turn it around. I made gun crews out of my passengers. Even the marines volunteered, and soon they were all in good repair and shining like all the rest of the marines' equipment. I never expected to use either the guns or the crews on my trip from Gibraltar back home to England."

Jeris stood up and paced up and down, occasionally flexing his wounded knee. Then he sat down again. "I'm just trying to ease the pain in my old wounds. Go on."

"As you know from my report, we sighted the French brig *Toulon* about a hundred miles south of Portsmouth. She was apparently on patrol, and I'm sure she thought we were just an old undermanned transport and an easy mark. I kept my gun ports closed on purpose to lure her in. I changed course to make her think we were trying to evade her. She came roaring toward us, all canvas on. I tried to lower my speed by lowering my jib. She couldn't see it because we were headed away from her, and she must have thought we were still trying to escape. When she was in range, I raised my starboard gun ports, changed course to starboard to unmask my starboard battery, and gave her everything we had. All my guns had been rigged to fire to starboard. I knew it wasn't enough, and in spite of the damage we did to her rigging and the men we killed on her weather decks, she kept coming on like a dog after a bone."

"How did she come to board you?"

"I wanted her to, and I offered little resistance. I kept most of my sailors and marines below as she came alongside. They were all well armed with cutlasses, axes, and pikes. We had only a few guns and pistols, and I gave those to the marines, who were then double-armed.

"Just as she came alongside and threw over grapnels, I ordered my men to come up from below when the French boarded. Those few remaining topside had taken shelter behind the hammock nettings, and the officers and men of the Frenchman discharged their weapons against the nettings, doing little damage to my men, but lodging a lot of balls in the hammocks. I made no attempt to throw off the grapnels and all of us on the quarterdeck made a big show of cowering behind the bulwark.

"With their weapons empty, the crew of the Frenchman swarmed aboard, shouting French oaths. My men below, augmented by our passengers, surged up from the lower deck. We outnumbered them on our decks, and it was soon all over. All of the Frenchmen on our deck were soon killed, and I ordered my men to board the French ship and take over, but not to kill all the sailors or officers. We would need them to help our prize crew sail the ship home."

"And then?"

"My prize crew brought her in, and you see her lying at anchor astern of us."

"Yes, and a handsome ship she is. The inventory you sent with your report said she was carrying a considerable amount of gold bullion aboard."

"Yes, the French officers said they were transporting it back to France."

"Then the French captain got greedy and tried to bring you in, too."

Kilburnie laughed. "He caught a bigger fish than he baited his hook for, as you used to say when you were fishing with us in Scotland."

Jeris nodded. "Exactly. Now the question is to protect the big fish for you."

"I don't understand."

"You know very little about this, but luckily you are in Plymouth where your prize will be surveyed by an honest expert who is beholden to me. I am sure the Admiralty will decide to buy the ship. All French ships are well built and faster than ours. Now comes the bad part. What we call 'head and gun' is that part of the prize money to be paid based on the numbers of guns and men on the prize. It will be shared equally by all members of your crew and your passengers, but the proceeds of the sale of the ship and the bullion will be distributed in eighths.

"Fortunately, you were not operating under an admiral, who would ordinarily get an eighth, so now you get that eighth and two more eighths because you were commanding, for a total of three-eighths. Your officers will divide another three-eighths and the crew will split the rest of the money among them. Altogether, the prize money will be handsome, and the officers and crew will be well rewarded."

"I haven't thought much about such things. Will my share be substantial?"

Jeris smiled. "I should think it would be. Several thousand pounds, more or less. If you want me to do so, I'll send your share to your father and suggest that he buy an adjacent farm for you."

"Uncle, I want to share this with you. Anything I've done I owe to you."

Jeris shook his head. "No, lad, Martha and I are well fixed. All I ask is that you invite me to share any salmon fishing there may be on your new farm. Maybe I'll even ask your permission to build a small house on it."

Fergus laughed warmly. "You have a standing invitation, both to visit us and to build a house of any size you want to build. But there's a qualification."

Jeris's eyebrows shot up. "Yes?"

"I won't guarantee the fishing."

Jeris laughed. "Fair enough, since you haven't even seen it yet."

Fergus asked the question that had been foremost on his mind. "What news of the family, Uncle Jeris?"

Jeris's face was pained. "I'm afraid your grandfather is not well. Even the most robust of constitutions eventually breaks down, and I'm afraid this is happening to your grandfather. Still, he derives great pleasure from hearing about your exploits, and I keep him informed."

"What of Mother and Father?"

"They are well and are constantly telling me how thankful they are to be away from Ireland, with its Popery and rebellion."

Fergus decided not to ask about Ireland, but he was certain Jeris would know about the affairs of Donegal and the fortunes of Lord Inver. "What of the Irish rebellion, Uncle?"

Jeris's tone became grim. "Naturally the peasants—Papists and Presbyterians—took it as an opportunity to settle old scores. Their actions were drowned in a welter of blood. The rebellion was put down in the same manner as in '45, which is to say with brutality and great execution."

"I was told that the Irish did win some battles."

"Indeed."

Fergus decided to move to a happier topic. "What about the previous prize money that is owed me?"

Jeris smiled knowingly. "You will be happy to know I was able to get your money out of the prize agent. Anyway, I paid your debt to Lieutenant Kittrelle, who now commands a thirty-six-gun frigate out of Plymouth. All of your debts are paid in full."

"Leaving me?"

"The tidy sum of thirty-seven pounds."

"Oh, I almost forgot. I have a large bag of dispatches for the Admiralty. Can you take care of them?"

Jeris's jaw dropped. "What? We have been here jawing while the Admiralty is waiting for such important information?"

Fergus laughed. "Calm down, Uncle, a few hours won't hurt."

The next day Jeris was back again. After Fergus had settled him before a brandy, Jeris began to talk. Fergus had never seen him so agitated. "What's the matter, Uncle, has someone tried to steal my prize?"

"Oh, no, that's in the hands of the prize court. It will be safe for you no matter how many senior officers try to horn in on the proceedings. The prize court crew has already taken the ship over."

"Yes, I know. My men came back from the prize this morning, and they said the Frenchies had been taken ashore to a prison camp."

"Yes, they'll be ransomed soon."

"Then what's the trouble?"

"A special messenger brought a communication to me from the Admiralty this morning. I returned your dispatches from Admiral Nelson to the Admiralty with him. The communication said there are at least ten captains waiting in the Admiralty waiting room and making a huge fuss with the Third Professional Sea Lord to take over your ship, and that I am to get back as soon as possible to write orders for one of them. There's no doubt my boss means it."

"My God! What do I have to do to keep a command?"

"Be about four years older, have about five more years' service, and be English, preferably titled."

"I can't do any of those. I wasn't born that way. Is there any other hope for me?"

Jeris gulped down his brandy and asked for another. Fergus poured him a stiff one. "Yes, I've sent back word that I'll be down here on urgent business for three more days. You will have to load your ship and leave for the Mediterranean in forty-eight hours. I'll have to write orders for a new captain when I get back, but he'll have to catch you."

Fergus shrugged. "I guess he will."

"Maybe. Maybe not. And at least you'll have your command for several months. That's a lot of time for opportunity to knock. Maybe something good will happen in that time. You seem to have the same kind of luck Admiral Nelson has."

"But I can't just leave port without orders."

Jeris pulled an envelope out of his pocket. "You'll have these. They came in the same pouch as the communication to me. Open it."

Fergus opened the official-looking envelope and read the orders. "It says the *Aberdeen* is to load as soon as possible, get under way, and proceed to the Mediterranean and report to Admiral Nelson."

"You can hide down there for months. The new captain may never find you."

Fergus got up out of his chair. "I don't seem to have any other choice. I'll be ready to go."

Jeris said, "Well, that's settled. Give me another brandy to keep the others company, and tell me more about the Battle of the Nile."

"You mean it's not common knowledge back here?"

"No, it isn't. I understand Admiral Nelson was badly wounded in the battle and his ships were so badly damaged they had to stay in Aboukir for two weeks before they were able to get under way and leave."

"I can see that could be possible. We went alongside several ships to deliver mast parts and other supplies. Several of our ships were dismasted and many badly damaged. Also the French ships he captured had to be made ready for sea so they could be brought back as prizes, and they were in worse shape than ours by far. But couldn't he have sent word back by a brig?"

"I guess you mean a frigate. That's what we call brigs these days now that they are bigger."

Fergus raised his eyebrows. "Well?"

"No. He had only one frigate, and it was damaged, too. He couldn't even pursue the four ships that escaped in the darkness."

Fergus laughed, but then sobered. "We found them, even though we didn't want to."

"That's when Captain Leeks got killed?"

"Yes. He was the only casualty. I still feel bad about it. I think he was near retirement."

"He was. We were going to carry him for another year and then let him go."

"You knew he drank heavily?"

"Yes, we knew, but when he was young he was a tiger. The navy owed him a few years out to pasture, and when I heard the news that you were sailing with him, I thought it would be a good opportunity for you."

"I feel better about it. He didn't bother me, and in effect I learned to be a captain under him."

Jeris got up. "I've got to go ashore and hide for three days from Admiralty messengers carrying urgent messages. I won't see you again for a while. Good luck, and don't give up."

Fergus saw Jeris off and went forward to oversee the loading of supplies from a barge. "Let's get at it," he said to Lieutenant Young, his first lieutenant, who was in charge of loading supplies. He then turned to the boatswain. "We leave in forty-eight hours. Are you ready?"

The boatswain shrugged. "Not as ready as we could be in four days, but we'll sail all right."

Fergus went below to where the crew was lashing the extra guns tightly to the bulkheads to make room for the extra cargo coming below. He walked up and down, patting the pomelions at the ends of the guns affectionately. The gunner, following him, grinned. "They did a good job. Do you think we'll ever have enough luck to use them again, sir?"

Fergus laughed. "Luck is where you find it, and we'll be going a lot of places."

"Good, sir, the boatswain has stowed the stuff so we can move it if we have to. We'll be able to use half the guns, maybe more."

Fergus looked around the gun deck on one last tour and went back to the quarterdeck. A message was coming in from a nearby ship of the line. The signalman read it. "Sir, you've been invited for dinner."

"Thank you. Please accept."

At dinner Kilburnie enjoyed the large cabin and its beautiful appointments. Two other captains from nearby ships were also present, and Kilburnie was the center of attention, answering a barrage of questions about the Battle of the Nile and the adventures of his own ship.

Fergus ate and drank lightly, hoping to be excused early to get back to his ship before some foraging captain could show up to claim it.

His sleep was fitful, and he listened carefully for strange footsteps on deck. At 3:30 A.M. he could sleep no more, and he rose and prepared for the day.

17

İn Command

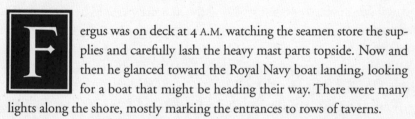ergus was on deck at 4 A.M. watching the seamen store the supplies and carefully lash the heavy mast parts topside. Now and then he glanced toward the Royal Navy boat landing, looking for a boat that might be heading their way. There were many lights along the shore, mostly marking the entrances to rows of taverns.

At dawn he still had not seen any boats headed their way, and the Royal Navy signal tower, though lighted, was quiet. He had the boatswain called, and soon he could hear the familiar cry along the decks, "All hands, stations for getting under way."

The *Aberdeen* slipped quietly out of the harbor at dawn, well within the forty-eight-hour limit Jeris had given him.

When the ship was secured for sea, and all sails were trimmed and drawing properly, Fergus heaved a sigh of relief. He might not be the regularly ordered commanding officer of the *Aberdeen,* but in his eyes and in the eyes of his officers and crew he was her captain and would be for some time.

He looked aft at her wide-spread sails and then glanced forward along her upper decks. She was slightly broader than other more modern ships of her size, and therefore not as fast, and some of her timbers and a bit of her bottom, where teredos had long ago penetrated a slight gap in the copper bottom sheathing, were on the verge of rotting, but she was still beautiful to Fergus. Any passing ship, not knowing she was no longer a ship of the line, would probably think she was one as long as her gun ports were closed.

The master came aft to the quarterdeck to consult Fergus about the weather and the use of the sails. He noticed that Fergus was preoccupied, and he stood beside him for a few moments without talking, watching the foretopmen come down from aloft. Then Fergus noticed him standing there quietly beside him and said, "Yes?"

"I think you were admiring your ship," the master said. "She's a beauty."

"Yes," Fergus said, "I'm very lucky."

"So is the crew. They look forward to serving under you."

Fergus laughed. "I hope they don't expect us to take a prize every cruise."

"No. They haven't spent all their money from the last one yet, but they know you'll run toward, not away from, any opportunity you see."

Fergus laughed. "They've got that right."

As they sailed south toward Gibraltar, the weather grew warmer day by day. It was now early August 1798, and the summer was at its height. Gibraltar was sweltering as they lay at anchor, awnings rigged to keep off the worst of the sun. Fergus was glad to get his orders there to proceed east to find Admiral Nelson's fleet. He asked the admiral of the port, "Where do you think I should look for him?"

The old admiral raised his eyebrows and smirked. "Naples, of course."

Fergus was puzzled. "Sir, why would he be there?"

The admiral laughed. "I guess you haven't heard the latest gossip. He's there to see Lady Hamilton."

"Who's she?"

"The wife of a diplomat stationed there."

"I still don't understand."

"Don't worry about it. Apparently Hamilton doesn't object. If you've seen the lady, you'll agree he probably needs some help, if you take my meaning." He laid a finger alongside his long red nose.

Fergus, now getting the drift of the conversation, said, "Thank you for your advice, sir. I'll leave tomorrow and head for Naples."

On September 23 the *Aberdeen* sailed slowly into the busy port of Naples. Vesuvius loomed threateningly behind the harbor. Fergus shuddered. "I don't like that damned big mound of hot rock so close."

The master laughed. "It's been there a long time, and it looks safe now."

"Yes, and according to my history books it has killed a hell of a lot of people over many years, and they just keep on staying around it."

"I'm more worried about dodging these damned Neapolitan ships. They don't seem to have any idea of the laws of the sea and who has the right of way."

Still sweating profusely in the September heat, the master managed to anchor the *Aberdeen* without major damage, although a small ship dashed across her bow just before she was to drop her anchor and managed to scrape her starboard side slightly, making a long thin scar.

The Italian captain leaned on her bulwark and laughed as he viewed the long scar on the paint on the side of the *Aberdeen*.

The boatswain, in the bow, let out a string of oaths and shook his fist.

The Italian skipper laughed again, answered with an even longer string of Italian oaths, and gave the boatswain the Italian salute with his middle finger.

Fergus shook his head sadly. "A different world," he said.

When the anchor was safely down, Fergus looked around the harbor. On the way in he had not seen any British war ships, but now, with a closer look, he could see the *Vanguard*, Nelson's flagship, anchored behind a line of Italian ships. A British frigate was moored alongside. He examined the ships through his long glass. After a few seconds, he whistled.

"Anything wrong?" the master asked.

"My God! The *Vanguard* is still a shambles topside. I think she needs our help. Call away my gig."

The midshipman on watch shouted to the boatswain, and his whistle sounded immediately. "Away the gig!"

Thirty minutes later the *Aberdeen*'s gig pulled alongside the flagship. Fergus was piped aboard and met by the admiral's aide.

The aide said, "Is that the *Aberdeen* you brought in?"

Fergus answered, "Yes, but I am not a captain. I am commanding her as a lieutenant."

"Amazing! I would have thought one of that flock of buzzards roosting in the Admiralty waiting room would have found your ship by this time."

The aide escorted Fergus below. He said, "The admiral would like to see you as soon as possible."

Admiral Nelson was reclining on a settee in his cabin when Fergus was presented to him. "Lieutenant Kilburnie, commanding officer of the *Aberdeen*," the aide said.

Nelson was obviously still recovering from his wounds received at the Battle of the Nile. There was a pink scar in his scalp where a flap of skin had been sewed back. "Please forgive me for not rising," he said. "My wounds are a little demanding at times." Then he looked closely at Fergus. "Ah, I remember you from when your ship remasted me off San Pietro. I understand your captain was killed in a battle later."

"Yes, sir. I was sorry to lose him."

"And now you are in command temporarily?"

"Yes, sir. I understand a captain is on his way to take over the ship."

Nelson's dark face cleared. "No, he isn't. He was bound here on a transport and was killed in a fierce action with a Spanish frigate. I am sure you will be in command for quite a spell. As a matter of interest to you, I am sending off a communication to the Admiralty recommending your immediate promotion to captain and that you remain in command of the *Aberdeen* permanently. I don't think it will go amiss. As of now, you have the rank of captain to go with the size of your ship. I will confirm this with the Admiralty."

Fergus beamed. "Thank you, sir."

Nelson, obviously tiring, smiled wanly. "And now bring your ship alongside and start transferring supplies and equipment to us. You could see when you crossed the quarterdeck how much we need them." The admiral brightened. "Oh, by the way, didn't you take a prize on your last cruise?"

"Yes, sir. I had a lot of help from my passengers and some extra guns I was carrying."

"Have you unloaded the guns?"

Fergus reddened. "Well, no, sir. I was pressed for time in my last port."

Nelson laughed. "I won't bother you over them. Keep them. I also have some passengers for you. The flagship is keeping fifty wounded seamen who are veterans of the Battle of the Nile with me and who need to be sent home to the hospital. I want you to take them with you."

"Of course, sir. Are they badly wounded?"

Nelson shrugged. "A few are. Most of them are ambulatory, and if they think you might take another prize, they'll get well in a hurry."

"I see, sir," Fergus said.

Nelson looked up at the overhead, his good black eye sparkling in his pale face. "Let me remind you that you will be under my command until you reach home. Therefore, I am entitled to one-eighth of any prize money you win."

Fergus nodded. "Of course, sir."

Nelson was somewhat apologetic. "Ordinarily I'm not concerned about such things as prize money, but lately my—ah—expenses ashore have been considerable and some prize money would be welcome."

Fergus grinned. "Sir, we'll try our best."

Two days later the *Aberdeen* was empty, and Fergus took his departure from Admiral Nelson and set course for Gibraltar. The trip to the Big Rock was uneventful, and the *Aberdeen* turned north for England.

For the first three days the *Aberdeen* sailed before a gentle southerly breeze on a northeasterly course. The water was calm and blue like the Mediterranean and filled with porpoises. Fergus spent his daylight hours watching them frolic around the bow like small children. Over them were agile white seagulls and soaring terns, dipping to the surface of the sea occasionally and quickly snatching a bit of green seaweed or an unwary small fish cruising on the surface.

While he was lazily watching the sea and its attractions, he thought about Shannon. He also wondered about the farm in Scotland his prize money had bought. Surely it would have a house on it, in addition to a salmon stream, and he thought briefly about getting out of the navy and going back to Ireland to see if Shannon would leave her husband and join him on his farm. After all, Nelson had done the same thing, with little reaction from the Admiralty.

A shout from the masthead interrupted his reverie. "Sail on the starboard bow!" the lookout yelled.

Fergus swung up on the bulwark and then up on the ratlines. Then he thought better of it, dropped back down to the deck, and sent Midshipman Puller aloft in his place. Puller was maturing fast and needed more responsibility and challenge.

On deck, he looked to starboard and watched the sail grow in size. He thought briefly about turning to port and running away from it. After all, the *Aberdeen* was only a partially armed transport and not expected to do battle with a French warship. Quickly he rejected that course of action, remembering what Captain Waterbury had done months ago in the same but more favorable situation when he had deliberately avoided action with a French ship. He, Captain Kilburnie, would not avoid action, no matter what the odds. Admiral Nelson never had, and he had succeeded wildly. Kilburnie would follow Nelson, not Waterbury. He knew his crew wanted the action as well as the prize that might follow it. He could see men nearby glancing at him and smiling with expectation.

Puller came sliding down the ratlines, disregarding the tar accumulating on his white stockings. "Sir," he said, "it's French and a good-sized frigate."

Fergus turned to MacGregor. "Master, keep her steady as she goes."

Then he said to the first lieutenant, "Lieutenant Young, make all preparations for battle."

"Shall I beat to quarters?"

"By all means."

The first lieutenant looked slightly puzzled. "You're sure she's French, sir."

"I'd stake my life on Midshipman Puller's assessment. That's why I didn't go aloft."

Young grinned. "I agree, sir."

Fergus nodded confidently. "Now we'll take her."

The French ship came on steadily on a westerly course, all sails set. Fergus studied the wind and knew he would have to lure the Frenchman to a southerly heading. "Master, two points to starboard, please."

MacGregor bawled out the necessary orders in his lowland Scottish accent, and some of the seamen left the guns temporarily to help the sail trimmers.

The French ship also turned two points but to her starboard to keep the direction and rate of closing unchanged. The speeding Frenchman was now due east of the *Aberdeen* and about five miles distant.

Fergus said to Midshipman Puller, standing next to him, "Put a long glass on the quarterdeck of the French ship and keep it on her no matter what happens. I want to know what the French captain is doing, where he's looking, how he looks, and, if you can do it, tell me what he's thinking. Also let me know anything else important you see."

Puller laughed. "I speak French, but he's too far away for me to read his lips."

Fergus, also studying the Frenchman with a long glass propped on the bulwark, said, "My God! He's bigger than I thought. At least thirty-eight guns."

The master heard him. "Captain, are you sure you don't want to change your mind about fighting him? I don't think we could outsail her, but we could delay the inevitable and she might even give up and let us escape."

Fergus laughed. "To hell with the inevitable. We're going to make something happen."

The master shrugged and put his hands behind him. "Well, whatever you're going to do you'd better do it very soon. We're just about in her gun range."

Fergus turned to his first lieutenant, who was in charge of the starboard gun battery. Lieutenant Young was indeed an older officer, both in years and in outlook. For years he had been waiting for promotion while serving on a ship of the line, and for years he had been passed over in favor of "those blighters hanging around the Admiralty," he had said. Now he was serving out his tour on a second-class ship until he was eligible for retirement. Fergus liked him, but he needed constant prodding. Fergus thought perhaps that was the reason he had never been promoted. Now Lieutenant Young stood looking at Fergus, his lined, anxious face set in a grim line. But today Young also seemed to be unusually enthusiastic, and Fergus hoped he had been able to change Young's attitude.

He asked the waiting Young, "Do you have all preparations made, and the extra guns on the gun deck rigged to fire to starboard?"

"Yes, sir, the passengers are ready, too, and eager for the action to start."

"Can they do any good with all those wounds?"

"Yes, sir. They know all about the prize we took before. They have confidence in you. Most of them have forgotten about their wounds. There are several veteran gun captains among them. They can lay a gun even though they're wounded. They'll be better than the French gunners."

Fergus clenched his hands lightly. "I'll try not to disappoint them. They'll be firing soon." He turned to the sailing master. "Change course eight points to port."

MacGregor gave orders to the helmsmen at the wheel and sent the seamen sail trimmers scrambling aloft to change the sail positions and trim. The *Aberdeen* swung to port rapidly, leaving the Frenchman on her starboard side. The Frenchman tried to turn to starboard to close the *Aberdeen,* but she was slower than her opponent. The *Aberdeen*'s large beam prevented her from making higher speed, but instead gave her the ability to turn more quickly than a faster ship.

Fergus grinned and shouted, "Commence firing!"

The gun captains checked the laying of their guns and as soon as they were sure they were on the turning Frenchman the guns boomed out. Even though they were at maximum range, several of the balls passed high in the Frenchman's sails, from forward aft, and at least one sail burst into tatters, the pieces fluttering in the breeze.

Fergus was exultant. "Most of the hits on the sails came from the lower deck guns manned by our passengers!" he said to Puller. "Great shooting!"

Puller answered, "They're paying their passage."

The French ship was so slow in coming about that a second group of flying balls met her just as she came broadside to the speeding *Aberdeen*.

Puller shouted, "I could see at least four shots hit her, mostly on her sails and rigging."

Kilburnie said, "Yes, that's why I've got the gunners firing on the up roll."

Puller said, "I see. You don't want to damage her hull so you can sail her in and you want to slow her down."

The master came up behind Fergus. "Captain, I think we've damaged her sails and rigging enough so that we can outsail her and get away."

Fergus guffawed. "Dammit, Master, stop worrying. We don't want to get away. We're going to take her."

MacGregor grinned. "Just testing you, sir."

The two ships were slowly closing. Now the Frenchman got off her first ragged salvo. Most of the balls passed high through the sails, but one entered the hull forward. In the relative silence between salvos, it could be heard bounding around.

Puller laughed, his young English face coloring light red. "No guns or gun crews up there now. Didn't do a bit of damage. Maybe we can fire the ball back."

Fergus ran forward to the twelve-pounders on the upper deck and talked to Lieutenant Young, who was sporting a wide grin. Fergus had never seen him display so much enthusiasm. He said to Young, "Keep after her sails and rigging."

Young's face fell and his smile collapsed. "Sir, don't you want to try to sink her?"

"Hell, no. Just like I told you. Keep your gunners firing on the up roll. She's like a prize salmon. We don't want to throw her back. We want to keep her."

Fergus ran back to the quarterdeck. "Puller, anything new?"

"No, sir."

The after guns crashed out. Fergus watched the balls fly off in gentle arcs like black pheasants scudding over the sea-green moor.

Then Puller shouted, "I'll be damned. A shot hit her steering wheel and binnacle. Their captain is down, too, and several men are lying around."

Fergus flexed his tired leg muscles. "Lucky hit, but we'll take it."

Fergus turned to the sailing master. "Come to starboard slowly so that we close her, but not so much that we mask any of our starboard guns."

Fergus grabbed a long glass from the binnacle and trained it on the Frenchman. He studied the ship's rigging and the officers and seamen on her topside carefully. Several men were standing around the captain, and the gun crews on the upper decks seemed to be disorganized. Most of them were frantically waving their hands and looking aloft. A few men were looking over the stern toward the rudder.

Fergus said to Puller, "I think she's lost steering control. Watch the leading edge of her sails carefully. If the rudder won't hold her up into the wind, the wind should blow her around to her starboard."

The firing from the *Aberdeen's* guns continued, but the French rate of gunfire was decreasing. Then Puller said, "The leading edges of her sails are beginning to flutter. She's definitely luffing."

"Good!" Fergus shouted. He turned to Lieutenant Young, who had come aft. "Lieutenant Young, be ready with your bow chasers and any other guns that will bear. You'll be able to rake her from astern in a few minutes."

When the Frenchman had turned enough so that her stern was to the *Aberdeen,* Fergus shouted to the busy master, "Head right for her and close her even though you mask our starboard battery. Our bow chasers outnumber their stern chasers, and we'll give her hell right up her butt."

The Frenchman, now with the wind out of her sails, lay dead in the water. The bow chasers of the *Aberdeen* kept up a steady fire, and the remaining sails of the Frenchman came down on deck in pieces, one by one, followed by yards and rigging.

"She's helpless," the master shouted. "She's got to strike her colors soon."

She did, but not before one of her stern guns had hurled a final twelve-pound ball at the *Aberdeen.* It hit the bulwark abreast of the binnacle and shattered the wood in it into hundreds of sharp splinters. Fergus felt some of them beat like angry bees against his left shoulder. There was not much pain at first, but he looked down and saw blood beginning to soak his shirt. He tried to lift his arm, but he couldn't.

The master, who had been shielded from the deadly hail by Fergus's body, looked at him. "Good God! Captain, shall I call the surgeon?"

Fergus shook his head. "Not now. I can't miss this. I'll be all right."

The *Aberdeen* slowly pulled alongside the struck French ship, her colors now down. Her sails were in a shambles and the officers and men on her deck were disorganized. Fergus was beginning to feel pain, and a faintness crept over him. He braced himself against the binnacle and took a deep breath to steady himself.

The sailing master backed the sails, and the *Aberdeen* stopped neatly alongside the wallowing Frenchman, a hundred yards away. Fergus held on to the binnacle. "Puller, take ten seaman, five marines, and any of the passengers who volunteer. You will be the prizemaster, and you can practice your French on the bastards on the way home."

Fergus turned to Lieutenant Young, who had come aft. "Lieutenant, lower a boat. Arm the boat crew and the men who will go to the prize."

While the boat was being lowered and the prize crew rowed to the Frenchman, Fergus studied the crippled ship. Then he swore. "The ship is in terrible shape topside," he said to Lieutenant Young. "As soon as the boat comes back, send the boatswain, the carpenter, and the sailmaker and some of their mates over there. Also some seamen if they say they need them. Tell them we'll pick them up on the way home as soon as they are through repairing the worst of the damage."

Fergus sent for the carpenter and gave him his long glass. "Take a look at the wheel and binnacle, Chips. Do you think you can fix it?"

The carpenter, unused to using a long glass, took a few minutes to adjust it, twiddling the focus ring and batting his eyelids. Then he said, "Captain, easy. I can see from here everything I need to know. The rudder itself looks intact. I can easily reeve a new set of ropes and I could even build a jury wheel. I figure about twenty-four hours."

Fergus asked, "How about the masts and spars?"

The carpenter, now waving the long glass about with ease, said, "Maybe another twenty-four hours. Then you'll have at least three knots. Maybe more."

"Good," Fergus said, "Off with you, and I will guard you and the others carefully until you are back."

The carpenter wiped his sweating brow. "Captain, I'd go aboard a flaming wreck if you asked me to."

When the boat came back from its second trip, and both ships were still lying to, Fergus left Lieutenant Young in charge and went below to see the surgeon.

The surgeon was Pollitt, the same young Welsh doctor Fergus had served with on the *Athena*. Having him transferred to the *Aberdeen* was the one favor Fergus had asked of his Uncle Jeris.

Jeris had said when Fergus had asked him to do it, "Easily done, lad. He's so young no other captain would want him."

Pollitt had been a great help to Fergus and served the crew well. His biggest contribution was making the crew take the newly prescribed lime juice to prevent scurvy. Through Jeris, Fergus had ordered a large number of butts of the juice. Not a single case of scurvy had occurred. Pollitt's rich Welsh voice also added to the infrequent Sunday morning divine services conducted. He made up for the lack of a chaplain and relieved Fergus from the duty of giving a Sunday morning sermon, which he hated to do.

The surgeon had Fergus laid out on a series of sea chests he was using as an operating table, cut away his shirt, and began to examine him. He whistled. "Captain, some of this is big and deep. I'll get all the splinters out, but I can't sew you up because this is so deep infection might set in. I'll have to keep the cavity open and pack it with lint. It will heal up from the bottom over time and hopefully without infection. At sea, splinters coming from topside wood are exposed constantly to salt water and sunshine. They seldom produce septicemia."

As Pollitt worked on him, Fergus moaned from the mounting pain, but managed to say between gritted teeth, "Let's get on with it. I want to be back on deck soon."

The surgeon frowned. "I don't know about that. I'll give you some laudanum while I work on you. You may not feel like fresh air after I'm through."

The laudanum helped, but Fergus had to set his teeth on a twisted rag. Even then he passed out twice.

When the surgeon was finished, he said, "Do you still want to go on deck?"

"No, but I have to. Can I sit in a chair there?"

"I don't advise it, but I know you're a stubborn Scot. If you do, have somebody tie you in it. I don't want you to fall and start the bleeding all over again."

Fergus forced a grin. "I promise. The only thing worse than a stubborn Scot is a stubborn Welshman. How long will this take to heal?"

"Depends upon your constitution. A little luck is involved, too. In any event you'll have to go to the hospital when we get in port."

When Fergus had been helped topside and tied in a chair, he looked over at the French ship, still wallowing in the seas a hundred yards away. The *Aberdeen*'s artisans were swinging aloft, directing their own men and the French crew. Rigs were being put in place for hoisting spars and mast parts.

The sailing master said, "They're in a hurry to get back to port. The carpenter just signaled that he's rigged a jury steering system, and it is working. I can see new spars and sails going up."

By the next morning the two ships were making a steady four knots toward England. Fergus, with no sails in sight, had finally allowed the surgeon and his steward to put him in a hammock rigged in his cabin in lieu of his cot. The pain was worse, but bearable with repeated doses of laudanum.

A week later the *Aberdeen* arrived in the Thames Estuary and anchored off Gravesend. By now Fergus was feeling better, and he stood proudly on the quarterdeck as they came in. The prize anchored nearby under an equally proud Midshipman Puller as prizemaster.

This time it was almost noon before Jeris arrived on the wharf, took a pinnace out to the ship, and clambered aboard.

He was so eager to board he almost fell from the sea ladder. After he had been retrieved by the side boys and hauled up the remaining steps, he looked at Fergus and said, "My God, laddy, are you making a habit of this? Do I see another prize over there?"

"Yes, Uncle, only this time I wasn't able to send word ahead to you."

Jeris looked more carefully at Fergus. "Lad, what happened to your arm? Are you hurt bad?"

"The surgeon thinks so, and he's about to take me to the hospital."

"Well, let's go. If you can get down the ladder with one arm, we'll use my carriage."

"If you can do it with one arm, I can."

Fergus turned to Lieutenant Young, standing erect on the quarterdeck. "Take over command of the ship. Enjoy it. You've earned it."

18
RECUPERATION

ergus traveled in Jeris's carriage to the hospital, the driver carefully trying to avoid the worst of the potholes in the well-worn
cobblestones. Jeris left him at the entrance. "I've got to get to
the Admiralty. I'll come back to see you tomorrow," he said.

The chief surgeon of the hospital took Fergus in tow and soon had his upper
clothes off and his body stretched out on an operating table under a bank of
gas lights in reflectors. The surgeon carefully stripped off the bandages. Then
he looked at the blood-soaked lint packing the wound caused by the largest
splinter. He whistled softly. "I'll give you some laudanum before I take this out."

An hour later, after Fergus had passed out twice, the surgeon looked
down at him as he opened his eyes. "It's all over. I've emptied and cleansed
the wound and put in a drain. You're lucky, and your surgeon did a good
job of cleaning and packing your wounds. There's no sign of infection, and
healing from the bottom has started. I've bandaged it, and if you feel like it
you can get up and walk around."

Fergus breathed deeply and the faintness lessened. "How long will I
be here?"

"About two weeks, I'd say. Maybe three."

Fergus tried to shrug, but his wound hurt. "That's not too bad."

The surgeon said, "Who's your ship's surgeon?"

"Doctor Pollitt."

The chief surgeon rubbed his chin. "Don't know him. Is he young?"

"Very, and a Welshman."

"He's very good. He really cleaned and packed your wound well. You could have had a nasty infection."

"Thank you. I'll tell him."

The chief surgeon rubbed his chin again. "I'd like to have him here, but I'm sure you'll say you can't spare him."

Fergus grinned. "That's what I'd say, sir. We really do need him."

"But you're not a full war ship. You shouldn't have many wounded men."

Fergus pursed his lips. "That's all relative and depends on what you do. So far we've fought more in the last year than any first-line frigate I know of."

"And I hear you took a prize."

"Two, as a matter of fact."

"Well, I'm barking at the wrong door, as my old Welsh father used to say, but if you can ever spare him, please let me know."

Fergus laughed. "Funny, my old Scottish grandfather used to say the same thing about barking at the wrong door. Dogs must be the same the world over."

The next morning Jeris arrived at the hospital beaming. "How are you feeling?" he asked. "I've got a package of food from Martha for you."

After a long breakfast of all the delicacies he had missed during his long time at sea, Fergus sat up and said, "Please thank her. I'll take it on this afternoon after a nap. I'm dry-docked for two or three weeks. Will that make me lose my ship?"

"Lad, you don't have to worry about that anymore. She's yours as long as you want her."

"I don't understand. Not long ago I was hiding in the Mediterranean."

"Well, since that time the Admiralty has received a communication about you and your actions from Admiral Nelson. He made it clear that you were to be promoted to captain and retain command of the *Aberdeen* as long as he was at sea. It's not official yet, of course, but it could be soon."

Fergus sighed. "I'd like that."

Jeris was not through. "When the Admiralty heard yesterday that you had brought in another prize, they tried to outdo Nelson. When I told them about the extra eight guns you had been hiding aboard, they wanted to give you eight more and the personnel to fire them."

Fergus grinned. "Eight more would make sixteen. That's a thirty-two-gun broadside. Together with four at the bow and eight astern that would make us the equivalent of a forty-four-gun frigate."

"That's what the Admiralty seemed to think. As short of fighting ships as the Royal Navy is, they wanted to turn you into a fighting ship while continuing to be a transport as a secondary mission."

Fergus laughed. "That sounds good, but I can't be so lucky all the time. I'll keep the extra guns I have and do the best I can. At least I don't have to worry anymore about losing my ship."

Jeris said, "There's more to this than you're telling me. How did you run across Admiral Nelson?"

"Simple. I had something he desperately needed. A ship full of mast parts."

"And he didn't have any? I don't understand."

"His flagship was completely dismasted in a violent and sudden storm in the northern Mediterranean. I found him just at the right time for both of us."

"But that can't be all?"

"No. He knew about my time on the *Athena*. I think Admiral Jervis told him. He told me I could keep the *Aberdeen* as long as he was in command of the Mediterranean fleet."

"There was more?"

Fergus laughed nervously. "There was a bit about his wanting a part of my prize money if I won any. He reminded me I was under his command and therefore he rated it."

"He doesn't usually take any of the prize money of ships under his command."

"That's what I heard, but I understand now he's got the need for some in Naples."

"Ah, I understand. There's been a rumor or two."

Fergus tried to ease his sling. "More than that, but I suggest that you and I not be the ones to pass it on."

He then asked of Essex and his father, Lord Satterfield. Uncle Jeris cheerfully replied that Essex was doing splendidly in his now not-so-new command. "He is developing an enviable reputation as a daring commander and an able captain who treats his crew like men and not like dogs. Of course, having his father in Lords is of no small assistance in this matter."

"And his father?"

"Essex's father is a master in politics and electioneering and has connections with all parties—the Tories, the Whigs, the king's men, and even the Jacobins. Still, he is one of the more vocal proponents of a hard war against the French whom he views as being, as he puts it, 'infected with ideas more dangerous than the Americans have.'"

Fergus leaned back in his chair. "Uncle, I am amazed at your knowledge of Lord Satterfield's political abilities. How do you come by it?"

Now Jeris smiled slyly. "Fergus, being an Admiralty clerk demands that I have knowledge of many men and their politics. As I told you, on occasion I am asked for advice. That advice is not necessarily confined to the workings of the dockyards, if you understand my meaning."

"I was considering paying a call on Lord Satterfield while I was in London. Now it seems I'd be a fool not to."

Jeris nodded. "Well put, Lieutenant Kilburnie. You'll not be a lieutenant forever if you do. I think he would want to see you, bandages or no."

Later that night Fergus lay on a feather bed, somewhat disconcerted that the bed didn't swing like a hammock. He considered how he would approach Lord Satterfield. A note, perhaps, asking if his lordship would be available for a call. Damn! Why did advancement in the navy depend on such a powerful patron? It wasn't that he disliked Lord Satterfield, for he liked him very much. It would seem so transparent what he was doing, cultivating a man with political power in hopes of gaining promotion and perhaps even a better ship. As he drifted off to sleep he considered what the wording of his note should be.

In the morning Aunt Martha sent him a enormous Scottish breakfast, porridge, blood pudding, boiled eggs, oat cakes, and many cups of strong tea. Afterward, Jeris seated him to write a note to Lord Satterfield. "I'll take it to the office and have it delivered, but ask his lordship to answer to this address."

Fergus took up the pen and carefully wrote the following: "Dear Sir: As I have lately returned from service in the Mediterranean, and have been recuperating in hospital from a wound, I would appreciate it if you would allow me to call upon you so that I may describe the events of the Battle of the Nile which I witnessed at close range. I would also like to enquire about your son, my close friend. I am, sir, your obedient servant, Fergus Kilburnie, Lieutenant, Royal Navy."

Reading it, Jeris nodded approvingly. "Good. His lordship will undoubtedly appreciate this."

"Why so, Uncle?"

"Why, Fergus, those who have seen the Battle of the Nile are few and far between in London, and his lordship will appreciate any first-hand information he can glean from you. It might give him a political advantage, and in that area those in politics appreciate any edge over their rivals."

The next day an orderly came into his room and handed Fergus a letter addressed to "Lieutenant Fergus Kilburnie, Royal Navy."

Fergus turned the letter over to unseal it and noticed that the seal bore a nobleman's coat of arms. Involuntarily he came to his feet in excitement— Lord Satterfield! He broke the seal and hurriedly unfolded the letter. It was short and to the point, a letter of a busy man.

Lieutenant Kilburnie—Many thanks for your letter. I would indeed be pleased to meet with you and hear of your account of the victory enjoyed by Nelson's fleet over the French as well to interview you regarding your plans for future service in His Majesty's Navy. Please meet with me tomorrow at seven o'clock at my club—White's. I thank you for your consideration. I remain your obedient servant. Satterfield.

The next evening, Fergus found himself in front of White's, one of London's most exclusive clubs. Known throughout the city—and probably the world—as a place at which congregated the men who held positions of property and power in Britain, it was not a place Fergus approached with confidence. After all, a lieutenant in the navy would seem quite out of place in an establishment that had as its members men who were at ease at the highest levels of government and trade.

As he approached the door, the porter—a large fellow with a nose that seemed to have been broken more than a few times—came forward and bowed slightly. "Yes, sir." His face betrayed nothing, not distaste, not approval—nothing.

"Good evening. I am here to meet with the earl of Satterfield at his lordship's invitation."

At the mention of Lord Satterfield's name, recognition flickered across the doorman's eyes. "Yes, sir," the porter replied, stepping back to open the door. "The hall porter shall assist you in finding his lordship." He smiled, displaying a few gaps in his teeth. Fergus started to thank him, but the porter had already turned his attention to another man approaching the door. As Fergus stepped through the door, he heard the porter call, "Good evening, m'lord."

As he entered the entrance hall another man, more slight than the door-man and a bit older, materialized beside him. "Good evening, sir. Allow me to take your hat." He plucked Fergus's hat from his hands. "I trust you are Lieutenant Kilburnie."

"Uh, yes, yes, I am," said Fergus, somewhat taken aback at the man's knowledge.

"Ah, good," the hall porter said. He stole a glance at the clock in the hall. "And at the appointed hour as well. His lordship will be pleased." He motioned for a footman to approach and when the man came close, he said, "This is Lieutenant Kilburnie. He is Lord Satterfield's guest. Please take him to his lordship presently."

The footman bowed slightly. "Please follow me, sir." Fergus did as he was bid and followed the man through a number of rooms in which men were loudly discussing or quietly conversing. Other men were sprawled in chairs, sleeping with hats drawn over their eyes. Everywhere was the smell of tobacco smoke. Fergus found himself wishing that he knew who these men were for he had the distinct feeling that a great many of them were power-ful men indeed.

Lord Satterfield was alone in a relatively quiet corner, reading a newspa-per and drinking a glass of claret when Fergus approached. "M'lord," the footman said with great gravity, "Lieutenant Kilburnie."

Satterfield dropped the newspaper and looked up at the servant and then at Fergus. To Fergus's relief, his lordship broke into a smile when he saw him. "Ah," he said jovially, "a hero of the Nile! Well, Admiral Nelson is not in London, so you sir shall have to do, in spite of your bandages!" He winked. "Let us repair to the dining room. I am famished from all this politics. I have to get back to the country or I'm sure to develop the gout." He let out a burst of laughter and stood. "Come, Kilburnie!"

Fergus followed Lord Satterfield into a large room where tables were arrayed and at which many men were eating, drinking, and talking. As they sat Fergus mused that upon first glance some people might think it was almost any tavern in London, but after a moment the room's understated richness and high quality of the men's dress would make it evident that this was no common room.

Lord Satterfield led Fergus to a table at which were four chairs, lowered himself into a chair, and gestured for Fergus to do the same. A man bustled over with a bottle of claret and two glasses, which made Satterfield beam. "Ah, good, I see you remembered," he said to the servant and then turned to Fergus. "I gave instructions that I was to be served claret here unless I directly asked for something else. I had too much punch here one day, fell asleep over a newspaper, and missed a vote in the House. The prime minister was not at all pleased, I'm told, but seeing as I control more than a few votes in Commons, there is just so much he can say." He chuckled and Fergus wondered what it must be like to control votes in the House of Commons and to not concern yourself much with the opinion of the king's first minister. The sense of the wide gap between him and Lord Satterfield, and Essex, made it even more amazing to him that Lord Satterfield would invite him to this club.

Fergus looked meaningfully at the empty chairs and Lord Satterfield beamed. "Ah, a keen observer. I have taken the liberty, Kilburnie, of inviting some friends of mine to hear your tales of fighting the French. London is abuzz with rumors and stories as well as what has been published in the newspapers—Nelson's dispatches and all that. Therefore, they would like to hear what an actual participant saw."

"Well, sir, my ship, the *Aberdeen,* was not in the thick of the action as was the *Vanguard* or the *Bellerophon.* When darkness fell it was difficult to see things because of thick smoke from the guns and the burning ships."

"I understand, Kilburnie," said Lord Satterfield benevolently. "I remember how confusing things could get on a battlefield. I can just imagine what could happen at sea with no sergeants to get people back in ranks." He sipped some wine. "So, while we wait, tell me of your plans. I take it you plan to stay in the navy."

"Yes, sir. Besides, as we are at war, I cannot conceive of leaving the service."

"Admirable sentiment, Kilburnie, admirable. Does your present ship suit you?"

Fergus hesitated for a moment. Was Lord Satterfield offering him help to get to a new ship? Yet, if he said he did not like the *Aberdeen* and Captain Leeks, would that be taken as disloyalty? If he said it suited him fine, would Lord Satterfield consider the matter closed? "Ah, sir, the *Aberdeen* is a fine ship. Captain Leeks was an excellent captain and a good man."

Lord Satterfield smiled, "But?"

Fergus flushed hotly and then gave a sheepish smile. "I am, of course, always, uh, open to other considerations."

A grave look flashed over Lord Satterfield's face. "My boy, I am sorry for asking such a question. As a soldier, you always have loyalty to your regiment no matter if the officers' mess is a collection of blackguards and the men a parcel of rogues. It's the Tenth Foot or the Sixteenth Light Dragoons or nothing! I keep forgetting the sailor's life is different. Quite thoughtless of me. You have my apologies, sir."

"Ah, no offense taken, sir," Fergus said with immense relief. "What of your son?"

"Ha! That young rascal! Well, Kilburnie, as your uncle knows," at this Satterfield winked, "he has commanded a cutter for some time now. The ship is attached to the Channel Fleet, 'special duties,' my son says. Whatever that means, anything so secret must be rather dangerous." He paused for a moment and looked worriedly into his wine. Fergus knew that Satterfield was correct to be worried; "special duties" included raiding and the landing and rescuing of agents along the French coast, highly dangerous indeed.

Lord Satterfield looked back up. "It's a good job for a high-spirited lad like him. No one looking over his shoulder, telling him what to do." He laughed as if at some private joke. "His older brothers are, of course, mad with jealousy and I must admit I am a bit envious myself. Yet, war's a young man's game, eh?" Smiling slyly, he observed, "No doubt you wouldn't mind having such a ship yourself, eh, Kilburnie?"

"Quite frankly, sir," Fergus announced firmly, "I'd like nothing better."

"Good man," replied Satterfield. "I didn't think service on an armed transport would suit a man like you forever."

Kilburnie was getting noticeably fatigued. Satterfield kindly said, "I know you would like to get back to your hospital bed. I will tell my guests you will meet them another time. It has been kind of you to accommodate me tonight."

Kilburnie nodded gratefully. "Thank you, sir, and I hope to see you again."

"Oh, yes, and I will be following your career closely."

After his meeting with Lord Satterfield Fergus was released by the hospital to spend a few days recuperating at home. He awoke one morning to a knock on the door. The maid said, "I have water for your shaving, sir," and smiled shyly as she came in with a pitcher and replaced the one from the night before. "Good morning, sir," she said as she left. He stood by the dresser and prepared to shave.

He worked up lather from the soap and spread it over his beard. He opened his razor and then began shaving. He stopped suddenly as the razor came to a place on his neck where a rope would be placed if he were hanged. He put the razor down and took a breath, then shook his head, trying to shake the memories of the men he had seen hanged.

Chuckling at the memory of Lord Inver's florid, angry face that day in the churchyard, he picked the razor back up and began to shave again. "Besides, Fergus," he announced to his reflection, "you're too lucky to be hanged."

The aromas of another of Aunt Martha's enormous breakfasts met him as he came down the stairs. "Well," Aunt Martha said in mock seriousness, "the day's half over and you're just getting round to coming down to breakfast."

"It is seven o'clock, Aunt Martha; the day is hardly wasted."

Fergus decided not to argue the point further and sat down. He filled a cup with tea and started filling his plate with food when Aunt Martha fished a letter out of her apron. "Oh, yes, one of the liveried servants who seem to hang about this house like flies now that you're with us brought this by early this morning."

"One of Lord Satterfield's servants?"

"Oh, no, sir," the cook piped up. "This one was in a blue coat with a lovely row of gold buttons."

"Thank you," Aunt Martha said archly at the cook's unbidden intrusion, causing to the cook to flush and turn quickly back to her duties. "As I was saying, Fergus, it was delivered this morning."

The seal on the envelope was relatively simple, no coat of arms to denote a nobleman; however, the paper was thick and smooth. Fergus hurriedly broke the seal and read the contents. His surprised expression caused Aunt Martha to ask if the letter bore bad news. "No, but I have been invited to a levee at the house of the Honorable Mr. John Phipps to 'celebrate the late victory of our fleet under the command of Admiral Horatio Nelson.'"

"Let me see that," Aunt Martha snatched the letter from his hand. After reading the letter for a moment, she observed, "It is in a fashionable neighborhood, although I'm not familiar with the name." She glanced again at the letter. "Goodness, Fergus, this is tonight!" She looked about the kitchen and started snapping out orders for water to be boiled and irons heated. "Where is your best uniform, Fergus?"

"Upstairs."

"With your best linen?" Fergus nodded. "Good." She turned to the maid. "Go get the uniform and linen. Now!" Just then the yardboy came in bearing a load of wood. "You there! Go and fetch my nephew's shoes and give them a proper cleaning." She held up a hand. "Wait!" She turned to Fergus. "Do you have pumps?"

Pumps? Dancing shoes? This was going too far. "What do I need those for?" he asked incredulously.

Aunt Martha sighed impatiently. "In case you have not noticed, Fergus, we live in a city and you cannot step anywhere without stepping into something vile—be it garbage or manure of some sorts. You don't want to be trailing manure on some fine gentleman's carpet, do you?"

This was getting too much, Fergus thought. "What's wrong with using a boot scraper?"

Aunt Martha put her hands on her hips. "Do you want these people to say, 'There's that Scottish oaf, Kilburnie, reeking of dung, clomping around like some farmboy in the stable yard?'"

"Who notices shoes, Aunt Martha?"

Aunt Martha took an exasperated tone. "Plenty of men of quality—and their women, that's who. There's many a man baying for advancement in the navy like hounds after a fox and if a man of influence, or his wife or his mistress—and there are a great many men who depend on the opinion of women—decides you appear to be a rude country boy, despite your fine linen and uniform, you'll never get a ship."

"Surely things aren't done in such a fashion," Fergus said incredulously.

Aunt Martha snorted, "More times than you'd think, my boy." She wagged a finger at him. "You might have seen some of the world, Fergus Kilburnie, but you don't know all of its ways." She paused, shaking her head. "I'll see if your uncle has any upstairs that might fit you. If I cannot find any, you'll just have to mind where you step tonight."

Hours later, Fergus's uniform was brushed, polished, and shined as best as the efforts of Aunt Martha and her maids could make it; his shoes were cleaned and polished to a deep gleam and the buckles shined brilliantly. His hat had been carefully brushed and awaited him in the hall. A pair of pumps had been found ("From when your uncle and I visited people—before this accursed war kept him at his office so much") and had been worked into a condition that, in Fergus's opinion, would pass an inspection by the most scrupulous admiral in the fleet, but which Aunt Martha described grudgingly as "adequate." Uncle Jeris came home and when he innocently asked the reason for the commotion had been banished into the parlor along with Fergus, a large helping of bread and cheese, and two tankards of beer. "Keep out of the way, Jeris," said Aunt Martha. "Keep Fergus out of the way and make sure he eats. I don't want people thinking he is attending this ball because otherwise he would not be able to get a meal." Jeris obeyed these orders with a wink to Fergus and a wry smile. "Come, my boy, the little hen must be free to bustle about."

Settling into the parlor chairs, the two men fell to eating the bread and cheese and drinking their beer before talking. "So, Fergus, what was the name of this man who is holding the ball?"

"The Honorable John Phipps." Fergus showed him the letter.

Uncle Jeris furrowed his brow. "Well, he's a nobleman's son; that's where the 'Honorable' comes from, but I'm not familiar with the name." He shrugged and handed the letter back to Fergus. "Did you give some thought to what I said about your prospects? I did not mean to scare you, Fergus; I know the prospect of command is enticing, but you should be aware of just what might await you."

"I'm aware of why you did it and you have my thanks."

Jeris raised his tankard. "Well, then, Fergus, here's to your next ship—whatever her name may be!"

Fergus raised his tankard in response. "Thank you, Uncle. May she be fine of line and fast."

In the carriage, Fergus checked his shoes for what was probably the tenth time and brushed the sleeves of his uniform coat yet again. He checked to see if the baize bag in which his uncle's pumps rested was where it had been—what?—a minute ago. He took a deep breath and admonished himself yet again for being nervous. "Damn it," he said aloud, "you've been in action and stared down a Spanish three-decker. Why should attending a party bother you?" Still, his nervousness remained. Damn. He looked out of the windows of his uncle's cabriolet cab. Although the autumn sun had set, in the dusk there was enough light left for him to see the press of humanity on the streets. Whenever his carriage slowed, some man or woman ran up, hawking something. More than once, he was thankful for the cudgel the cabman had placed on the seat. A couple of doxies, reeking of gin and wretched perfume, had asked lewdly if he wanted to "lay alongside" them "like Admiral Nelson done with the Frenchies." When he angrily shooed them away, they replied with a torrent of abuse that would have made a bosun blush.

Just as Fergus began to wonder if the cabdriver had lost his way, they arrived on a street lined with finely built, brilliantly lit houses. It soon was obvious which house was hosting the party as a long queue of carriages was near the front of one.

After a few minutes Fergus's conveyance came up to a group of liveried servants. An unseen hand opened the door and another man bent to lower the folding steps. While Fergus was making sure he had his pumps and his hat, one servant, older and probably senior, looked impassively at Fergus and asked for his name. "Lieutenant Fergus Kilburnie, Royal Navy," Fergus replied, hoping his voice did not betray the nervousness he felt.

The servant's face changed not a wit. "Yes, sir." He gestured to the door. "This way, please, sir."

Fergus moved up the walk to the grand doorway at which another servant was posted and who opened the door at his approach. Stepping through the doorway into an anteroom, Fergus was dazzled momentarily by a flood of light thrown out by dozens of candles and a burst of noise—the drone of conversations, punctuated by laughter, music, and the treads of scurrying servants. The noise seemed to come from another room and Fergus could see people coming in and out of doorways.

A servant came up to him, "Your hat, sir?" Fergus gave it to him wordlessly. A flicker of approval crossed the man's face. "Ah, I see you've brought your pumps. You'll want to change." The man gestured to a chair in the anteroom. "I'll see no harm comes to your shoes, sir."

After changing into his pumps, Fergus moved through the door of the anteroom and was guided by a footman to the room in which the Phippses and their guest were gathered. He stood in the doorway for a moment, searching for a familiar face, but saw none. Instead, he saw a great many men and ladies beautifully dressed—and no small number of fellow officers. He lost count at fifteen and was distressed to see that the most junior was a commander who looked younger than he did and that at least two admirals were in attendance. None of the men he recognized, which, he considered, wasn't all to the bad; Captain Waterbury could have been here.

Damn him. A servant announced, "Lieutenant Fergus Kilburnie, Royal Navy."

Well, no going back now, Fergus thought, and moved into the room. Not knowing whether or not to approach the other officers, he decided that the safest place was where drink was being dispensed. Before he could find it, however, a servant materialized beside him, in his hands a tray with drinks. Fergus selected a glass of wine and began wandering about the room, taking pains not to gawk at the paintings, fine furniture, or the women, who were sumptuous in both dress and figure. A particularly fine-looking woman— almost jet-black hair and china blue eyes with a firm chin—smiled flirtatiously at him, and when Fergus returned the smile she came over to him. Perhaps, Fergus thought, Nelson's victory has made sailors fashionable this year. Whatever the reason, he was happy with the attention.

"Good evening, Lieutenant."

Fergus bowed. "Lieutenant Fergus Kilburnie, Royal Navy, ma'am. At your service."

"Oh, you're a Scotsman," she said brightly and for a moment Fergus wondered if he was about to be insulted. "Just like the gallant Lord Cochrane." A smile shone; clearly, this woman was not offended by Scotsmen. Thus heartened, Fergus decided to continue the conversation. But what to say? He was thankful when the lady put a hand to her mouth. "Oh, how silly of me! You do not know who I am."

"Indeed, ma'am, you have the advantage of me."

"Oh, I doubt anyone could get the advantage of you," she purred, lightly touching his arm with her hand. Fergus felt a chill run down his spine. "I am Honoré Phipps, the sister of the man hosting this party. Tell me, Fergus Kilburnie, on which ship are you an officer, or are you still looking for one like so many of these poor wretches on half-pay, condemned to wander seaports looking for a ship?"

Fergus replied, "I am most pleased to say, ma'am, that I am an officer on His Majesty's Ship *Aberdeen*."

Honoré's brow furrowed as she thought for a moment. "*Aberdeen*. I seem to recall the name. Was that one of the ships at Aboukir Bay?" She leaned toward Fergus and whispered conspiratorially, "My brother thinks I do not read the newspapers, but I do. Most avidly."

"Indeed, she—the *Aberdeen,* that is—was at Aboukir Bay." Now he leaned forward and whispered, "Although we were not part of the battle line precisely."

"Oooh," Honoré squealed, "how utterly delightful! Here we are having a party to honor a victory and one of the men who was there is in our midst." She linked her arm under Fergus's. "Come, you must meet my brother."

Fergus and Miss Phipps stood on the fringe of the group of men. There was no doubt who the brother was in the group. The Honorable Mr. Phipps and his sister shared the same dark hair and blue eyes and strong chin. "Brother," she announced. The men fell silent and turned their attention to her. "May I present Lieutenant Fergus Kilburnie, Royal Navy, of His Majesty's Ship *Aberdeen* and a man who fought with Admiral Nelson in Egypt?"

At the magical words "Nelson" and "Egypt," all conversation ceased in the group and all heads turned toward Fergus. He felt Miss Phipps's arm slide out from his and immediately he became the center of attention. With a look of great pleasure Mr. Phipps grabbed his hand and shook it vigorously. "Well, well, well," was all he said. But if Mr. Phipps was not a nimble conversationalist, the other men unleashed a torrent of words upon Fergus. "Splendid!" "Well done!" "Superb!" "I hope the army can do as well!"

Phipps said, "You shall have to tell us all about the battle!" A chorus of affirmation went up instantly.

Before Fergus could say anything Phipps had taken him by the arm, spun him around, and led him to a large table upon which rested all sorts of food. "You must show us, Lieutenant," he said cheerily. He turned to the guests. "Lieutenant Kilburnie here was with Nelson and the fleet at Aboukir Bay! He has consented to describe the battle to us in some detail." A loud murmur of approval greeted this announcement and the guests began to converge on Fergus. Phipps waved his hands at the servants. "Clear this here!" The servants bustled up and moved dishes and trays, making a space on the snow-white tablecloth. Phipps's gaze fell on a bowl of nuts. "Here," he scooped up a handful, "let the walnuts be the French ships. And," he grabbed a bowl of sweetmeats, "these shall be our ships."

Wondering as to just when it was he had consented to describe the battle, Fergus began to protest. "Truly, sir," he said, "I cannot add anything to what you and all these learned people have already read." A storm of polite protest greeted his words. "Oh, please, Lieutenant Kilburnie," said Mr. Phipps. "I'm sure the ladies will enjoy."

"Oh, indeed," piped up Honoré, who stood across the table from Fergus. She lightly clapped her hands. "Oh, please, Lieutenant."

Fergus hesitated. What to do? Then a deep voice that could have carried from binnacle to topgallant without aid of speaking trumpet boomed out. "Yes, Lieutenant, please tell us."

Fergus looked to Honoré's right to where stood a florid-faced man with wiry, bushy eyebrows and an admiral's uniform. The admiral gestured lightly. "Let these people know what the navy is capable of, Mister Kilburnie." There was no menace to the admiral's tone, but by the emphasis on "mister" Fergus knew that he had just received an order.

"And leave out no detail," said a familiar voice. Fergus whipped his head to his left. There stood Lord Satterfield, a broad grin on his face and a gorgeous woman on his arm. Lord Satterfield gestured with his eyes, as if saying, Well, get on with it.

Strengthened by the smile of Miss Phipps and the presence of Lord Satterfield, Fergus's confidence welled up. He drew himself up. "Well, if I am do this properly, I shall need to set the scene." A murmur of satisfaction went through his audience.

Fergus pointed to a bottle of wine. "Let me have that, please." He placed it on the table near him. "Now let that be Aboukir Castle and these," he snatched a number of napkins from where they lay near some dishes and arranged them in a shallow, elongated crescent, "shall serve to outline the bay." He took the walnuts and laid them in a line, trying to reproduce the positions of the French. When they were in a satisfactory place, he took up the bowl of sweetmeats. "Now, it was about sunset and the wind was coming from here." He gestured to show the wind's direction. "On the *Aberdeen*—which was about here," he stabbed the table with his finger, "we were wondering just what Admiral Nelson would do. It had been months we had been looking for the French, 'tis true, but the sun was setting, meaning a night fight if the attack was made."

He began placing the candies on the table, near what represented the bay's entrance. "Then just as the lead ships were approaching the entrance, up went the signal for the attack from the *Vanguard*." Involuntarily, he smiled at the memory of that day. "Well, you can imagine the tumult on board. The men—and the officers—cheered themselves hoarse and some began singing." Inexplicably, Fergus felt his throat tighten with emotion. That was quite a moment, wasn't it? A great victory and he was there. Then, remembering where he was, he cleared his throat and coughed.

"Oh, please forgive me. Here," said Mr. Phipps thrusting a glass of wine into Fergus's hand, "we cannot have you getting a parched throat." Laughter twittered about the table.

"Thank you, sir," said Fergus, at once thankful for the wine and the fact that no one seemed to notice how the memories had affected him. He took a draught. "Much better, sir." And with that Fergus began a narration of the battle, spicing the tale with vivid descriptions of the major events—the British van's navigation of the tricky passage round the head of the French line, the explosion of the massive *L'Orient,* the morning escape of the remnants of the French fleet. He made sure to tell the tales of the French admiral's desire to die on his quarterdeck, the refusal of one captain's son to leave his mortally wounded father, and the tenacity and dogged courage of some of the French crews. He paused to take some wine occasionally and, when he did so, he made sure to examine the faces of his audience. All seemed to be held in rapt attention, even the other officers—to include the admirals.

When he finished with a description of the *Aberdeen's* move against the French frigate coming down at the *Bellerophon,* he made sure to play down the *Aberdeen's* role, giving the lion's share of credit to the *Zealous* and her timely appearance. After he told that tale, he took another mouthful of wine and said, "Well, that is all I have in the way of a narration." The men voiced their approval and the ladies clapped politely; out of the corner of his eye Fergus could see the two admirals exchange approving nods. Well, he thought, at least I've upheld the honor and reputation of the navy. He had little time to ponder his triumph (such as it was) for almost immediately he was surrounded by people who peppered him with all sorts of questions.

Just as Fergus was wondering when the barrage of inquiries would ever end, Phipps came to his rescue. "Come now, ladies and gentlemen, there are other entertainments beside exhausting Lieutenant Kilburnie here." Some of the women gave little groans of displeasure, but Phipps ignored them. "Now, now, I'm sure that Mr. Kilburnie knows why some men prefer to run at the mouth of a cannon than walk into a London levee." Laughter bubbled up at this remark. "But let us allow him a rest at least." He nodded toward a quartet of musicians seated in the corner; they quickly brought up their instruments and began to play. The buzz of conversation increased and the people began to break into small groups.

Phipps smiled at Fergus warmly. "Thank you, sir, for your most enlightening description of the battle. Please excuse me for throwing you to the lions as I did, but all of London is starved for information and, besides, you came well recommended." Before Fergus could ask the meaning of that remark, Phipps excused himself hurriedly, "Oh, there's someone leaving, a man my father expects to be treated most delicately lest he take his votes somewhere else come next division in Commons. Please take some refreshment."

Fergus turned gratefully to where wine was being poured and was happily sipping a glass when he heard Lord Satterfield's voice close by. "Well done, Kilburnie, well done." Fergus turned to see Lord Satterfield standing there, the stunning woman still on his arm. She was no girl, but a mature woman with an ample figure, her eyes bright and sharp. Fergus bowed slightly, "Thank you, my lord."

"Please forgive me, Kilburnie, but it was I who arranged your invitation to this affair. As soon as I told Mr. Phipps of your experiences, he was most ardent that you attend."

"Ah, so that's what he meant when he said I came 'well recommended.'"

Lord Satterfield gave a grin. "Indeed. Besides, there are people here who could be important to your prospects." The lady with Lord Satterfield cleared her throat. "Oh, my apologies," Satterfield said. "Here this lady asks to meet you and I prattle on about business." He gestured to Fergus. "Lieutenant Fergus Kilburnie, may I present the Countess du Montclair. My dear countess, Lieutenant Kilburnie."

The woman smiled warmly and extended her hand; Fergus took it lightly, bowed, and said, "Your servant, madam."

The smile grew even warmer and the eyes danced with delight. "I want to thank you, sir, for all you did in defeating those . . . those . . . ," the Countess du Montclair said in a voice heavy with an accent Fergus assumed was French. She paused searching for the words. "Those villains!" she declared, her eyes now blazing with anger.

Fergus paused. He assumed she meant the French and guessed that she was one of the many expatriates—nobles and commoners—who had made their ways to safety in England since the revolution in France and the wave of executions and imprisonments that some described starkly as "the Terror." Rather than risk offense by saying something gallant or expressing some sympathy where none might be required Fergus bowed again. "Thank you, madam."

Lord Satterfield broke in. "Like most of our officers, madam, Lieutenant Kilburnie is somewhat bashful when it comes to acceptance of thanks for a service well done—even from beautiful women."

"Especially from beautiful women," said Fergus with a firmness that brought a slight smile to the countess's face and a look of absolute delight to Lord Satterfield's face. "It's just that in the navy so much depends on the entire crew that it is somehow wrong to take all the credit for yourself."

"Oh, but Lieutenant Kilburnie, you are a most skilled diplomatist," said the countess. "It should stand you well in your profession."

Fergus felt himself blush. Of all the things he considered himself, a diplomat was not one of them. "Thank you, madam, but I am determined to develop my skills as a sailor more than those of diplomat."

The countess gave another dazzling smile. "Very admirable, my dear lieutenant, but great victories are often won by a well-chosen word."

"Oh, ho, Kilburnie," chuckled Lord Satterfield, "the countess has you there."

Fergus bowed slightly. "Indeed, she has, my lord. I stand corrected."

Satterfield smiled and gestured to the crowd about the room. He dropped his voice a bit, "Very impressive, Kilburnie, your performance. I am hopeful it was not lost on the some of the more—shall we say—senior guests."

"I hope not, too, sir," answered Fergus truthfully. "Even in a war, it is apparent a man needs help to gain even the chance of advancement."

"All too true, Kilburnie," said his lordship seriously. After a slight pause, he turned to the countess. "Come, my dear countess, I need you to charm a banker I know. He needs to see the worth of another loan to the Crown."

Fergus bowed. "Good evening, countess, and good evening, my lord."

19

Shannon

wo weeks after Kilburnie returned to the hospital, the sur-
geon removed the dressing from Fergus's wound and exam-
ined the red patch of healed skin. "This has healed nicely,"
the surgeon said, "and I'm going to put on a light bandage
to protect it."

"When I can go back to my ship?"

"Maybe in another week. I want to make sure the skin is tough enough
to resist infection."

Fergus sighed. "I'll be bored out of my shoes."

"Ah, well, I have the solution to that. The Admiralty sent word over to
send you and any other senior officers well enough to attend a ball to be
held tonight in honor of Admiral Nelson's latest victory."

"He'll be there?"

"Well, actually no. It seems he's been detained in Naples, but it is still
being held in his name."

Fergus laughed. "I can understand that, but I really don't want to go."

"Certainly a Scot can dance, and you've been to social affairs."

Fergus colored. "Naturally. All Scots can dance. But I may not be familiar
with all of those fancy English dances. Reels and bucks and all that sort of thing."

The surgeon laughed. "You won't have any trouble. You are famous as a fighting man and certainly are handsome. You'll have to fight off all the young ladies volunteering to teach you the latest dances."

Fergus laughed. "Thank you for your prognosis, Doctor. I guess I'll have to go in honor of Admiral Nelson if the Admiralty wants me to go."

"They do. Enjoy it. I've had your steward bring your dress uniform here. It was a little moldy, but we've given it a little treatment with hospital chemicals. The mold is out, but it may smell a little odd. You'll be all right. The ladies will think it is an exotic seagoing smell."

Fergus laughed. "If I know the ladies, they'll be wearing so much perfume they'll never notice me."

"Where did you get the captain's uniform?"

"I sort of inherited it from a captain I really admired, Captain Burbage, and I wanted to wear it some day. I've carried it with me all this time, and someday I'll give it to his wife. I suppose it gathered a lot of mold down in the hold in my sea chest."

That evening Fergus put away his hospital garb and grudgingly got into Captain Burbage's dress uniform. A young nurse helped him ease it over his still slightly tender shoulder. The sailmaker had done his best to alter it. The linen was clean, starched, and freshly pressed, but the gold-trimmed jacket smelled of some strange chemical the hospital nurses had used to clean it and to kill the mildew. Fergus borrowed Jeris's dancing pumps again and wished he could be attending the ball in softer, more comfortable civilian clothing.

Jeris, who had heard of the Admiralty's requirement that Fergus and other senior naval officers now present in London attend the ball in Admiral Nelson's honor, loaned Fergus his driver and carriage for the evening. Fergus boarded the specially polished and cleaned carriage at the hospital entrance under the watchful eye of the chief surgeon and his nurse and arrived at the ballroom in fine style, but still not happy at having to spend the evening that way.

"I won't be long," he said to the carriage driver.

The driver grinned. "You look grand, sir, and I think the ladies will keep you busy until at least midnight, but I'll stand by before then."

The carriage waited in line briefly before pulling up to the ballroom entrance, and he got down carefully, moving uncomfortably in his full dress uniform.

Fergus reluctantly entered the large ballroom. The orchestra was in full swing and dancing had already begun. A member of the ball committee, a middle-aged lady in a low-cut gown with a red ribbon stuck in her décolletage to denote her position, met him just inside the door and immediately introduced herself and then took his arm and introduced him to a pretty young lady.

"Ah, are you the famous Lieutenant Kilburnie?" she asked, corn-blue eyes open wide.

Fergus laughed. "I'm Kilburnie, all right, but I don't think I'm famous for anything."

The young lady, from behind her fan, examined him carefully. "Well, I like you anyway, and I think you will be able to dance well."

Fergus grinned. "Thank you. I'll be glad to dance with you."

The dance ended and he took her hand and escorted her to a place in the next reel.

After a set of English reels, Fergus excused himself and went to the other side of the room to the refreshment table. Halfway across the room, his heart almost stopped, and he felt a dryness in his throat. The lady several feet in front of him, busy talking to an older man, had to be Shannon Inver. The long, dark-red hair, now carefully coiffed and put up on top of her shining head in accordance with current fashion, the green eyes, the fair complexion, the beautiful figure encased in a dark-green silk gown, were all one of a kind.

He stood still in the midst of the milling dancers for a few minutes to be sure, and then he made his way toward her side, pushing through couples as he went. Halfway there he stopped next to one couple. "Pardon me. Could you tell me who the lady is over there?" he asked.

"Where?" the lady replied.

Fergus pointed discreetly. "The beautiful red-headed one in the green gown."

The lady looked toward Shannon and said, "Oh, certainly I can. That's Lady Shannon Malin."

"Thank you," Fergus said, and he continued on across the crowded floor toward Shannon.

She turned slightly, looking toward him, and saw him approaching. Her eyes widened, and Fergus was sure she had recognized him.

He came to her side, bowed deeply, and said, "I'm Fergus Kilburnie. Do you remember me?"

Shannon threw her arms around him, as impulsive as ever. "Of course, how could I forget you?"

Fergus's heart began to beat faster.

Shannon said, her arms still around his neck, "I'm so glad to see you again."

Fergus was aware of the man standing next to her and was afraid that Shannon's warm greeting might have offended him, particularly if he was her husband.

She released him, apparently aware of his concern. She looked at the man at her side and grinned. "Uncle, this is a young man I knew when I was a girl. I hope you'll forgive my behavior, but we were very close."

Fergus felt relieved and held out his hand. "Captain Fergus Kilburnie, sir."

The older man smiled and took Fergus's hand. "I know of you. You are famous, sir. I'm Shannon's maternal uncle, Clevis Strathan of Donegal."

Shannon took Fergus's arm and smiled disarmingly at her uncle. "Thank you, Uncle. Please excuse me for a few minutes while I dance with Fergus."

Her uncle bowed. "I'll be sitting with the chaperons if you want me."

Shannon said behind her fan as they walked away, "Don't believe a word of that. He'll be dancing with every pretty woman he can catch."

The first dance was a waltz, and Fergus was forced to hold Shannon at a considerable distance, as was the new custom. Fergus was not accustomed to the waltz, and he asked Shannon what it was.

"It's a new German dance," she said. "They introduced it to the French. Some of our embassy members stationed in Berlin brought it back to London, but it's not popular yet. I think that will be the last waltz of the evening."

Fergus held her as close as the dance would allow. "We can't get very close with this dance. The Germans can keep it."

She was still close enough. Memories of the early days in Donegal flooded in on him, and he wondered if she felt the same. After the second dance, not a waltz, he asked, "Is there some private place where we can talk?"

Shannon took Fergus by the hand and led him outside. They walked about the beautiful formal garden, lined with stone benches placed in alcoves, but the private areas were all occupied. Finally Fergus found a low wall for them to sit on, distant from the walk.

Fergus started the conversation. "Was that really your uncle you were talking with?"

She laughed. "Yes, but my husband is nearly as old. He wasn't able to be here tonight, though."

"You have children?"

"Two girls, two and three," Shannon said. "And I suppose you are married, too."

"No. I'm still alone."

"I'm surprised no one has found you."

Fergus shrugged. "Not much chance of that since I've been at sea all the time. I suppose you had to marry someone your father picked out."

Shannon sighed. "I fought him as long as I could. I knew you would never come back to Ireland, and if I couldn't have you it didn't matter much whom I married."

"Did you marry anyone I knew?"

"I'm not sure if you knew Finian Malin. When you were in Ireland he was away somewhere at school or traveling. He's now a lord. His father, who was English, and my father came to Ireland when they were young to raise racehorses. It was the only thing they liked to do and they had enough money for it. When my father died a few years ago I inherited his estate, which is where we live now. You remember the grounds and the big house."

Fergus grinned. "And the stables and the paddock where we used to meet."

Shannon sighed. "The best days of my life. I'll never forget them."

"Are you happy now?"

Shannon shrugged. "I don't know. Finian is a nice person and a good father. But after the children his interests are politics and horses, in that order. I come after them. It's been this way so long that most of the time I don't notice anymore. But when I get too lonely, I can't help thinking how it could have been if you and I had been together all this time."

Fergus moved to get a better look at Shannon. She was as he remembered her, but her green eyes and beautiful face were far more mature. Her gown accentuated her slim but well-formed figure, still elegant in spite of having borne two children, and in the style of the times her full breasts were barely covered. He wanted to hold her in his arms, even if briefly. "Will you dance with me again?" he asked.

"Of course."

They danced many times and talked some more. Toward midnight Shannon said, "My husband is in Ireland for two days. Something about horses."

"But you live in London?"

"We have a townhouse here. He comes to London when Parliament is in session to follow the debate about the merging of the Irish and English Parliaments. My husband has a grand passion for helping the Irish people."

Fergus took a chance. "Could I see your townhouse?"

Shannon took a deep breath. "I thought you'd never ask. I was about to suggest that."

They found Shannon's uncle dancing with a beautiful widow. Shannon said, "Uncle, Captain Kilburnie does not have a place to stay tonight in the city, and I'm going to take him home with me."

Fergus spoke up, "Sir, I have a carriage waiting, so you won't have to leave with us."

The uncle looked relieved. "I am, er, busy here, as you can see."

Fergus grinned. "I see, sir, and I wish you luck."

Her uncle nodded. "I don't need luck, my boy, just opportunity, and you've given it to me."

Uncle Jeris's carriage and driver were waiting. The driver grinned knowingly at Fergus, but Fergus pointedly ignored him and handed Shannon into the carriage. Fergus sent the driver back to find Shannon's driver and direct him to wait for her uncle. When he returned Shannon gave the driver her address and he started out, chuckling quietly to himself.

When they arrived at Shannon's house, she said to Fergus, "You can send the driver along. You can use my carriage whenever you want it."

The driver started to grin, but Fergus looked at him sternly, and he straightened his face and drove off.

Shannon took Fergus's hand and led him up the entrance stairs, took out a key, and unlocked the door. Inside the house a low fire was burning in a grate in the library. Shannon said, "Please shake up the fire and add some coal. There is a large cabinet in the next room full of glasses and all kinds of drink. You'll find everything you need in there. I'll be back down soon."

Fergus brought the dormant fire up with a shake and a few lumps of channel coal and poured himself a glass of Scotch whiskey from the liquor cabinet. Just as he settled himself before the fire, Shannon came back into the room, wearing a green silk dressing gown and matching slippers.

Fergus said, "Sorry you changed. I thought you were beautiful in that ball gown."

Shannon laughed. "You men are all alike. Ball gowns and what goes under them are very uncomfortable for women. Now take off your jacket, too, and we'll both feel better."

Fergus hung his dress uniform jacket over a chair, and poured another glass of Scotch whiskey and added a small amount of soda water. He handed it to Shannon. "I hope this kind of whiskey is what you wanted."

"Yes, that will be fine for now. Maybe later I'll find some champagne. Now sit down next to me and tell me all about your career and all those years you spent in the navy. I've tried to follow your career, but it has been difficult. They say you've become famous. Are you as famous as Admiral Nelson?"

Fergus laughed. "Now you're teasing me, just like you used to do. I'm just a plain captain in command of a transport, the *Aberdeen*. A week ago I was a lieutenant, and I've just got promoted this afternoon."

"But haven't you captured two French frigates? Transports aren't supposed to be able to do that, or at least that's what my Uncle Clevis tells me."

"Just luck and a good crew."

Shannon sighed. "I wish we'd had some of that luck when we were young in Ireland."

Fergus shook his head. "I was unlucky to have had to leave Ireland, but leaving you set me on the way to the navy."

"You went right to sea?"

"Yes. I was really low after I left you, and I wanted to get away."

She laughed. "You certainly got away. Where did you go?"

"Mostly to the Mediterranean. I also went as far west as the Indies, but I never had a chance to go to the South Seas or any of those other romantic places. Most of the time I cut circles in the Atlantic Ocean off of Gibraltar, and the sea gulls and porpoises were always the same."

"I don't understand."

Fergus shrugged. "I think the public is not well informed as to what the navy does."

Shannon laughed. "You sound like a stuffed shirt."

Fergus ignored her. "The first ship I served in I started as a seaman and I stayed there until I was promoted to lieutenant. The ship was a frigate, a medium-sized, fast ship designed to patrol and intercept and destroy or capture French warships and merchantmen. We spent a lot of time patrolling the same area, waiting for a ship to come by. On the chart our track looked like a bunch of circles. I never left the ship in all that time, either."

"Did you succeed?"

"I did personally, I suppose. I was promoted from seaman to gun captain and eventually to lieutenant, all on the same ship, the *Athena*."

"You captured a lot of prizes with that ship?"

"No. Only one."

"Did you get much prize money?"

"For that one only a little. Lieutenants don't get a very big share."

"And captains do better?"

"A lot better. After I became a temporary captain of my present ship, we took two prizes, one a brig full of bullion, and the amount I was awarded was much more than I expected. I got three-eighths of the value of the brig, her cargo, and bullion she was trying to carry home."

"Did it come to much?"

"Twenty thousand pounds."

"What did you do with it?"

"I bought a large farm in Fairlie, Scotland, next to my family farm. With part of the money from my second prize I am building a large house on the farm near a salmon stream."

"Oh, yes, all you Scots like salmon."

"And you Irish like Atlantic cod."

Shannon laughed. "Remember, I'm not really Irish. My mother was, but my father was English. They were married in the Church of England."

Fergus got up and fixed another drink. Shannon said, "Leave the water out of this one."

Fergus sat down again and raised his glass. "Here's to the Scots and the Irish, and the devil take the rest of the English."

Shannon moved closer to him. "Tell me about the women you met."

Fergus laughed. "What women? I talked to a young Irish girl when I was traveling home to Scotland from Ireland, but I didn't do anything about her. I was still thinking about you. I don't think you realize what it's like in the navy in wartime. I haven't been ashore since I joined the navy except for a trip to the Admiralty to take my lieutenant's examinations and now to enter the hospital. Well, maybe a short stop in Gibraltar."

Shannon shuddered. "That's terrible." Then she laughed. "You must be, er, charged up."

Fergus colored. "That's one way of putting it. Just looking at you sets my blood to boiling."

"Mine boils, too, and I haven't even been to sea."

Fergus wasted no more time. He took her in his arms, and she came to him willingly. Their kisses were deep, repeated, and passionate, as if they were trying to make up for all the years they had lost in their youth.

The dressing gown fell away, and Fergus found she had removed all of her clothes. He thought of the time in the old churchyard when he had come so close to possessing her and he could stand it no longer. He threw off his clothes and kissed her deeply again. She was all he had wanted all those years, and he took her, at first gently, and then with all his might, on the carpet in the library in front of the roaring fire. All the years of denial, regret, and remorse fell away.

Later, lying in his arms, she noted the red patch on his left shoulder. "What happened?" she asked.

He told her about his wounding, and when he had told her as much as he could stand he got up and brought two glasses of whiskey back to her. She downed hers straight again, not even making a face.

Fergus laughed. "You'd have made a hell of a Scot the way you drink their whiskey."

Shannon shrugged her shoulders. "I also drink Irish whiskey straight. It's a habit I picked up trying to forget you. The bottle next to the Scotch is Irish whiskey. Let's try it next time."

The alcohol loosened their tongues, and they lay in each other's arms talking until dawn.

Then Shannon said, "Come up to my bedroom. The servants and children will be stirring soon."

In the warmth and privacy of her bedroom, they made love again, but they were so aroused by the night that they couldn't sleep afterward.

They dressed and went downstairs. Shannon had the servants prepare an enormous breakfast. The children were already out in the garden playing. Fergus watched them from the dining-room window. "Wonderful children," he said.

"Yes," Shannon said, "I've been fortunate. They are what holds my marriage together."

"But you said you were not happy. Would you divorce your husband and marry me? We could have a wonderful life living on my farm. I remember that you liked to fish. We'll have the best salmon stream in Scotland right at our door. I'll keep as many horses as you want. We might even have enough money to keep a townhouse in London."

Shannon cried openly, making no attempt to control the tears. Fergus gave her a handkerchief.

"Thank you, my dear," she said, "but nothing can help me at the moment."

"I don't understand. Why not?"

Shannon started to cry again, but controlled herself quickly. "I'd like nothing better than to spend the rest of my life with you, but I can't."

Fergus was perplexed. "Why not?"

"Divorce would ruin my husband's career, and even though there's very little romantic attachment between us, I couldn't do that to him. He has always been straight with me and loves our children very much. And I have to think of the children. They would be outcasts, particularly back in Ireland."

"I don't understand that. You can't perform the sin of divorce, yet you are willing to carry out the sin of adultery with me."

Shannon sighed. "There is a difference. If I got a divorce, I would be hurting other people, my children and husband, and I couldn't do that. If I am adulterous, I hurt only myself, and I can do that."

Fergus shook his head sadly. "Here I've finally found you again and I can't have you. I feel almost as bad as I did that day in Ireland when I had to leave you."

"You can have me today and tomorrow and whenever you come back to England. Send word to me, and I'll find an excuse to leave home right away and come to you anywhere and stay as long as you like."

Fergus shook his head. "That's not much. Two or three days twice a year."

She sighed. "Then let's make the most of the next two days we have."

When their passion had been sated temporarily, Shannon said, "Let's take a ride in my carriage."

"What about the children?"

"They'll be happy with their nanny."

"I'd like to get to know them."

Shannon sighed. "I don't think it will be good for you to get too attached to them yet."

Fergus got up and dressed. "All right, then. Let's get on with it."

They rode about London and its parks for several hours and past the palace, the Parliament, and finally past the Admiralty. Although Fergus had been glum, he perked up when they passed by the yellow buildings.

"What's so interesting?" Shannon asked.

Fergus told her about his first entrance into the Admiralty building, and about his Uncle Jeris and Aunt Martha. "You'd like them," he said.

She turned and kissed him so passionately Fergus was afraid the driver would notice. When he could disengage himself, he said to the carriage driver, "Back to madam's home, please."

The second night was even better than the first. Fergus knew he would have to carry the memory of it for many months, and he caressed her passionately, from her dark red hair to her slim legs.

Toward dawn, he awoke, dressed, and left the bedroom quietly. He went out into the garden and paced up and down, wondering if he could remember the flower and grass arrangements later when he paced his quarterdeck.

When the sun rose, he went back inside, awakened Shannon with a kiss, and they had a final breakfast.

This time Fergus insisted on meeting her children, and they spent the morning with them in the garden.

About noon, Shannon said, "I know you are about to leave. Remember what I said. When you come back from sea, send word to me. I'll be there as soon as I can."

Later that day Shannon's carriage returned Fergus to the hospital. Fergus got out of the carriage and walked to the entrance of the hospital in a trance. The chief surgeon met him. "My God! Kilburnie, I was about to send out a search party for you. Why didn't you come back the night of the ball? You said you wouldn't stay long. From the sad look on your face I'd say the ball was quite a trial."

Fergus managed a sad smile. "No, it was successful beyond my wildest dreams. I found the wonderful girl I left in Ireland years ago."

"Then what happened?"

Fergus shrugged. "I found paradise that night and lost it two days later."

20
Back on the Aberdeen

t the end of another week, Fergus's wound was declared healed, and the surgeon said, "I've cured your wound, but I can't do much about your sadness. If you won't talk to me and tell me what happened, I can't help you."

Fergus tried to grin, but the effort was useless. Instead he shook his head sadly. "Sorry, I can't tell you what's wrong. Nothing can cure this disease. Maybe the passage of time and traveling on a lot of saltwater will make it at least bearable."

"I know it's some affair of the heart. I'd like to say I've been happily married for several years, and I might be able to solve your problem using my past experiences. I note from your medical record you're unmarried and only twenty-six. You have many years left to look for someone else."

Fergus nodded. "That's correct. If I can't go on with life this way, I may ask the Admiralty to be retired early, or I may have to resign my commission."

The next day Fergus returned to the *Aberdeen.* Lieutenant Young met him on the quarterdeck. "Glad to see you back, sir. We've missed you. All of our repairs have just been completed, and our stores are loaded. We're ready for sea in all respects now that you're back."

Fergus looked around the topside at the new rigging, all taut and tarred, and the patched woodwork. A few seams were still visible but would probably soon disappear under the careful ministrations of the carpenter and a few coats of varnish.

Fergus said, "She looks ready to go. You and the crew have done a fine job."

"The yard has done most of it, sir."

"Good. This is a fine navy yard, but you deserve the credit for putting it all together."

"Thank you, sir. Now all we need is orders."

"We'll get them soon."

Lieutenant Young beamed. "Good, sir."

"How's the crew?"

"Fine, sir. We didn't need to press or recruit anybody from the local prisons. Even the ones in the hospital came back early. They don't want to miss a cruise under you."

"Why not?"

"They think you're lucky."

"Wouldn't they settle for just liking to fight?"

"They would, but the lucky part helps."

Fergus sighed. "They don't know how unlucky I am in affairs of the heart."

Young grinned. "I think the enlisted men have different standards. They think you're lucky to be able to get back to sea a single man."

The next morning Jeris boarded the *Aberdeen* at the wharf. "Walking up the brow beats climbing up that damned ladder," he said.

Fergus grinned. "Being wounded gave me a new appreciation of how difficult it is getting around a ship and up a ladder with only one arm."

Jeris nodded. "I'd rather lose an arm than a leg. Come below, and I'll give you your next orders. By the way, you look like you've lost more than an arm."

When they were settled below before their customary brandies, Jeris said, "I hear you danced most of the night with the most beautiful lady at the ball. Martha wants to know all about it, and so do I."

"Yes, she was Lady Shannon Malin. I knew her when she was Shannon Inver and only sixteen."

Jeris's eyebrows shot up. "Oh, oh, that's the filly who got you thrown out of Ireland."

"Not exactly. I was equally to blame."

"And you spent time with her?"

"Oh, yes, two days."

"And nights?"

"Yes, and it was wonderful. Like we had never been apart, until. . . ."

"Until?"

"Until I asked her to get a divorce and marry me and she reminded me that she couldn't do it. It was hell on earth for a few minutes after she told me."

"And after you had just found her again."

"Yes. Now I don't know what to do."

"You will have to keep on going with your career. The navy needs you, and now more than ever you will have to depend on the navy to help you get over your problems. As a matter of fact, this may be for the best. Not many captains your age are married. Life in the Royal Navy, particularly in time of war, isn't much fun for a wife, and Shannon might not have liked it if she had chosen to divorce her husband."

Fergus sighed. "It wouldn't have been much fun for a husband either."

"Most Royal Navy captains wait until they retire to get married."

Fergus smiled wryly. "That's the only alternative I have, but even then I'll have trouble."

Jeris frowned. "Why?"

"Because she thinks a divorce will ruin her husband's career and her children's reputation."

"Not good. How old is her husband?"

"I don't know for sure, but he is considerably older than she is."

"Maybe that's your answer. He won't live forever."

"Forever might be a long time, but I don't have any other alternative."

"Maybe you could do what Admiral Nelson is doing."

"Live with her openly even though she's married? I'd do it, but Shannon wouldn't because of her children."

Jeris said, "I see."

"I've got to stay at sea."

Jeris said, "I agree."

"Do you have my orders?"

"Yes, I almost forgot them. Here they are." He passed an envelope to Fergus.

Fergus read the orders, wrinkled his eyebrows, and read them again. "I don't understand this. We've never put transports, or even merchantmen, in convoys before. At least the transports have always sailed singly and successfully."

Jeris explained, "There's a new turn in the war at sea. The French have been avoiding combat at sea with our ships of the line when either force is in numbers. Instead, they have sent all of their ships out in small groups to prey on our merchantmen and transports. The answer is to bunch our ships in convoys and to protect them with squadrons of our ships of the line."

"That certainly does cut down on the chances to display initiative."

"If you mean the chance for you to take more prizes, I certainly agree."

Fergus got up and walked up and down. Jeris watched him. "You have an idea?"

Fergus stopped walking. "Yes, I may decide to retire from the navy soon, and I'll never give Shannon up. But I'll try a convoy or two first."

Fergus sailed his ship in three large convoys composed mainly of merchantmen from England to the Mediterranean and back. On the first two nothing unusual happened.

On the third, a small group of French ships attacked the convoy, but were driven off by the British escort of three frigates. Fergus champed, pacing up and down and swearing under his breath, hoping to see action, but there was no opportunity for the *Aberdeen,* stationed far to the rear in the convoy, to get at the French warships.

On the next convoy the ships circled through the Irish Sea on the way home and entered Liverpool, avoiding the usual French force waiting at the western end of the English Channel. Again there was no action.

The crew was becoming restive, sensing a change in the pattern of the war. Fergus, too, was unhappy at the lack of action, and the long days and nights at sea were filled with memories of Shannon and their all-too-brief time in London. As he paced the quiet quarterdeck in the long hours of the night, he relived every moment of their passion and even of their earlier days in Ireland. The exercise of walking against the roll of the ship failed to dim his memories or quiet his feelings, and eventually he went below to the doubtful solace of his lonely cot. He slept only when exhaustion overcame him, and then lightly, with dreams very near the surface.

The *Aberdeen* returned from the fifth convoy again without incident. Fergus asked Jeris to find out about Lord Malin. After a few days of investigating Jeris told him, "The old boy is still spry, although he doesn't ride his horses in races anymore."

Fergus said, "I know he puts riding even above Shannon. That may mean something."

Jeris shook his head. "I wouldn't put too much faith in that. Englishmen are like that."

"What did you find out about Shannon?"

"Since Parliament is not in session, she's in Ireland with her family."

"How does she look?"

"Those who have seen her say beautiful, as usual."

"But beside that?"

"I don't think any of my investigators are experts on the happiness of women, but one talked to someone who had seen her out riding."

"And?"

"He said she spurred the hell out of her horse."

Fergus nodded. "She's unhappy. She always takes it out on her horse."

"Well, if that's what she's like, maybe you're lucky she isn't riding you."

Fergus laughed. "She wouldn't do that to me. She's an impulsive woman, and I'll take a chance with her if it's given to me."

Jeris sighed deeply and stretched his wounded leg. Obviously this emotional conversation was getting to be too much for him. He said, "Lad, I don't think you can count on that. You'd better stay at sea for a while longer."

Fergus decided to go on at least one more convoy, and the *Aberdeen* departed a week later, the only transport in a covey of fat merchantmen.

For this convoy, the overconfident Admiralty reduced the convoy escort to a single frigate. Fergus drilled his gun crews hard and tried to speed up the ability of the sail trimmers to tack against the wind. He hoped the change might give the ship a better chance to see action.

On the third day, with the convoy well south of the entrance to the English Channel, the wind shifted to the south and began to increase.

Fergus called Lieutenant Young, MacGregor, and Danbury to the quarterdeck for a conference. "Gentlemen," he began, "I don't like this weather."

MacGregor interrupted. "Captain, this is the beginning of hurricane season. In this part of the Northern Hemisphere, at this time of year, we always get heavy winds and long swells."

"I agree," Fergus said, "and this looks like the beginning of a corker."

Lieutenant Young had been looking at the merchantmen of the convoy. He shook his head, "We think we have it tough tending sails and lines with only two hundred men. Those merchantmen have to do the same thing with only one hundred men and sometimes not that many."

Fergus nodded, buttoning his oilskins tighter around his neck against the increasing wind. "And the frigate up ahead has at least three hundred men. They don't have much sympathy for the rest of us."

MacGregor shook his head. "We'll have to tack repeatedly against this wind from the south, and even then we won't make much distance to the south."

Fergus said, "All right, gentlemen, let's get about securing the ship for heavy weather."

The wind increased steadily from thirty, to forty, to fifty, and finally to sixty knots. The long seas rolled up from the south, lifting the *Aberdeen*'s bluff bow, passing under her keel, and leaving her astern with a flip to her rudder that made her yaw wildly. Because all the ships were sailing sixty degrees across the wind, much of the motion caused by the passing seas was from the side of the hull and the ship, even though steadied somewhat by her spread of wind-filled but reefed canvas, still rolled heavily and unpleasantly. In such weather there was no comfortable position, and Fergus usually found a small space near the lee bulwark where he could wedge himself between the bulwark and the mizzen shrouds.

Fergus had ordered the topmasts struck below on the first day, and the *Aberdeen* was scudding along under reefed main courses and a storm jib. The merchantmen were similarly rigged, but the frigate had retained her topmasts and had smaller reefs in her sails.

MacGregor looked at the frigate, moving from side to side at the front of the formation. "Look at that silly rooster. He doesn't need to sail her like that. He knows we're all doing the best we can."

Fergus turned to keep the salt spray out of his mouth. "When you were below, she came back to the merchantmen and to us. Made some signals to us to sail closer to the wind."

"What did the merchants do?"

"One sent back a signal telling him they were doing the best they could. The others didn't even bother to answer. I don't think that frigate captain was very happy."

On the third day the wind steadied at sixty knots, but the rains came. The wind blew the stinging drops into every opening of the oilskins of the men topside. Fergus was wet to his skin in ten minutes. Fortunately the rain was not cold.

As the *Aberdeen* made her next tack to starboard, the merchant ships tried to follow her, but some of them lost sight of her in the driving rain. It was almost four hours before the formation came together again.

Fergus had been tacking at the change of the watch so the men could have as much time below as possible. The merchant captains followed his motions. Now it was time for the next tack, and the process started all over again just as the formation was back together again.

Most of the time now Fergus abandoned his more comfortable position near the lee bulwark and stood by the weather bulwark, peering up-wind, because that was the side an errant merchantman would probably come from. There was little protection from the wind, and the seas came roaring along the weather side. The tops caught briefly in the ratlines extending over the side where they joined the bulwark abreast of the feet of the three masts. Tops of the waves caught at Fergus, and then the main part of the waves smashed into the rear section of the bulwark. All Fergus could do was shut his eyes when he heard the sea was coming, hang on to the bulwark, and wait until the green monster had passed aft enough so that he could open his salt-reddened eyes.

On the morning of the fourth day, the wind began to abate, and by dusk it was a steady twenty knots. The rain stopped suddenly, and the gray overcast parted briefly to let a reluctant sun peep through.

The long rollers still came on, but they were a little lower and it was not as far between crests. By the next morning the sea had returned to normal and the wind had shifted to the east.

MacGregor watched the changed direction of the long rollers, now from the east. "That shows the storm has passed to the east. We should have good weather now."

He was right. The next day was perfect. Bright sun, ten knots of wind, and a decent six-foot sea.

Fergus stumbled below, threw off his wet clothing, and crawled into his hammock, rigged to use instead of his hanging cot in such weather. He slept for twelve hours.

A week later the huge Rock of Gibraltar was sighted, and the first part of the trip was over.

On the trip back from the Mediterranean with a new group of merchantmen but still with a single escort, Fergus was rewarded when a lookout reported two sails to the north. The sails closed fast, and soon under them appeared the hulls of two frigates. They were undoubtedly French, although still too far away to make sure. Fergus rubbed his hands and sent Lieutenant Young forward to check the guns and their crews.

The lookouts reported two more sails behind the first two. Fergus pursed his lips and clenched his hands. This might be too much of a good thing. He watched them come on, and soon Lieutenant Young, returning from aloft, said, "Two more French frigates."

The single British escort, the frigate *Imperious,* struck out boldly under full canvas, heading for the approaching enemy. The convoy was ordered to turn northwest, obviously to transit around Ireland and enter the Irish Sea from the north through the North Channel rather than try to circle around to the north of the oncoming enemy ships.

Without direct orders Fergus kept his course and increased speed by hoisting some more sails. He followed the British frigate toward the oncoming enemy.

After a few minutes, the *Imperious* seemed to notice the *Aberdeen*'s movements and frantically sent a signal to the *Aberdeen* to carry out her orders.

The master said, "Sir, shall I change course and reduce sail?"

Fergus said, "No. Stand on at this speed. I take full responsibility."

"But sir, we can't take this large a force on directly. They'll murder us."

"Neither can one British frigate. If we don't help, she and a lot of our ships will be destroyed or taken by the French ships coming at us."

The *Imperious* was faster than the *Aberdeen,* and drew ahead slowly. Fergus chewed his lower lip, hoping to be able to help, or at least to divert some of the oncoming ships from the fleeing convoy, still relatively near.

When the four French ships were about six miles away, there was a fluttering of signal flags on what was obviously the flagship of the squadron, and two of them turned to a northwesterly course, apparently to chase the scattering merchantmen. The other two French ships continued to head under full sail for the *Imperious.*

Midshipman Puller, standing next to Fergus, said, "They're after the merchantmen."

Fergus nodded. "So we'll have to intercept them." He turned to MacGregor. "Master, head for the two French ships to the north."

MacGregor gave the necessary orders, and the *Aberdeen* swung quickly to a course across the bow of the oncoming pair of French frigates.

Puller watched them intently. He said, "Sir, they're diverging. The northernmost ship will try to get around us and get to the convoy while the southernmost comes south to take us on."

"We'll have to try to engage both of them."

In half an hour, Fergus knew he could not. The French frigates were too fast. The northernmost would soon pass to the north, and there was nothing the *Aberdeen* could do about it. She was too slow. The merchantmen would have to continue to scatter, and the loss of some of them would be inevitable. The best the British force could do was to occupy the remainder of the French force long enough to permit most of the merchantmen to escape or to scatter, or at least to avoid capture or destruction until darkness covered them.

Fergus bit his lip. This wasn't what he had wanted. Maybe his luck was running out. Or maybe he had used it all finding Shannon. Then thoughts of Shannon flooded his mind. Shannon at the ball, whirling gracefully in her green ball gown with him, Shannon beside him on the carpet before the fire, Shannon downing the glass of straight Scotch whiskey.

Someone was talking to him. It was Lieutenant Young. "Sir, shall I man the starboard battery?"

"Yes. I'll turn to port when we're in gun range."

Puller, next to him, said, "Sir, a few more yards and we'll be in range."

Fergus, eager to join battle, turned to MacGregor. "Master, six points to port, please, sir."

Puller said, "That should do it, sir."

The master began shouting orders, and the *Aberdeen* quickly swung to port. Although she was not fast, the design of her broad hull that took away her speed added to her ability to turn quickly.

When Fergus was sure the gun captains had enough time to lay and aim their guns, he shouted, "Starboard battery, commence firing!"

The broadside seemed to take the Frenchman by surprise, and he had to change course to clear his broadside so it would bear on the *Aberdeen*.

The *Aberdeen*'s first broadside was a little short, throwing up empty geysers. One shot skipped twice and bounced harmlessly off the Frenchman's side, its force and speed taken away by the contact with the water. Fergus growled to himself and cursed his overeagerness.

The second broadside went out at the same time the Frenchman fired his first broadside. The smoke prevented Fergus from getting a good view of any damage to the Frenchman, but a lookout called down, "Her foresail is down, sir."

The first French salvo put two shots in the gun deck forward. One pierced the bulkhead and caromed harmlessly around the inner bulkheads before settling in a corner. The second scattered splinters among the gun crews and put two guns and part of their crews out of action.

Fergus scowled when he got the report of damage from the carpenter. This engagement wasn't going the way he wanted. He shouted words of encouragement to the gun crews on the upper deck, and they redoubled their efforts. Still, the Frenchman seemed to be relatively undamaged, and more and more shots flew through the upperworks of the *Aberdeen,* carrying away rigging, sails, yards, and even the upper portions of the fore- and mainmasts. The falling rigging and mast parts put some of the guns on the upper deck out of action until the wreckage could be cleared.

The speed of the *Aberdeen* was dropping. The sailing master worked frantically to send up new sails, cursing in Gaelic as he worked, but shifting to English to give his orders to the hard-working crew.

Fergus, losing patience, grabbed a long glass and climbed up the rigging to get a better view. The frigate they were engaging now seemed to be as battered as they were. Her sails were all tattered, and her masts shortened. To the east, he could see that the *Imperious* was giving the two French frigates everything she had, but was getting battered on both sides by the circling Frenchmen.

Fergus gazed quickly to the northeast. The merchantmen had scattered, but the fourth French frigate was firing relentlessly at a straggler.

Fergus went back below. Lieutenant Young asked, "How is it going?"

Fergus shrugged. "We're in trouble. This is going to be a disaster. The Admiralty will hear about this. They never should have reduced the number of escorts."

The firing continued, but the Frenchman, although winning the exchanges of broadsides because of her superior number of guns, seemed to be losing her will to fight. Many of her guns stopped firing.

Fergus looked up at the *Aberdeen*'s rigging and sails. All of the sails, even the replacements, had been holed. Some several times. Tatters of burned sailcloth hung down from the mizzen sails. The foremast was down, and the mainmast barely upright, held by the boatswain's temporary rigging. The rudder had been hit and part of it carried away, but the ship could still be steered, although with difficulty. For a moment Fergus wished he still had Poston, his old quartermaster, to take over the steering.

The gunner reported that they were running low on powder and balls and even had no grape shot left, but Fergus knew the Frenchman must be running low on ammunition too. Both ships had fired about all of what would be their normal allowance of ammunition.

Suddenly the firing from the Frenchman stopped, and she turned away to the east. Fergus watched her go. "Damn! I'll wager she ran out of ammunition."

Fergus turned his attention to the *Imperious* and her circling opponents. The *Imperious* was battling hard, but it was obvious that she was losing her battle slowly. Suddenly the firing stopped there, too, and the French frigates turned away and sailed slowly off to the east and joined their comrade, now almost hull down.

The *Imperious* was wallowing in the seas, dead in the water. Fergus asked the master, "Can we make enough way to close him?"

The sailing master went forward to confer with the boatswain and the carpenter, who were busy making repairs. When he came back he said, "I can give you two knots in about an hour. We're badly hurt."

"Any flooding below?"

"A little. I'll make a more thorough inspection as soon as I can."

"Then you should be ready soon?"

"We're ready now."

"Then we'll close her."

Two hours later the *Aberdeen* slowly pulled alongside the *Imperious*. Up close the damage was worse than it had appeared at distance.

Fergus picked up a speaking trumpet. "Do you need assistance?" he yelled.

The captain of the *Imperious* called back, "We'll need several hours and maybe an extra day to make enough repairs to get us to Portsmouth. Please see what you can do to overtake and reform the convoy. Take it around Ireland and through the North Channel. Good luck."

Fergus replied, "I'll try to chase the fourth frigate off, but I'm low on ammunition. Good luck to you, too."

The *Aberdeen* sailed slowly northwest, hoping to follow the track of the merchantmen of the convoy. Fergus occasionally climbed the ratlines and joined the lookouts aloft but the horizon remained clear.

On the second day, just before darkness, and just before Fergus had given up, a lookout shouted, "Sail one point on the starboard bow!"

Fergus went aloft and watched it grow in size. In the growing dusk it closed rapidly, and soon Fergus was sure it was the fourth French frigate.

The Frenchman changed course to the northeast, obviously to avoid the *Aberdeen*.

Fergus came to the north to try to intercept the Frenchman, but the crippled *Aberdeen* could only make two knots. It would be some time before the two ships could meet.

Fergus noted that the carpenter had disappeared. "Where's Chips?" he asked Lieutenant Young.

"Below, I think, sir. Shall I send for him?"

"Please do."

Soon the carpenter appeared, following the messenger Young had sent. The carpenter was wet to his waist, and water dripped on the deck from his trousers and shoes. "Sir, you sent for me?" he asked.

Fergus said, "I take it from your state of dress that there's something serious going on below decks."

The carpenter grimaced. "Yes, sir, and if you can leave the deck I suggest you come down below with me and see it for yourself."

Fergus left Lieutenant Young in charge and followed the carpenter forward and down the ladder to the gun deck. He looked around. "Looks all right to me."

The carpenter was already on the ladder down to the orlop deck. "Down here," he said.

Fergus could see three carpenter's mates and several seamen frantically stuffing mattresses and oakum behind stateroom doors placed against the inside of the hull and on either side of a badly shattered thick oak rib. A shot had hit the ship at the waterline. Not only had it penetrated the thick outer planking but it had also destroyed the futtock rib on which the planking was carried.

"Look at that," the carpenter said.

"I see it. Every time the bow plunges it carries the hole underwater, and a hell of a lot of seawater comes in the hole," Fergus said.

"Yes, sir, and if you'll look down the ladder to the holds below you'll see a lot of water already aboard. The pumps are going steadily, but if we don't get the inflow under control we'll have to stop so the bow doesn't plunge until we can make better repairs."

"How long to fix it?"

"As you can see, I've got a spar across the ship from the patch to the opposite side planking. We're putting in wedges between the other side and the end of the spar against the patch. They'll help tighten the patch seal."

Fergus nodded. "I'm going back on deck. Let me know what happens."

After he was back on the quarterdeck, Fergus paced nervously, expecting to get the word momentarily from the carpenter that he would have to take way off the ship while more permanent repairs could be made. If he did, the French ship would pass to the north easily. If he could keep going he had a chance, no matter how small, to intercept her.

In twenty minutes the carpenter appeared on deck forward. As he came aft, Fergus could see a smile on his face. "Fixed?" he asked.

"Ah, yes, sir. For the moment, but it won't hold up in heavy weather."

"Thanks," Fergus said. "We'll have to pray."

Lieutenant Young heard the conversation. "Sir, shall I send for Surgeon Pollitt? Maybe he could sing a hymn."

Fergus laughed. "No, I think this takes more than just a hymn."

Midshipman Puller was listening. "Sir, I used to be a choir boy, and I know most of the standard prayers."

Fergus turned to him. "Puller, you've done a lot of things for me over the years. Now go ahead with that prayer."

Puller grinned. "Sir, what shall I pray for?"

"Good weather, dammit. Now get on with it."

While Puller prayed Fergus sent for the boatswain.

Danbury came running aft and said, "Sir?"

"Look at that bastard. Can you do anything to give us more speed?"

The boatswain stroked his chin. "Sir, I've tried everything I can think of."

Fergus said, "Try rigging a spare jib as a staysail forward of the mainmast."

"Sir, the spare jibs are long gone."

"Damn!" Fergus said.

"I'll tighten the sheets and throw a little water on the sails. That might help."

Nothing helped, and in a few minutes the Frenchman passed to the north, just at gun range. Fergus ordered the bow chasers to fire, but the shots fell harmlessly short, the shots bouncing on the water at least twice before sinking.

The French ship threw a contemptuous broadside at them as it speeded to the east. It also fell well short, and the balls only bounced once.

Young said, "He must be running out of powder. That wasn't even a full charge."

Fergus shook his head. "That bastard doesn't want to fight either. He could have taken us easily if he'd tried. He has more guns and more men than we have."

Puller said, "Even if we ran out of ammunition, he'd have to have boarded us."

Fergus grinned. "And you'd have stood him off?"

Puller was serious. "Yes, sir. My cutlass is well sharpened and ready."

The French frigate disappeared in the darkness to the east. Fergus secured the crew from quarters. He turned to Lieutenant Young. "We're so slow we'll never overtake anybody tonight. Let the crew get some sleep."

The *Aberdeen* sailed slowly to the northwest in the darkness. Fergus paced the quarterdeck, waiting for his nervous system to quiet so he could go below and sleep. Even then, he was not sure he could sleep. Somehow his luck was deserting him, and he thought it had changed when he left Shannon, but he had had no alternative. He had to play the hand he was dealt.

21
RESPITE

he next morning there were no merchantmen of the convoy in sight. Fergus sent for the boatswain, who came to the quarterdeck bleary-eyed and sleepy. "What happened to you?" Fergus asked.

Danbury smiled sleepily. "Nothing, sir, I've been up all night."

"Did you do any good?"

"Yes, sir. I think we're up to four knots."

Fergus turned to the master, tiredly leaning on the binnacle. "What does the log slate say?"

MacGregor looked at the slate. "Four knots, sir. It's been increasing steadily all night."

Fergus asked, "Where's Lieutenant Young?"

MacGregor said, "Forward, I think, sir. He's been on an inspection tour."

Fergus sent a messenger after him. When he came to the quarterdeck Fergus asked, "How does she look?"

Young said, "Much better. I think we can make a little more speed soon."

"We're keeping ahead of the water?"

"Yes, sir."

"Are the pumps working all right?"

324

"The pumps are fine, but the men are tiring."

"Tell them it's better than swimming."

About noon a lookout reported, "Sail ho! Dead ahead!"

Fergus went aloft again, his weary legs hardly supporting him as he climbed, and soon identified the sighting as a British merchantman on the same course as the *Aberdeen*.

It was the next morning before the plodding *Aberdeen* could overtake the slightly slower merchantman. Fergus passed on her port side about a hundred yards away. It was evident that it had been recently fired at and was one of the convoy they had been escorting.

Fergus hailed the merchantman. "What ship?" he bellowed through the speaking trumpet.

The captain, who was bandaged heavily and was leaning on the binnacle for support, replied in a subdued tone, "British Merchant Ship *Proteus*, recently of your convoy, and now proceeding independently to Liverpool."

Fergus asked, "Were any other of our merchantmen damaged or sunk?"

The merchant captain replied, "Yes. The *Phaeron* was sunk by a third frigate to the west of us. The French ship attacked both of us, and after she stopped firing we went back and rescued survivors."

Fergus said, "You were lucky. Your orders now are to rejoin the convoy if you can; otherwise to proceed independently around Ireland and through the North Channel to Liverpool."

Slowly the plodding *Proteus* dropped astern as the almost equally slow *Aberdeen* continued to the north.

The next morning the lookouts reported the sails of four ships ahead. Slowly the *Aberdeen* overtook them.

Fergus spent the morning in the foretop trying to identify them. By noon he was sure they were the ships of his convoy.

By evening the *Aberdeen* was ahead of them, and Fergus sent a signal to them that he was resuming escort duties.

The next morning three other merchantmen were overtaken and ordered to join the formation. Fergus looked back proudly at his convoy. "A great sight," he said. "A few more, and we can be ready to arrive in Liverpool."

Just outside Liverpool they overtook three more merchantmen who settled in the formation astern, and the convoy sailed proudly into Liverpool intact, less the ship that had been sunk.

The *Aberdeen* was ordered to moor at a wharf in the shipyard. When all lines were secured and doubled up, a young man dressed in civilian clothes was the first to board. He asked to see the captain immediately on urgent business and was escorted to Fergus in his cabin.

"Yes?" Fergus asked him.

"Sir, I'm a messenger from the Admiralty. I've been on the road day and night to bring this to you." He held out a bulky manila envelope to Fergus.

Fergus asked, "Should there be an answer?"

The young man said. "Sir, I don't know what's in it, and Mister Fairlie said not to wait."

Fergus smiled. "How is the old boy?"

"Very well, sir. He sent his personal regards and said he hoped you would like what is in the envelope."

Fergus cut the large outer envelope open. Inside were several smaller ones. The labels on the outer sides were all in Jeris's fine hand.

There was a loose letter outside of the envelopes signed by Jeris. Fergus read it.

Dear Nephew:

It is my pleasure to send to you the enclosed documents. First, there is a commission for you as a post captain. The larger envelope contains a golden epaulette to add to the one you already wear as a captain. Now you must wear two. As you know, this privilege is usually extended only to captains with three years' service. The Admiralty has extended this privilege to you now as a mark of recognition for your conduct recently in the action with the four French frigates. They recently have received the information about that action with pleasure and much admiration.

The second envelope contains a commission as captain for your Lieutenant Young. He is to relieve you immediately as commanding officer of the Aberdeen.

Before you go off on a Scottish snit, read the contents of the third envelope. It orders you to proceed when relieved to London and to assume command of the frigate Imperious. You may delay five days on leave before reporting.

I am sure you will know all about the Imperious. At least her captain knows about you. She put in at Portsmouth for emergency repairs for a few days after she left you. Her commanding officer sent us a report by fast mail about the action with the four French frigates. He praised you to the skies, and every member of the Admiralty decided it was past time to promote you to post captain and to give you a first-class ship.

The Imperious is now at a navy yard on the Thames at Gravesend and will be ready for sea in about a month. Unfortunately, her captain developed a serious infection in a leg wound and may lose his leg. Obviously he must be relieved of command.

You are to assume command after your leave. After Lieutenant Young has relieved you, take the fast stage to London. Martha and I will not be here. We are off on a vacation to Scotland. We will be at the small cottage you allowed us to build on your farm. I will also keep an eye on the construction of your house.

More to the point, when you get here, go directly to our flat. It is yours for your leave period. You will find everything you need in it. My next-door neighbor to starboard has the key and will keep it cleaned up.

I have sent word to Shannon that you will be here in about a week and where you will be. Parliament is in session, and she is in London. You can expect she will meet you at our flat.

No matter what, good luck both on your leave and in your new command when you go to sea. Now you have proved that a Scot, if he is good enough, can rise to the highest ship command in our navy in spite of the system. Who knows, you may be a flag officer some day.

Fergus put down the letter and looked around the cabin. He had learned to love the *Aberdeen,* but it was time to move on to other challenges. He sent a messenger for Lieutenant Young.

Young knocked on the door a few minutes later and came in, hat in hand, and with a smile on his broad face. "You sent for me, sir?"

Fergus grinned broadly. "Sit down, Captain, and open this envelope." He turned one of the manila envelopes over to Lieutenant Young.

Young looked confused, but tore open the envelope. When he had read the contents, he grinned but his voice shook. "Sir, I owe this to you."

Fergus shook his head. "No, you don't. You earned it. I just gave you the chance."

Young said, "Now what do I do?"

"You relieve me of command of the *Aberdeen.* I have to leave for London on the next fast stage. I have one request. I'd like to take Midshipman Puller with me for service on my new ship. I understand that is the privilege of a post captain, and I'll make it legal with the Admiralty."

The relief of command was quickly done, but in a dignified ceremony, and Fergus left a smiling crew that afternoon. A swelling "Three cheers for Captain Kilburnie" followed him as a hastily rented carriage took him up the wharf. Midshipman Puller sat next to him, and their luggage filled the rear seat.

Four days later the stage, having stopped overnight at Stoke on Trent, Birmingham, and Northhampton, rolled into a tavern yard in London. Puller helped him take his baggage to a rented carriage before leaving to stay with friends until Fergus would report to his ship. Then Fergus was on his way to Jeris's and Martha's flat.

As the carriage rolled up to the door, Fergus could see lights in the windows, and he knew Shannon was there. He threw some bank notes at the driver. "Please put my baggage on the stoop," he said over his shoulder, as he dashed up the steps.

The door was unlocked, and Fergus turned the knob and pushed it open. "Shannon!" he shouted.

Shannon was in the parlor sitting before a small fire. She leaped up and ran to Fergus.

Fergus took her in his arms and kissed her deeply. Shannon responded, holding him tightly in her arms.

After a few minutes, Fergus stepped back and looked at Shannon. "Ah, you're wearing the same robe you wore in your house."

"Yes, I am."

Fergus grinned. "And I suppose you're wearing the same thing under it."

Shannon laughed. "You've been to sea too long." She let the belt go, and Fergus pulled off the robe.

They made love on Aunt Martha's Turkish carpet in front of the fire. After a while, Fergus got up and went to search for a drink. Shannon said, "For heaven's sake, find yourself a robe. You'll freeze away from the fire."

Fergus found one of Jeris's robes and a bottle of Scotch whiskey and brought back two glasses. He sat down next to Shannon and poured out two stiff drinks. "The first drink is to you," he said. "You are as beautiful as the first day I saw you in Ireland."

Shannon laughed. "The first day you saw me I was a thirteen-year-old stick."

"You were the most beautiful stick I'd ever seen, and I loved you even then."

"Enough of me. What has happened to you?"

"You must have been thinking of something else when I came in the door."

Shannon colored. "I must admit I had eyes only for your face."

"And?"

"Well, maybe for your body, too."

"And anything else?"

"Stop teasing me."

"Well, I was wearing two gold epaulettes."

"I don't follow all that naval stuff."

"It means I've been commissioned a post captain."

"Oh, I see! That's wonderful! Let's have another drink to your promotion."

When they had downed another straight Scotch whiskey, Shannon said, "Does that mean you're going to another ship?"

"Yes. That's why I'm in London."

"Your Uncle Jeris just sent me a note that you would be here about five days on leave. I dropped everything and came here, like I said I would."

"Does your husband know you're here?"

"No. He thinks I'm visiting a sick aunt in Bristol."

"Did Jeris tell you I'd have a few days leave before taking over the ship?"

"Yes, but he didn't say what ship."

"She's the *Imperious,* here at Gravesend. I go to her at the beginning of the sixth day."

She laughed. "Five whole days. We'll do every thing we want to do."

Fergus took her in his arms, bowling over the empty glasses. "They can wait," he said.

Later that evening Fergus helped Shannon explore Martha's pantry and kitchen. It was filled with wonderful baked goods, fruit, and even some fresh vegetables. Cheeses and a roast of beef were in a cooler. Shannon said, "This will last us for a while, but I'll have to shop for some fresh food and a few other things in a couple of days. I know how hungry you are for fresh food after your time at sea."

Fergus said, "Jeris's carriage is in back. We'll take a trip to the market when you're ready."

Shannon grinned. "Just like an old married couple."

"I wish we were. I got a letter from my father describing my new house. He picked out a nice location, and the builder started to dig the foundation. He found a lot of old stones that had been part of the foundation of an old castle that had been built on the same location."

"Will it be finished soon?"

"About six months."

"Does it have a view?"

"Oh, yes. From the front windows you can see the Firth of Clyde."

"And Ireland?"

"No. It's eighty miles away. But you can see the Isle of Arran on a clear day, and the Ayrshire shore stretching to the south is beautiful."

"You'd miss the sea."

Fergus laughed. "Not for long. I could always sit on the front porch and watch the traffic going to and from Belfast to Glasgow on the Firth of Clyde."

Shannon snuggled closer to him. "I think I could keep you busy most of the time."

Fergus finished another drink before the fire while Shannon put together a superb dinner. "Martha and her cook did very well by us," she said as she called Fergus to the table.

After dinner, Shannon found two vanilla custards left by Martha in the cooler. They ate them before the fire.

Shannon said, "Tell me about my latest rival, this new ship of yours."

Fergus began, "She's a thirty-eight-gun frigate, the *Imperious,* a fifth rater."

Shannon bridled. "I don't like that. After all you've done for the navy you should have a first rater."

Fergus laughed. "A first rater is a battleship of more than one hundred guns. Almost a thousand men. A veritable city. I'm not ready for that old fogey stuff yet."

"You mean a fifth rater can be first-rate. And you want a ship that is small and fast. I know you."

"Yes. That's a frigate. The *Imperious* is a big frigate, about as big as they get. She's smart and fast, and I've seen her in action."

"When?"

"On my last cruise. I helped her fend off four French frigates."

"You didn't take a prize?"

Fergus laughed. "No, I don't need any more. I've got enough prize money to take care of all of our needs for the rest of our lives."

"The *Imperious* was damaged?"

"Yes. She's in the navy yard at Gravesend. She should be ready soon."

"And you'll be back to sea?"

"Yes, but let's enjoy my leave now."

"But how long before you'll be back in England?"

"About six months."

Shannon shrugged. "That's a long time, but if you get leave like this every six months I think I can wait."

Fergus shook his head. "It won't be like this. In wartime I can't come ashore in England. You'd have to come down to the ship and live with me in my cabin."

Shannon shook her head and threw her glass into the fireplace. "I'd live with you anywhere else, but that would be too open."

"Well, maybe you could pay me long visits."

Shannon began to cry but soon recovered. "Sorry," she said, "I didn't meant to ruin our first night together."

For the next four days Fergus and Shannon rode in the carriage daily through London's parks. They took picnic baskets into the countryside to locations recommended by Jeris's driver, now firmly on Fergus's side. This was the best time of Fergus's life, and he enjoyed every minute of it.

On the fifth day they had a final dinner in front of the fire, and early in the morning of the sixth day, Fergus kissed Shannon deeply and left in the carriage.

It was over.

22
THE IMPERIOUS

Fergus looked back at the windows of Jeris's flat. He could see Shannon's face at a window, and he waved. Shannon took her handkerchief from her face and waved back.

Fergus was using Jeris's carriage to take him to the ship. He stopped off at the office of the master-attendant of the shipyard opposite the berth of the *Imperious* to draw a commission pennant, which he would fly on the *Imperious* day and night as long as he was in command. It would only be taken down if he was killed in action or relieved of command.

With the narrow, swallow-tailed, red and white pennant in hand he returned to the carriage and had the driver take him to the brow of the *Imperious*.

While the driver took his luggage up to the quarterdeck, Fergus walked the length of his new ship. At the bow he could see the newly gilded figurehead, a replica of a Roman warrior. The figure thrust its ample chest upward and outward and held its head proudly backward. There was a metal helmet on the top of the head. Like most figureheads, it had no arms. Its upper body was encased in armor, and the top of a sword snuggled against the hips.

Fergus laughed. "An imperious old bastard, all right. I'll have to live up to him," he said aloud. He walked back to the brow, looking at the gun ports as he went. They and the sides were recently painted and looked to be in good shape. In accordance with Admiral Nelson's example, the ports were painted white and the sides black.

By now the midshipman on watch on deck had seen him and had the side boys ready. As he climbed up the brow, he looked back at the wharf. By Royal Navy custom, he could not return ashore in England until the end of his cruise when the crew would be paid off. The only other option was the Admiralty sending for him. When he told Shannon that, she had thrown her glass across the room in anger. He grinned in memory of the incident and hoped the glass had not been one of Aunt Martha's best. He shrugged off the memory and climbed up the brow and through the ornate gangway in the bulwark.

The boatswain called out, "Attention, Captain arriving," and shrilled his pipe after ordering the side boys to salute. Fergus saluted the colors aft and then saluted the officer of the watch, a midshipman. Until he arrived and assumed command, he was just another visiting officer, and he properly asked, "Permission to come aboard, sir?"

The officer of the watch returned his salute and replied, "Permission granted, sir."

Fergus stepped over to a lieutenant, standing rigidly at attention and saluting. "I'm Post Captain Fergus Kilburnie, reporting aboard to assume command."

The lieutenant finished his salute and said, "Welcome aboard, sir. I'm First Lieutenant Grantham. I'm ready to turn over command to you."

Fergus grinned pleasantly. "Thank you. Let's go below and talk this over."

"Let me escort you, sir."

"Please do."

In the cabin, Fergus sat down on one of a pair of carved wooden chairs and invited Grantham to sit next to him in the other. Before he could say anything, a gap-toothed, elderly man knocked and entered without waiting for an invitation.

"Sir," he said, "I'm Wattle, captain's steward. I was Captain Natal's steward for over five years. Would you be keeping me on, sir?"

Fergus looked carefully at the man. He was clean and apparently healthy apart from the loss of some of his teeth. Fergus suspected a case of scurvy in the past. He said, "Are you a good cook?"

Out of the corner of his eye Fergus could see Lieutenant Grantham squirm, but Fergus ignored his discomfort and let Wattle answer. Wattle paused and said, "Not very fancy, sir, but you won't starve. I understand you're a Scot, and I don't know much about haggises."

"How about oatmeal porridge?"

Wattle said, the gap in his teeth showing, "Now you're in my territory, sir. I'm also good with cornbread as long as the meal lasts and the worms don't eat too much of it."

Fergus laughed. "I've eaten many a weevil."

Wattle looked surprised, but went on. "I'm also good with lamb and mutton, even without curry powder."

Fergus laughed, knowing how cooks at sea usually used curry powder to disguise rotting meat. "You'll do, Wattle. You're on as steward. Now please bring us some brandy."

Wattle shifted from one foot to the other. "Sir, there's only this one bottle here on the sideboard left. Captain Natal wasn't much of a drinker, so I didn't keep a very large cellar for him. I'm a teetotaler, in case you're wondering if I drank all of the captain's supply."

Lieutenant Grantham broke in. "I'll vouch for that, sir, but Wattle is good with wine for flavoring meat."

Fergus reached in his pocket and pulled out a wad of currency. "Wattle, go ashore and buy a dozen bottles of good brandy. Also an assortment of wines, red and white, and some port and sherry. I don't drink much, but I like to have wine with dinner when there are guests. Also buy all the necessary food for a cruise. Make it wholesome, not fancy. Get as much fruit and vegetables as we can keep from spoiling. Also a butt of lime juice. Fill the manger with as much livestock as we have room for, but not at the expense of the wardroom and crew. They come first."

Wattle pocketed the money and left grinning.

Lieutenant Grantham said, "He doesn't look like much, but you've made a good decision, if, as you say, you just want plain fare. He'll take care of you."

Fergus said, "Thank you."

Lieutenant Grantham was still obviously uncomfortable. "Sir," he said, "have you decided about me?"

"You?"

"Yes, sir. I understand you can pick your first lieutenant when you assume command."

Fergus laughed. "I just did. You're it. I saw what a great job the *Imperious* did a month ago."

"But, sir, I was just the first lieutenant."

"I know you were, and I know that the captain of a ship always gets all the credit. The captain bears a heavy responsibility and should get corresponding credit. I've been in both positions, and I don't argue with the theory. I can also guess that while the captain was leading and inspiring your crew you trained and prepared it. I think you will continue to do that for me, and I look forward to a continuing relationship with you. My first lieutenant on the *Aberdeen* was just commissioned a captain, and I hope to do the same with you sometime in the future."

Fergus opened the bottle of brandy Wattle had left and filled two glasses. He raised his. "Here's to our success and to the *Imperious*."

There were tears in Grantham's eyes and he had difficulty speaking. "I second that, sir," he finally managed.

Fergus tried to cover for him. "Now tell me about the other officers."

Grantham said, "We are allowed three lieutenants, and at present I am the only one aboard. One was killed in our last action, and the other is in the hospital with several serious wounds."

Fergus said, "I have one in mind. A Midshipman Puller will be reporting aboard this morning. I brought him from the *Aberdeen*. As soon as we get to sea, I will have the authority to promote him as an acting lieutenant, and I will do so. He is a fine young officer and is maturing rapidly. I've seen him in battle, and I stand by him personally. In the meantime, I'll look over the present crop of midshipmen we have aboard. Do you have a schoolmaster?"

"Yes, sir, and he's a very good one."

"How about the master?"

Grantham took a swig of brandy. "His name is Lombardi. Good voice. Can yell clear to the maintop even in a storm. He knows everything there is to know about sailing. He has only one fault." Grantham paused and scratched his chin.

Fergus said, "Go on."

"When he gets excited he forgets his English and lapses into Italian and a lot of it."

Fergus whistled. "What do you do then?"

"I don't have any trouble understanding him because I understand a little Italian. Also I'm an opera buff. I interpret for the crew."

Fergus laughed. "I guess my school Latin will pull me through."

Grantham said, "I'll help you if necessary."

"What about the other officers?"

"The boatswain is named Alberts. From Chelsea. Good man. The carpenter and gunner are well qualified. I'll tell you more about them later. The purser is always a key man. Ours is sharp, and, actually, that's his name—Sharp. He's Cockney, but you can understand him. Now he's over in the shipyard finishing our revictualing arrangements. We are bound to do well with him in charge."

"He's that good?"

Grantham laughed. "Actually he is, but the yard victualler is his cousin. The cousin always makes sure we don't get old barrels of salt beef and biscuit that returning ships have turned in. While what we get may not be much good, it's the best the navy has."

"Is he honest?"

"I stand by him."

Fergus was getting impatient. He said, "I can't wait any longer to assume command. Please go up and call the crew to quarters. Don't make them change uniform."

Half an hour later the first lieutenant knocked. "The crew is at quarters, sir."

Fergus followed Grantham topside. The crew was in ranks around the quarterdeck and in working uniform. Fergus walked around the ranks, carefully looking at each man. The crew looked fit to him, although somewhat dirty because they had not had time to clean up.

Fergus read his commission and orders to assume command, addressed the crew briefly, and ordered the first lieutenant to dismiss the crew.

When they dispersed, Fergus walked to the after bulwark with the first lieutenant. "Now that I've seen them, tell me about the crew."

Grantham said, "We have an allowance of four hundred men based on the number of guns we have. We lost twelve seamen in our last battle and have fifteen more in the hospital. Eight of them should be back. That means we will be short nineteen men. We need to fill our allowance. Would you like me to send out a press gang or ask the Lord Mayor of London to furnish us with some of his inmates?"

Fergus laughed. "I'd rather go to sea short than do either, but I don't think we will have to. Please send the surgeon down to my cabin."

Half an hour later there was a knock on the door.

"Come in," Fergus said.

A young man wearing a white surgeon's coat came in. "Captain, Surgeon Denton Melville, sir. I want to apologize for taking so much time to get here. I was up in the manger inspecting the newly arrived animals, and I don't think you'd have wanted to see me in that state."

Fergus laughed. "I was raised on a farm, but just the same I appreciate your consideration. Where did you go to medical school?"

"The University of Edinburgh."

"Ah, a Scot? You don't sound like one."

"No, sir, English. I just wanted to get the best education and training possible. Now you see why I'm wearing a white coat. It's a new tradition at the medical college."

"Good. Now I have a job for you. Go over to the naval hospital and ask to see the senior surgeon."

"Aye, aye, sir."

"Ask him as a favor to me to look over the patients who are due to go back to duty soon. Maybe some of them will be willing to be—shall we say—pressed."

The surgeon laughed. "I understand, sir, and I'll be off right away."

Later that day Doctor Melville brought back eight men. Two limped a little but looked sound. Fergus went up to the quarterdeck to meet them. To his surprise, Poston, his old quartermaster shipmate on the *Athena,* was among them. Fergus strode over to him and shook his hand. "My God! Poston, where'd you get that scar on your face?"

"The *Athena* had a run-in with a French frigate, and all of us here were wounded."

Fergus looked at the others and recognized a few familiar faces. He said, "Are all of you from the *Athena*?"

Poston answered for them, "All, sir. The ship left us here and is now in the West Indies. I don't think the captain wanted any of us back."

"That's good."

"We're all free to ship over on any vessel we want to, and I talked them into serving under you."

Fergus laughed, "Well, at least they won't have to worry about the gratings."

Poston nodded. "They know you are against that, and I vouch for all of them."

"Did you ever learn to navigate?"

"Oh, yes, thanks to you, and I'm pretty good now."

"Well, you're about to be a lieutenant as soon as we get to sea."

"I don't understand, sir."

Fergus laughed. "Trust me, and don't buy anything from the purser until we get under way."

During the next week, one or two men walked up the brow each day to serve under "Lucky Captain Kilburnie."

By the end of the week the allowance was filled; the ship was loaded and ready for sea far ahead of schedule. Fergus ordered all the women and peddlers off the ship. He holed up in his cabin for several hours to avoid the noise while Lieutenant Grantham dealt with the women. Soon Grantham knocked on his door. "All clear, sir, they're gone."

Two days later a messenger from the Admiralty brought orders. Fergus read them and passed them to a waiting Lieutenant Grantham.

The first lieutenant read them carefully and grinned. "Shall I station the detail for getting under way, sir?"

"Please do. The wind is off the wharf. Just to speed our departure put a boat in the water ready to tow our bow out."

Lieutenant Grantham tested the breeze and said, "Captain, do you want a pilot?"

Fergus shook his head. "No, all we need are some line handlers from the navy yard. I'd also like to put my gig in the water. First, I want to see what the gig crew is like, and second, I want to have it to tow the bow out."

Grantham sent a messenger to the navy yard to ask the master to furnish a line-handling party and had the boatswain call away the gig crew and lower the gig into the water alongside the outboard side of the ship. Fergus looked the members of the gig crew over carefully as they climbed over the bulwark and down into the boat, now lying alongside to starboard. He noted that all the members of the crew wore white duck trousers, blue and white horizontally striped jerseys, and short-brimmed black hats. All were reasonably well matched. He knew that some captains required fancy uniforms for their gig crews, but this crew seemed neatly and conservatively dressed, and Fergus decided he liked them as they were.

Lieutenant Grantham came up beside him. "Sir, the line-handling party is standing by. Shall I have the gig take us in tow now?"

"Please do. Have them head straight out. Also take in all lines except the stern line."

The first lieutenant shouted the necessary orders, and the men on the mooring lines slacked them so the line-handling party could throw them off the bitts on the wharf. As soon as they were off the large iron bitts, the men on deck ran them in and flaked them in neat patterns on deck so that they could dry before being put below for storage.

The gig crew began to pull on their oars to the exhortations of the gig coxswain. Fergus could see the bow start to move out from the wharf. The gentle breeze helped to move it. The light airs carried memories of the navy yard as its smells wafted across the wharf—tar, paint, oakum, and machinery oils. Fergus was glad the breeze was not toward the wharf, because it would have brought the unpleasant odor of the mud flats across the river and would have made getting away from the busy wharf harder.

Fergus said to Lombardi, the master, "You can begin to make sail. Start with the jib and the lower courses. That should be enough to get us out."

Lombardi nodded and began to bellow the necessary orders in his resonant voice.

Fergus listened to him and grinned, wondering how his Latin would do when Lombardi lapsed into Italian. But by now the master was quiet and competent, and the sails were up and filling with the breeze.

The ship was headed across the Thames. Fergus said, "Master, when you're ready, come to starboard and then head down river. We'll hoist the boat now." He then turned to the first lieutenant. "Take in the stern line and avast towing. Hoist the gig."

Fergus went to the starboard bulwark to see what he could of the gig coxswain's handling of his boat. He could hear the coxswain yell, "Oars," and the crew stopped rowing and held their oars horizontally. "Cast off the tow line," and a man aft leaned forward and threw the towline off the cleat in the stern and into the water.

The coxswain called, "Give way together," and the oarsmen began to row, carefully following the stroke oar so that all the oars hit the water at the same time. The coxswain brought the boat around to head for a position alongside the slowly moving *Imperious.* As it approached, he said, "Port side, toss oars." The port oarsmen stopped rowing, took their oars out of the holes on the sides of the boat, and hoisted them overhead. The starboard oarsmen continued to row.

As the boat came alongside, the coxswain ordered, "Port side, boat your oars." The port oarsmen lowered their oars to a horizontal position and stowed them inboard alongside themselves. The bow oarsman took a line known as the sea painter being tended by a seaman on deck and secured it to a cleat in the bow. The boat fell back slightly and began to be towed by the sea painter. The coxswain ordered, "Starboard, boat your oars."

Two additional lines were secured to the boat fore and aft to pull it into the side. Now the boat was ready for hoisting, and all but two of the crewmen scrambled up the rope ladder thrown over the side.

In minutes the boat was up and in its cradle.

Fergus was pleased. If the rest of the crew was as well trained as the gig crew and the members of the deck force hoisting it, it would be a fine cruise.

In fifteen minutes the *Imperious* was on course east down the channel of the Thames Estuary, all sail hoisted and making a steady six knots by the log.

In two hours she was passing Sheerness to starboard, and soon the merchant ships of her convoy could be seen coming out astern to join them.

When the convoy was formed, Fergus set course east to round the North Foreland. The next morning, with a good fix on Margate, Fergus changed course to the south, and the convoy rounded up behind him.

The two weeks of the trip south were a pleasure for Fergus. The weather was reasonable. Every day he became more acquainted with the crew. He concentrated on gunnery training, firing the guns at least every other day at targets made of empty barrels lashed together and released over the side. The crews of the merchantmen seemed to enjoy the show.

Fergus became very close to the gunner. His early time as a member of a gun crew and as a gun captain helped him to be able to assess the skills of the gunner, a middle-aged Irishman named McClarty. The gunner knew his business, and was a good man with the crew. Fergus trusted him.

The two new lieutenants, Puller and Poston, needed the most training. They had always been aware of the guns, but had concentrated on navigation. Now each had a gun battery to command as well as a watch to stand.

One morning just after dawn, the lookout shouted, "Sail on the horizon, three points on the port bow!"

Fergus dashed up the ratlines with a long glass and looked at it from the masthead. Lieutenant Puller followed him. Fergus said, "It looks like a small French ship, probably a sloop. If we can catch it, we might get in a little gun drill and even a little prize money."

Puller said, "Lieutenant Grantham tells me this ship has never taken a prize."

Fergus laughed. "Let's go below and see what we can do about that."

Fergus ordered Lombardi to turn to port toward the French sloop and put on all sail. Lombardi responded, and soon the *Imperious* was boiling along at ten knots, scattering plumes of spray.

After twenty minutes, Fergus knew it was a lost cause. The sloop had turned away and was as fast or even faster than the *Imperious*. Fergus estimated that it would take them twelve hours to catch it, even if they could, and he could not leave the convoy that long. He reluctantly ordered Lombardi to reverse course. The crew was obviously disappointed, and the sail trimmers, who had responded eagerly when the chase had begun, now went about their duties of reducing sail slowly and without enthusiasm.

In two hours they were back ahead of the convoy.

By the time the convoy reached Gibraltar, Puller and Poston were ready as lieutenants, and the whole crew functioned well. Fergus was pleased and invited all the lieutenants to dine with him the night before they were to raise Gibraltar. Wattle produced a passable if plain dinner, and as Wattle plied the group with wine he had chosen in Gravesend the mood became very pleasant. Fergus was sure his officers were first rate.

The convoy entered Gibraltar Harbor without incident, and Fergus released them after anchoring. Then he took the gig ashore and called on the captain of the port.

The captain of the port had orders ready for the *Imperious* to leave in forty-eight hours with a convoy of eight merchantmen to be taken around Ireland to Liverpool. Fergus brought his orders back and showed them to Lieutenant Grantham.

Grantham read them with interest. He said, "I'll send your steward and the purser ashore to see if they can pick up some fresh stores. Otherwise, we're ready to go."

Forty-eight hours later, as per his orders, Fergus gave the order to get under way. The eight merchantmen they were to escort weighed their anchors and left the harbor following the *Imperious*.

Fergus paced the quarterdeck, comfortable in the gentle breeze blowing off the mainland of Spain and bringing strange and pleasant smells with it. He could detect orange blossoms, lime blossoms, cut grass, and several other sweet and unidentifiable odors.

Fergus said to Lieutenant Grantham, "The captain of the port said the French are concentrating on stopping our sea traffic up the English Channel to London and the channel ports and also through Saint George's Channel and thence to Liverpool. That's why convoys are being ordered to go west around Ireland and then to approach Liverpool through the North Channel into the Irish Sea."

Grantham said, "That's farther, but anything to dodge the damned Frogs."

"Maybe we won't manage to miss them. They're smart enough to figure out what we're doing. I think we'll run into a couple of frigates."

"A couple?"

"Yes. The captain of the port says the French are operating in pairs since we started escorting convoys with single frigates."

Grantham pulled at his chin. "Then we've got our work cut out for us."

"You handled four frigates the last time out."

Grantham laughed. "But we had you helping us."

The first day was pleasant as they coasted along Spain and Southern Portugal in mild weather. The smell of orange blossoms and other fruit continued to be carried to them on the afternoon breeze.

On the second day the convoy turned north as it rounded Cape St. Vincent. Fergus looked at the cape and spent a pleasant hour describing to his officers the Battle of Cape St. Vincent as he had seen it.

The long reach north toward Ireland took almost two weeks because the wind was persistently from the north and the ships of the convoy had to tack repeatedly.

Fergus figured the French ships would find them as they passed the Bay of Biscay, but they were almost to the southern coast of Ireland at Cape Clear when the lookouts cried, "Sail on the starboard quarter! May be two ships, sir!"

Fergus knew instantly that they had to be French frigates. No British ships would be sailing in pairs now that ships were in such short supply. Just to be sure, he climbed the ratlines, closely followed by Lieutenant Puller. When they reached the fore truck, Fergus said, "Puller, we've done a lot of this sort of thing together."

Puller was already studying the oncoming ships. "Yes, sir," he said, "and those are French ships all right."

Fergus nodded in agreement. "Then let's go below and get ready."

Back on the quarterdeck, Fergus directed Lieutenant Poston to hoist a signal to the convoy to scatter and proceed as previously directed.

Grantham asked, "Shall I beat to quarters, sir?"

"Please do, sir, and make all preparations for battle."

Fergus spent the next fifteen minutes, as the Frenchmen closed them, studying the situation. The convoy was now fleeing to the northwest. The Frenchmen, now almost due east, obviously would round up to the northwest to chase the convoy. That put the *Imperious*, now on a northerly course, between the convoy and the French ships.

Puller said, "Are you going out to meet them, sir?"

"No, we're going to stay astern of the convoy. The French will then have to pass us to get at our merchantmen."

"I don't understand," Puller said.

"You will. Just before the French ships are in gun range of us, I'm going to change course to follow the convoy."

"That will put the French directly behind us and on the same course."

"Yes. They'll have to pass us to get to the convoy."

Fifteen minutes later Fergus was satisfied he had the relative positions he wanted. "Master, change course to northwest," he shouted.

Lombardi had been listening and quickly shouted the necessary orders. When the *Imperious* was settled down on course he came over to Kilburnie. "Sir, what do you want me to be ready to do next?"

Fergus liked his eager black eyes, ready for anything. "Lombardi, I want to stay between the convoy and the enemy at medium speed. When they try to pass us, I'll go after both of them with our stern chasers and occasionally order you to change course quickly so we can get in a broadside. If we are good enough or lucky enough we can keep them from passing us."

"I see, sir. We have more stern chasers than they have bow chasers put together. But what if they diverge and try to pass on either side?"

Fergus pursed his lips. "They will. Then our seamanship and gunnery become even more important. I will direct you to close one or the other by about three points course change. As soon as we are steady we will give them a broadside or two. Then we'll change course in the other direction about six points and go after the other ship. While we're headed away, the Frenchman on that side will have only our stern to shoot at. A small target. There will be a lot of noise around us. I will hold up three fingers and point to starboard. That means change course three points to starboard. Likewise six fingers and pointing to port means change course six points to port."

Lombardi grinned, showing his white teeth. "I've got it."

Puller, standing nearby, said, "You'll be trading distance along the course for a chance to fight them one at a time."

Fergus grinned. "That's right. But it also depends on our ability to slow them both down with damage to their sails so they can't pass us."

The master grinned, his white teeth still flashing in his swarthy face. "Captain, I'm ready. I think I can do what has to be done with the crews of our bow chasers added to my sail trimmers and won't have to use any of the broadside gun crews. With your permission I'll go forward and make all the arrangements."

Fergus nodded. "We won't need the bow chasers unless we let the Frenchmen get ahead of us."

As Fergus expected, the French ships began to separate, and soon there was one on each quarter on parallel courses.

Puller, watching them, said, "They've got all the canvas they can pile on. With the wind astern they must be making eight knots."

"I'm glad they have all their canvas up. All the more for us to shoot at."

Around the quarterdeck the stern chaser gun crews were ready, shirts off, rags tied around their heads, guns loaded. Fergus walked quietly among them. To each crew he said, "The better you do the more chance we have of holding them back. Fire on the up roll as I told you. Shoot for their sails."

The stern chasers divided in half, each two carefully laid and aimed at the large spreads of canvas.

The Frenchmen opened fire with their bow chasers, but were not yet in range, and the balls skipped twice and sunk ignominiously.

Fergus had the gun captains put their extra quoins under the forward carriage wheels of the stern chasers to give them a small extra amount of elevation and hence range.

When he was sure they were in range, he ordered, "Commence firing!"

The guns boomed and ran back against their lashings. The smoke cleared forward, and Fergus eagerly watched the French ships for signs of damage. Some of the balls fell short, but a few holes were visible in the lower courses. The question was how much damage the balls had done after they had passed through the large lower sails.

The next French salvos also missed, but Fergus could tell the ships were gaining on the *Imperious.*

The master came running aft. "More sail, sir?"

"No. I want to let them close the range on us with all their sails up as targets."

Two more salvos went off from the *Imperious*. More holes appeared in the sails of the French ships. Fergus thought he could see a tear developing in the fore course of the left-hand ship, but he couldn't be sure. "Puller, put your glass on the fore course!" he shouted.

The next salvo of two balls from the left-hand French ship hit near the water line aft. For a moment Fergus thought the rudder might be damaged, but the quartermaster reported he still had steering control.

Wattle burst out of the captain's cabin. "Sir, the bastards put a ball in your cabin. It's a hell of a mess in there."

Fergus wondered why Wattle had not cleared his cabin. "Then you don't have to do anything more in there. Report to the master. He can use all the help he can get."

Wattle went forward mumbling, obviously happy to get out of the cabin when he looked over his shoulder and saw what had been shooting at him.

The French tried a new tactic and changed course slightly to put them parallel to the *Imperious* and at maximum gun range.

Puller watched them change. "Just like you said they would," he said.

Now their aspect was such that they presented a wide target, and the *Imperious* poured out the salvos on both broadsides as well as from the chasers.

Puller said, "I can see damage now. Their sails have been reduced by at least one sail per mast and there are holes and rents in many others."

Now the range had closed so that the French could reach the *Imperious*. Shots began to whistle through the mizzen and fore courses.

Fergus had to admit he was happy the quarterdeck was no longer the primary target of the French gunners.

By now it was evident that the French ships were still gaining and were now almost on the quarters of the *Imperious*.

Fergus looked at Lombardi, raised three fingers, and pointed to starboard. Lombardi was ready. "Change course three points to starboard!" he yelled at the helmsmen, and he trotted forward to supervise the change in trim of the sails. Maneuvering with the wind almost astern was relatively easy, and in seconds the ship was steady on a course across the bow of the northern Frenchman. The southern Frenchman was astern, and her target was relatively small as she looked up the retreating stern of the *Imperious*.

As soon as the ship steadied, and Fergus was sure the gun captains had time to lay and aim their guns, he called out to Lieutenant Puller, "Starboard battery, commence firing!"

Puller relayed the order below, and the starboard battery crashed out. Fergus could see balls passing through the sails of the French ship and some seemed to penetrate the side. After another salvo, Fergus gestured toward the sailing master, raised six fingers, and pointed to port.

"Steer six points to port!" Lombardi yelled to the helmsman, and again Lombardi went forward.

The helmsman leaned on the spokes of the big double wheel, and the ship swung rapidly to port. Now her stern was pointed to the northern Frenchman and her port broadside was open to the southern Frenchman.

Lieutenant Poston, on the port battery, was ready, and as soon as the ship was steady Fergus gave the order to fire. The port battery opened fire with a rolling crash.

Again, Fergus could see damage to the sails and rigging of the Frenchman and stayed on that course long enough to get off another broadside.

Two broadsides came back, and Fergus could see some damage to their own rigging and possibly to their hull. Some of the shots passed harmlessly overhead where the sails would have been had the *Imperious* been carrying as much sail as the French ships.

Fergus ordered a change back to starboard, and while the *Imperious* was swinging he tried to make an estimate of the damage to the French ships. He realized that with one ship engaging two the *Imperious* should have sustained twice as much damage as either of the French ships, but by his tactics he was in effect fighting only one side of each ship whereas his ship was using both batteries, a fairly even match. If, as usual, the British gunnery was better than the French, he should win, barring lucky shots.

Still, the French ships were almost up to the beam of the *Imperious,* and he would have to damage at least one of them heavily so he could concentrate on keeping the other from the convoy.

He ran up and down shouting words of encouragement to the gun crews to speed up their rate of fire, but he was not sure he was doing any good. They were already doing their utmost, sweat pouring from their bodies, and feet slipping on the bloody decks. Five guns were out of commission, and other gun crews were running short as wounded and dead were carried below to the surgeon.

On the next tack to the north, Fergus held on until four salvos had been fired, and he was sure the northern French ship's masts, sails, and rigging had been heavily damaged. She was definitely slowing.

But when he turned south, the southern French ship was clearly on his bow, and he held on toward her as the port battery poured salvo after salvo into her. He cursed and clenched his hands, hoping one of her masts would fall, and on the sixth salvo her foremast toppled, spreading sails all over her topside. She definitely slowed, and Fergus turned north again. This time the northern ship seemed to be doing better with her guns, and several shots penetrated the *Imperious*'s hull. One cracked the mizzenmast badly, but it did not fall, and the carpenter rushed aft to put extra shrouds on it.

Fergus pressed toward the northern French ship, and he could see shots pouring into her hull with every broadside.

Just as he thought he had the upper hand, a salvo boomed out from the southern French ship astern, and Fergus could feel the impact of several balls on their stern.

The quartermasters on the wheel called out, "Lost steering control, sir."

Fergus shook his head. Victory had been in his grasp, and now he had lost it. If the French found out he couldn't steer, one of them would leave for the convoy and the other would stay around and finish off the *Imperious*.

Fergus rushed aft and looked over the stern bulwark, but before he could get a good look at the rudder, the master yelled, "Sir, the French have turned away! They're sailing away to the east!"

Fergus straightened up and looked toward the French ships. It was true. They were leaving. They had had enough. He laughed exultantly. How would the French captains explain this to their higher command? He knew they'd tell the French admiral exactly as much as they wanted him to know. He didn't give a damn. It was over, and he had won. That was what counted.

23

STORM CLOUDS

Puller came back from his battery and Lombardi joined them. All of the officers stood together watching the French ships leave. From behind them there was a welling, ragged cheer as the gun crews realized what was happening.

Lombardi broke the feeling of elation. "Captain, look to the south."

Fergus turned to the south. Aloft in the distance he could see broad bands of clouds stretching toward them. He thought he could detect the beginnings of a long swell. "Gad!" he said. "Somebody look at the barometer."

A midshipman bent over, opened a cabinet door in the binnacle, and read the barometer. When he straightened up, his face was solemn.

"Well?" Fergus asked.

"Twenty-nine hundred," the midshipman said. "Down a whole inch, sir."

"Damn!" Fergus said. "This could be a hell of a mess."

Lieutenant Puller said, "Maybe that's why the French left in such a hurry."

Lombardi bridled. "No. We beat the devil out of them."

Fergus shrugged. "Who knows why a Frenchman does anything? At least they're gone."

Puller persisted. "Sir, maybe they are trying to avoid the coming storm by leaving to the northeast. Maybe we should be doing the same."

Fergus laughed. "It's going to be several hours before we can go anywhere. When we can move, we'll follow our convoy to the northwest."

"But, sir," Lombardi said anxiously, "we'll go right up the track of the storm."

"And you wouldn't?"

Lombardi shrugged. "We Italians are more practical. We've done our best to protect our convoy. Now we have to look out for ourselves."

Fergus nodded. "I see your point, but we Britishers look at it a little differently. My orders are to escort the convoy to Liverpool, and I must do my best to carry out those orders, despite some risk to this ship."

Lombardi looked disappointed, but didn't say anything.

Fergus called Lieutenants Puller and Poston, the master, the boatswain, the carpenter, and the gunner back to the quarterdeck for a conference. When they were assembled, he said, "We will make all possible sail as soon as possible to proceed northwest to find the convoy. Now tell me what we have to do. Chips, you start off."

The carpenter cleared his throat nervously. "First, our steering system is in horrible shape. The leather steering lines are parted in three places. I have some of my mates splicing them now. This is possible to do, but it is a slow process to make the splices smooth enough to pass over the sheaves easily. Worse, the rudder has been shattered. I'm going to put some of my men over the stern on stages and see if it can be repaired. It will be a tough job working down there and must be done before those seas out there get too big. You can see that the mainmast is almost totally destroyed. I don't think we can do much with it, but I'll try later. Our one spare mast part must go to repair the foremast."

Fergus looked forward. "I see what's left of it."

"Also, the mizzenmast is badly cracked. It's still standing. The boatswain should take down the upper masts and I'll use them to try to brace the mizzenmast and maybe the mainmast. With additional shrouds, the mizzenmast may support the mizzen course sail. However it was badly cracked with a shot. I'll rig a temporary splice around it with spare spars and wrap it with hemp line, but I don't really have enough spare spars to do it right. I will also add spare shrouds from the masts to the bulwarks.

"The mainmast is whole but weak. I will have to use the last spare spars to put a preventer splice on it in case it goes later.

"I will also have to put a temporary splice on the foremast, but I don't have any spare spars for it. I'll have to improvise something."

Fergus looked up at the mizzenmast above him and shuddered. "I'll try to remember not to stand under that one."

The master said, "If it comes down it could wipe out everyone on the quarterdeck."

Fergus said to the boatswain, "How about you, Boats?"

The boatswain said, "I've got the sailmaker breaking out all of our spare sails. As you can see, we don't have much but rags aloft."

Kilburnie said, "Keep the old sails. We may have to use them and some old yards to make a sea anchor and stream it astern if the wind gets too high or the repair to the rudder doesn't hold."

The boatswain went on, "Aye, aye, sir. We have enough sails left to put up courses on the foremast and mizzenmast after I make my splices. We can keep the jib and maybe rig a staysail or two. Most of the shrouds, halyards, and sheets are shot, but we'll work as fast as we can to replace them."

The carpenter interrupted. "Oh, by the way, sir, we've got a lot of water coming in below. Some of my mates are working at patching the holes."

"Are there many?" Fergus asked.

"A hell of a lot. I haven't counted them, but I'd guess a dozen, and some are at the waterline. Water comes in on every roll. I'll get to them first thing."

Fergus nodded and looked nervously to the south. "Try to plug them before the weather coming on makes us roll more of them under."

Fergus turned to Lieutenant Puller, who was acting as first lieutenant while Grantham was below getting his wounds dressed. "Puller, as soon as your guns are safely double-lashed, turn as many men as possible over to the carpenter and boatswain. We've got to get control of this ship back in a hurry. That storm won't wait. Let's go!"

The ship's officers quickly scattered, and Fergus began pacing the littered quarterdeck. He soon became impatient and strode aft to look over the bulwark where the carpenter and his mates were working on a hastily improvised and lowered scaffold. Fergus could see the rising swells cover their lower bodies up to their waists.

Fergus cupped his hands and yelled, "What progress?"

The carpenter heard him and looked up. "Sir, it isn't good. The best we'll be able to do is jury-rig a few planks to the rudder post with nails and line lashings. Most of the rudder is gone."

"Will it work?"

The carpenter shrugged. "Not very well, and a good storm will probably carry it away."

"Do your best," Fergus shouted.

Fergus walked over to the base of the mizzenmast just forward of the quarterdeck. Before he got there, Wattle burst out of the cabin door. He had just gone in to the cabin after being dismissed from quarters. "Captain! Captain!" he shouted. "You've got to come to your cabin!"

Fergus turned toward him. "Calm down, Wattle, nothing can be that bad."

Wattle shook his head. "Wait until you see it."

Fergus followed Wattle into the cabin. The door was torn off its hinges and was lying on the deck. Fergus stopped just inside the entrance.

Wattle, still wild-eyed, said, "Look, Captain, you ain't got a single piece of furniture left. It's all splinters."

Kilburnie said, "You didn't put all my furniture below."

Wattle said unhappily, "I didn't have time to get it all down before I had to man my station."

Kilburnie shrugged. "Well, it wasn't much good anyway." He looked around the cabin. Wattle was right, although Fergus thought one of the carved chairs, now upside down, might be salvaged. Overhead his hammock swung undamaged. Fergus said, "Well, at least I can sleep in my hammock."

"Maybe so, but you're going to have trouble eating and drinking. All your crockery is busted, and your wine and brandy bottles are broken."

Fergus smiled. There was a strong odor of alcohol. Fergus looked around the cabin again. In one corner was a black iron ball under a sideboard. Fergus laughed. "Wattle, you can turn that ball over to the gunner. We're a little low on ammunition."

There was a big hole in the stern bulkhead where the ball had entered. Fergus put his hand in it. "Wattle, you'd better plug this. We're going to get a lot of wind and rain from astern soon."

Fergus left his devastated cabin and went forward to the mizzenmast. The boatswain was busy directing several seamen rigging additional shrouds. Fergus watched the men work. Finally he said, "Boatswain, will it hold up?"

The boatswain shook his head dolefully. "Not very long. We'll have to baby it. A large roll or shock may bring it down."

Fergus pursed his lips. "If that's the best we can do, I'll have to keep it in mind. Now come forward with me and see what else has to be done."

The mainmast was broken off at its upper tree. The boatswain said, "It's long enough and strong enough to carry a main course sail after I splice it."

Fergus asked, "Can we carry a staysail between the foremast and the mainmast?"

"I think so. The foremast is better off than the other two masts and can carry its course and a jib."

"How long before we can get some way on?"

"As fast as the masts, sails, and temporary rigging are done. About two hours."

Fergus nodded. "That will take us northwest where we want to go, rudder or no rudder."

Fergus sent for Grantham and went to the forecastle. It seemed to have suffered less damage than the rest of the ship, and Fergus and Grantham went below. All the remaining animals in the manger were dead, the result of a caroming ball. Fergus looked at them. "We'd better eat them as soon as possible."

Grantham grinned. "The crew will like that."

Down on the orlop deck there was chaos. The carpenter's mates were running back and forth, shouting at each other. Grantham stepped in. "Calm down! Let's get organized."

One man ran over to him. "Sir, we've got eight holes down here near the waterline and a few extra."

Grantham turned to another man. "Find the gunner and tell him to man the pumps on the double."

Fergus looked below. The water was rising slowly in the bilges. "Just in time," he said. "We've also got to get on with stopping up these holes."

Grantham sent another messenger to summon the carpenter, and soon he appeared, clumping down the ladder. Before Grantham could say anything, the carpenter said, "I know about these holes, sir, and I'll get right on it. I wanted to get my men started on the rudder first." He moved off, shouting orders to his assistants.

Fergus looked at Grantham. "I think he's got a start on this, but I'll feel better if you stay down here until you're sure he really has it in hand. It won't do us any good to be able to move if we sink in the meantime. I'm going back up topside. The weather worries me."

Back on the quarterdeck, Fergus read the barometer again. It had lost another quarter of an inch. He swore softly and looked at the sky to the south. The high streamers had become solid overcast. The seas had become long and evil-looking on the surface, and the wind was up to twenty knots.

Fergus sent for his oilskins, and Wattle brought them out.

"Captain, these ain't much good. They've got a two-foot gash in the back."

Fergus stuck his hand through the rent and laughed. "Get the sailmaker for me."

The sailmaker was on deck working on a replacement main course. He came aft carrying his needles, awl, and sail thread. "Yes, sir?"

Fergus showed him his oilskins. "Can you fix this temporarily?"

The sailmaker laughed. "Easy, sir, after that big sail I've been working on. This ain't nothing."

The sailmaker sat down on the deck, put the jacket on his lap, and with deft stitches closed the hole.

When he handed it back to the captain, Fergus said, "Thank you. That's going to keep me dry."

Wattle had been waiting. When the sailmaker finished, he said, "Sir, if you'll come back to the cabin, I'll give you a little supper."

Fergus raised his eyebrows. "With what?"

Wattle smiled. "Come and see, but it ain't fancy."

In the cabin Wattle had lashed the one surviving carved chair together and had placed a battered chest in front of it. On the chest was a cracked pottery plate, a bent silver goblet, and some obviously straightened silverware.

Wattle said, "That's all that was left in here, and it will have to do."

Fergus grinned appreciatively and sat down. "This looks good. What is it?"

"Fresh mutton stew. We've got a lot of it. The whole crew is having it tonight."

"Yes, I know. I saw it lying around the manger." Fergus started to eat. "My God! This is great! How did you make the wine sauce?"

"I salvaged some from the broken bottles and in the scuppers. Sopped it up with one of your clean handkerchiefs. There's also a little in your—er—wine glass."

Fergus shook his head in amazement. "Wattle, I'm certainly glad I took you on as steward."

After supper, Fergus went back on deck. The weather was steadily worsening, but the carpenter's gang was climbing back on deck astern, and Fergus could see two course sails up and drawing. He looked over the side.

Lieutenant Puller, who had the watch, joined him. "Maybe two knots, sir?"

"I'd guess so. Thank God we're going where the storm is going."

The barometer continued to drop, and the large swells from the south became huge oily monsters. As they passed under the *Imperious*'s stern, it yawed from side to side, the swells hissing as they passed down the sides of the ship.

The sky grew an even more ominous gray, and the barometer fell to a low Kilburnie had never seen before. He ordered the temporary shrouds on the masts doubled, sacrificing sheets from the sails and the rigging. He took in or reefed all possible sails until the *Imperious* seemed to be scudding along under bare poles. The ship wallowed on, all of her men huddled just below the weather deck, afraid to go any farther below.

The corkscrew motion made the hull joints and the mast stumps groan alarmingly.

The rains increased, blotting out the sky. Kilburnie felt like he was wallowing in a gray sack with someone belting him with a staff. It was the worst storm he had ever been in or even heard of.

Just before dark Fergus went into his cabin and dragged out the remnants of the chart showing the west coast of Ireland. Although no one had taken any sights for twenty-four hours, he reckoned that they were fifty miles west of Dingle Bay and making two knots on a northerly course. The nearest possible bay of refuge was Galway Bay, about one hundred miles north. Even at three knots that would require thirty-six hours. Fergus knew his only hope was to try to change course to the northeast as they passed the entrance to Galway Bay. If the rudder held, they might make it into the shelter of the bay and make repairs later. Otherwise, they would continue to be swept to the north by the implacable storm. If they did not have enough maneuverability with the rudder at that time, Donegal Bay was another hundred miles north and would require another fifty miles of sailing to the northeast after rounding the edge of Bermullet Island.

Anywhere they would go would depend on the direction of the storm and its winds and the strength of the rudder. "Damn the rudder!" Fergus muttered. "Our lives depend on the strength of that pile of planks back there on the rudder."

Fergus went out on deck. He walked over to the wheel and asked the men on watch, "How does it feel?"

The two helmsmen shrugged. One said, "Not very good, sir."

Fergus took the wheel and tried to steer for a few minutes. The action of the rudder was soft and mushy. Fergus sighed and sent a messenger off to find Lieutenant Poston. When Poston arrived, Fergus said, "Poston, you don't have to steer, but please stay close to the wheel and let me know immediately of any change in our ability to steer."

The captain then went forward from the quarterdeck and looked up at the straining mast remnants supporting the few patched sails that were hoisted. The twenty-knot wind from astern was filling them completely. Even so, Fergus doubted they were making more than three knots, and he shook his head apprehensively. It would be close.

Forward he could see that the gunner had organized a bucket brigade to supplement the pumps. Soon the carpenter came aft. "How's it going, Chips?" Fergus asked.

The carpenter started to speak but then looked over Fergus's shoulder toward the black clouds to the south. "My God!" he said. "That looks like a lot of trouble over there."

Fergus interrupted him. "It is. How are things going with the holes in the hull?"

The carpenter turned his attention to the captain. "Sir, one to go. The gunner is holding even with the water level. A lot depends on that storm. If the ship pitches too much, some of the patches will be under the waterline. I'll keep my men watching all of them for leaks."

"Thanks," Fergus said. "Keep at it."

The winds increased to thirty knots as complete darkness fell, and Fergus could feel the increased amplitude of the rollers from the south.

Suddenly splats of rain pelted his oilskins, and by dark they were in a downpour.

Fergus paced the quarterdeck all night, feeling the steady increase in the velocity of the wind and sensing the growing wave heights. Wattle occasionally brought him hot tea and a few ship's biscuits filled with thin slices of mutton.

At dawn the winds were at fifty knots but the rains relented and the long swells lifted the *Imperious* from astern, passed under her straining and creaking hull, and dropped her thirty sickening feet as they passed away from her bow.

Fergus ordered the boatswain to rig additional stays on all mast stumps, but he doubted that would help.

All that day the *Imperious* moved north as the wind increased to sixty knots. One of the midshipmen tried to cast the log, but the wind, current, and movement of the ship made his guess of three knots uncertain.

When Fergus judged it was time to try to turn to starboard to attempt to enter Galway Bay, he and the master went over to the wheel where Lieutenant Poston was still hovering. Fergus said, "Take the wheel, Poston, and try to bring us to the northeast."

Poston took the wheel and turned it slowly and easily. The ship began to turn, and for a moment Fergus thought they might make it. Then there was a cracking sound aft, and Poston said, "It's gone, sir, I've lost steering control."

Fergus shook his head. "Now we're at the mercy of the storm. We'll have to go where it takes us." He turned to the boatswain. "We'll have to rig a sea anchor and keep our stern to the swells so we won't broach and roll over. Use any of the spars and sails you need, even take some from the mast splices."

Fergus watched as the boatswain directed his men to put a sea anchor together. Working in the driving wind was difficult, but the men first lashed together three spars. Then they lashed to this framework two sails. A small anchor cable was walked aft and passed around the capstan, out a gun port, back up on deck, and connected to the sea anchor. It took ten men to walk the contraption to the edge of the bulwark and ease it over the side. The boatswain directed that thirty fathoms of anchor cable be payed out, using the capstan, and then stopped off.

Kilburnie looked aft at the floating structure as it took a strain and began to pull back on the ship's stern. The long rollers began to pass under the keel and the stern stayed steady pointing aft. Fergus heaved a sigh relief. "Nice work, Chips. It works fine."

The ship gradually returned to its downwind course. Fergus rapidly calculated in his head what might happen. He said, "Another twenty-four hours and we'll be clear of Bermullet Island, the westernmost point of Ireland."

The master nodded, wiping the spray off of his unshaven chin. "But what if the storm changes to the northeast, as they usually do?"

Fergus shrugged. "Then we'll be blown into Donegal Bay."

For the next day and night the wind blew unceasingly at sixty knots, and the seas rolled on under the laboring *Imperious*. She began to groan even more loudly as the twisting motion loosened the joints in her hull structure and planking, but the sea anchor held and she did not broach.

Fergus spent most of his time by the compass binnacle anxiously trying to determine the direction of the wind. Soon it was evident that the storm had changed direction and they were indeed being blown into Donegal Bay. Fergus called his officers aft. "We're in for it," he said. "The best we can do is to try to get the anchor down before we are blown ashore. There isn't much chance because the bay is deep right up to the shore."

The master said, "Yes, that's right. Donegal Bay is very deep."

Fergus said, "It's our only chance."

There came a time when he knew the *Imperious* was doomed. Even the fully reefed sails had blown out. The rudder was gone. Some of the holes in the hull were leaking through the patches put on by the carpenter, and the hull had begun to leak around the old timbers that should long ago have been replaced. The carpenter came up from below shaking his head and shouted in Fergus's ear over the roar of the wind, "It's coming in faster than we can pump it out."

Kilburnie shouted back, "Keep pumping it out as long as you can. Don't let any of your men be caught below if she starts to go down."

Fergus warned the other officers, and they in turn conveyed the word to their men. There was nothing more that could be done. The wind and waves were carrying them steadily into the inner part of Donegal Bay.

Fergus knew where they were in general, but he was unable to tell exactly. When the high rollers calmed, he knew they were inside Donegal Bay and the southern arm of the bay was catching the rollers. It didn't really make that much difference. They were going aground somewhere in Donegal Bay no matter what he did.

As the day passed, Fergus could feel the wind lessening, but it was too late. They were still doomed. Fergus went to the port bulwark, straining his eyes to try to see through the thick grayness.

As darkness approached, Fergus thought he could see rocks ahead, and in twenty minutes he was sure of it. They were dead ahead of the laboring ship. He shouted to those on the quarterdeck, "We're going aground! Grab a line and hold on tight!"

The sound of the ship sliding up on the rocks was horrible, worse than any battle sound he had ever heard. The hull planking ground and screamed as the black rocks tore holes in it.

The sound of the collision with the rocks was devastating to Fergus. He felt like his own guts were being torn out. The ship he had loved so much was now in great pain and slowly dying. He suffered with her as she moved across the sharp rocks below. The rocks ground through the old hull, groaning as they chewed the oaken timbers of the hull planking. The ship heeled over sharply, and Fergus heard the cracking of the fore- and mainmasts as they broke away from their splices. The masts and the bare and broken rigging came crashing to the deck just forward of the quarterdeck.

Fergus was so preoccupied with watching the devastation forward that he failed to remember the carpenter's warning about the mizzenmast.

Suddenly there was a crack like the firing of a gun just forward of the quarterdeck. Fergus knew what it was, but he couldn't do anything about it. He managed to look up just as the lower part of the mizzenmast and its lower spars crashed down around him. He felt a terrible blow to his shoulder and a lesser blow to his head, and he knew something in his shoulder had been broken. Slowly the gray of the storm turned black and he lost consciousness.

The ship shifted on the rocks, beginning to roll over on its side. Fergus began to wake as saltwater engulfed his body. He could feel the wreckage beginning to lift off of his chest and his body float free in the cold saltwater.

Then blackness came again.

24
RESCUE

ady Shannon Malin lazed in front of a large wood fire in her parlor. She was still dressed in her black riding habit, having waited all afternoon in front of the fire for the storm to end so she could go riding about the estate. Now, with full darkness coming on, she gave up the thought of going out and called to the butler to bring her tea. Her husband, Lord Finian Malin, was a few miles away, visiting with his uncle on the Malin estate. Shannon had protested when he decided to ride off during the height of the storm, but he was very eager to see a newborn foal.

Shannon picked up a London magazine but before she could open it and start to read, she heard a loud banging on the front door. She knew the butler and kitchen staff were busy preparing her tea, so she put down her magazine, rose, settled her riding habit skirt, and went toward the front door. The banging began again with more urgency.

She said to the butler, who was coming out of the pantry, "I'll get it."

"But, ma'am, it's night."

Shannon's eyes flashed. "Doesn't make any difference. I'll go."

The butler rolled his eyes impatiently and went back to the pantry.

The opened door revealed an oilskin-clad man from the village. She started to say something, but the man couldn't wait. "Lady Malin," he said in an urgent tone, "is Lord Malin in? I have an urgent message for him from the mayor. He's very anxious."

Shannon shook her head. "He's at the Malin estate and should be back soon. I'll take the message."

The villager shook his head, obviously upset. "I have to see him, ma'am."

Shannon became impatient. "What's the trouble?"

"There's a big navy ship that's been wrecked in the storm out at sea and washed ashore on the beach just below the old churchyard. The mayor is there with most of the villagers and the village priest, but he needs to have Lord Malin tell him what to do with the survivors and the injured that he's sent up from the beach."

"I can tell you. Take them to the church or to the school building."

"Thank you, ma'am. We've already done that. We need to know what to do with them after that."

"Well, then, I suggest you ride over to the Malin estate and tell him. I'll go on down to the beach and see if I can help."

Shannon closed the door and shouted for the butler. He appeared, carrying a tray. "I'm coming, Lady Shannon. Here's your tea."

"No. Forget the tea. There's been a shipwreck on the beach below the old churchyard, and I'm going down. Please tell someone at the stables to bring up my horse as soon as possible."

The butler put down the tray and left.

She nibbled at the cakes, ignored the tea, and poured some Irish whiskey into a glass, downing it in an unlady-like gulp. "I'll need this," she muttered.

Shannon put a rain cloak over her riding habit and paced the foyer impatiently, occasionally hitting her boots with a riding crop. Ten minutes later a knock on the door announced the arrival of the stablehand. Shannon flung open the door, ran down the steps, and mounted the horse. She spurred it down the road to the old cemetery. The horse knew the way well, even in the dark, since Shannon frequently rode to the old cemetery with a picnic basket, and she arrived without trouble.

Shannon turned her horse into the lane leading down to the church between the crumbling gateposts, and the horse picked its way between the tilted grave markers to the edge of the churchyard above the beach. She began guiding her horse to the trail leading down to the beach, but soon realized she should not ride a horse down there in the darkness. She dismounted and tied the horse to a small tree, raised her skirts, and started walking carefully down the steeply sloping trail. The occasional beams from the lights in the lanterns moving about the beach below reflected off the stones in the trail's surface, giving enough illumination so that Shannon reached the beach without falling.

She turned and headed toward a group of men walking about the beach. Their lanterns showed the broken mast stubs and punctured hull of a large ship a hundred yards off the beach. Spars, pieces of line, and shreds of canvas littered the beach together with debris from the inside of the ship.

She ran toward the group of men. Those in the back standing together parted to let her in. "Can I help with anything?" she asked.

No one answered, and she shook the arms of two men in front of her. One said, "Yes?"

She pointed to the two men in front of them. "Who are they?" she asked.

"The mayor and the priest, ma'am."

The mayor and the parish priest were bending over a form lying on the coarse sand. Finally the mayor heard Shannon and said, "Yes, Lady Malin, we're glad to see you here, but we need Lord Malin more."

Shannon bristled. "Why?"

"Well, ma'am, we've already sent about one hundred and eighty men to the village school. The women of the village are taking care of them. But we need to know what to do with them later. We've also got ten bodies over there." He pointed to a double row of figures lying on the sand under a flapping piece of salvaged sail. "I'd like to be able to move them soon. The tide is coming in."

Shannon nodded. "If the tide rises before my husband arrives, move them farther up the beach. But he should be here soon." She noticed a still form on the sand covered by two coats. "What about that one?"

The parish priest shook his head and said, "That's the captain of the ship. He may be in a bad way and probably won't last long. His chest may be crushed. The doctor couldn't tell whether the blood in his mouth came from his chest or a gash in his mouth."

"Do you know what happened?"

"A little. One of the men told us the ship, a Royal Navy frigate, was escorting a convoy around Ireland bound for Liverpool. They got in a big battle south of Ireland with a French squadron and were badly damaged. Lost a lot of men, had a good many wounded, and were shot up pretty bad.

When they were trying to go north around Ireland to get back to England the storm overtook them. With their masts gone and the rudder damaged they couldn't make much speed. The storm drove them into Donegal Bay. Just as they hit the rocks, a jury-rigged mizzenmast fell and damaged the captain's chest. He was lucky enough to get washed ashore on some wreckage."

Shannon shook her head slowly. "Poor soul. Maybe I can make him more comfortable."

They walked over to the recumbent figure and bent over him.

Shannon said, "Did he give you his name?"

"Says he's Captain Fergus Kilburnie."

Shannon gasped and leaned over the quiet figure. "Give me a lantern," she ordered.

The priest held a lantern close to Kilburnie's head so she could see his face. She pulled the coat back from his soaked head.

The priest said, "He may not have long to go."

"Where's the doctor from Donegal?"

"He was here and saw that man. He didn't think he could help him so he went off with the other wounded to the schoolhouse where he could see to operate."

Shannon leaned over Fergus and said softly, "Fergus, darling, hold on. It's Shannon. I'll take care of you."

The priest shook his head. "He's in pain."

The mayor nodded. "Maybe not long now."

Fergus's eyes opened slowly and then widened as he recognized her. His lips formed her name, and he coughed as he tried to speak. Blood welled up slowly and trickled down the side of his cheek, mingling with the rain. Shannon leaned even closer and pulled her scarf from her neck, wiped the blood away from his mouth, and tried to shield his face from the wind and rain. "Do you know me?" she asked.

Fergus began to whisper, and Shannon put her ear close to his mouth to hear him. "I lived a whole lifetime with you . . . ," he whispered.

Shannon smiled, tears welling up in her eyes. "I'll never forget it."

Fergus struggled to whisper. "If only . . . my farm . . . Scotland."

"As soon as you're well we'll go there for the rest of our lives."

Fergus managed a smile before losing consciousness again.

Shannon bent over him and wiped the blood off his mouth with her scarf. She felt along his rib cage and then his shoulder as if he was one of her horses. "Your chest is intact. You've got a bad gash on your mouth and a bruise on your head. Your mouth is bleeding and your collarbone is broken." She took her bloody scarf and bound Fergus's arm to his chest.

Fergus opened his eyes while she moved him. With great effort he said, "Bury me in the old churchyard."

"No, Fergus dear. I won't need to do that. You're going to live. I've already lost our son, I can't lose you, too."

With enormous effort Fergus opened his eyes and said, "Son?"

Shannon sighed and bit her lip. "No one knows, darling. My husband thought it was his. We lost him to typhoid as a baby."

Fergus laid his head back and closed his eyes. As she pulled the coats over him, Shannon heard the creaking of leather saddlery and the scrabbling of a horse's hooves as a rider came recklessly down the path. As the horseman approached the group, the mayor recognized the rider. "Lord Malin!" he yelled. "I'm glad to see you."

Lord Malin dismounted, handed the reins of his horse to a villager, and strode over to the group. "Shannon! What are you doing here?"

Shannon pulled her rain cloak closely about her. The rain was letting up, but the cold wind was still blowing on the beach. "A messenger came to get you. I sent him to your father's and came down here."

"Yes, he found me."

The mayor said, "Father Duveen and I have done all we can. Now we need your help. There are about a hundred and eighty Royal Navy survivors being cared for in the village school. Some are wounded and all are hungry and wet. The doctor from Donegal and the ladies of the village are feeding them and giving them dry clothes. I need to know what to do with them after they are taken care of."

Lord Malin nodded. "I'll pay for outfitting them and sending them back to England."

Father Duveen interrupted. "I've got ten bodies over there to bury. What shall I do with them?"

Shannon interrupted. "Why can't we bury them all in the old churchyard?"

Father Duveen gasped. "But that's consecrated ground reserved for Catholics, and we don't know the religions of these people here."

Lord Malin was obviously irritated. "No. It isn't all consecrated. I paid for some of it for Church of England members. Besides, does that matter? They all gave their lives in the service of their king, their navy, and their country."

Father Duveen and the mayor exchanged looks but said nothing.

Shannon said, "If Captain Fergus Kilburnie here dies he should be buried next to our son, Fergus Malin." She could see by the lantern light that her announcement startled her husband.

He pulled her aside. "Shannon, what is this all about?"

Shannon said, "This is Fergus Kilburnie, a young man I used to know. I want to take him up to my house and wait for the doctor to come back. I don't think he is as badly injured as the doctor thought. He didn't have time to examine him properly."

Lord Malin was quiet for a minute. Then he said, "Fergus Kilburnie? You had an affair with this man?"

"Yes. His name is Fergus, which is why our child is named Fergus."

"I never liked that name."

Shannon let the full story spill out. "Three years ago when you were back in Ireland and I stayed on in London Fergus came to London on sick leave when he had been wounded. We knew each other when we were young, on my father's estate. We were deeply in love, but my father caught us in a passionate moment and made him leave Ireland.

"Later, when we met at a ball in London, our love grew again."

"And young Fergus resulted?"

"Yes. I wanted to tell you the truth, but you wanted a son, and you loved him so."

"I did," Lord Malin said softly. Then he shook his head. "Obviously it's all over between us. All I ask is that you don't divorce me for the sake of the children. I'll go to your house and clear my things out."

Shannon sighed. "I promise not to divorce you." She turned away from the men and walked over to Fergus. The priest soon joined her. He said, "You know, I think he's going to live after all."

Shannon smiled weakly. "I'll take him home and nurse him. Let's take him up the path on a stretcher."

The priest said, "I'll have him put in a wagon and taken to your home. When I get to the village I'll ask the doctor to drop by your house as soon as he can. I think he'll be surprised."

Shannon nursed Fergus day and night. His mouth healed quickly, but his arm was still not usable. The doctor had set his collarbone and strapped his arm closely to his body, saying, "Six weeks, and then we take that strapping off."

Precisely six weeks after the loss of the ship, the doctor came out to see Fergus. "Now we have a launching, as you sailors would put it," he said.

Slowly the strapping came off. "How does it feel?" the doctor asked.

Fergus flexed his shoulder carefully and slowly. "Stiff and sore," he announced.

The doctor laughed. "About as I expected. Exercise it daily."

Shannon asked, "Can he travel?"

"Yes, in a carriage, but not on horseback."

A week later Shannon packed Fergus and her two children into a carriage and a mound of baggage into a second carriage.

Fergus tried to hold down his smile when he saw the amount of baggage. "Do you plan on staying in Scotland long?"

Shannon's laugh sounded like Fergus remembered it. "Forever, my dear."

After a leisurely, week-long trip by carriage and ship, they arrived in Glasgow. Shannon had left her estate in care of a relative and sent the carriages back there.

Fergus hired two other carriages in Glasgow and the group set out for Kilburnie.

They stopped on the hill above Kilburnie farm, and Fergus pointed out the various farms and buildings.

Shannon asked, "Where is your own farm?"

"Down there is the family farm, but my estate is over there on the second hill beyond the woods. I haven't seen it yet. Let's go."

The driver of the first carriage followed Fergus's directions, and soon a large house came onto view around the bend in the road.

Shannon gasped. "It's huge. About as big as my house."

"It is. That's the way I asked my Uncle Jeris to have it built. Let's go see it."

Fergus knocked at the door and a maid answered. His mother was close behind her, and she took Fergus in her arms. When she could control her tears, she stepped back and looked at him. "Fergus, I'm so glad to see you." Then she noticed Shannon and her two children standing behind Fergus.

Fergus tried to bridge the gap of embarrassment. "Mother, you remember Lady Shannon Malin. These are her two children, Mary and Margaret."

"Come in," his mother said warmly. "You'll like this house."

Two days later, now comfortably situated, Shannon sat with Fergus on the broad porch facing the Firth and watched the children coming back from the woods.

Shannon asked, "Is that where the salmon stream is?"

"Yes, and it was full of salmon when I walked over there yesterday."

"Do you think the local people will resent us as long as we live together and are not married?"

Fergus shook his head, "Scots usually mind their own business. Besides, when you've got a stream with salmon jumping from it almost asking to be caught, all of your neighbors will be your friends."

Shannon looked off in the direction of the Firth. "You have a remarkable view," she said.

"Yes. I can sit here and see all the sea-going traffic going to Glasgow."

"What is that ship down there?"

Fergus picked up his grandfather's old long glass he had borrowed and looked carefully at the ship. "It's the daily packet from Liverpool."

"And it will bring mail regularly?"

"Yes."

"And someday it will bring a summons for you from Admiral Nelson or the Admiralty?"

"I suppose so."

"Will they want to court-martial you for losing your ship? Or maybe give you a new one?"

Fergus bristled. "Why should they want to court-martial me? I carried out my orders to the letter and then some. I got the convoy to its destination in spite of two French frigates and a terrible storm, even if I lost my ship."

She laughed. "I don't know about those things. As far as I'm concerned, they should give you a big new ship."

"If any word comes, that will be it. Uncle Jeris knows where I am, and if they need help they'll send for me. In the meantime, I expect to enjoy life."

Shannon smiled wickedly. "Oh, you will. I'll keep you busy."

A week later the mail ship brought a large envelope for Shannon. She opened it nervously. "Very official looking. Must be from lawyers," she said. "I don't like it."

She read it slowly and began to cry.

Fergus looked at her closely. "What's the matter?"

She wiped her eyes. "Finian, my husband, is dead. He was killed in a hunting accident—his horse threw him." She shook her head. "I told him he was too old to ride like that."

He put his arms around her. "Would you like me to tell the children?"

"No, just give me a few minutes to recover. They loved their father."

Fergus was at a loss for words to comfort her, but he suddenly blurted, "This may not be the right time, but we have waited for so long. Will you marry me?"

She wiped her eyes again and a slow smile spread across her beautiful face. "Any time is the right time. Yes, I will."

"Will a Presbyterian service in the town kirk do?"

"Oh yes, I don't want to get married as a Catholic again anyway. But we should wait at least a month. We don't want to shock the villagers."

"Nothing much shocks a Scot, but you are right. We should wait."

"We'll have many years together—and children!"

"I hope so. But you understand the day may come when a large brown envelope may be delivered to me, too?"

"Yes. With the Admiralty seal."

"And you'll still love me if I leave you to go to sea?"

"I did so before, and I'll do it again."

ABOUT THE AUTHOR

Vice Adm. William P. Mack graduated from the U.S. Naval Academy in 1937 and served in battleships, destroyers, and amphibious forces. He served in many capacities, including assignments as aide to the secretary of the navy, aide in the general planning group, chief of information, chief of legislative affairs, and deputy assistant secretary of defense. He also commanded the Seventh Fleet during the mining of Haiphong Harbor and ended his career as superintendent of the Naval Academy.

Admiral Mack began his writing career by writing articles for the U.S. Naval Institute and speeches for the president, the secretary of the navy, and members of Congress. He coauthored three manuals for the Naval Institute. His first attempt at fiction was a Book-of-the-Month Club award-winner titled *South to Java* that he wrote with his son, William P. Mack Jr. Five other books about destroyers in World War II followed and then a book on the Revolutionary War.

Admiral Mack won the Navy League's Alfred Thayer Mahan Award and several other literary awards. He is currently working on a sequel to *Captain Kilburnie.*

The Naval Institute Press is the book-publishing arm of the U.S. Naval Institute, a private, nonprofit, membership society for sea service professionals and others who share an interest in naval and maritime affairs. Established in 1873 at the U.S. Naval Academy in Annapolis, Maryland, where its offices remain today, the Naval Institute has members worldwide.

Members of the Naval Institute support the education programs of the society and receive the influential monthly magazine *Proceedings* and discounts on fine nautical prints and on ship and aircraft photos. They also have access to the transcripts of the Institute's Oral History Program and get discounted admission to any of the Institute-sponsored seminars offered around the country. Discounts are also available to the colorful bimonthly magazine *Naval History.*

The Naval Institute's book-publishing program, begun in 1898 with basic guides to naval practices, has broadened its scope in recent years to include books of more general interest. Now the Naval Institute Press publishes about one hundred titles each year, ranging from how-to books on boating and navigation to battle histories, biographies, ship and aircraft guides, and novels. Institute members receive discounts of 20 to 50 percent on the Press's more than eight hundred books in print.

Full-time students are eligible for special half-price membership rates. Life memberships are also available.

For a free catalog describing Naval Institute Press books currently available, and for further information about joining the U.S. Naval Institute, please write to:

Membership Department
U.S. Naval Institute
291 Wood Road
Annapolis, MD 21402-5034

Telephone: (800) 233-8764
Fax: (410) 269-7940
Web address: www.usni.org